Kou Keikou

Kou clan military officer / Reirin's oldest brother

"Exciting? How?!"

Shu Keigetsu

Maiden of the Shu clan

Kou Reirin

Maiden of the Kou clan

"Hee hee... This is so exciting!"

Kou Keishou

Kou clan military officer / Reirin's 2nd oldest brother

SOUTHWARD, FOR THE HARVEST FESTIVAL!

Unran

Chief of a southern village

Reirin faces her greatest crisis yet in Keigetsu's body!

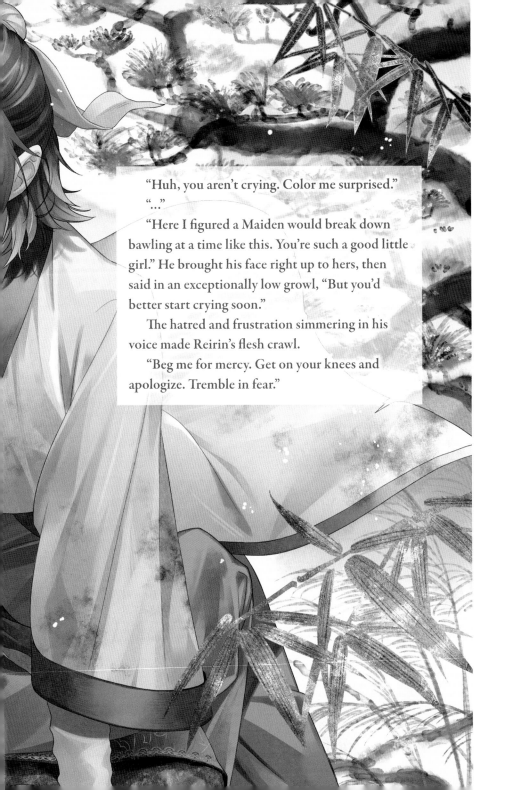

"Huh, you aren't crying. Color me surprised."

"..."

"Here I figured a Maiden would break down bawling at a time like this. You're such a good little girl." He brought his face right up to hers, then said in an exceptionally low growl, "But you'd better start crying soon."

The hatred and frustration simmering in his voice made Reirin's flesh crawl.

"Beg me for mercy. Get on your knees and apologize. Tremble in fear."

Table  Contents

THOUGH I AM AN INEPT VILLAINESS

Tale of the Butterfly-Rat Body Swap in the Maiden Court

3
NOVEL

WRITTEN BY
Satsuki Nakamura

ILLUSTRATED BY
Kana Yuki

Airship

Seven Seas Entertainment

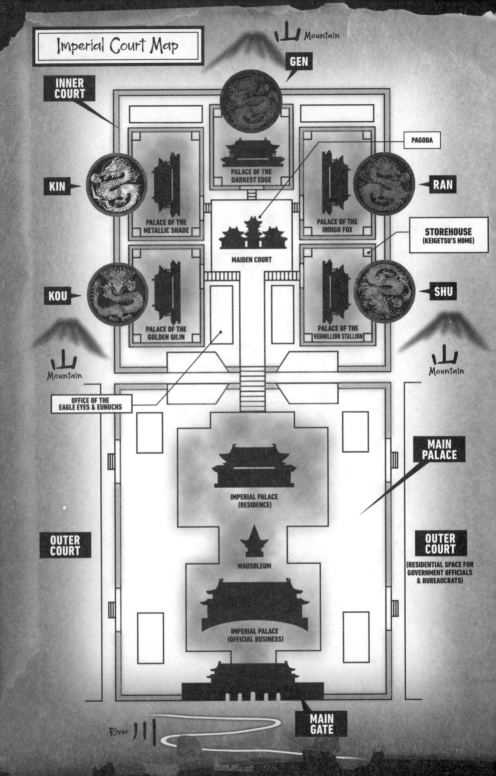

The clan that governs the lands to the west and rules over metal. Their signature season is autumn, signature direction is west, and signature color is white. Chops wood and collects water. Divided into two factions of pragmatic merchants and artists. Mainline descendants tend to be artsy types who prize aesthetic and philosophy. People who can make a profit from extolling beauty.

The clan that governs the lands to the north and rules over water. Their signature season is winter, signature direction is north, and signature color is black. Dampens (suppresses) fire and nourishes (enhances) wood. Aloof and unfazed by carrying out the most inhumane of acts. On the other hand, can latch on hard to the right target. Many are proficient in the military arts.

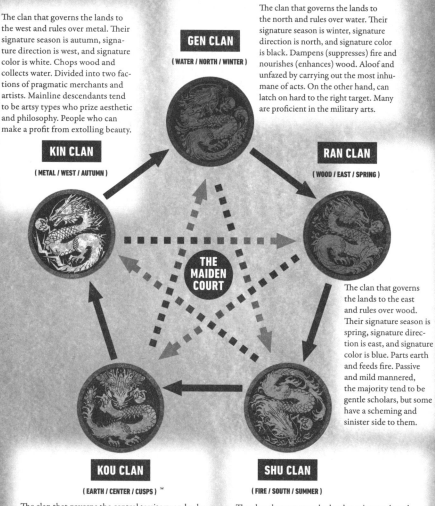

GEN CLAN

(WATER / NORTH / WINTER)

KIN CLAN

(METAL / WEST / AUTUMN)

RAN CLAN

(WOOD / EAST / SPRING)

THE MAIDEN COURT

The clan that governs the lands to the east and rules over wood. Their signature season is spring, signature direction is east, and signature color is blue. Parts earth and feeds fire. Passive and mild mannered, the majority tend to be gentle scholars, but some have a scheming and sinister side to them.

KOU CLAN

(EARTH / CENTER / CUSPS)

SHU CLAN

(FIRE / SOUTH / SUMMER)

The clan that governs the central territory and rules over earth. Their signature season is the four cusps, signature direction is the center, and signature color is yellow. Obstructs water and bears metal. Straightforward, unpretentious, and full of natural-born caretakers. Mainline descendants tend to have a pioneering spirit and be as steadfast as the earth itself. People who can make it through the biggest of catastrophes with nothing but a "dearie me."

The clan that governs the lands to the south and rules over fire. Their signature season is summer, signature direction is south, and signature color is red. Melts metal and produces earth. Full of intense personalities and show-offs. Prone to wild mood swings and value emotion over reason. People who hate and love with equal intensity.

ENHANCE

SUPPRESS

Kou Reirin

BODY SWAP

Shu Keigetsu

The Kou Maiden. Beautiful and benevolent. Beloved by all, which has earned her the nickname of the prince's "butterfly." Frail and often sick.

The Shu Maiden. Has a freckled face and wears thick makeup. Reviled by all, which has earned her the nickname of the court "sewer rat." Jealous of Reirin.

Ei Gyoumei

The crown prince, handsome and well versed in both the pen and sword. Reirin's cousin. Has loved her since they were both children.

Shin-u

Captain of the Eagle Eyes, the enforcers of discipline in the inner court, and a ruthless executioner. A descendant of the emperor.

Leelee

A low-ranking court lady who serves as Keigetsu's attendant. Violent-tempered, she slips into street talk when she gets excited.

Kou Tousetsu

Reirin's head court lady. Level-headed and unexpressive, but has pledged a deep allegiance to Reirin.

Kou Kenshuu

The empress and Reirin's aunt. Dignified and takes a clear-cut approach to most things.

Shu Gabi

The Noble Consort. The second highest-ranked after the empress. Widely considered to be mild mannered and compassionate.

Kin Seika

The Kin Maiden. Fancies herself the second favorite to win after Reirin.

Gen Kesui

The Gen Maiden. The oldest of the group and competent in all she does.

Ran Houshun

The Ran Maiden. The youngest of the group and a skilled poet.

Futsutsukana Akujodewa Gozaimasuga Vol. 3
© 2021 Satsuki Nakamura. All rights reserved.
First published in Japan in 2021 by Ichijinsha Inc., Tokyo.
Publication rights for this English edition arranged through
Kodansha Ltd., Tokyo.

Seven Seas press and purchase enquiries can be sent to
Marketing Manager Lianne Sentar at press@gomanga.com.
Information regarding the distribution and purchase of
digital editions is available from Digital Manager CK Russell
at digital@gomanga.com.

Follow Seven Seas Entertainment online at
sevenseasentertainment.com.

TRANSLATION: Tara Quinn
COVER DESIGN: H. Qi
INTERIOR LAYOUT & DESIGN: Clay Gardner
COPY EDITOR: Jade Gardner
PROOFREADER: Cheri Ebisu
LIGHT NOVEL EDITOR: T. Anne
PREPRESS TECHNICIAN: Melanie Ujimori, Jules Valera
PRODUCTION MANAGER: Lissa Pattillo
EDITOR-IN-CHIEF: Julie Davis
ASSOCIATE PUBLISHER: Adam Arnold
PUBLISHER: Jason DeAngelis

ISBN: 978-1-63858-976-1
Printed in Canada
First Printing: March 2023
10 9 8 7 6 5 4 3 2 1

Prologue

IT WAS YET ANOTHER DAY plagued by a blanket of thick clouds and a light drizzle.

"What the hell are we supposed to do?"

Fields grazed the foot of a steep mountain, and hidden amid the green stood a shabby hut. The haggard voices of several men echoed inside. They had chipped teeth and gaunt frames. Hair that hung disheveled around their shoulders, striking in its messiness. Clothing peppered with patches. These men—recognizable as paupers at a glance—were sitting in a circle around an old straw mat, more sighs escaping their lips the longer their meeting dragged on.

"There's only one thing *to* do. If our taxes go up any higher, how are we supposed to get by?"

"As if this year's cold spell hadn't done enough damage already, it's been so overcast that the rice hasn't grown at all. If we don't do something soon, disease'll do all the plants in."

"Are you saying we should get on board with this insane plan, Gouryuu?"

When the rest of the men continued to hem and haw, the bulky man occupying the seat of honor—Gouryuu—pounded the floor in frustration and raised his voice. "What hope do we have if the top three village officials behave like a bunch of cowards? Now that my brother is dead, we're the only ones who can protect our home. You hear me? There's only one way forward! We kidnap Shu Keigetsu, the villainess who brought this disaster to our doorstep, and torture her! That's the only way to stop these acts of divine punishment." His booming voice cracked through the room like thunder.

Gouryuu was the village chief's younger brother. Now that said chief had passed, both he and his nephew had been thrust into leadership positions.

The three officials glanced out the paneless window with tension etched onto their faces. Upon observing the incessant fall of the rain outside, the men clasped their hands in a prayer to the dark skies, mumbling, "O heavens above, we ask that you calm your anger."

Perhaps owing to their wealth of fire qi, these villagers—no, all denizens of the Shu clan's southern domain—were an emotional sort. Impressionable and easily spooked, they lived in fear of curses and calamities.

Gouryuu looked out the window with a frown, then dropped his voice to mask his own trepidation. "According to the township magistrate, we defiled the Imperial Court when we shoved an unqualified woman into the role of Maiden, and this cold spell is our divine punishment. It makes sense when you think about it. Ever since Shu Keigetsu was appointed our Maiden out of the blue last year, it's been one calamity after another down here in the south."

The men then began chiming in.

"That's true. First we had that drought, and now it's a cold spell."

"And after that, the pride of our southern domain—that beautiful, kind Noble Consort—suddenly got the boot. This hike in taxes has to be because the Shu clan incurred the wrath of the emperor, right? How's that fair to us?"

"The capital is supposed to send us congee when starvation runs rampant, but we haven't seen a single bowl. You think it's Shu Keigetsu's fault that our rations were cut too?"

"That's what the magistrate said," Gouryuu confirmed with a nod. "We'll punish her for forgetting her place on behalf of the Heavens. Once the deed is done, the skies will clear and the sun will shine on our fields once more. The magistrate even said that he'd halve our taxes as a reward for a job well done."

The men's eyes lit up. "*Halve* them?!"

Their lives were hard enough to begin with. The drought and cold spell had pushed these villagers to their breaking point.

"Now that's a generous cut!"

"Still, kidnapping and torturing a noblewoman? That could be what really lands us divine punishment."

"Who would even take on such a heinous task?"

If it meant a way out of abject poverty, the men were more than happy to jump on the township magistrate's proposal. On the other hand, they feared that turning to villainy might earn them the wrath of the gods.

Fed up with his irresolute coconspirators, Gouryuu gave a click of his tongue before casting a glance edgewise. "Hey, Unran! Don't you have anything to say about all this? *You're* the one my brother named his successor."

In a corner of the hovel, a young man lounged upon a matless section of the dirt floor. He looked to be around twenty years old. Much like the rest of the group, he wore hand-me-downs and kept his hair short, but he alone had scooped the top section of his sun-kissed auburn hair into a bun. This laid his swarthy, wild good looks bare to see, which never failed to draw the eyes of the neighborhood women.

"Nope. You can take the lead on this, Uncle Gouryuu," Unran drawled in response. He was the perfect picture of a provincial prodigal son, resting his head on his folded arms and chewing on a twig to keep his mouth busy. Rolling lazily onto his side, he flicked his gaze over to the group. "It's not like you *want* me making decisions for you, right?"

His contemptuous smile hid all the bite of a carnivorous beast. The sight of it had the other men seething.

"Watch your attitude!"

"How did the chief ever consider someone like this a son?"

"That was the fool's first mistake. Looking back on it, this whole disaster might have begun when he accepted a half-blood like him into our vill—"

Ptoo!

The three men stopped talking the moment Unran jerked upright and spat out his twig. Pariah though he was, they dreaded the consequences of provoking the mercurial young man's wrath. His vigorous, well-toned body and sharp wits were unmatched within the village.

Narrowing his eyes, Unran drummed his fingers on the knee he'd folded in front of him. As the men looked on in breathless suspense, he suddenly said, "Let's get his word on that."

"What?" Gouryuu and the others gaped at him, lost.

Unran rose to his feet, dusting himself off. "A contract, I mean. We'll make the magistrate write, 'I ordered these villagers to see the job done. I pinkie-promise to lower their taxes in return.' Otherwise, he'll foist the blame onto us untouchables when the whole thing goes south."

"Huh? Oh..."

"I know how to read, so I'll make it work. Ha ha, it really does pay to be learned. Makes it easier to blackmail people." His sharp gaze narrowing, he stared at the clouds gathering outside the window. "Shu Keigetsu... Tormenting that one woman is all it'll take to save this entire village. Sounds like a good deal to me. Don't worry, I'll handle that part of it myself. Not like any of you cowards have it in you."

By the time he turned back to the group, a sneer adorned his handsome features.

"What's so scary about tormenting a Maiden? Every girl is the same once you strip her bare. Even those uppity ladies from the township are happy to spread their legs after a bit of sweet-talking. Same goes for almost all women."

Gouryuu blanched. "U-Unran! What are you suggesting?!"

"Don't like the idea of defiling her? Then how about stoning her? Is beating her, cutting her hair, or shoving her into a cesspool out of the question too?" Unran snorted. "That's kind of you. Here *we* go through that sort of thing all the time."

A hush fell over the hut.

Unran dragged out his words, letting his voice permeate the silence. "While we've been groveling and licking the townspeople's shoes, Shu Keigetsu has been walking all over people and letting her money burn a hole in her pocket. While we've been tilling our meager fields, she's been busy taking care of her skin. All those times we've starved, suffered, stressed, or lost loved ones, how was that Maiden of ours enjoying life in the capital, I wonder?"

"..."

The longer he went on, the deeper the anguish and hatred on the men's faces became. The room was filled with starving villagers, men pushed over the edge by heavy taxes and storm clouds that showed no signs of lifting. In their struggle to find adequate sustenance, some had even lost family members to disease. It was in their nature to believe in and fear misfortune. Igniting their barely repressed hatred for the nobility was easier than setting a spark to tinder.

"We've been starved, scorned, and treated like trash. We're just doing exactly what's been done to us. Why should that land us divine punishment? Don't be stupid," Unran spat bitterly, then curled the corners of his lips into a smirk.

It was an eye-catching smile that surely would have landed him a job as a popular actor had he been born in the capital.

"Let's teach that disaster-wreaking villainess exactly how her subjects feel."

With those red-brown eyes peculiar to the southern domain flashing in threat, Unran chuckled low in his throat.

THOUGH I AM AN INEPT VILLAINESS

Tale of the Butterfly-Rat Body Swap in the Maiden Court

"ON TO QUESTION number thirty-two, then. Let's suppose you have a fiancé, but out of the blue, another handsome gentleman confesses his love to you. What do you do? One: give him the brush-off. Two: go home and think it over. Three: accept his affections," an exceptionally cheery voice rang out. It was coming from a garden pavilion in a corner of the gorgeously landscaped courtyard of the Maiden Court.

That voice, as clear and beautiful as the tinkle of a bell, belonged to a girl dressed in an elegant gold robe, the Maiden of the Kou clan—Kou Reirin. Her features were as sigh-inducingly gorgeous as ever, but the way she clutched a brush in her hand and leaned across the table had an almost intense air of overeagerness to it.

"Hey, don't distract me right now! Great...now I've forgotten the last move I made."

The girl biting her nails in frustration across the table was the Maiden of the Shu Clan—Shu Keigetsu.

It was a midafternoon just past the height of summer, the time of year when heat still lingered in the air. The two girls were spending their one weekly day of rest enjoying a game of chess beneath the pavilion.

"You just moved your soldier from here to there, Lady Keigetsu. And then I moved my horse like this. Now, to get back to my question—"

"I told you to be quiet!"

No, perhaps Keigetsu was the only one focused on the chess match. Reirin had been bombarding her with questions the entire time, clearly itching to chat with her friend.

"Excuse me, Lady Reirin, but this is supposed to be a tutorial match. How about you let up and give Lady Keigetsu a chance to concentrate?" the scarlet-clad court lady attending Keigetsu's side—Leelee—cut in with exasperation, unable to stand by and watch this. "Lady Keigetsu of all people is trying her best to master the four arts. I'd appreciate it if you didn't break her spirit by trouncing her as an afterthought. I almost have to pity her for making an honest effort."

She certainly wasn't mincing her words. Keigetsu's face twitched. "Are you trying to back me up or put me down? Pick one."

The gold-clad court lady who was serving the tea beside Reirin—Tousetsu—poured salt on the wound by coolly adding, "She has a point, Lady Reirin. While I understand your frustration at wasting the time you might otherwise spend with your gamboge golds on mentoring Lady Keigetsu, a true superior must always give her all for her students."

"Would you please stop dragging your grudge against me into everything, Tousetsu?" Keigetsu said, her eyes narrowing into a squint.

Every single one of Tousetsu's scathing comments used to leave Keigetsu a cowering mess, but it seemed she'd grown used to the tongue-lashings as of late. It spoke to just how often Tousetsu had been putting her through the wringer.

Hee hee. I'm glad to see Lady Keigetsu getting closer to Leelee and Tousetsu.

Reirin broke into a smile at the sight of this "heartwarming" conversation between her favorite people. Though the exchange felt a touch vitriolic in nature, the fact that they could speak their minds freely and fire off comebacks without missing a beat was a sign that they had opened up to one another. That was how Reirin saw it, at least.

I've been spending a lot more time with Lady Keigetsu ever since the switch. It's been so much fun.

A month had passed since the body swap on the night of the Double Sevens Festival and Noble Consort Shu's subsequent exile. Although it was once the second-biggest powerhouse after the Kou Palace, the Palace of the Vermillion Stallion still had no consort to lead it. If its Maiden hoped to restore it to its former glory all on her own, she couldn't stay the "talentless sewer rat" she was—and thus had Keigetsu been turning to Reirin for all manner of guidance in hopes of refining her skills.

Some of the nastier ladies of the Maiden Court had appraised Keigetsu's abrupt change in attitude as "learning to suck up," but for Reirin's part, she couldn't have been happier to have her beloved friend relying on her.

"Personally, I don't feel great about running to you for help with every little thing," Keigetsu said, putting her next move on pause as her face twisted into a frown. "But neither the Shu clan nor the other Maidens are willing to lend me a hand. I don't have any other options."

Hearing the frustration in her voice, Reirin amended her previous happy-go-lucky thought. *That's right. Coming to me was an agonizing choice for Lady Keigetsu. I mustn't celebrate it.*

Indeed, due to her past misconduct, Keigetsu had no one but Reirin to turn to if she wanted to improve her skills. It had more or less been Shu Gabi's unilateral decision to make Keigetsu a Maiden in the first place. When she first came to the Maiden Court, several members of the Shu clan had protested that the consort ought to have picked a girl more worthy of the prince's favor, which had in turn irritated Keigetsu to the point of purposely squandering the Shu clan's fortunes. It went without saying that the two parties were not on the best of terms.

With the Shu clan's dependence on the ex-Noble Consort's good standing leaving them on shaky ground, that was truer now than ever. As they scrambled to hang on to their political capital, there were no doubt several voices calling to replace their current Maiden with someone easier to control. Despite Keigetsu's stated intent to polish her Maidenly credentials, no one had bothered to send her an instructor.

That left her the option of going to the other clans for

instruction and taking the chance to deepen those bonds—which Keigetsu likewise struggled to consider. She had gone too long considering the other Maidens little more than "rivals to dethrone." She had gossiped about Seika—her self-styled superior—whenever the opportunity presented itself, and she'd torn into the timid Houshun every chance she got. She'd never even managed to carry a conversation with the impenetrable Kasui from the sound of it.

Keigetsu had insisted that it was too late to go crying to them for help. In practice, she still rarely spoke to the other three girls.

It's such a shame. Each Maiden has her own area of expertise. If she were to absorb all their know-how, I'm sure Lady Keigetsu could become a wonderful Maiden in her own right.

Her chess piece still clutched in her hand, Keigetsu looked away in a sulk. It reflected her childish nature, but Reirin chose to interpret it as a show of competitive spirit. The girl had insatiable ambition and the strength to fight in the face of adversity.

If only everyone else would come around to seeing her good points, Reirin thought with a faint half smile. "It doesn't bother me in the least. As a matter of fact, I'm honored that *I* get to be the one to teach you...and I feel a little guilty too."

"You feel guilty? Why?"

"Because I'm sure the other Maidens would make for even better teachers."

Reirin was being sincere, but Keigetsu gave a snort as she rested her chin in her hand. "Too much modesty comes across like sarcasm. Who, pray tell, do you think would be better than you?

Lady Seika is a splendid dancer, but that's all she has going for her. Lady Kasui is as terrible a conversationalist as I am. And Lady Houshun is just a wimpy coward."

For someone who knew the pain of being ridiculed, Keigetsu sure had a knack for bad-mouthing other people.

Reirin frowned, upset to hear her so readily write off the other Maidens. "That's not true. Lady Seika studies dance theory, so I'm sure she'd be good at teaching it. Lady Kasui may not say much, but she'll take the time to sympathize with your concerns. Though Lady Houshun seems like the reticent sort, I'm sure once you get to know each other—"

She swallowed the rest of her sentence upon seeing Keigetsu shrug. Every time she spoke in the other girls' defense, her friend was always quick to snap something like, "You're such a goody-goody."

In fairness, most people wouldn't take well to being pushed toward someone they didn't get along with. Reirin read the room and opted for a change in topic. "But if I'm the only one you feel you can trust, I'll consider that a privilege. I'm more than happy to keep you all to myself."

"Wha...?!" Keigetsu boggled before turning red to the tips of her ears. She was such a precious girl.

"There she goes again..." Leelee muttered from beside her gaping mistress, a weary look on her face. This had long become a familiar sight.

"G-give me a break! *Must* you spout those embarrassing lines the first chance you get?!"

"It's not embarrassing. It's the honest truth."

"S-sure it is. I bet you're just trying to get on my good side because you're after my magic and more time in my body!" Keigetsu shouted back as she looked off to the side, her embarrassment having reached critical mass.

Reirin's face fell. "How could you suggest that? While it's true that I've had the opportunity to switch places with you twice in the past...or had the pleasure of it, perhaps I should say...that isn't..."

Losing her confidence, Reirin averted her gaze as she trailed off. Now that her intentions had come into question, she felt she may have enjoyed their swaps a little *too* much to be sure that wasn't her true motive.

"It's happened more than twice. If we count the Double Sevens Festival, it's been three times. The first was when we got dragged into the consort's plot. The second was when you were aching all over from tilling the garden too much. The third was when you stayed up all night mixing herbs and couldn't get up in the morning. Don't tell me you've conveniently forgotten."

"Hrk... I have nothing to say for myself..."

"Each time we switch places, you always promise me it'll be the last time. So how did we get to this point again? Talk about a bald-faced lie. Are you that eager to get found out by His Highness? Oh, I get it now. Your real goal was to rile him up so he'll make you his as soon as possible! Wow, what a cunning villainess!"

Keigetsu's insults grew nastier as she flashed back to their previous switches. All three times, she had taken a browbeating from Tousetsu while Reirin was off stretching her wings with Leelee.

And all while stressing over if and when Gyoumei might show up, no less.

Sweating bullets, Reirin scrambled to make excuses. "B-but His Highness has yet to stumble upon us—"

"We keep getting lucky, that's all. There won't be a next time!" Keigetsu snapped, silencing her protest.

As for why Keigetsu had become so wary of trading places despite instigating the swap in the first place, it was because she was afraid of Gyoumei seeing through their switch.

"Should you manage to catch me in the act of trading places with Lady Keigetsu, I promise to go back to calling you my 'dear cousin,' as shall I swear to remain your Maiden forevermore."

Reirin had made a bet with Gyoumei on that fateful summer day. She had her own reasons for proposing it, of course, but she'd assumed that Keigetsu would stand to benefit from the wager as well. If there was a chance the girl he was talking to could be Kou Reirin, Gyoumei was bound to treat her with greater care. It would encourage him to make frequent visits to the Palace of the Vermillion Stallion too. That would help keep the forces looking to undermine the Shu Palace in check.

Still, there's a heavy price to pay if we get caught. A bet isn't a bet without proper stakes, after all.

To remain Gyoumei's Maiden "forevermore" meant making up her mind to become his wife. She would cease to be a Maiden—a candidate who could have another girl take her place if she ever so desired—and instead become an official consort.

Put bluntly, it meant she would have no grounds to protest Gyoumei taking her to bed. That was the secret wish of nearly every Maiden: to be chosen by her man and become a de facto consort in advance of his accession to the throne.

But that would simultaneously lock in the hierarchy of the "unchosen" Maidens. The hitherto ambiguous ranking of the five girls would be formalized with the Maiden he bedded in the top spot. Since Keigetsu had yet to display any talent worth mentioning, she would go from the Maiden rumored to become the lowly Worthy Consort to the lowest-ranking of the five.

A drop from Noble Consort to Worthy Consort would all but guarantee the Shu Palace's downfall. Now that she was struggling to keep the palace afloat in the absence of its consort, Keigetsu dreaded the thought.

I assumed I would be the only one affected if I lost the bet. I never imagined it would put so much pressure on Lady Keigetsu.

Watching Keigetsu whine, "I don't want to be the Worthy Consort! Anything but that!" made Reirin feel just terrible. *She* wasn't too hung up on the ranking of the consorts, for her part, and the current Worthy Consort—Gen Gousetsu—appeared to take her status in stride, so she never would have imagined that Keigetsu would be so averse to the position. The girl's preoccupation with titles had completely slipped her mind.

On the other hand, she didn't understand why Keigetsu was being so pessimistic. People wouldn't mock her just for being the Worthy Consort. It wasn't even a sure thing that she would come out on bottom. Keigetsu was a wonderful, earnest girl brimming with ambition. If she had her sights set on the top spot, Reirin was confident she could turn things around with enough effort.

The idea that she would end up in last place if the decision were made now was nothing more than Keigetsu's personal opinion. She seemed to have a bad habit of envisioning the worst possible outcome and then conflating that with reality.

Besides, all I have to do is make sure I don't get caught, Reirin smoothly concluded, ever the pragmatist and advocate of hard work. She thrust the paper in her hands before Keigetsu. "It'll be fine! I'm working hard each and every day to ensure our switches go undetected."

It was an honest attempt to reassure her worrywart of a friend.

"I've filled fifty scrolls with the answers to questions I could potentially be asked when we trade places," she went on. "Not to mention that I've been practicing my impression of you day in and day out. The only future I can see is one in which I utterly outwit His Highness."

"The only future I can see is one of total doom!" Keigetsu cried. Evidently, Reirin's earnest assurances had fallen on deaf ears.

Reirin leaned forward, injecting even more enthusiasm into her voice. "Don't be silly! Here, look at the angle of my neck. You have a habit of tilting your head ever so slightly when you're listening to someone talk. You lift the corners of your lips like this when you smile. When you're mad, you tend to slam your fan down at this approximate angle. As for your laugh, you always put the most emphasis on the first syllable, like so: '*Ha* ha ha ha ha! Serves you ri—'"

31

"Stoooop!" The moment Reirin attempted to show off her best impression, Keigetsu screamed hard enough to scatter the pieces on the board. "Please tell me you're not recording the answers to questions this dumb on that cheat sheet of yours."

"Of course I am. The devil is in the details. By accounting for even the least possible scenarios and learning the patterns in your thought process, I'll be able to improve my impression even further."

"So you're saying a man trying to woo me is 'unrealistic,' is that it?!" Keigetsu was glaring daggers now.

Reirin flapped her hands back and forth, flustered. "No, not at all! We simply have little chance to interact with men other than His Highness—that's all I meant. Still, the scenario comes up often enough in love stories that I figured it was worth asking."

In truth, Reirin had never held much interest in love stories. She'd spent most of her life under the impression that she would grow up to marry Gyoumei, after all.

"We don't, eh?" For some reason, Keigetsu shot back a dubious look. "You blockhead," she muttered under her breath.

Reirin hadn't caught that. "What?"

"Nothing." Keigetsu sighed—only for her lips to curve into a smirk as a sudden idea struck her. "Fine. Then I suppose it's worth answering. What would I do if a handsome gentleman made a move on me, you asked? Why, I'd use every trick in the book to seduce him into becoming my personal love slave."

"Huh?!" Reirin was so surprised that her eyes nearly popped out of her head.

"Hear me? I'm not a little goody-goody like you. If a man tries to seduce me, I'll return the favor. I'll give him my best bedroom eyes, run my fingers over his skin, and never let him take his eyes off me for a second. I have a feeling it's not a trick *you* could ever pull off."

It was such an obvious bluff that Leelee and Tousetsu had to stop themselves from bursting out laughing. Forget being wooed—Keigetsu had hardly even spoken to a member of the opposite sex before. Even with Gyoumei, her voice would crack the moment their eyes met. Shin-u's handsome face had dazzled her enough to make eyes at him in the past, but even then, the most she had managed was shooting him longing glances from afar.

Still, Keigetsu had been so firm in her response that Reirin took her at her word.

"Get it now? You could never pull off a perfect imitation of me. Don't get ahead of yourself."

"You're right... My apologies. I took the task too lightly."

Keigetsu had so many things she didn't. No doubt she was far more experienced in *that* department too. Swallowing her friend's lie without question, Reirin jotted down the answer in her neat handwriting.

Little did she know that would become both her and Keigetsu's undoing later down the line.

Once she'd set her brush aside, Reirin broke into a smile. "This is so much fun, Lady Keigetsu! The better you get to know someone, the more hidden depths reveal themselves. Why, I don't think I'll ever tire of asking these questions. I'm so glad I got to learn about a new side of you today."

Keigetsu shoved her chin into her palm, sullen. "Just so we're clear, no matter how well you get to know me, I'm not switching places without a seriously compelling reason ever again."

"That's fine!" Reirin replied with a giggle.

The time she spent in Keigetsu's body was truly magical, of course, but Reirin considered the afternoons spent chatting with her no less precious.

"Hee hee. That reminds me, we'll be deciding the site for the Harvest Festival today. This will be our first-ever outing as Maidens. What do you say to spending our free time together?" Reirin asked, directing the topic to the upcoming event as it popped to mind.

"Oh, right. The Harvest Festival..." Keigetsu lifted her face with a listless expression. She squinted in the direction of the main palace—the complex where the men of the imperial family administered the affairs of the state. "I wonder if a shaman is predicting our future with a turtle shell as we speak."

With the Ghost Festival behind them, the Harvest Festival was the next event that awaited the Maidens. Toward the beginning of autumn, the crown prince and his Maidens would pay a visit to a remote farmland to pray for a bountiful harvest. It was tradition for the rite to be held in one of the five clans' territories, but there was no set turn order. Whichever place the shaman saw in her oracle—meaning the region where the flow of qi had been most disrupted—was selected as the venue. The imperial family, the bearers of the dragon's qi, and the Maidens, the acting priestesses, would then go there to restore the balance of yin and yang.

Today was the day the shaman would determine that location.

"Where do you think it's going to be, Lady Keigetsu? It would be the highest of honors to receive His Highness's visit. I've even heard stories of some clans bribing the shaman just to lure the prince to their domain."

"Give me a break. You must realize that the Shu clan can't afford to celebrate a visit from the prince right now," Keigetsu said curtly, a stark contrast to Reirin's excitement.

She couldn't bear the responsibility of being the host at the moment. Settling the greatest disturbance of qi in the land—which was consequently the place where the crops were in the greatest danger of failing—would help bring peace to the entire kingdom. To that end, a good deal of arrangements had to be made in advance of the visit.

The one responsible for making those arrangements was none other than the hosting Maiden herself. She was expected to toil away at the festival preparations and demonstrate her qualifications as a future consort. That involved setting up the altar and stage for the rite, soliciting offerings from the other clans, and distributing congee to her starving subjects ahead of time to strengthen the region's allegiance. What's more, she was to put on a personal performance dedicated to the god of agriculture for the pre-celebration, then offer a prayer alongside the crown prince during the actual rite. Naturally, it was also her job to arrange transportation and prepare the banquet.

A Maiden with a competent guardian could leave most of the work to her consort, so the other girls dreamed of being chosen as the hostess, longing for the honor of bringing the crown prince to their own domain. A month ago, even Keigetsu might have bribed the shaman for a shot at hosting the Harvest Festival in the southern territory. But as things stood, she didn't have the time or attention to spare.

"The Shu Palace court ladies have been resigning one after another, complaining they don't want to work in a palace that only has a 'sewer rat' to lead it. So far no one has even stepped up to be my ceremonial officer for the trip. Hosting it would be out of the question," Keigetsu said bitterly, her gaze dropping.

Not long ago, the former Noble Consort, Shu Gabi, had been abruptly exiled on the grounds of "a grave insult." The suddenness of it had thrown the entire Shu clan for a loop. If the truth of the matter ever came to light—that Shu Gabi had tried to assassinate the empress with a curse—the result would be far worse than a minor bit of scrambling.

Confusion invites mistrust. Mistrust breeds defection. Add to that the poor reputation of the consort's successor, Keigetsu, and it was little wonder the Shu Palace court ladies were leaving their posts in droves.

It was Harvest Festival tradition for each clan to put forward at least one ceremonial officer, a military official of a high enough rank to accompany a Maiden—most often a relative of hers—but apparently even that was still up in the air.

"Oh, Lady Keigetsu..."

"I'm so sick of this. All anyone ever does is mock me for being a 'sewer rat.'"

"Well, um... That doesn't have to be a *bad* thing! Just picture the critter and its adorable little squeak—"

"Are your nerves made of steel or what?!" Reirin's honest effort to cheer Keigetsu up earned her a snarl, shortly followed by a sigh. "It must be nice not having to worry about these things."

"That's not—"

Keigetsu tended to drop a lot of jealousy-fueled comments about Reirin. Sarcastic praise too. Each of those times, the thought of *I'm not that impressive a person* niggled at the back of Reirin's mind, but saying as much would only draw more of her friend's ire.

Reirin instead gave an awkward half smile and steered the conversation elsewhere. "If you're worried about finding a ceremonial officer, I'd be happy to lend you one of my brothers. There's no rule that it has to be someone from your own clan. Both of them volunteered upon returning from their most recent conquest, so feel free to help yourself to one."

"Help myself? What are they, vegetables?" Despite the wise-crack, Keigetsu sheepishly raised her head. "That would help me out a lot, if I'm being honest. Are you sure?"

"Absolutely. In fact, I would be most grateful if you took one of them off my hands."

The immediacy of her response drew a skeptical look from Keigetsu. "What's that supposed to mean? Do you not get along with your brothers? All the rumors said that the three of you were really close."

37

"Oh, we are! It's just, well..." Reirin trailed off uncomfortably.

Tousetsu finished that sentence for her. "They're overzealous."

"Huh?"

"It's nice to see that they inherited the Kou clan's love for hard workers, but they'll abscond with Lady Reirin every chance they get, disregarding her schedule to shower her with attention... Plus, their training sessions always focus purely on building muscle. They don't know the first thing about the beauty of martial arts."

The taciturn court lady was in an unusually talkative mood. Despite her fervent loyalty to the Kou clan, the glazed look in her eyes showed that, in a rare display, she couldn't be bothered to hide her irritation with the men of the house she served.

Across from her, Leelee gave a perplexed tilt of her head. "But both of Lady Reirin's brothers have made quite the name for themselves amid multiple conquests—and at an awfully young age, at that. Given how many court ladies dream of becoming their brides, I hear rumors of their exploits float around the Shu Palace now and then."

"Hmph. I have no bone to pick with their military accomplishments, but I don't approve of them forcing their *unique* methods of training upon Lady Reirin. And that's not to mention them overstepping their bounds as military officers to wait on her hand and foot. That's a court lady's job."

"So it's just jealousy talking?" Leelee noted, but Tousetsu stood her ground.

"No. We each have our own role, that's all."

"As you can see, my brothers and Tousetsu are both very good to me, but it's easy for conflicts of interest to arise with so many overprotective sorts in one place..." Reirin stared off into the distance as she gave her explanation. She wondered if it would be too brazen to come out and say that it always ended in them fighting over her. "Erm..."

"There you are!"

While she was struggling to come up with a more neutral phrasing, a voice cut in from the side—the orotund tones of a man.

"Your Highness?!"

Arriving on the scene was none other than Prince Gyoumei, with Captain Shin-u of the Eagle Eyes in tow. No sooner had the girls turned their heads than they scurried out of the pavilion and greeted him with a bow.

"It's a pleasure, Your Highness."

"Enough. No need for formalities."

Gyoumei looked as gorgeous as ever with his hair tied into its usual neat topknot, the heat-laden breeze passing over him like it was nothing. It was a rare occasion for him to visit the Maiden Court on a day of rest, and the unanticipated encounter had Keigetsu fussing with her hair next to Reirin.

"I imagine you'll want to jump into the preparations right away, so I'll cut straight to the point. We've determined the site of this year's Harvest Festival."

"Huh?"

Reirin and Keigetsu exchanged glances. If he was going out

of his way to personally inform them, the venue had to be either the central or southern territory.

"So it's the Kou clan's central territory, then." Such was Keigetsu's interpretation of his announcement, and a wave of relief crashed over her.

Reirin took the news with disappointment. As great an honor as it would be to host the prince, the central territory was directly adjacent to the capital, so going there wouldn't make for much of an excursion.

But his next few words made her snap back to attention.

"No. It's the southern territory."

Keigetsu's jaw dropped. "What...did you say?" came her vanishingly small murmur.

"I said it's to be held in the Shu clan's southern domain. It'll be in a township called Unso on the southeastern outskirts," Gyoumei replied mercilessly, though there was a trace of pity in his eyes as he looked down at her. "His Majesty has made his decision in accordance with the shaman's oracle. Shu Keigetsu—I advise you to assume your duties as the hosting Maiden at once."

A silent, tepid breeze swept through the courtyard, and so went that peaceful afternoon two weeks before the start of autumn.

No matter how extravagant a carriage was or how slowly it rolled down the path, it was going to bounce up and down the moment it hit an unpaved road. As Keigetsu's rising nausea taught her that lesson the hard way, she fought to keep her eyes trained on the scroll in her hands.

"Only when the crown prince, a descendant of the dragon, and the Maiden playing the part of his favored priestess...offer their prayers to the god of agriculture...will the balance of yin and yang be restored..."

Since they'd crossed into the southern territory, it had grown so oppressively hot that not even opening the window or asking Leelee to fan her had done much to cool her down. Though Keigetsu had been accustomed to this climate only a couple of years back, she found the sticky heat unbearable to return to.

"To harmonize yin and yang during the Harvest Festival, one must strictly enforce a division of the two sexes... During the pre-celebration, the prince and his men will dedicate a meal to the god of agriculture, while the Maiden and her women will offer up a performance... On the day of the festival, a stalk of early-blooming rice, a clean robe, and a dance should be presented... alongside the prince's prayer... Blegh!" Keigetsu clamped a hand over her mouth and doubled over.

"Why don't you take a look out the window, Lady Keigetsu?" came a worried voice from the opposite seat. It belonged, of course, to Kou Reirin, who was dressed in plain traveling clothes and accompanied solely by her head court lady. "Can you please tell her to stop, Leelee? Trying to read in a bouncing carriage is only going to make her motion sickness worse. Come, haven't we gone over the details a dozen times already? You'd do better to get some rest instead."

Her attitude was quite the breath of fresh air for someone trapped in such a humid carriage.

Reirin leaned forward to pluck the document from Keigetsu's hands before pointing out the window. "See that, Lady Keigetsu? We're closing in on the township capital. Look at the big river running through it! That cluster of buildings must be the heart of the town. I can see a drum tower looming far above everything else."

Maidens weren't permitted to leave the imperial capital save for official excursions and two visits home per year. Reirin's frail constitution meant that she'd hardly had the chance to travel prior to her time in the Maiden Court, so this was her first ever visit to another clan's domain. She sounded more animated than ever. Her eyes dancing with curiosity and a light flush on her cheeks, she looked so beautiful that Keigetsu almost forgot how nauseated she was in her awe.

"Look, a bird just flew by! It's so big! Oh my, the spider crawling along our windowsill is on the large side himself. The flies, the ants—all the insects I've seen have been so enormous!"

"Excuse me, could you please not let bugs inside our carriage?!"

Looks aside, she had a habit of saying the weirdest things. Keigetsu had to wonder *why* Reirin was so happy that the bugs were bigger.

"Sorry! Hee hee. I'm just having too much fun. But it sure is hot, isn't it, Lady Keigetsu? Not even stripping down or getting fanned is enough to beat this heat. Hee hee... This is so exciting!"

"Exciting? How?!"

Reirin certainly seemed to be enjoying the journey. Every little thing she saw or touched provided a fresh new experience for her, and she'd been on cloud nine ever since the group had boarded their carriage.

"You sure are animated, Lady Reirin..." Fan held in her hands, Leelee was practically wilting. "This is my first time...hopping around from boats to carriages for multiple days in a row. I'm so done..."

Tousetsu dismissed Leelee's whining from the seat across from her. "Enough complaining. If this is enough to make you motion sick, you clearly lack discipline." It seemed her Gen clan roots had granted her quite the robust constitution, as she had yet to show the slightest sign of fatigue.

"Come, Tousetsu, don't be so harsh," Reirin chided her. "She's not used to traveling. It's only natural that she's feeling tired. Here, I'll help cool you down. It must be hard to be stuck on fanning duty all day," she said, plucking the fan from Leelee's hands and gently waving it in the direction of the group.

"I'm surprised *you're* not feeling sick. I thought you'd be the first one to retch or pass out," Keigetsu muttered under her breath, her voice dripping with resentment.

"Who? Me?" Reirin gave a blink of her long lashes. "Oh, of course I'm feeling sick and dizzy. I'm used to that, though. It's easy enough to overcome with a little fighting spirit."

Keigetsu gave a silent groan when Reirin oh-so-innocently flexed her biceps. Getting a glimpse of what a meathead her friend was underneath those delicate good looks made her feel like she'd been scammed by the universe itself.

"Say, Lady Keigetsu, how do you plan to spend your free time? I imagine you'll have your hands full as the hosting Maiden, but do you think you could take about half a day to relax? Tonight is the pre-celebration. The main event won't be held for five more days, so sometime between now and then might work. Her Majesty sent me off with some rare candies and liquor, so why don't we have ourselves a tea party?"

"Sure, whatever you want," Keigetsu curtly replied.

Still, the fact remained that she had been given some measure of solace by this girl whose entire being was emanating an aura of excitement.

"Some measure"? "Total" is more like it.

Keigetsu stared out the window. As the hostess, she was riding in the carriage at the head of the cavalcade. Immediately behind her rode Prince Gyoumei, followed by the other Maidens' carriages and the clusters of guards protecting them.

It was Keigetsu's job to keep everyone occupied for the length of the trip by providing refreshments and ordering the cavalcade to stop at scenic spots along the route. However, down a guardian to show her the ropes and at odds with the rest of the Shu clan, she hadn't the faintest idea how to make those arrangements. It was only thanks to all the advice Reirin had given her (while apologizing for "sticking her nose in") that Keigetsu had managed to deliver what was expected of her.

I ended up turning to the Kou clan for a ceremonial officer too.

As she gazed at the ceremonial officers riding gorgeous white steeds alongside their respective clans' carriages, Keigetsu heaved a sigh.

In the end, not a single Shu had stepped up to be her ceremonial officer. The Eagle Eyes and the local soldiers would be the ones handling the actual security, so going without a guard was unlikely to affect her personal safety to any serious degree. Still, bringing one along was meant to be a show of charisma—another way of saying, "I'm a Maiden worthy of this gallant military officer's protection." Hence why the clans picked their most competent, good-looking, and high-ranking men for the job.

Her chin in her hand and her elbow on the windowsill, she took turns studying each of the families' mounted officers.

The Kin clan sent...Lady Seika's uncle, I think. Talk about one dignified lady-killer. If memory serves, the Gen clan went to the trouble of holding a martial arts tournament and picked the winner for the task. Now that's what I call manly good looks. Ah... Even those late-blooming Rans found someone drop-dead gorgeous: a slender man whose defining feature is the mole under his eye. I heard he's Lady Houshun's older brother. Gee, aren't they lucky to be blessed with such capable relatives?

She didn't know their exact titles or track records, but if nothing else, each man carried himself like a full-fledged ceremonial officer. Any one of them had the potential to become center of the women's attention, if only the man guarding Prince Gyoumei's carriage—Shin-u, the captain of the Eagle Eyes—hadn't boasted looks stunning enough to put them all to shame.

45

Of course, mine could certainly give him a run for his money.

Keigetsu flicked her gaze to a spot a short distance from her window. The front of her carriage was flanked by two military officers on first-rate horses. The brawny man outside the window Keigetsu was leaning against was Kou Keikou. The petite, slender man on the opposite side was Kou Keishou.

The two of them were Reirin's older brothers. Having racked up achievements amid several foreign conquests at their young age, the pair was hailed as the cream of the Kou crop and the right-hand men of the emperor-to-be. What the two of them lacked in elegance they made up for in their virile good looks and proud bearing. Between their talent, promising futures, and masculine charm, it was little wonder that so many court ladies loved to fantasize about them.

But then again...they can *be overzealous.*

The true nature of these "dreamy" military officers had quickly revealed itself to Keigetsu over the course of the trip.

Both of them were obsessed with their sister. Each one was as obnoxious about it as the other.

No, the elder Keikou was at least true to his instincts. He'd scoop his sister into a hug while screaming about how cute she was or pat her head like crazy whenever he saw the chance. If she protested, he'd brush it off with, "Ha ha ha, that's even cuter, Reirin!" Keigetsu had given him the secret nickname of "Mr. Musclehead."

The younger Keishou didn't tend to get quite as physical. Instead, he'd take every opportunity to launch into a rambling accolade of his sister, recounting long-winded stories like: "Oh, you've always been such a kind girl! That spring when you were only five years old..." Keigetsu had dubbed *him* "Mr. Clingy."

The pair had attached themselves to Reirin for the duration of the boat ride, escorting her from place to place in their arms. On land, they had plucked whatever beautiful flowers they found blooming as a gift to her.

Even after the trio was split up between carriage and horseback, every other second it was "Have some sweets" or "Here's a cold hand towel" or "Check out this sword I forged from my love for you" or "I brought you your favorite doll." All Reirin had to do was stretch to get them flinging the window open from the outside and offering, "Why don't you get out of that carriage and come ride with your big brother?!"

If the girls weren't careful, they might see their carriage filled to the brim with gifts and Reirin snatched away on a horse. During each pit stop, Tousetsu would mercilessly jettison their offerings while Reirin dodged her brothers with a smile that bordered on deadpan. That was the only thing keeping their road trip relatively sane.

Due to the frequent intrusions upon their carriage, Reirin had driven her brothers off with a request: "Please keep to the front of the carriage." Only now that they had left her line of sight had Keigetsu finally managed to relax.

Indeed, their "overzealousness" wasn't the only reason that Keigetsu wanted to avoid them.

"Why the long face, Lady Keigetsu?" Reirin asked from the

THOUGH I AM AN INEPT VILLAINESS

opposite seat, leaning in with concern. "If our conversation hasn't made for a sufficient distraction, I'm afraid I must apologize."

"I'm not expecting you to entertain me or anything," Keigetsu shot back, ever the contrarian.

Suddenly, Reirin snapped her head up as an idea struck her. "Should I have my brothers do some tricks for us? They're great at impressions, animal taming, and feats of strength. People say that they can get a laugh out of just about anyone, so—"

"Don't!" Keigetsu rushed to stop Reirin when she placed a hand on the window, ready to call her brothers back over. "Just leave it. I'm begging you, please don't make this weird. I don't want to talk with them more than I have to."

"But I'd hoped you three would take this opportunity to get to know one another better..."

"I don't want to. I bet they don't either," Keigetsu flatly asserted.

Reirin gave a confused tilt of her head. "I don't think my brothers have any reason to *dis*like you, at least..."

"You seem to have forgotten that I *am* the same girl who pushed you from the pagoda."

"But His Highness hushed the whole incident up, didn't he? Since my brothers were fighting on foreign soil at the time, they shouldn't have any way of knowing what happened... Why else would they have agreed to guard you without a second thought? Neither I nor Father nor Her Majesty went out of our way to inform them, and they haven't mentioned anything about it." Reirin rambled on and on, her head still cocked to one side.

"I guess." Keigetsu cut the conversation short with a frown, then looked off to the side.

I hate to break it to you, but they found out a long time ago.

She thought back to five days earlier, when she had received a secret summons from Gyoumei prior to their departure. Given what a busy man he was, it wasn't every day that he called upon a Maiden other than Reirin. When Keigetsu came running, racking her brains for what this could be about, he had a surprising message for her: He'd warned her not to get on her ceremonial officers' bad side.

"Both Keikou and Keishou are incurable sister fanatics who couldn't care less about anything but Reirin. Knowing that, I found it a little odd that they'd volunteer to double as your ceremonial officers. I ran into them during a meeting this morning, so I took the chance to inquire about the reason for the change of heart." On most days, Gyoumei didn't bother to meet Keigetsu's gaze, but for once he was looking straight into her eyes. "They claimed they wanted to get an up-close look at the girl who threw Reirin from a pagoda. This *despite* the gag order I imposed regarding the events of the Double Sevens Festival. Now why would that be?"

Keigetsu went pale in the face. She didn't need to stop to wonder why—she was the one who had told them about the Seventh Pagoda incident.

Upon switching places with Reirin, she had been so tickled by her "brothers'" enthusiasm for sending letters and gifts that she'd gone to the trouble of imitating Reirin's handwriting and written them back a sob story. She had oh-so-sadly "confessed" to the terror of being pushed from the pagoda, the humiliation of having her diary stolen, and several other fabricated instances of harassment. Then, enough times to imprint the idea upon their minds, she had ended her letters with: *"I'm too powerless to stop her. I can only wish that you two might punish Shu Keigetsu in my stead."*

The ensuing mayhem had left such an impact that she'd forgotten all about doing that. Who could have guessed it would come back to bite her after all this time?

One look at Keigetsu's pale face probably gave Gyoumei a rough idea of what had happened. Though he'd heaved a deep, unimpressed sigh, much to her surprise, he hadn't criticized her. Instead, he'd said, "My attending Eagle Eye will look out for you during the rite proper. Just keep your head down and let the Kous do their job while we're split up."

Gyoumei endeavored to be a just and fair ruler. Since Keigetsu had already served her sentence, he must have deemed it unreasonable to punish her further. Or perhaps because she'd already made herself so many enemies, he'd chosen to go easy on her so as not to push her past her breaking point. Looking at it from another angle, it meant that Keigetsu's circumstances were dire enough to elicit Gyoumei's sympathy.

I am just reaping what I sowed, but still... Agh. Why did I ever do something so stupid?

She hated her idiotic past self.

"Don't look so sad, Lady Keigetsu," Reirin said in a gentle tone, concerned to see her brooding. "You shouldn't just assume that everyone hates you."

"I'm not *assuming* anything," Keigetsu countered without missing a beat. "I've been the most hated person in the Maiden Court since forever. The total lack of support I'm getting says it all. Here His Highness is, gracing us with his presence, and the Shu clan won't lift a finger to help me. The patriarch won't even make the trip to greet him. My own clan has turned their backs on me."

"That's not your fault, Lady Keigetsu. Maidens have yet to become official public figures, so it's common practice for the clans to stay out of our affairs. It prevents us from being used for political purposes. From their point of view, this is little more than a rehearsal for when you become a consort." Reirin's response was mild. "You're doing the best you can. I'm positive your passion and sincerity have come through loud and clear."

Somehow, the sight of her gorgeous, serene smile further sizzled away at Keigetsu's heart.

Reirin was a beautiful girl. A girl who had been steeped in enough love and care to burst. No one had ever hated her, so she couldn't comprehend the despair and frustration that made Keigetsu want to claw out her own chest.

"How about you see what it's like to be me?"

The words sounded almost like a curse. Not a second after she had let that slip, Keigetsu rushed to clamp a hand over her own mouth. It was the stupidest thing she could have said.

"Excuse me, Lady Keigetsu?"

"What did you just say?"

To no surprise, Leelee and Tousetsu were glaring at her with an air of threat.

"Um... Th-then..." Meanwhile, Reirin pressed her hands to her flushed cheeks, utterly failing to hide her excitement. "Should we go ahead and trade places?"

"No!" Snapping back to her senses, Keigetsu slunk back in her seat as if to protect herself. "It was a slip of the tongue! Besides, didn't you say the last time would be the *last* time?!"

"Well, yes...but it's a different story if you want to do it too."

Sensing that she was on the defensive here, Keigetsu tacked on another believable justification. "I wouldn't agree to it even if I wanted to. We can't switch bodies while we're here in the south. The spell is too likely to spiral out of control."

"Really? It's harder to handle in your own territory?" Reirin blinked her long lashes. This was a surprising bit of information to learn.

It wasn't every day that Keigetsu had something to teach Reirin, so a hint of smugness crept into her voice as she explained. "Amateurs, I tell you! Listen, it takes qi to use the Daoist arts, but that doesn't mean more is better. The fire qi in this region is too strong. To make matters worse, we're on our way to an area where the energy flow is a particular mess. When there's too much of one element, spells will sometimes run out of control. It's much easier to use my magic in the capital, where there's a proper balance of the five elements."

"Oh, I see." Reirin gave an earnest nod, then smiled with a twinkle in her eye. "I had no idea. You're so smart, Lady Keigetsu!"

"..."

It was this sort of thing that made Reirin so hard to handle.

Just a few words and a well-meaning smile, and she could charm her way into anyone's heart.

The wind taken out of her sails, Keigetsu fidgeted as she corrected her posture.

Well... I guess there's no point in being too negative.

Suddenly, she found her nerve. She stared down at her own hands—hands that had the power to cast spells at will.

The situation isn't great, but this isn't the worst-case scenario.

Keigetsu thought long and hard about her current predicament. It was no easy feat to host the Harvest Festival without a guardian, sure. Still, she had a busybody friend in Reirin to give her whatever advice she needed. Gyoumei was on her side too.

The Shu clan hadn't sent her a single ceremonial officer, and the Shu patriarch wouldn't be appearing—but that also meant that no one could blame her for screwing up. The Kou brothers supposedly had it in for her, but at the very least, they were taking a wait-and-see approach for the time being.

And this township...

Keigetsu gazed at the landscape beyond the window. This was a small township called Unso, located on the eastern end of the southern region. It was uncharted territory for Keigetsu, who—despite her southern roots—had grown up in a township closer to the imperial capital.

It looked to her like an idyllic countryside. Most of the land was surrounded by mountains and rivers, and the humid subtropical climate was said to provide its residents a generous harvest every year. That unfortunately wasn't the case this year

53

due to clouds shrouding the sky all summer long and a cold spell that had gripped the area, but the neat rows of austere houses still looked safe and orderly from a distance.

"I've heard that Lord Koh is a true gentleman, one who's tirelessly devoted himself to the backwater township assigned to him... Out of all the places in the south it could have been, perhaps I should count myself lucky that *this* was picked as our destination," she mumbled.

Reirin's face lit up, and she was delighted to hear Keigetsu thinking positively at last. "That's true. In places where yin and yang are unbalanced, it's not uncommon for subjects to grow so agitated that they rise up in revolt. Yet word has it that here in Unso, the people are living peaceful lives under their magistrate's just rule. I'm sure they'll be proud to welcome you as their hosting Maiden."

"Let's hope so." Feeling her own mood steadily brightening, Keigetsu gave a shrug of her shoulders to keep her expectations in check. "But this township also has a den of lowly criminals called the Untouchable Village. The only thing separating it from the township capital is a river, so here's hoping the villagers don't step out of line."

Every township had its haunts for criminals and lowlifes. Stamping those out provided an easy win for any magistrate, so each time misfortune befell the kingdom, a good number of townships would burn those villages to the ground in the name of a "cleansing." Lord Koh had instead mercifully settled for cutting them off from the township proper, permitting their continued survival and even providing them with work.

Keigetsu could only hope that his graciousness wouldn't come back to bite them during the festivities. As that thought crossed her mind, the carriage finally passed through the township limits.

The same road that had once been a mere mud puddle slowly but surely began to even out. Soon it grew from being almost too narrow for a single carriage to squeeze through to being wide enough for two coaches to pass each other with ease. Though it couldn't hold a candle to the ones found in the imperial capital, it even boasted a gate built of stone and roof tiles. That had to be the entrance to the heart of the township.

On either side of the gate, a single-file line of men and women in dark red robes prostrated themselves before the incoming carriages. That was their welcoming committee, by the looks of it.

"Your Highness and honored Maidens, we are truly humbled to receive your visit," came the resounding greeting of the elderly man at the front of the procession—probably Lord Koh, if one had to guess. He was a thin but genteel old man, his hair neatly gathered into a topknot and his long, white beard well trimmed.

Mirroring their magistrate's polite bow, the townspeople awkwardly ground their foreheads into the dirt.

It looks like he's done a good job keeping them in line, Keigetsu thought, relieved.

She ordered the carriage to move a little ways off to the side, then stopped it there. Upon fulfilling her role as guide, the hostess was to let the prince, the other Maidens, and their guards go ahead, making her the last one to set foot in the township.

"Well done, Shu Keigetsu," said Gyoumei.

"Thanks for the arrangements," said Kin Seika.

"I had a fun time on the trip," said Ran Houshun.

"Excuse us," said Gen Kasui.

Each offered a word of thanks from their carriages before disappearing into the town ahead. When Keigetsu noted that the townspeople flanking the gate had kept their heads bowed for the entire length of the procession, she was both relieved and impressed.

What a courteous and scrupulous township.

If their behavior to this point was any indication, the townspeople were sure to lend her a hand with the Harvest Festival.

Once everyone else had passed through the gate, it was time for Keigetsu and Reirin's carriage to head into town. In a rare show of enthusiasm, Keigetsu leaned her head out the window. Though this was her first time meeting them, these were her subjects. She thought it might lift their spirits to show her face and offer them a grateful smile.

"Good work, everyone! You can raise your heads—"

She swallowed her words mid-sentence. The townspeople had all risen to their feet and looked in her direction before she could give the order. Not a single one of them was smiling.

Huh?

No, worse than that—it looked almost like they were mumbling something under their breath with a glare.

What's their problem?

She was still frozen in shock as her carriage rolled past the humble gate. Was it her imagination, or were the gatekeepers looking the other way?

A tepid breeze blew in through the open window. There was no sun to shine warmly upon them, only the humid sort of heat that clung to the skin and made it hard to breathe.

Keigetsu couldn't help her pulse quickening with a sense of foreboding.

THOUGH I AM AN INEPT VILLAINESS

Tale of the Butterfly-Rat
Body Swap in the Maiden Court

2 | Reirin Sees Red

THE ARRANGED PLATES boasted sticky rice cooked in safflower extract, wild vegetable stir-fry and soup, and deep-fried coriander. There was not only kuai made with sliced raw fish from the river but grilled pork and chicken to go with it. Tinted in the light of red-hot bonfires, the appetizers served for the pre-celebration looked nothing less than lavish.

"My, I saw chrysanthemum rice served for the Tomb-Sweeping Festival, but I didn't realize they dyed their rice red in the south. I've never seen anything like it before."

"Me neither, Lady Seika. It looks so festive that it's almost a shame to eat it."

"You'd do better to partake in the food than stare at it, Lady Houshun. Eating meat will help you grow bigger."

"Y-yes, Lady Kasui!"

There was a brand-new stage complete with an altar, and the ground had been gorgeously repaved in stone. A red carpet had been laid out over the floor, and atop it sat a horizontal row of tables and chairs that faced the stage.

Seated with their backs to a partition screen emblazoned with their respective clan's crests were the four Maidens—excluding the Shu Maiden. In their capacity as acting priestesses, the girls were to spend the pre-celebration partaking in a meal before an altar dedicated to the god of agriculture, a ritual through which they offered their prayers and gratitude.

The gong had just announced the hour of the monkey, which simultaneously signaled the start of the pre-celebration feast. The Maidens had kept their foreheads to the ground and their expressions schooled for the duration of the opening remarks given by Keigetsu and Lord Koh's wife. Only now that they were seated and had their meals in front of them did they finally have a chance to unwind.

"But I must say, it's been exhausting to jump straight into the festivities after arriving," Seika complained as she massaged her aching knees. "We've hardly even had time to unpack our things."

"It had to be this way, Lady Seika. The pre-celebration has to take place on the most auspicious date possible."

"She's right. And Lady Keigetsu is going to be performing for us before she's even had a bite to eat. If you consider what a heavy responsibility *she* bears, we're fortunate that all we have to do is relax and enjoy our meal."

Houshun and Kasui took turns pacifying her.

"Fair point," agreed Seika, though she still cast a glance behind her. "But facing an altar and eating in full view of an audience is a bit draining in its own right."

60

Behind the partition screen to their rear, close to a hundred women from the township were kneeling in rows, prostrating themselves as they recited their prayers. This meal was more than just a simple welcome banquet—it was a rite. The Maidens had to eat in a manner befitting their supreme status, and the towns-women had to remain on their knees and pray the entire time.

Aside from the Maidens' ceremonial officers, there wasn't a man to be found in the vicinity of the altar. The Harvest Festival was a rite in which the crown prince became one with the god of agriculture in order to bless the earth and balance the forces of yin and yang. Because those forces weren't to be brought into harmony before then, yin and yang—that is, women and men—had to be kept as far apart as possible in the lead-up to the main event.

Each time one of those warm night breezes so typical of the southern territory swept through, the bonfires cracked and popped.

Shu Keigetsu, the hosting Maiden, wasn't seated because she would soon take the stage and dedicate a performance to the Heavens. Her plan was to play the erhu, so she had gone back to her assigned room to get changed. Perhaps the harmonious atmosphere was owed to the absence of the court nuisance.

Or maybe not. In one corner, there was a table that went past "harmonious" and was better described as "bustling."

"Look, Reirin! This grilled meat looks real tasty. Open wide!"

"No thank you, Brother Senior. I'm perfectly capable of holding a pair of chopsticks on my own."

"Hm? I'm not sure how fresh this meat is, Brother. How about I bring down the bird that just flew past you and we cook that instead?"

"With all due respect, Master Keishou, I must ask that you refrain from killing animals near the festival site. Here, Lady Reirin, try some of this broth."

It was Reirin's seat. Her two older brothers had been making a huge fuss over her since the banquet began, forgetting their place as bodyguards and even brushing aside her personal attendant of Tousetsu to feed her dinner. The ceremonial officers had been given special permission to attend the pre-celebration despite the "no men allowed" rule, but no one else had gone so far as to stick to his Maiden's side and wait on her. The other clans' bodyguards were shooting them befuddled looks from a path a short distance away.

The three Maidens whispered among themselves.

"I'd heard the rumors about the Kou clan, but that truly is an impressive display of overzealousness—or, *ahem*, familial love."

"I-I feel a little bad for Miss Reirin..."

"No wonder she's developed a tolerance for compliments and come-ons."

Back in the Maiden Court, Reirin had shrugged off every last one of the passionate gazes and compliments Gyoumei directed her way. The rest of the Maidens had always wondered what her secret was, given her otherwise innocent disposition, but something told them they'd finally found the answer to that mystery.

No one would have blamed the girls if the excessive display of affection put them off, but there was something so pitiful about the glazed look in Reirin's eyes that they instead watched her in commiseration.

Agh... This is so embarrassing.

Meanwhile, Reirin was deeply ashamed of being fussed over from three different directions. The Kou clan prided themselves on standing on their own two feet and doting upon others. She hated being on the receiving end of a one-sided spoiling.

The biggest reason for their protectiveness was that she spent so much time hovering on the verge of death, but she had a feeling that this was also a natural result of having three natural-born caretakers in the same place. It was like a three-way game of tug-of-war.

This is precisely why I asked Lady Keigetsu to take one of them with her, she inwardly whined at her missing friend.

Despite Reirin going to the trouble of offering Keigetsu a ceremonial officer, she had left both Keikou and Keishou behind, insisting, "I don't want an unfamiliar man following me to where I'll be getting changed."

I don't blame her...but I think it would be safer to keep someone by her side for now.

As Reirin dodged a pair of chopsticks that was about to get shoved into her mouth, a shadow passed over her face. Ever since coming to the township, Keigetsu had seemed more high-strung than ever. It was likewise concerning that the townspeople seemed to give Keigetsu and only Keigetsu a frosty reception. It wasn't overt enough to qualify as mistreatment, but Reirin sensed hidden implications in the looks they gave her or the things they said.

Reirin was concerned that with all that stress and frustration built up, Keigetsu's emotions would explode the moment she was left alone. She wanted nothing more than to slip away and go check on her in her room.

"Reirin! Say, Reirin, you've grown even prettier in the six months since I last saw you. And boy, have you grown up! Why, it was just yesterday that you were following me around like a little duckling and calling me 'Big Big Bwother'..."

"Oh? What happened to the other fifteen years of my life?"

"Oh, Reirin! Rest assured, as one of the few intellectuals among the Kou clan's military men, I've kept a careful record of your growth down to the most minute detail. But I do so adore that worrywart side of yours, Reirin. Oh, Reirin..."

"Please stop saying my name so much."

Unfortunately, her brothers were too firmly glued to her side to let her go anywhere.

Is Lady Keigetsu going to be all right? It was long past time for the performance of tribute to start.

Just as Reirin turned her gaze to the stage before her, she heard an angry shout from nearby.

"How did this happen?!"

The voice was Keigetsu's. It seemed she had already made her way to the pavilion that connected to the stage. The women behind the screen were so startled by her sudden screech that they stopped praying.

"I sent you the erhu for the performance way in advance! Why isn't it here?!"

"I-I'm so sorry, milady! I left *this* woman in charge of guarding your room, and now it's nowhere to be found!"

"Forgive me! We don't know what happened either..."

Kneeling before Keigetsu were two women. One was from the township, and the other was an elderly woman who appeared subordinate to her. It seemed that the erhu for the performance had gone missing, and the woman put in charge of supervising the luggage was taking the heat for it. Leelee was doing her best to calm Keigetsu down, but she was too upset to listen to reason.

"How could you mess this up?!" she shrilly demanded.

The townswoman bowed her head low and pointed to the old lady beside her. "Our township has been suffering from a food shortage due to last year's poor harvest. Even rounding up all the able-bodied people in town couldn't get us the manpower we needed to build the stage in time, so we entrusted some of the work to the untouchables we don't usually allow in the township. And then—"

"You're telling me this old woman stole my erhu?!"

"No! Absolutely not!" the old woman who had been referred to as an "untouchable" shouted, exposing her chipped teeth.

The townswoman covered her mouth, openly disgusted. "It's not surprising. Her kind lives in a barren land where even rice is hard to grow. Those good-for-nothing riffraff would do just about anything to line their pockets."

"Th-that's not true! We—" The old lady tried to cling to Keigetsu's leg in desperation, but the latter stepped back to avoid it on reflex. The woman lost her balance and went tumbling over the stone floor. "Urgk..."

"Why did you put people like that in charge of my instrument?!"

"We were shorthanded... I'm so sorry."

The Maidens frowned as they overheard this conversation from a distance. The Harvest Festival was a rite dedicated to the Heavens, so the preparations had to be thorough. Still, did that give her the right to slam an old woman against a hard stone surface in her anger?

"There's no need to keep yelling after she apologized..." Houshun murmured in a frightened squeak.

That comment set off a wave of whispers among the women kneeling behind the partition.

"The Ran Maiden is right. Does she have any idea how hard this was for us? We're the ones who had to get everything ready for the festival when we're already starving and dealing with heavy taxes."

"We even brought the untouchables into our town to get the preparations done, but all she does is make more demands..."

"I heard that our current Maiden is known as the talentless 'sewer rat' of the imperial capital. How good of a performance was she going to manage even if we *did* have her oh-so-important erhu?"

It seemed that Keigetsu's bad reputation had made it all the way to the township. The women must have let their guard down because of the partition. Forgetting that they were in earshot of the other Maidens, they broke into hushed gossip about the offerings each of the clans had brought.

"Not to mention that all the Shu Maiden brought with her was liquor and snacks. That doesn't help anyone but the elites who get to enjoy them. And she was so stingy with the amount of congee she sent us beforehand."

"At least the Kou Maiden brought enough fertilizer to share with the whole township. And the Ran Maiden brought seeds, as befitting her clan's knack for agriculture. The Kin Maiden gave us gorgeous ceremonial garments—not all that many, no, but at least it's something that benefits the entire town. Even the supposedly boorish Gens brought us hundreds of farming tools made by skilled craftsmen."

"Lady Shu Keigetsu just isn't fit to be a Maiden. That's what made the Heavens furious enough to send the Noble Consort away. I bet it's her fault the qi is out of balance here too," someone spat. Several other women nodded their heads in instant agreement.

"This *is* divine punishment."

The strength of the assertion was a sign that the women had repeated that phrase dozens of times before.

"Wow, she's really unpopular."

"Maybe I didn't need to get revenge, after all."

Beside Reirin, Keikou and Keishou gave a disillusioned shrug of their shoulders as they watched the spectacle unfold.

Revenge...? Reirin's heart leapt at the ominous word, but she didn't have time to worry about that. She stood from her seat.

Keigetsu wasn't a bad person. She was just having trouble controlling her emotions in the face of an unforeseen disaster.

Her screaming didn't come from a place of anger—it was a cry for help. Nevertheless, even if all she'd done was step aside, leaving an old woman lying on the stone pavement was only going to make her look worse.

She needs to calm down before the townspeople's resentment spreads any further.

Unfortunately, Reirin was so distracted by her brothers' conversation that she reacted a moment too late.

"For heaven's sake, Lady Keigetsu, we can hear you all the way over here. If something's happened, why don't you come here and give us an explanation instead of yelling at the poor townspeople?" Seika mockingly called out to her, standing from her seat and dabbing at her mouth with a handkerchief. "It's the hostess's job to ensure that the festivities proceed without a hitch, even in the face of unforeseen circumstances."

She had jumped on her chance to tear into Keigetsu.

"Um... We heard what happened. You lost your erhu for the performance of tribute, right? I understand why you're upset..." Houshun likewise rose to her feet, perhaps hoping to ease the tension in the air. "But music isn't the only art that can be dedicated to the god of agriculture. If you don't have an erhu, why not put on a different performance instead?" It was a flexible proposal, but one that only served to further corner a girl as untalented as the Shu Maiden.

Keigetsu looked up, snapping back to her senses the moment she realized the other Maidens had been listening. That was when she *should* have taken the opportunity to offer the old woman a hand. But instead, she silently dropped her hands to her sides and hung her head, the picture of a girl with her back to the wall.

Be it an instrumental performance or a song, she had to offer up some kind of performance as the hosting Maiden; however, she wasn't skilled enough to perform a different art on command. That was the whole reason she had spent the past month practicing like crazy to get her almost-passable erhu skills up to snuff.

"Why so quiet? How long do you plan to keep your kneeling subjects and the god of agriculture waiting?" Seika asked, her eyes narrowed like a cat toying with its prey.

Kasui cut in to defend her. "I have an idea, Lady Keigetsu. Why don't you dance for us? You put on such a wonderful performance for the Ghost Festival. I'm sure that would suffice to please the god of agriculture."

"That's right! Don't you have that gorgeous ceremonial garment the Kin clan provided us? Its shiny metal embroidery alone ought to be worth ten thousand pieces of gold. I'm sure you could perform the most brilliant dance in that," said Houshun, clapping her hands together. "The robe and its sash are both of the finest quality. The simple act of wearing the garment should be enough to please the god to whom it's dedicated."

Upon hearing that, Keigetsu whipped her head up, furrowed her brow, and fled the scene altogether.

"Lady Keigetsu?!"

"Oh dear. Running away? How very unseemly." Seika sat back in her chair and examined her fingernails with a huff. "Here I was hoping she'd have what it takes to bounce back from this blunder. What a letdown."

"She might have run off to do exactly that," Reirin cut in, unable to sit back and listen to this any longer.

"Pardon?"

"Lady Keigetsu has a strong sense of responsibility. Please don't accuse her of running away." She then took off running after Keigetsu, heedless of the other Maidens' wide-eyed astonishment. "I'm going to go check on her!"

"Lady Reirin?!"

"Wait, Reirin!"

"Please put the townspeople's minds at ease, my brothers! Tousetsu, provide assistance to whoever needs it!" she shouted over her shoulder when the trio in question made a move to stop her, urging them to stay put.

I'm coming, Lady Keigetsu!

Reirin's heart ached even more than the strain on her lungs. She knew that Keigetsu had stood strong and put in a tremendous amount of effort over the past month, barely even taking the time to sleep. Even if her past actions were to blame, her court ladies had treated her coldly, and she'd been stuck without a consort to guide her. Finding no support from the Shu clan, the prideful girl had gone so far as to turn to Reirin—the Maiden of another clan—to make the arrangements.

In keeping with precedent, she had secured the necessary funds, double-checked with Tousetsu to confirm what needed to be done, and sent off order after order. The amount of "welfare congee" she had sent beforehand to nourish the townspeople should have been more than sufficient, based on the approval documents.

Something was afoot. And a malicious sort of something, at that.

Keigetsu was probably rattled from having that fact repeatedly thrust in her face in the short time since they'd arrived. Add the loss of her erhu on top of that, and she'd lost control of her emotions.

"Are you there, Lady Keigetsu?!"

Reirin was completely out of breath by the time she reached Keigetsu's assigned room. The wooden door had been pulled firmly shut, and Leelee was standing outside it, looking lost.

"Leelee! Where's Lady Keigetsu?"

"She bolted the door as soon as she went inside..." Leelee looked torn between annoyance and sympathy. Pursing her lips into a conflicted frown, she gave a shrug of her shoulders. "She won't listen to me. If we had a guard around, I'm sure he could force open the door, but no such luck."

The redhead cast a glance around the empty cloister. The area *should* have been posted with guards supplied by the Shu clan and the township in addition to Keigetsu's ceremonial officers. Yet there was no one to be found. That alone spoke volumes about how unpopular Keigetsu was.

But...there's no point lamenting the circumstances.

Reirin chewed on her lip, then tugged her ornamental hairpin loose. "I really struggled with this decision, but I'm left with no other choice. I'll use my hairpin to pick the lock."

"Hold on, I didn't see you struggle for a second!"

"I'm lucky that it has a flat design," said Reirin, tuning out Leelee's shout with a solemn look on her face. Then she inserted her hairpin between the gap in the door and lifted the bolt. "I'm coming in, Lady Keigetsu," she gently called out as she stepped into the room.

Reirin had expected to be greeted with either a shriek or flying furniture, but the room was dead silent.

"Lady Keigetsu—"

In the darkness unlit by even a single candle, the girl Reirin had come looking for was standing near the window. When Reirin saw her figure illuminated in the moonlight, the rest of her words caught in her throat.

Keigetsu was crying.

"The erhu, see..." she said softly before she'd even bothered to turn around. She could tell the intruder was Reirin from the sound of her voice. "I figured I'd go look for it myself. If I couldn't find it, then I'd push past it and put on a dance instead. As long as I had the right outfit, that was still an option. I could see the festivities through. I was sure that as long as I kept a cool head, I could figure something out. But..." Her voice cracked.

She was staring down at the erhu that lay in the path of the moonbeams shining through the window. Its neck had been snapped in two.

Next to it was a garment torn from its hanging rack and drenched in mud. It was the ceremonial robe and sash gifted to her by the Kin clan, so lavishly embroidered with gold and silver.

Keigetsu had been planning to wear it for the Harvest Festival rite in five days.

"How awful..."

"Why do you think this always happens, Kou Reirin?" Keigetsu's tone was almost unnaturally even. "It's true that I don't have talent, and I won't claim that my past conduct has been beyond reproach. But that's exactly why I thought hosting this ceremony might be a good opportunity for me. No, I was determined to *make* it one... I thought maybe I could start over."

As she hung her head, a tear trickled down her cheek. The robe and sash lay abandoned on the floor. The mud slung across them reeked faintly of excrement.

"I thought I could do it if I tried...if I worked hard enough. If I did it the right way, if I didn't cheat...if I faced things head on... then I thought for sure things would work out this time..."

The broken erhu was useless. If she wore a flashy enough robe, she might have been able to put on a decent-looking dance despite her meager skills, but even that was no longer an option. Worse yet, she was bound to come under fire for ruining the Kin clan's offering.

"Who would even do this?"

"Don't you get it?! All of them would!" Keigetsu suddenly raised her voice, then whirled on Reirin. "The court ladies! The townspeople! The guards! The Maidens! Everyone! All of them are out to get me! Do you realize why the Shu clan left me in the lurch?! They're waiting for me to fail. Then they're going to push all the blame onto me so they can replace me with a new Maiden!"

"Please calm down, Lady Keigetsu. If no one else, the Kou clan is in on your si—"

"Then what's this?!"

Keigetsu picked the robe off the floor and hurled it away. A beat after the cloth fluttered back down, there came the light *thunk* of something hitting the floor.

"What?"

"It's a tassel. A yellow one," Keigetsu spat.

Reirin sucked in a breath.

A tassel was a braided cord noblemen used to tie the jade pendant denoting their rank to their sashes. Of course, even these were color-coded by clan.

A yellow tassel belonged to the Kou clan.

"No way..."

"This filth strewn all over my robe is manure. Ring a bell? Yeah, it's the Kou clan's offering! Either Lord Keikou or Lord Keishou... no, it could have been both of them...but *someone* from the Kou clan muddied my robe and broke my erhu. It was their revenge for the time I almost shoved you to your death!"

Reirin couldn't assure her she was wrong.

Revenge...

After all, she had just heard her brothers utter that exact word.

"Let's both stay calm. We need to cool our heads and think—"

"You've got to be kidding me!" Reirin had been half talking to herself, but Keigetsu tore into her for it. "How do you expect me to stay calm?! I...I'm under attack from every angle! I don't even know how much of this was the work of the Kou clan.

For all I know, the townspeople, or the court ladies, or the Maidens had a hand in it too. It's all the same in the end! Everyone hates me!"

The tears spilling down her face one after another really did make her shriek sound like a cry for help.

"Oh, Lady Keigetsu..."

When Reirin noticed Leelee approaching them with a face taut with tension, she shot her a look that said to stop right there. The redhead looked worried that her mistress might go on a violent rampage, but it was more important not to provoke Keigetsu at the moment.

"I get it, Lady Keigetsu. Then—"

"You *get* it?! You don't *get* anything! You're always so calm and composed! Everyone else loves and protects you! You have no idea what I'm feeling!" Reirin had been careful not to argue back, but it wasn't enough to stop Keigetsu from flying into a rage, her bloodshot eyes narrowed into a glare.

The moonlight pouring in through the window turned a shade darker.

"You should get a taste of my suffering..."

Why was it that something in her trembling voice sounded as ominous as the rumble of earth?

"I've had enough! I'm so tired of all this!"

"Lady Keigetsu—"

"I just wanted to be like you!"

It happened the moment she screamed hard enough to make her throat sore.

Fwoosh!

All the candles in the room lit up at once, flames blazing.

"Eek!"

Which girl had been the one to scream?

A moment later, the fires that had been raging fiercely enough to warm the entire room died back down without a sound. In the ring of moonlight that had once again begun to shine through the window, both Reirin and Keigetsu crumpled to the floor.

"Wha...?! Are you all right?!" As she snapped back to her senses, Leelee rushed over and lifted Reirin in her arms. "I can't believe this! What the hell were you thinking, Lady Keigetsu?! Are you out to burn Lady Reirin to a crisp?!" Forgetting to watch her language, she glared at Keigetsu, only for her eyes to widen with shock in the very next moment.

"Huh? Oh dear..."

Why? Because the same "Shu Keigetsu" who had unleashed that onslaught of flame looked strangely calm as she tilted her head to one side.

"My oh my..."

There was also the way she put a hand to her cheek in bemusement.

Meanwhile, the so-called "Kou Reirin" in Leelee's arms all but groaned, "You've got to be kidding me... I triggered the spell with no preparations at all?"

"Th-then that means..."

It was clear what had happened, whether she liked it or not. Leelee's face froze in horror, while Shu Keigetsu—or Reirin in her form, that is—nonchalantly remarked, "It looks like we've switched bodies again."

"Wait, NOW?!" Leelee shouted. And who could blame her?

They weren't back in their home of the Maiden Court but in the midst of a grand excursion—in an environment that was dreadfully hostile toward "Shu Keigetsu." There was no telling what might happen to Reirin if she stayed in Keigetsu's body, and to make matters worse, Gyoumei was right around the corner. There was danger on all sides.

Hence, Leelee grabbed Kou Reirin—or rather, Keigetsu—by the shoulders and shook her back and forth. "Hey! Hurry and switch back! This is no time to be swapping bodies!"

"I-I know that!" Keigetsu-as-Reirin mumbled, contorting her gorgeous, delicate features into a grimace. "But I can't... I don't have enough qi."

"Huh?! Why not?! You clearly had enough of it to go berserk!"

"It's *because* it ran out of control! I triggered the spell without reciting an incantation or doing any proper preparations, so it drained me of all the qi I had!"

Leelee didn't really get the mechanics of the Daoist arts, but she knew from the fear in Keigetsu's voice that she was telling the truth.

"You're kidding. What do we do, then? How long will it take to replenish your qi? A few hours? A full day? Is Lady Reirin supposed to spend that whole time being 'Shu Keigetsu'?"

"Fire qi is plentiful in these parts, so the actual process of replenishing shouldn't take too long. But it'll be unbalanced, so

I'll have to mold that qi extra carefully in order to cast the spell right."

"And how long is that going to take, exactly?!"

Cowed, Keigetsu replied in a tiny voice, "Four or five days..."

"You've gotta be—"

"Now, now," an airy voice cut in just as Leelee had grabbed Keigetsu's collar in a flash of anger. It belonged to Reirin in Keigetsu's form. "There's no point getting upset about what's already come to pass. The blame lies with the disturbance in the qi more than Lady Keigetsu herself. It was out of our hands."

Her smile was gentle and benevolent.

"Hee hee...hee hee hee... Indeed, it's out of our hands. There's nothing we can do about it."

No... The way she had pressed her hands to her cheeks didn't look *benevolent*, exactly—it was more of a helpless sort of smile, like she couldn't contain the joy bubbling up within her.

"L-Lady Reirin?"

"K-Kou Reirin?"

Leelee and Keigetsu called out to her in unison, each girl feeling a mysterious shiver run down her spine.

Reirin smiled wider, then gracefully rose to her feet. "You were absolutely right to say that I should put myself in your shoes. And I don't have any desire to stand back and watch as my dearest friend gets hurt." Her gaze narrowed as the moonlight hit her cheeks.

Ah... Leelee flashed back to an old memory the moment she saw that face. *It's that look she gets with the aphids!*

Indeed, Reirin hadn't choked out all those insistences to stay calm because she was beside herself with sadness. It was because she knew she wouldn't be able to keep a lid on her boiling anger otherwise.

"It seems my dear, dear friend who forewent both sleep and pride in her efforts to succeed..."

"Erm, wai—"

"...has been disrespected by her subjects, scorned by her court ladies, and driven to despair by the other Maidens."

"H-hold on, Kou Reirin."

"Worse, my brothers—two *Kou* men, of all people—stooped to such vile methods to bring a poor girl to ruin."

Heedless of Keigetsu and Leelee's panic, Reirin cast a slow glance around the ransacked room. Then, she stared down at the yellow tassel clutched in her hands.

Shrrrk!

"Eek!"

The tassel gave a small screech as she ripped it in two.

"I refrained from suggesting we trade places because I didn't want to trouble you...but this must be the hands of fate. I can almost hear the Great Ancestor's voice in my ears."

Leelee and Keigetsu clasped each other's hands on instinct as the remains of the tassel fluttered to the floor.

After gazing upon it gently for a moment, Reirin inclined her head to one side. "It's telling me: 'Finish them.'"

Just as he had brought a full cup of liquor to his lips, Prince Gyoumei abruptly lifted his face.

Captain Shin-u of the Eagle Eyes leaned forward from his place at the prince's side. "What's the matter, Your Highness?"

"Was that a disturbance in the qi I felt?"

Shin-u blinked at the prince's half-soliloquy of a question. After a moment's thought, he carefully said, "I'm afraid I couldn't say as one who doesn't bear the dragon's qi. It *is* within my power to pick up on bloodlust or ill omens, however."

His blue eyes—a rarity in the Kingdom of Ei—darted around the room. He looked down upon the men crammed together over the red-carpeted floor, kowtowing as they recited their prayers, and then calmly concluded, "If nothing else, no one here seems foolish enough to do you any disrespect. Though a few do seem eager to finish up the banquet and get to drinking as soon as possible."

"That's no surprise." Gyoumei gave a small sigh, then leaned back in his chair.

Just like the Maidens, he too was currently partaking in a feast before an altar. Whereas the girls would proceed to dedicate an art to the Heavens, the prince would be sharing drinks and appetizers with the townsmen after his meal. It was plain to see that these scrawny men weren't eating well on a regular basis. Though they kept their foreheads pressed reverently to the ground, their feverish anticipation of what would come next was almost palpable.

"It looks like the south's cold spell has done more damage than I thought."

"The townspeople's qi does indeed seem to be in chaos. I'll bet being chosen as the Harvest Festival site is the only thing that stopped them from rising in revolt. The hosting township receives a greater helping of welfare congee than is standard, after all."

Though the men's prayers were sure to drown out their voices regardless, the pair conversed in whispers so as not to be overheard. The only two men eating in the room with the altar were Gyoumei and the township magistrate, Koh Tokushou, who was seated at a table one step below him.

As he watched Lord Koh bow his head toward the altar with each bite, Shin-u added, "Or perhaps it's owed to the rule of Lord Koh, who is so famed for his virtue."

Lord Koh was a lean but vigorous man whose white hair and beard were his defining features. His calm demeanor made him look more the part of an old scholar than a township magistrate.

It was rare for the site of the Harvest Festival—in other words, a region with enough turbulence in its qi to qualify—to have such tight control over its population. Since the current generation of Maidens had only just been assembled last year, this was Gyoumei's first time performing the rite; however, the populations of several townships visited by his predecessors had turned hostile due to rampant starvation, and there had even been instances of disrespect done to the imperial family.

But as evidenced by the way the men were keeping their heads bowed low, *this* township's loyalty to the throne was impeccable. The altar was remarkably well put together for a community of this scale, and the people's attitude toward Gyoumei was shockingly reverent and hospitable.

"They must be in awe of your regality," Shin-u said, thinking back to how pious the townspeople had seemed.

"No..." Gyoumei furrowed his brow a fraction. "If I had to say, it feels more like they're being cautious."

"What?"

Instead of answering Shin-u, Gyoumei took a sip of his drink. He side-eyed the prostrate men as he began turning over thoughts in his head.

The townspeople were reverent, but only toward Gyoumei and four of the Maidens. Since their arrival in town, he had noticed those same people repeatedly shooting disdainful looks Shu Keigetsu's way. Even if she didn't see them on a regular basis, she was still the Maiden of their domain. They ought to have had some measure of attachment to her. For instance, if this were the Kou clan's central territory, the townspeople would have been sure to smile and kneel before Reirin no matter which part of the land it was.

Do they resent the Heavens for sending them that cold spell? No...then their grudge would be against me, the son of the emperor. Why are they being so civil to me while they glare at Shu Keigetsu?

Another thing that bothered Gyoumei was the unusually large altar and hall. It looked like a huge undertaking for a backwater township that subsequently had a limited number of craftsmen to do the work.

The drum tower was likewise impressive for a township of this size. It had no doubt been renovated to prepare for the crown prince and Maidens' visit, but how could a region suffering a cold spell afford to do that?

It doesn't sit right with me.

The bad blood against Shu Keigetsu was something he particularly needed to keep an eye on. There was a risk that a Maiden as emotional as her might raise a fuss over a minor quarrel and escalate it into a huge debacle.

Earlier, when the page posted outside had reported to him that "Lady Shu Keigetsu lost her erhu for the performance of tribute, screamed at a townswoman in public, and went back to her room," he'd wanted to bury his face in his hands. Excluding family members, men and women were meant to avoid contact until the main event five days later, but in the worst case, he might have to go check on what was happening by the stage.

Just then, however, the ecstatic-looking page returned with the update that "Lady Kou Reirin successfully convinced her to return to the stage," providing Gyoumei some modicum of relief.

"It sounds like Lady Reirin saved the day. It won't be long before the banquet ends and the townspeople are served their drinks and appetizers. We should have an easier time moving freely after that...so should we go reprimand Shu Keigetsu?" Shin-u said in hushed tones, putting out feelers.

Gyoumei gave a thoughtful hum as he stroked his chin, then nodded. "Yes, I think I'll leave my seat for a bit—but it's Reirin I'll be going to see. Call her over for me, and be discreet about it."

"Why?" his half brother asked with a dubious frown.

Gyoumei chuckled. "If Shu Keigetsu is standing on the stage, it means she made it through her greatest crisis. She might be ashamed of her lousy performance, but that's trifling in the grand scheme of things. Even if the townspeople turn on her, the Kou clan will protect her from harm. I'm more concerned about Reirin losing her temper when she sees everyone mocking her friend."

Shin-u lapsed into silence. Most of the Maiden Court couldn't even imagine the prince's elegant "butterfly" getting mad, but he had learned Kou Reirin's true nature via the recent body swap. It was rare for her to lose control of her emotions, but the moment she lost her temper, she'd plunge into a series of bold actions with a staggering impetus and tenacity. If her friend Shu Keigetsu came under attack, it was entirely possible *she* would be more furious than the girl in question.

"Yes... I could definitely see her going on a rampage."

"Right? So I'm going to give her a warning."

"As you wish."

Once the captain of the Eagle Eyes had turned swiftly on his heel and left, Gyoumei huffed a small sigh. Perhaps that series of orders would seem excessive from an outside perspective. Still, part of him was convinced that he needed to keep Reirin in check. For all that she was sweet and ladylike, she was also shockingly reckless.

And now that she's on her very first trip, she seems to be cutting loose more than ever before. While there's no doubt that Reirin is capable, the truth is that she's still a sheltered girl who has barely seen the outside world.

A rueful smile rose to his face as he thought back to how excited his cousin had looked each time he'd caught a glimpse of her from his carriage.

Reirin had changed a bit as of late. She seemed to wear her heart on her sleeve more than she used to. That was a good thing, to be sure, and it only added to her charm—but on the other hand, she might find herself dragged into trouble if she didn't learn her limits.

"Good heavens."

He took the cup back in his hand, elegantly sipping his drink.

THOUGH I AM AN INEPT VILLAINESS

Tale of the Butterfly-Rat
Body Swap in the Maiden Court

3 | Reirin Strikes Back

"H A HA, hear that? She called us 'good-for-nothings.' And she's the one who broke the erhu on accident too. Can't believe she pointed fingers at Old Kyou without even batting an eye."

The townswoman remained kneeling on the floor long after Shu Keigetsu had fled the scene; it was only when a few other women came to comfort her that she left the pavilion at last. Left behind, the old lady—Kyou—scrambled to her feet and tottered after her. Meanwhile, Unran commented under his breath as he watched this play out from his high ground.

That's right: high ground. He was sitting atop a beam of the stage that had been built for this very occasion. The beam wasn't a particularly sturdy one, having been formed from the trunk of a single old tree. Someone afraid of heights might have fainted from the mere act of climbing up there, but you'd think Unran was perched atop the earth itself from the way he was lounging cross-legged and resting his chin in his hand. The bottom half of his wild, eye-catching face was swathed in black cloth. He was dressed almost like a bandit.

"They never would've constructed the stage in time without the help of us 'good-for-nothing' untouchables either. The townspeople get to hog all the credit while they foist the dirty work and responsibility onto us. Lucky bastards," came the guttural voice of the other person sitting on the beam. He was a middle-aged, unruly-looking man who boasted a sharp gaze—Gouryuu. He was likewise wearing a black cloth over his face.

Untouchables—that was their status within the township.

They were the residents of a village composed of criminals, refugees, and their descendants. Though their kind hadn't been "cleansed," as often happened in other territories, they were still strictly segregated from the townspeople in terms of the jobs they could get, the clothes they could wear, and even the length they could keep their hair. They were the societal underdogs who had been relegated to a particularly barren part of the township under the pretext of protection, then forced to give thanks for their circumstances. That was their lot in life.

Most days, they'd be stoned just for setting foot in the township capital. The reason they were allowed to be there now was, of course, so that they could carry out the secret mission given to them by the magistrate.

Tonight, at the pre-celebration venue, these two men would abduct Shu Keigetsu and abscond with her to their village.

"Nah, Uncle Gouryuu. The real lucky bastard is the girl who kicked up all this fuss over a single instrument. Did you see her fancy robe and hairpin? I can't even guess how many years of our taxes those must have cost," Unran all but spat.

Gouryuu nodded back. "Good point. No question that the Maiden is the most rotten one of the bunch. She's got an ugly mug and too much ego to give a damn about anyone but herself. It's just like the rumors said. I'm not surprised *she* brought all these calamities to our doorstep."

"Just thinking about how our taxes go toward dressing up a girl like *her* is enough to make me cry."

"You said it."

Their voices oozed with what could well be described as hatred.

"If we unleash divine punishment upon Shu Keigetsu...we'll be saved," Gouryuu muttered, the words sounding as heavy and viscous as a curse—perhaps because he had repeated them to himself so many times before. "Brace yourself, Unran. This hall is crawling with skilled guards. We'll have to catch them by surprise if we want to make it out of here with Shu Keigetsu."

"Yeah, that's exactly what *I* said. Are *you* going to be all right, Uncle Gouryuu? Your hands have been shaking this whole time," Unran shot back with a look of indifference.

He had him there. "Can it. I'm not good with heights, that's all." In an effort to hide his embarrassment, Gouryuu bad-mouthed his coconspirators as he rubbed his hairy arms. "Bastards. I get why *you're* here, since you volunteered to take the lead, but how did *I* get shoved into the role of kidnapper? This is the hardest part of the whole damn scheme. I'm not confident I'm gonna make it back to the village alive."

"You'll be fine. Aside from those 'ceremonial officers,' there's no one here but a bunch of girls. And thanks to my escapades

THOUGH I AM AN INEPT VILLAINESS

with the townswomen, I know escape routes that the men don't. I told the magistrate to relax the security to make the kidnapping easier too. No need to sweat it," Unran said in a languid but smooth drawl.

Gouryuu gave his nephew a surprised look. "Heh... You sure have become dependable," he said in self-deprecation. "I remember back when you'd spend all your time messing around in the mountains or the township, refusing to work in the fields and constantly picking fights with my brother. Now here you are, our village's last hope. Guess you never know what the future'll hold."

Unran shot his uncle a glance but didn't otherwise respond to his soliloquy.

The moment someone down below lit a short candle with the preprepared tinder, he said curtly, "Don't drop the oil pot, Uncle Gouryuu. We'll wait until Shu Keigetsu begins her performance to scatter the oil around and set it ablaze. If we're aiming to make a distraction, the fire's got to be as dramatic as possible."

"I know. Jeez...you're the only man brave enough to come up with a plan to set fire to a god's altar. Aren't you afraid you'll get cursed?" his uncle asked, a frown crossing his face.

"Oh, c'mon, not you too. We're just punishing a woman who affronted the Heavens. Who would curse me for that? I bet the god of agriculture'll be glad he doesn't have to suffer through her second-rate performance," replied Unran, dismissing the man's concerns out of hand.

"Look," he went on, jerking his chin toward the square. "Does anyone here seem concerned about Shu Keigetsu after she yelled at an old lady and ran off in disgrace? Obviously the townswomen don't, but not even her would-be 'friends' among the Maidens seem to care. Only one court lady ran after her, and none of the guards has so much as budged. *Nobody* likes her."

"True. The only one who went after her was that drop-dead gorgeous Kou Maiden. Now if only the Shu Maiden had been a looker like her..." Gouryuu sighed.

Just then, Unran sat up straight and covered his candle with a hand to keep the light from leaking out. "She's here."

In the corner of his vision, he saw that Shu Keigetsu had returned to the pavilion that led to the stage. Based on the lack of screaming, she seemed to have regained her composure. Perhaps the Kou Maiden who had gone after her earlier had managed to console her.

She's got guts for returning to the stage, I'll give her that.

He gazed coldly upon Shu Keigetsu as she gracefully strode ahead. His whole plan would have fallen apart if she'd locked herself in her room, so he was glad to see she'd pulled herself together. That was the first and last positive impression he was ever going to have of her, though. He was, after all, about to capture and punish her on behalf of the Heavens.

The Shu Maiden leisurely approached the stage. Her attending court lady hung back in the pavilion, and her only guards were the two ceremonial officers she'd borrowed from the Kou clan. The two men were standing on either side of the stage. It looked like each was keeping watch over one of the two bonfires.

THOUGH I AM AN INEPT VILLAINESS

Unran and Gouryuu simply watched as she took the stage as quietly as a beast before its prey, until at last the pair raised an eyebrow in unison.

"Doesn't she seem...different somehow?"

"Yeah."

Each man placed a hand atop the beam as he stared at the stage below. There, Shu Keigetsu prostrated herself before the altar near the back, then glided to center stage as elegantly as if her dance had already begun. She looked infinitely more confident than she had just earlier.

Even stranger than that, however, was the garment she was wearing.

"What's *that* about?"

Rather than don her precious ceremonial robe, she had merely draped it over her shoulders. What's more, it became clear in the light of the bonfire that most of the once-beautiful robe was caked in mud. It certainly wasn't fit for a dance of tribute.

"What is she planning?" Unran muttered.

In the same moment, Shu Keigetsu signaled the ceremonial officer standing to one side of the stage. Confusion plain on his face, he proceeded to cover one of the bonfires with an iron box.

Losing one light source dimmed the stage, lending it a greater air of mystique.

Perhaps sucked into her rhythm, the townswomen stopped their gossiping and fixed their eyes upon the stage. All that could be heard was the crackle of the one remaining flame.

"May the god of agriculture receive the goddess of fertility in the coming autumn days."

The moment after she announced her dance in sonorous tones, the two men sitting atop the beam let out a gasp.

Let's turn back the clock and return to the Maidens' seats in the square. Left to fret after Reirin had run off to comfort Shu Keigetsu, Keikou and Keishou were relieved to see the girls return together.

"Oh, Reirin! You're back!"

It appeared their little sister had successfully pacified Shu Keigetsu and brought her back in one piece.

The same girl who had been shrieking her head off earlier approached them calmly and offered a deep bow. "I apologize for losing my temper back there. I'll be returning your sister now."

"Sure..."

The pair gaped in surprise, getting the sense that she'd changed an awful lot in a brief span of time.

Before he could put a finger on what felt different, however, Keikou noticed how pale his sister looked and said, "What's wrong, Reirin? You don't look so good."

"Huh? Oh. Um... I'm a little tired, that's all." In contrast to Shu Keigetsu, *she* looked like she'd been wrung out in an equally short period. "Erm, since I had to run after Lady Keigetsu and all..."

The brothers frowned at how feeble she looked. Reirin was the crown jewel of the Kou clan. They wouldn't tolerate anyone weighing their sister down, not even with a mere bit of fatigue.

"It seems you made quite a bit of trouble for our sister on the way back here, Lady Shu Keigetsu. Looks to me like your reputation for being the biggest nuisance in the Maiden Court was well deserved," Keikou accused her, sharpening his gaze.

Your average woman would burst into tears upon being threatened by a man as burly as Keikou. A girl rumored to be as emotional as Shu Keigetsu shouldn't have lasted two seconds.

Yet oddly enough, Reirin was the one to squeal, her lovely face contorted with fear as she clung to him in a panic. "Lord K— Brother Senior! P-please don't say that. You mustn't provoke her. Let's keep things amicable. Peaceful! Please?"

"Your kindness is one of your best features, Reirin. But what's wrong with telling the truth? I've heard the rumors about the talentless 'Maiden Court sewer rat.' What's with that dirty robe she's wearing, anyway? It reeks of mud. Is our little rat planning to show off a few tricks in *that*?"

"Brother Senior, please!" his sister screamed, going white as a sheet. It was so like her to stop someone from bad-mouthing her friend.

And as for Shu Keigetsu, she simply heard him out before murmuring, "A talentless 'sewer rat,' hm?" For all the screaming she'd done earlier, she appeared awfully calm.

Or, no...

"Is that right?"

"Urk!" The thin smile that rose to her face was enough to intimidate even a military officer like Keikou. "You..."

"Mud is such a sinful thing." As Keikou instinctively tensed up, Shu Keigetsu shifted her gaze. She turned to look out over the Maidens and townswomen who were watching this all unfold. "No matter what beautiful fur lies underneath, one will be mocked as 'filthy' the moment they're caked in mud. Everyone hesitates to set foot upon a field of pure white snow, but no one minds slinging dirt at someone who's already soiled."

It managed to sound like both a speech and a soliloquy at once. A smile rose to her face as her audience fell silent in awe.

"A 'sewer rat,' am I? Very well. Then I shall make full use of the virtues buried beneath this mud and offer a performance sure to please the god of agriculture." Then she looked Keikou straight in the eye and asked, as if he were only expected to obey her commands, "I no longer have an erhu, so I plan to perform a dance instead. It's too bright with a bonfire on either side of the stage, so could I ask you to put out one or the other, my dear ceremonial officer?"

Keikou and Keishou were doing Shu Keigetsu a favor by doubling as her ceremonial officers, so she shouldn't have been in a position to make demands. And yet, she ordered them around with all the confidence of a Maiden to whom countless military officers had sworn their fealty. Strangest of all was how it felt like the right attitude for her to have in that moment.

Keikou nodded after a moment's silence. "As you wish." For some reason, he was overcome with the same apprehension and elation he felt facing a worthy opponent on the battlefield.

95

"Then I'll stand watch over the bonfire on the other side. Someone needs to make sure the pillar doesn't get knocked over during your dance," the younger Keishou quickly offered, sensing the tension in the air. He was probably concerned that Shu Keigetsu might take advantage of the ceremony to try something dangerous. "Tousetsu, watch Reirin for us."

"Yes, sir."

"Thank you. I'll be counting on you both, then," the Maiden said with an impassive nod, then headed straight for the stage. There was something almost invigorating in the way she looked straight ahead and tucked in her chin.

Taking that as their cue to head over to their respective bonfires, the brothers casually exchanged glances. Had this girl always been so beautiful?

Upon taking the stage, Shu Keigetsu prostrated herself before the altar before assuming center stage. Once Keikou had put out one of the bonfires, she kneeled quietly in the dim light.

"May the god of agriculture receive the goddess of fertility in the coming autumn days."

Her dignified preamble echoed across the silent stage. Keikou and Keishou—no, all those present—watched her closely, stumped as to what would happen next. After all, she didn't have her erhu. She claimed she was going to dance instead, but a dance without instrumentals was sure to lack punch, and the robe meant to ensure its splendor was inexplicably covered in mud.

Kin Seika, who until that point had been fiddling with her fan in boredom, went wide-eyed when she saw Shu Keigetsu kneel upon the stage. She leaned forward, feeling a shiver run down her spine. "That's more like it."

The Shu Keigetsu she was looking at now clearly wasn't the girl known as a "sewer rat." The girl standing there was the same one she had seen during the Ghost Festival—that steadfastly noble dancing girl.

"I see she's finally getting serious. But how do you plan to dance with no music, Shu Keigetsu?" Seika asked under her breath. She would soon have her answer.

Shu Keigetsu came to life upon the stage. She held up the robe she'd hung over her shoulders and hid her face behind the bodice. The muddied garment was just the right size to cover the length of her body.

"Dozing upon the warm earth..."

The soiled robe almost blended into the shades of night. The spectators gasped in unison when they heard a melodious voice sound from within.

A song!

This was the first time the Maidens had ever heard Shu Keigetsu sing so loud and clear. All the times she'd been asked to sing in the past, she had barely managed to squeak out a muffled, off-key performance.

"Petals of life / fluttering and fluttering / rife and abundant / as we long for a light / that shines from the east..."

The girl on the stage slowly rose to her feet. That one simple motion was enough to draw the audience's eye. Though the lyrics sounded improvised, the melody was beautiful. Having the performer's face hidden from view also made the spectators focus all the more intently on her song.

"We soon extend a hand / to the world beyond..."

She opened her arms outward. Then, the moment her face came into view and the audience leaned forward in suspense...

Fwp!

The robe fluttered loudly through the air, drawing a buzz from the crowd. It drew a gorgeous trail through the darkness as it sailed away, its golden embroidery reflecting the light of the bonfire. What emerged from within was neither a deep vermillion nor a drab mud-brown in color, but a glitzy green garment.

Shu Keigetsu was clad in a robe reminiscent of a sprout.

"O skies above / blow your winds in celebration / O clouds above / bring your rain of blessing..."

She whipped around and bent backward with an intensity far from the slow start of her performance. Entranced, the audience watched the dancing girl as she dashed all across the stage, spinning and twirling. She slid an arm up her sleeve in an almost suggestive gesture, and from it she pulled a shawl that had been stored inside.

"O light / beam down upon us..."

Whoosh!

The shawl was a pale orange. Billowing in the breeze and soaking in the glow of the bonfire, the sheer cloth looked almost like a ray of sunlight. Everyone in attendance saw the illusion of a sprout breaking through sludge and shooting straight toward the Heavens, bathed in warm light.

"Incredible..." Kin Seika eventually murmured, so captivated by her dance that she had forgotten to breathe.

She wasn't the only one. All the townswomen who had just been glaring at Shu Keigetsu—even the court ladies and military officers who should have been used to watching the performances of gorgeous young women—succumbed to her vivacious kaleidoscope of a dance one after the other.

"Wow... Do you think she's trying to send a message?"

"Yeah. I think she's supposed to be a growing seed...no, a sprout."

The ladies kneeling in the back whispered among themselves, leaning toward the gaps in the partition to get a better look. Even the townswomen too uneducated to know how to appraise sophisticated dances could sense that there was a theme to this performance.

"*O light...*"

When the girl in the limelight reached the edge of the stage, she suddenly let the shawl drop from her hands. Then, much to everyone's great surprise, she slipped past Keishou...and grabbed a log of burning wood from the bonfire behind him.

Gasp! A stir swept through the crowd when it looked like the Maiden had thrust her hand into the flames. Yet all she did was calmly adjust her grip on the log and then proceed to spin it around in a circle. Shimmering sparks danced in the air, and the vermillion afterimages formed a large ring in the darkness of the stage.

The whole crowd let slip an admiring "ooh." Ahh, they realized, this was supposed to be the sun.

"Give unto us the light..."

Flames held high overhead, she looked almost like a celestial maiden embracing the sun itself. The girl played with the fire until she at last reached the other end of the stage, where Kou Keikou guarded the second bonfire. She flashed him the most dazzling smile she could muster...

Swsh!

And then she hurled the firewood straight at Keikou's throat.

"Ngh!"

She'd moved so fast that he couldn't even see the afterimage of the flame. Her masterful dance was more like a martial arts demonstration than a performance. Keikou drew his sword on instinct and prepared to slice the log down. But despite the flames flicking their tongues to reach him, the wood stopped short of his neck.

"Hee hee," came a tinkling laugh, small enough to be drowned out by the crackling of the firewood. "Look at the aphid, so scared of fire."

"Ack!"

Only upon following her gaze did Keikou notice that he had pulled one of his legs back. He was as intimidated by this woman as if he were standing before a fearsome foe. They only made eye contact for a second, yet it was plain to see what she was trying to say through that smile filled with burning rage. If a talentless Maiden could be called a sewer rat, then wasn't a military officer afraid of some firewood no better than an insect?

"Wha...?"

Ignoring Keikou's gulp, she tossed the firewood into the extinguished bonfire as smoothly as if it were part of her dance. Now illuminated from both ends of the stage, the dancing Maiden turned her back on the speechless man, a silent declaration that she had no more business with him. The girl slowly made her way back to center stage. Her arms outstretched, she threw out her chest toward the Heavens.

"May we bear fruit."

Her voice practically melted into the air around her as she recited the final verse. It was clear what her pose at the end of the dance was meant to symbolize. The stage was bright again. Basking in the glow of the flames, her light-green robe took on an almost golden hue. Her back bent and her head hung low, she was the very picture of a drooping ear of grain.

Silence fell over the square for a few moments.

Eventually, Kin Seika came to her senses and started clapping, which set off a wave of applause among the other Maidens, the court ladies, and the townswomen. The clamor was almost deafening as cheers erupted from every corner.

After sitting there and watching her in breathless amazement, even Kou Reirin's—no, Keigetsu's—voice trembled. "So this is how she dances..."

She'd known that the Kou Maiden was an expert dancer. But that was supposed to entail delicate, graceful performances that were little more than pleasing to the eye. Never had she witnessed a dance so dynamic it made her heart rattle in her chest.

"This is your first time seeing *her* dance, isn't it?" Tousetsu quietly remarked from her side. When Keigetsu turned her head, catching the hidden meaning in the words, the court lady bent down to pour more liquor in her cup and whispered into her ear, "I see you've traded places again."

Of course she'd seen through it. Keigetsu's face froze, but Tousetsu didn't say anything more than that. Perhaps she couldn't be seen criticizing her Maiden in public. First Keigetsu thought to make excuses, then to apologize. But upon realizing that Tousetsu wouldn't tolerate either, she just followed her heart instead. That is, she applauded "Shu Keigetsu" with all her might. She clapped for that dazzling butterfly who stole the people's hearts with her playful dance.

"I wonder," she murmured amid the thunderous applause, "if *I'll* ever be able to dance like that."

Her voice was laced with longing and a faint hint of despair.

"Even a mud-dweller like me...who only ever gets mocked."

Tousetsu cast her a sidelong glance. Surprisingly, she didn't snort in response but just matter-of-factly said, "You can do it *because* you're bathed in filth."

"Huh?"

"That's what the dance was all about. It's because she was covered in mud at the start that the verdant robe underneath looked so dazzling. Don't you understand what she was trying to tell you?"

"Don't look so sad."

A mild voice replayed in the back of Keigetsu's mind.

"You're doing the best you can."

Her gentle tones always shone a light into the distance. Each time Keigetsu had given up and tried to abandon her efforts, Kou Reirin had been there to patiently admonish her. *It'll be all right. Calm down.* How many times had she heard those words?

Keigetsu finally understood. It wasn't purely out of spite that Kou Reirin had danced in that soiled robe and thrust a flame at her brother. Her true goal had been to encourage Keigetsu. She could cast aside the blanket of filth. With a fire in her heart, she could overcome any foe.

"Why, I'm almost jealous to see how much she cares for you," Tousetsu said somewhat sulkily. Tears pricked Keigetsu's eyes.

Dedicating a dance meant for the god of agriculture to me... What do you think you're doing, Kou Reirin?

Reirin was a villainess through and through. She acted like a good girl, only to disregard even the gods to do exactly as she pleased. She was daring and freewheeling, and she toyed with people's hearts all she liked. Keigetsu hurried to blink away her tears.

"Excuse me."

It was then that a subdued voice called out to her from behind, and she straightened up with a start. When she turned around, she saw it was Shin-u, the captain of the Eagle Eyes.

He cast a dubious glance around the excitement-filled square—fortunately, Reirin was currently bowing before the altar with her back to the audience—but as soon as he noticed Keigetsu's eyes on him, he swiftly stooped down and whispered, "His Highness is waiting for you inside."

Keigetsu thought she deserved credit for managing to swallow down her scream. She broke out into a cold sweat. *Why now? Oh no... Did he find out already?*

She gazed awkwardly up at Shin-u. Interpreting that look as a rebuke, he proceeded to explain himself. "I apologize for interrupting the rite. However, word reached us that you stood up for Shu Keigetsu in her time of need. His Highness is concerned that your righteous indignation might drive you to do something reckless."

He sounded much more polite than he generally did around Shu Keigetsu. Now wasn't the time to get indignant about that, however.

Neither was it the time to be entranced when Shin-u broke into a smile and, looking vaguely gleeful, added, "There *is* the precedent of the Bow of Warding, after all."

"Erm..."

When Keigetsu froze up, Tousetsu stepped in to answer for her. "Understood. Now that the tribute is over, we'll be heading into a short break. I'll tell everyone that Lady Reirin stepped out into the night breeze to sober up."

She took Keigetsu's hand and helped her to her feet, casually shooting her a meaningful glance.

Bluff your way through it. That was probably the rough translation. It seemed that Reirin's ever-faithful servant planned to guard the secret of the swap alongside Keigetsu.

I'm glad she's on my side, but...what am I supposed to do?!

Just the thought of seeing Gyoumei in this situation was

enough to make Keigetsu break into shivers. Running away wasn't an option, though.

Keigetsu walked silently ahead, accompanied by Tousetsu. As she followed Shin-u's lead, feeling like a chicken on its way to the slaughter, she soon caught sight of a figure standing in the cloister. Looking like a painting come to life as his cheeks glistened in the moonlight was none other than the gorgeous crown prince: Gyoumei.

"Hello there, Reirin. I'm sorry to take you away from the festivities."

"I don't mind, Your Highness."

Judging by his gentle cadence, he had yet to realize who she was. Keigetsu sucked in her gut. There was nothing left to do but get into her role as Kou Reirin and prepare for the worst.

"I hear that I've given you cause to worry," she said. "I'm afraid I must apologize."

For her first move, she placed a hand to her cheek in a demure manner. It felt a little forced, but that *was* the most recognizable element of Reirin's body language.

Keigetsu cringed when Gyoumei responded with a blink, but he soon broke into a smile. "Liar. You're not the least bit remorseful, are you?"

She almost panicked at the word "liar," but it didn't appear he'd seen through her act.

Gyoumei turned his gaze in the direction of the square. "I heard cheers coming from outside just now. Shu Keigetsu did well, from the sound of it. Did you set her up for success, Reirin?"

"I have no idea what you could be referring to," she responded with all the grace she could muster, sweating bullets on the inside.

Think, Keigetsu, think! How would Kou Reirin respond to that question?

She wouldn't boast about her own accomplishments, that was for certain. In fact, she didn't talk much about herself at all. She spent most of her time praising other people.

With a twinkle in her eyes, or perhaps a proud smile upon her face, Keigetsu said, "Lady Keigetsu simply demonstrated her own potential. All I did was offer a few words of encouragement."

"Oho."

Things seemed to be going well so far.

Keigetsu relaxed as Gyoumei gave a calm nod of his head, only to have her breath stolen a moment later when he brought his face to hers. "I'm glad to hear it. But I came here to tell you something, Reirin."

"What is it?"

Time and time again she had wished the handsome crown prince would close the distance between them. Never had she imagined she would feel so terrified when he finally did lean in close enough for her to feel his breath on her face.

"Our bet is off for the duration of this trip. I hereby forbid you from switching bodies."

" ..."

It was a stroke of luck that her throat locked up in panic and prevented her from making a sound.

It's too laaaate!

If she *had* managed to express her innermost thoughts, she would have ended up screaming at the top of her lungs.

"The southern townspeople resent Shu Keigetsu even more than I anticipated. I'm sure it's hard for you to watch her struggle, but don't so much as think about trading places with her and taking on her hardships. This isn't the Maiden Court. Even Shin-u and I might not be able to protect you from whatever happens."

That was the crown prince's keen eye for you. He'd predicted his cousin's actions down to the letter.

But he was too late.

It was all too late.

"I'll take steps to prevent harm from coming to Shu Keigetsu. It's up to me and the military officers to protect her, not a Maiden like you. Got it?"

Why was it that hearing her ideal man plainly say he would protect "Shu Keigetsu" only made her feel more trapped?

Drawing his own conclusions as to why Keigetsu tensed up, Gyoumei further hardened his features and whispered, "Not happy with that? I don't like throwing my weight around, but I will if I must. If you disobey this order of mine, Reirin, then I will consider that a violation of the crown prince's decree. Our bet will be immediately terminated..."

His breath tickled her earlobe, an almost seductive huskiness to his deep voice.

"...and I will take you as my empress right then and there. Or perhaps this threat will be more effective against you? If you defy this order, I will punish Shu Keigetsu for aiding you in your treason."

She hadn't even cast a spell, and still Keigetsu could feel her soul leaving her body.

"What...sort of punishment?" she managed to squeeze out, but the prince effortlessly dodged the question.

"Who knows? So long as you don't do anything as reckless as trading places, you'll never have to find out."

Aware that pushing the matter would only make her look suspicious, Keigetsu had no choice but to respond, "Very well."

"I'm sorry to be so tactless. But you have to understand that this is for your own safety," he said mildly, then turned his gaze to the grand hall once more. "I want to tell Shu Keigetsu the same, but there isn't much time."

"I-I'll tell her myself. Feel free to head back, Your Highness."

"Is that so? Still, if she performed a splendid enough tribute to draw all those cheers from the crowd, I really ought to offer her a word or two of praise. She *is* the type to seek approval. Well then, Reirin. Be sure to behave yourself."

"Your Highness, wait!"

Heedless of Keigetsu's efforts to stop him, Gyoumei gave Shin-u a signal before turning on his heel. None present had the authority to detain the prince.

Her eyes swimming with tears, Keigetsu berated herself. *I hate myself! I hate that he thinks I'm so needy, and I hate even more that he's exactly right!*

There was no use regretting the past, though.

"What should we do? If His Highness sees her onstage, there won't be any fooling him..."

The distress in Tousetsu's voice made Keigetsu panic in turn. For all that she was competent, Reirin was appallingly defenseless when it came to herself. There was little chance she'd make it through Gyoumei's interrogation without incident. If the pair came face-to-face, she was bound to slip up and give herself away in an instant.

All that awaited Keigetsu after that was her own ruin.

"There's a candle...ah, over there."

Her only hope was to tell Reirin to get out of there before Gyoumei could make it to the square. Also, she had to do it in a way that he and Shin-u wouldn't notice.

Keigetsu ran in the opposite direction of the square and put all her hopes into one of the candles in the cloister. She fixed her gaze upon its flickering flame, focusing her qi. For better or worse, using up so much of her qi earlier meant that she could cast even more intricate spells without fear of her powers running berserk.

"Kou Reirin."

She envisioned the girl she wanted to talk to on the other side of the flame.

Right about now, Reirin was bound to have her back turned to the audience as she presented incense to the candle on the altar. The images cast by a flame mirage spell were difficult to see from anywhere but point-blank range. So long as she didn't make the flame too big, it should've been possible to get Reirin's attention without alerting anyone else.

"Just hear me out and don't say anything—Kou Reirin!" Keigetsu called her friend's name in a hoarse voice.

Following the performance of tribute, the Maiden was to prostrate herself before the altar and offer up a stick of incense.

Dear god of agriculture, I'm so sorry for using my dance to you to fulfill multiple other objectives. Still, it's thanks to this opportunity that everyone has come to look kindlier upon my friend. I thank you from the bottom of my heart.

Pressing her forehead to the ground with a completely straight face, Reirin did her best to get back on the god's good side.

Judging by the applause she could still hear behind her, her dance won the hearts of the audience. Though it wasn't as if she'd had a say in the matter, she would've felt terrible if she'd stolen Keigetsu's spotlight only to bungle the performance, so she was glad the crowd had liked what they saw. She hoped it had raised Keigetsu's spirits a little too.

There was no lie in my desire to bring the southern territory a bountiful harvest either. Please accept my humble apologies on that point. Oh, what's that? You'll forgive me? How very benevolent.

Alas, the Heavens gave no answer, but Reirin took a guess that he'd accepted her apology. The gods' magnanimity was said to go beyond human understanding. Surely it would be fine.

When she rose to her feet and made to offer the incense at the altar, Keikou and Keishou came along either side of her and lit the space around her hands with wood from the bonfire. The show of diligence was a complete one-eighty from their earlier attitude.

"My, thank you," said Reirin, smiling.

Keikou grinned back and said, "Don't mention it. Even a lowly insect ought to do what he can to help." Reirin sensed a barely disguised bite to the words, but she brushed it off with a smile. So long as her brother had taken a moment to reflect on his actions, she didn't care what he thought.

"Watch out. You could get hurt if you don't hold it a little lower, Reirin."

"Oh, I'll be—"

Before she could finish that sentence with "fine," she cut herself off.

As she watched the slow burn of the incense stick, Reirin broke out into a cold sweat.

What...did he just say?

Was her brother so flustered he had gotten her name wrong?

"With all due respect, sir, my name is Shu Keigetsu."

"It's so strange. You have Shu Keigetsu's face, sure, but you're moving like a completely different person. There's only one girl in all of Ei who could unleash her inner beast and dance like such a madwoman, and that's my little sister."

"Sorry, *inner beast*?"

Reirin got caught up in her brother's description of her, but that was the least of her concerns at the moment.

This is bad. He's figured me out!

Realizing that the time had come to put all her practice imitating Keigetsu to the test, Reirin hurried to adopt a tone more reminiscent of her friend. "My, I see you underestimate me. Even

I'm capable of that much." She lifted an eyebrow, tilted her head at the same angle she'd practiced, and glared at Keikou. "Especially when I need to settle the score with a man despicable enough to muddy a woman's garment."

To her surprise, Keikou responded with a skeptical frown. "What?"

"Didn't you smear the mud on it yourself as part of the performance?" Keishou likewise asked from beside her, genuinely curious.

Reirin blinked in confusion, wondering what was going on—and right then, the contours of the flame in front of her swelled and billowed.

"Just hear me out and don't say anything, Kou Reirin!"

Nooo...

It was Keigetsu's flame magic—with the worst possible timing.

Keigetsu had made her reflection in the fire as small as a fingertip, probably so that only someone peering into the altar would be able to see it.

Sadly, she hadn't accounted for the presence of Reirin's two brothers.

Oblivious to the two boggling men, the Keigetsu in the flame leaned forward in a panic.

"Listen up. Just now, Hi...H-H-Hi..."

Hee hee hee...? Reirin frowned, concerned that Keigetsu was under this much pressure.

Keigetsu finally blurted out, *"His Highness called me out and said we're forbidden from switching bodies during the trip. If we*

113

disobey him, he'll take you as his empress on the spot, a-and I'll be severely punished!"

"Eep!"

"His Highness and the Eagle Eyes' captain are on their way to see you now. You won't be able to fool him. Just run. Do whatever it takes to get out of there! It's all over for us if they find out what happened!"

Reirin had a feeling it was all over for them the moment Keigetsu had made that flame call, but sure.

Perhaps to lower the risk of getting caught, the candle went out in a puff of smoke. As smoke lazily curled from the incense stick in her hands, Reirin sweated bullets.

"Oho?"

"Hmm..."

Keikou and Keishou each gave a sage nod. If anything, the conciseness of their reactions was proof of their total conviction. The Kou duo may have been notorious for their overzealousness, but neither one of them was a fool.

"Care to explain, *Reirin*?" her brothers asked in perfect unison, their voices low and threatening.

Reirin steeled herself. At this point, she was better off coming clean and enlisting their help than making a poor attempt to cover things up. Fortunately, she happened to be the best there was at getting these two particular men to coddle her.

"I'm sure you have a rough idea of what's going on, so I won't bore you with details." Placing the dwindling incense atop the hearth, she looked at each of her brothers in turn. Then, she slumped her shoulders and went on in a tiny voice, "I'm in a bit of a bind. It sounds like I'll be disciplined if anyone finds out I switched places with Lady Keigetsu. I don't want to be handed the highest throne as part of a punishment."

Fully aware of how sly she was being, she offered a thought to no one in particular: *You'll have to excuse me.*

"Besides, I'm not ready to stop being your little sister. Please help me, my dear brothers!"

The second she hit them with the finishing move of her best puppy-dog eyes, the men's faces turned deadly serious.

Logically speaking, Reirin's enthronement ought to have been a matter of celebration for her whole clan. But if she claimed she wasn't ready to make that change, it was in the nature of the Kou men—of her two brothers—to drop everything and say, "We won't let it happen, then."

Leelee leaned forward and shouted from the pavilion. "Milady! His Highness and the captain are coming this way!"

Hearing the footsteps of doom steadily approaching, Reirin straightened up with a start. This was the first time since making the bet that she'd be coming face-to-face with Gyoumei in Keigetsu's body. Something told her that her cover would be blown the instant they came into direct contact. Her chances were even worse after that incredible dance she'd just performed.

Whatever happens, I have to avoid getting Lady Keigetsu punished at all costs.

It was as Reirin drew her lips into a thin line that Keikou abruptly spoke up from beside her. "Let me get this straight,

Reirin. You don't want His Highness to find out about the switch, right? And it'd be bad if he saw you right now, yeah?"

"Huh? Yes."

"Got it. Leave everything to your big brothers here."

Reirin whipped around in surprise at the unexpected declaration. "Y-you're going to help me?"

"Of course. There's nothing we wouldn't do for you."

"But how?"

"That's what we're about to figure out. The three of us are such good boys and girls—surely the Heavens will lend us a helping hand somewhere."

Reirin cast a helpless glance heavenward. That answer was so like her brother. In that same instant, her eyes went wide as saucers. There, on the roof of the stage high overhead...sat two figures atop one of its beams.

"Huh?"

The pair was staring down at her, looking dumbfounded. Snapping back to his senses upon meeting her gaze, one of the men raised his arms high in the air and flipped over what looked like a pot.

Splish!

There came the splash of liquid, followed by the sound of something being thrown to the ground. In the next moment, the entire trail of spilled oil burst into flame.

"Eek!"

"This way!"

Reirin only narrowly avoided being engulfed in the roaring

flames when Keikou scooped her up into his arms. But it was then that the two figures swiftly descended from the beam and doused both Keikou and Keishou with the leftover oil.

"Don't move. Hand over that Maiden if you don't want to go up in flames."

"Oh, don't worry, we're not gonna kill her. We just need her to come with us for a bit."

The pair's faces were covered with black cloth. There were torches in their hands. Since they hadn't dumped the oil on Reirin herself, it was probably true that they didn't plan to kill her. It seemed their goal was to separate "Shu Keigetsu" from her guards and kidnap her. It was a very sticky situation.

And yet, the brothers' faces lit up as they whispered to Reirin, "Did you hear that? The Heavens have answered our prayers!"

"Let's leave it to these bandits to get you out of here—I mean, abduct you!"

"Huh?"

Did they really want her to take advantage of a kidnapping attempt?

"Um, b-but...I don't know about that... Wouldn't going off with a couple of perfect strangers be a little too risky?"

Even a girl as gutsy as Reirin was perturbed by her brothers' utter fearlessness.

"Aww, it'll be fine. As long as I tag along, I can lay those bandits flat in the blink of an eye," Keikou said in a show of extreme disrespect for the kidnappers.

Beside him, Keishou murmured, "We're out of time. His Highness is coming this way."

Lo, Gyoumei and Shin-u had made it to the entrance to the square.

"Captain! Go protect Shu Keigetsu at once! All ceremonial officers are to evacuate the Maidens and townspeople immediately!"

"Yes, Your Highness!"

There were Gyoumei's leadership skills in action; he took immediate command of the situation, unfaltering in the face of a sudden emergency.

As she watched Shin-u dash forward with a swiftness that lived up to his name as an Eagle, Reirin made up her mind.

Lady Keigetsu did *tell me to do whatever it takes to get out of here!*

The intensity with which Gyoumei and his guard were closing in on them was immense. Even Reirin was starting to think that she'd rather take her chances with the bandits than incur *their* wrath.

"L-Let's do it!" she said with a nod, clenching her hands into fists.

Her brothers dove right into their respective roles.

"Whaaat?! How dare you bandits attempt to kidnap Lady Shu Keigetsu under the cover of flame!" For starters, Keikou raised his voice in an exaggerated manner and highlighted the bandits' objective.

"Ugh, these guys are tough! We don't stand a chance when we're surrounded by fire! It's too hot!" Keishou lamented not a beat later, bemoaning their "predicament."

"Oh, to think they would take my ceremonial officers hostage! This is terrible—I don't want to be kidnapped! But I'd feel awful for the Kou clan if something were to happen to them, so I have no choice but to let these men take me away!" Reirin shrieked last of all, playing the part of the Maiden kidnapped against her will with all her might.

There was no denying an expositional quality to the whole thing, but the raging flames added to the gravity and persuasive power of their performance. Plus, the fire would make it harder to spot any unnatural behavior of theirs from the square.

"Hah, glad to see you're getting the picture. Come with us, Shu Keigetsu," the younger of the mysterious duo said with a jerk of his chin.

While she turned on the waterworks on the outside, Reirin said a polite *Don't mind if I do!* in her head, happily repurposing their schemes for her own ends.

"Noooo! If you're going to kidnap our Maiden, at least take me with you!" wailed Keikou, clinging to the second, middle-aged man with the over-the-top motions of an actor.

"Hey, let go!" came the man's gruff voice. "We've got no business with her guards. Don't make me torch you!"

"I'll never let go! If you want to set me on fire, take this!"

When Keikou threw his arms around the man and rubbed his oil coating on him, the latter gave up with a click of his tongue. If he started that fire now, the two of them would burn to their deaths together.

"Hey, Unran! This guy's clinging to me like a leech!"

"We haven't got time for this, Uncle Gouryuu. Just bring him with us."

When the man called Unran caught sight of a military officer—Shin-u, captain of the Eagle Eyes—closing in from just beyond the stage, he turned swiftly on his heel, perhaps sensing the impending threat.

"Wait, I won't let you get away! Ugh...I've inhaled so much smoke that it's hard to move! *Cough, cough!*"

"It's all right, Keishou! You stay here and tell His Highness what the bandits looked like!"

"Oh, Brother, I'm such a disgrace! I'll see it done, even if it costs me my life!"

And so the two bandits and the two siblings vanished into the flames engulfing the stage, Keishou's theatrics playing out behind them.

4 | Reirin Breaks New Ground

BEFORE YOU EMBARK on a journey of revenge, dig two graves. Keigetsu was pretty sure that saying was a load of bull.

"So there you have it: We can't let His Highness find out that the girls have already switched places. Head court lady Tousetsu, Shu court lady Leelee, do bear in mind that having turned a blind eye to the situation makes you both accomplices. Be sure to do everything in your power to keep the truth from getting out...if you value your own lives, that is."

It was late at night in the magistrate's residence. The group sat in a corner of the room assigned to "Kou Reirin."

In the dark space with only a single candle left to light it, Tousetsu and Leelee bowed their heads to Keishou, their faces glum.

"Yes, sir. I live to be of service to Lady Reirin."

"Sure... I'll take the heat for Lady Keigetsu's blunder..."

It was an hour after the bandits had set fire to the stage. Prince Gyoumei had cut the pre-celebration short and sent the Eagle Eyes to put out the flames. Based on what he heard from

Keishou, who'd stayed behind as a witness, he had then organized a search party to look for "Shu Keigetsu." He'd fired off order after order without missing a beat, as one would expect of such a wise ruler-to-be.

Now that they'd had the chance to calm down a fraction, the Maidens were staying in their rooms with their respective ceremonial officers. Keigetsu had likewise returned to her chambers as "Kou Reirin," bringing her head court lady, Tousetsu; the Kou clan's ceremonial officer, Keishou; and the stranded Shu clan attendant, Leelee, along with her.

The second she'd closed the door behind her, Keishou had done a one-eighty from his show of despondence and said with a smile, "Well then, Lady Shu Keigetsu, let's have ourselves a secret chat." He'd then forced her to tell him the full truth of the matter, thus bringing our story back up to speed.

"Good heavens, Shu Keigetsu. Just how do you plan to take responsibility for the situation we're in? It's because *you* flustered Reirin with your fire magic that we were forced to capitalize on the bandits' raid. Now look what a fiasco this has become," Keishou said with an air of exasperation, looking down at Keigetsu as she hung her head.

Still, there was a part of her that wanted to argue back like so: *I know she had to avoid running into Gyoumei, but was there any need to get captured by bandits?*

All Reirin actually had to do was leave the stage before Gyoumei got there.

"We learned about the swap after overhearing your conversation

in the fire. Reirin and my brother went with the bandits to keep from running into His Highness, and I stayed behind to help cover our tracks," Keishou had whispered into her ear soon after the fact. She'd nearly collapsed upon hearing it—and it wasn't because of her vessel's weak heart.

How did this happen?! I know I said to do whatever it takes to get out of there, but who would jump straight to "Fine, I'll go get kidnapped"? I was stupid to worry about her for even a second.

When Keigetsu saw the stage get swallowed up in fire and bandits appear on the scene, she was shocked to her core. As flames spread across the wooden stage and smoke filled the air, all the women present—herself included—had been paralyzed with fear.

Fortunately on their way over already, Gyoumei and Shin-u had jumped straight into action. Yet when Reirin was kidnapped before her eyes nonetheless, the shock had been enough to make Keigetsu weak in the knees, thoughts like *How could this happen?* and *Is she going to be killed in my place?* racing through her mind.

And then she found out that Reirin had gone with them of her own free will.

Thinking about it, this is the same girl who stayed totally calm after she was locked in a cage with a beast. If she has Lord Keikou with her, of course she wouldn't be afraid of a little kidnapping!

The sudden feeling of ennui that had washed over Keigetsu almost saw her collapse for a very different reason than earlier.

It seemed the Daoist arts were indeed not meant to be wielded against other people—or not against Kou Reirin, at the very least. Each time Keigetsu tried to do her harm, forget digging two graves—it always bounced right back to her and only her. And with heftier consequences, at that.

"Reirin should be fine as long as she has my brother with her. The worst-case scenario is that His Highness finds out about the switch and forces her to become his empress. Thus, for the four or five days until you amass enough 'qi' or whatever it is, keeping the situation under wraps should be our top priority." Keishou flashed Keigetsu a sweet smile.

Compared to his older brother, Keikou, he seemed like a slender and mild-mannered man, but there was a sharpness to his smiles that put Keigetsu on edge. At least Keikou made his hatred plain through the glares he shot her way. She had a harder time dealing with Keishou and his fake politeness. Especially when he was a man insidious enough to vandalize her robe.

When an awkward silence fell over the room, Keishou took the lead and chattered on, "At any rate, we should count ourselves lucky that His oh-so-clever Highness didn't personally join the search party. It's a good thing his status is keeping his hands tied. Then again, we wouldn't be *in* this mess if he weren't the prince."

He went on to mention that he was worried about what the Eagle Eyes' captain might do, or to wonder aloud about how they could divert the prince's attention, until at last Keigetsu cut in nervously. "Erm... There's something I'd like to ask you first."

"What is it?"

"Why are you helping me cover up the switch?"

Keishou just responded with a blank look, but this was something she needed to know. Keigetsu took a deep breath, scolding herself for nearly chickening out. "Wouldn't it be in the Kou clan's best interests to let the switch come to light? Your sister would get the throne as empress, and the girl you hate would be punished. You couldn't ask for a better outcome. Or did covering my robe in mud get it all out of your system?"

This had been bugging her for a while now. Keishou had explained it away with "we helped Reirin escape because she wasn't ready for the role of empress," but would a provider for his clan really act for such a selfish reason? Even if Reirin had reprimanded him with her dance, what reason did he have to cooperate with the girl who had thrown his precious sister from a high tower? Was this all some sort of trap?

That was what Keigetsu suspected, at least, but Keishou only blinked, confused. "Oh," he said. "Reirin said something to that effect too. So you didn't sling the mud over it yourself?"

"What?"

"Did you really believe we would do something so underhanded to avenge Reirin? Please. My brother punches the men he doesn't like and glares at the women he hates, and I'm the same way. Of course, I *do* happen to have more brains than my brother, so I got a little extra payback by tattling to His Highness."

"Huh?" Keigetsu was flabbergasted.

Keishou curved the corners of his lips into a smirk. "You pretended to be Reirin and sent us a letter during a previous switch, didn't you? You even imitated her handwriting. But in the end, an imitation is no more than that. I don't know about Brother, but you never stood a chance of fooling me. Not with that sloppy penmanship and uncultured vocabulary."

"Wha..."

"Incidentally, Brother took one whiff of the letter and worked out that something seemed off."

"Hrk?!"

Keigetsu was torn between yelling at *this* man for being so rude or trembling before the one whose instincts had led him to the truth. Either way, the one thing she knew was that the men of the Kou clan were not to be crossed.

Keishou gave a lazy shrug of his shoulders. "In her letters, Reirin seemed to have it in for a certain 'Shu Keigetsu.' Based on the rumors I'd gathered from afar, this girl had transformed into a much friendlier person around the same time. I had a hunch about what had happened—though naturally I couldn't be certain."

The number of Daoist cultivators had dwindled due to a previous emperor's persecution, turning the mystic arts into a thing of legend. It didn't seem realistic to think someone had wielded those against his very own sister.

"Brother was furious with 'Shu Keigetsu' for pushing our sister from a pagoda, but I couldn't shake the feeling that something didn't add up. As soon as we made it home to the capital, we went to see what was happening around the inner court. But by that point, Reirin was back to her usual self."

Then was it just a coincidence that the letter had seemed so strange?

However, as he picked up more detailed gossip around the inner court, Keishou learned that "Shu Keigetsu" hadn't been acting like herself for the ten days following the Double Sevens Festival. A peek at the storehouse to which she had been exiled revealed the neat rows of fields she had left in her wake. There were traces of someone training and growing herbs too. When he questioned Tousetsu, who had always been so proud to report anything that had to do with Reirin, she was strangely evasive.

Keishou had put all the pieces together, then gone to probe Gyoumei for answers.

"You went to His Highness?"

"He dodged all my questions, of course. But if anything, the secretiveness just confirmed my suspicions about the body swap." The man who prided himself as the brains of the Kou clan curled his lips into a smug smile. "From there, I steered the conversation to the Double Sevens Festival and mentioned that the letters I'd received from 'Reirin' at the time had been oddly mean-spirited. To be estranged from the prince is the greatest crisis a Maiden can face. Thus, *that* was my 'revenge,'" he easily confessed.

Keigetsu fell silent. She thought back to how Gyoumei had behaved before their departure. He'd seemed thoroughly unimpressed with her. That had to be because he'd known about the letters.

But...he didn't reprimand me any further.

Keigetsu gasped upon coming to that realization. He had kept his conversation with Keishou to himself. What's more, he had even offered to share his personal Eagle Eye with her. For all that Keigetsu felt like she'd been left in the lurch, someone had been looking out for her the whole time.

"I'm positive your passion and sincerity have come through loud and clear."

As a tender voice replayed in the back of her mind, Keigetsu clenched her hands into fists. Her chest felt hot.

But as Keishou went on, Keigetsu would soon feel like someone had doused her burning heart in a bucket of cold water. "Well then, I believe we've gotten off topic. You wanted to know why we would keep Reirin from taking the throne, as I recall. Did you think things would just go, 'Reirin becomes the empress and the Kou clan prospers happily ever after'? You must be a very simple person."

When Keigetsu looked up, she saw he was giving her a look several times colder than she'd ever seen on his face. "To be crowned empress is the highest honor imaginable. That much is true. And that's precisely the reason the five clans are so desperate to compete for the throne. If we Kous claim the title two generations in a row, can you imagine how much that will jeopardize the balance between the five clans? The pressure on Reirin and the risk of assassination would be higher than ever before. There's the danger of a civil war breaking out too."

His face twisted bitterly as he added, "For the record, the empress probably chose a sickly girl like Reirin as her Maiden to uphold the balance between the five clans. It looks better for the other families to 'worry' about a woman's ability to produce an heir than to insult her as a 'talentless girl.' Her Majesty went out of her way to hand her rivals an excuse."

"You're kidding..."

"To be frank, the Kous were the only ones who expressed concern when Reirin was appointed as a Maiden. The other patriarchs gave their unanimous approval and embraced her frail constitution. Though they claimed their enthusiasm was out of respect for her talent."

Distressed, Keigetsu said nothing in response.

No way... But everyone's always lauded her as the favorite to win the throne!

Kou Reirin had always been praised and adored by even the patriarchs of the other clans. Yet had that come from a place of disdain for her frailty all along?

"To begin with, descendants of the Kou clan are much better suited to a quiet life farming in some distant backwater. Aunt Kenshuu's appointment to the throne more or less fell into our laps, and the closer a Kou is to the main line, the less they're going to care about whether Reirin also becomes empress. If anything, she—" Keishou started to say something else, only to drop his gaze and shake his head. "Never mind. The point is, if Reirin isn't ready to take the throne, that's all the more reason we need to help keep the switch a secret."

His conclusion was a little forced, but what he was saying made sense. The Kou clan really wasn't interested in power. They took greater pride in the food they unearthed with their own hands than the favor bestowed upon them by the Heavens, and they preferred to dote on their loved ones than reign over a crowd. Perhaps their earth qi was to blame.

I can trust them, Keigetsu told herself. *And...there's someone else plotting to bring me down.*

Was it another Maiden, a member of the Shu clan, or perhaps even one of the townspeople? It wasn't clear who, but someone had bared their fangs against "Shu Keigetsu." As the one left behind at the scene, she had to figure out who it was as soon as possible.

Keigetsu confirmed the situation. "There are two things I can do right now: hide the truth of our switch to avoid His Highness's wrath...and find out who's out to harm me."

"Precisely. You're rather quick on the uptake," Keishou replied with a vigorous nod. "I'll do what I can to help. I look forward to working with you."

"Do you think Lady Reirin will be all right?" Leelee blurted out, having listened quietly to their conversation up to that point. "She may have gone along with them willingly, but those were still untouchables, right? I don't think a sheltered Maiden like her could even imagine what sort of lives those people lead or the sort of things they'd think to do."

"As strong-willed as Lady Reirin is, I must confess that I have my concerns as well." It wasn't just Leelee; even Tousetsu was chiming in with traces of melancholy upon her face.

Keigetsu's mouth twisted into a grimace. The court ladies had a point. Sure, Reirin hadn't lost heart in the face of her storehouse exile, but that was still within the safe and clean environment of the inner court. Even if Keikou defended her from acts of violence, there was little he could do about the hunger and un-sanitary conditions. There would be no shelter from the rain or dew, and her accommodations would be crawling in vermin and foul stenches. How difficult was it going to be for her to get by with no food to eat and no clothes to wear, surrounded by ruffians from dawn to dusk?

"Hmm..." In contrast to the girls' strained silence, Keishou gave a lazy tilt of his head. "She'll be fine, I think."

It was the last thing anyone had expected a man famed for his overprotective nature to say.

"Oh, I see the problem now," he said. "You three never knew Reirin before she came to the Maiden Court, did you?"

"Huh?"

The girls lifted their heads, sensing something foreboding in those words. Her behavior in the Maiden Court was outlandish enough as it stood. Had she been even worse back when she lived at her family's estate?

"But...she *is* a sheltered Maiden, isn't she?"

"Sure. She's always been sickly, she rarely ever left the house, and she never had much interaction with other people. She really *is* sheltered in that sense."

"But...?" Keigetsu hesitantly prompted him.

Keishou chuckled. "The problem lies with the company she keeps. My brother and Reirin hit it off so well that they get three times rowdier when they're together. She lets loose, one might say, or becomes even more of a daredevil..."

An uncomfortable silence filled the room.

Her voice trembling, Leelee eventually murmured, "More than she already is?"

131

That might have been what all the women present were thinking. The three girls glanced aside all at once, this time worried for those poor bandits' futures.

Those known as the "untouchables" were early to rise. As Unran stirred awake on the shabby bed in his hovel, he cast a groggy glance out the empty window. It was almost sunrise. The air was already thick with humidity, but judging by the dense clouds hanging overhead, it was looking to be another day without sunshine. He dragged himself out of bed with a languid sigh, while the man who had slept on the mat next to him stretched.

"*Yaaawn...* Morning already, huh? Damn, I'm sore all over."

The man scratching his bare chest as he got out of bed was Unran's uncle, Gouryuu, who was living in the same hut with him.

The pair headed into the living room sectioned off by only a single partition screen. "Morning, Gouryuu," someone called out from the section of bare dirt floor too small to be called a kitchen. It was an old lady cooking at the stove. Though she didn't spare Unran so much as a glance, she flashed her chipped teeth in a grin the moment she saw Gouryuu.

"Today's a special day. I put lots of fish balls I snagged from the township last night into the congee. Smells good, doesn't it? It was worth letting the townswomen kick me around."

This woman puffed up with pride was the same one the townswoman had accused of breaking the erhu the previous night—Old Kyou. In exchange for taking up residence in the village chief's hut, she was in charge of cooking all the meals. Her pathetic manner from the other night was nowhere to be found. She was all smiles now.

"You boys did a great job. Shu Keigetsu's kidnapping sent the whole township into an uproar. Nobody even noticed me sneaking into the kitchen last night. I got to swipe all the food my little heart desired."

The old lady wasn't one to settle for keeping her head down after getting attacked by the townswomen. She'd hold her breath and ride it out, then be sure to hit them back with a look of feigned innocence when her chance came around. Old Kyou's catchphrase was: "I've been part of this village since my grandmother's generation. I'm a born thief." She was a master pickpocket.

"I picked us up fish balls, vegetables, and liquor. Also grabbed the ceremonial robe and sash while I was at it. The stuff was caked in mud, but the golden embroidery was too pretty a sight to pass up. I rinsed 'em clean, and I've been playing dress-up ever since. I ought to thank the Ran Maiden for letting me know she had such a treasure in her room. Hee hee!"

"Old hags shouldn't try to dress up all sexy. Gives me the willies," said Gouryuu, frowning as he took his seat at the table. "Right?" He looked to his nephew to back him up, but Unran shot him back a lazy smile.

"Oh, I dunno. What's the big deal? Old Kyou snuck into the township alongside us, even if it *was* just for a chance to steal something. If putting on a robe is all it takes to put her in a good mood, then more power to her. I say it's cute."

"Gah! Cute? This old bag?! Spoken like a true lady-killer."

"Not sure I'd call myself a lady-killer, but I've at least got more game than you," Unran teased.

Never having had much luck with the ladies, Gouryuu scoffed. "You damn girly man. You'd better not go easy on Shu Keigetsu."

"My, you don't get it at all, Gouryuu," Old Kyou cut in with a snort as she was stirring the pot. "Men like him are the coldest toward women. Why, just the other day, a poor townswoman who was crazy about Unran got strung up by her husband when he discovered the affair, and the boy hardly even spared her a glance. I saw it happen."

"I figured it would only make more trouble for her if an untouchable tried to help," was Unran's shameless reply as he tied up his hair with a cord. "Besides, she wasn't serious about me either. Yet if I came forward, I'd be the only one to get killed. Doesn't seem fair to me. I appreciate that she fed me each time I came by to fool around, though."

The sheer chill in his voice stunned Gouryuu into silence.

Most untouchables would be stoned just for setting foot in the township, but it was different for Unran. His good looks, calculated friendliness, and guardedness of a stray cat made countless women forget their difference in standing to fall head over heels for him. But for Unran's part, he never seemed to open up to the ladies who came on to him.

In contrast to his charming appearance, he had quite the ruthless streak. Gouryuu stared at that nephew of his, conflicted, but he eventually wiped the look off his face and turned back to Old Kyou. "Anyway, you should present the robe and sash to the shrine. We burned the stage down. If we don't offer the god of agriculture a little something, we'll all be cursed."

Old Kyou wrinkled her nose at the nagging. "Hmph. I will when I've had my fun. I'll offer the robe to the shrine on the mountain and the sash to the shrine in the pond. Unlike you, I got up before dawn, cleaned off the stolen goods, and checked the fields, and now here I am making breakfast for a couple of deadbeats."

Unran and Gouryuu exchanged glances, then shrugged their shoulders in tandem.

"Who's a deadbeat? We were nearly up until dawn handling all the cleanup."

Indeed. After bringing the Shu Maiden and her Kou clan escort home with them, they'd had their hands full the previous night.

First of all, the man—his name was Keikou, apparently—had made so much noise along the way that he'd had to be blindfolded, handcuffed, and even gagged, which left Unran to carry him on his back. He probably ought to have abandoned or even killed him on the roadside, but he'd hesitated to do so in case it left clues for their pursuers.

To obfuscate the fact that the raid had been the work of the untouchables, the pair had left a Gen clan tassel behind on the stage.

The suspicion that it had been the work of another clan was sure to disrupt the investigation. They'd even sent a riderless horse along the road that led to the Gen clan's northern territory.

Plus, despite the Untouchable Village being located just one suspension bridge over from the township, the pair had taken a detour along the mountains. For a finishing touch, they'd cut the bridge that connected the township to the village. That move was to buy them time in case military officers from the imperial capital stormed in.

Finally, when at last they reached the village in the dead of night, they'd cleared out a second supply warehouse, then locked up and bound Shu Keigetsu and Keikou separately to keep them from escaping.

It was only after finishing all that work that they'd finally gotten to sleep.

"I never imagined things would go this smoothly," Unran muttered, stretching his arms.

"No kidding. I was worried we might be in for trouble when I heard how skilled the Kou clan's bodyguards were, but those guys were nothing." Gouryuu rolled up the sleeve around one of his stocky arms, flexing it with pride. Then, he said, "We really do have the Heavens on our side. The gods want Shu Keigetsu punished. We've got to make the little sewer rat who brought disaster to our southern domain suffer."

Unran shot his uncle a glance, then sipped from his chipped teacup. Gouryuu was a big man with a bad attitude, but he was a coward at heart. Unran understood why he was making such a point of lambasting Shu Keigetsu: It was his way of talking himself into what he was doing.

That dance last night...

She had looked beautiful standing upon the stage. The beam had been a considerable distance from where she was dancing, yet still her singing voice had tickled their ears, the flutter of her shawl keeping both men's eyes glued to the stage.

They were from a backwater township, and societal outcasts to boot. This was the first time they'd ever seen such a soul-stirring dance. Thus, they'd found themselves captivated for the entire length of her performance, completely forgetting to start their fire.

"Shu Keigetsu" was supposed to be a talentless sewer rat. The two men had been thrown for a loop, their whole image of her fundamentally overturned.

Not that it matters either way, if you ask me.

Unran propped his chin in one hand, playfully sending ripples through the cup he held in the other. The old teacup had once belonged to the hut's original owner and the former chief of the village: Unran's father.

No matter how well she can dance, Shu Keigetsu is still the root of all our misfortune.

As he gazed down at the undulations in the water's surface, Unran reflected on everything that had happened to this point.

Life had always been hard for the "untouchables." Driven off to the dimmest parts of the township and constantly struggling to cultivate their barren land, they were still taxed as much as the rest of the townspeople. Several of the villagers had been exiled on the grounds of disease or disability, so they had relatively few able-bodied workers to begin with. Even during the busy farming season, they were forced to do the jobs no one else wanted, and when they went to the township to get the work done, they were met with scornful glances, spit, and stones.

The villagers had stuck it all out, clenching their fists and telling themselves this was just their lot in life. But about a month ago, the township magistrate had dropped a bombshell on them: Their taxes would be going up even higher in the fall.

When Unran's father had managed to get an audience with the magistrate and asked for an explanation, he'd been informed that taxes were going up across the entire southern territory. The Shu clan had committed a grave disrespect against the imperial family, so the Noble Consort had been banished from the inner court and taxes on the south were to be doubled for the next three years.

No one knew what charges had been brought against the Noble Consort. Only the vague reason of "an insult" had been given for her exile.

To no surprise, Unran's small village had been distraught over the news. Things were hard enough for them at the current taxation rate. Doubling that amount just wasn't feasible.

The cold spell had put a strain not only on their rice production but their vegetable harvest too. The residents of the Untouchable Village were already starving by this point. In times of famine, the imperial capital was supposed to send congee as an act of charity, but now that Shu Keigetsu had incurred the wrath of the imperial family, the amount of food rationed out to the southern territory was half of what it had been in previous years.

In the face of the village's impending crisis, the chief had thought to procure some immediate sustenance by venturing into the Cursed Forest. The forest was located halfway up the mountain that split the township from the untouchables' district, and its eerie atmosphere had led the villagers to believe it was inhabited by evil spirits.

Only a few days after bringing home a deer from his hunt, the chief had died. The rest of the untouchables had blanched in fear, convinced there really was a curse, and shunned the late chief for fear that his affliction might spread.

"Why?!" the villagers had yelled at the sight of their leader's remains.

Why are we the ones who have to go through all this?

Why did the Shu clan do something so foolish?

There was no way for the untouchables to know the ins and outs of the Shu clan living in the imperial capital, but at the very least, complaints of their mismanagement and corruption had never traveled around the south until now. Their domain wasn't always blessed with bountiful harvests like their neighbors in the eastern territory, but the Shus had never made for especially great nor especially terrible lords.

If there had been but one exception—one whisper of discontent—that was when the current Maiden, the lowest-ranking

Shu daughter infamous for her lack of talent, was chosen for her position. The fact that the former Noble Consort, Shu Gabi, had been a woman beautiful enough to be nicknamed the "cotton rose" had made the people's disappointment upon hearing the rumors about Shu Keigetsu even more acute.

After all the work the Noble Consort had done to boost the south's status, this stunt of hers had brought its longevity back into question.

Each time the peddlers brought more rumors from the capital, the township's animosity toward Shu Keigetsu grew. With a poor harvest striking around the same time she'd entered the court, it was only natural that everyone would link the two occurrences together. Owing to their strong fire qi, residents of the southern territory had always been an emotional sort. Their love ran deep, but as the trade-off, they were a good deal more fearful, hostile, and superstitious than the average person.

Last year's drought had been terrible. Now they had a cold spell to contend with. The favored Noble Consort had been exiled. When the magistrate explained the misfortunes befalling them one after another as "divine punishment," the townspeople had believed him without question. In fact, they'd leaped at the chance to blame Shu Keigetsu, using her as an outlet for all their anxiety.

Shu Keigetsu had brought disaster to the southern territory.

Shu Keigetsu was the one who had pushed them to their breaking point.

If it weren't for Shu Keigetsu...

"If we make Shu Keigetsu suffer, the blight on the south will be lessened," Unran muttered to himself, looking down at his teacup.

That was what the township magistrate, Lord Koh, had said.

When Unran and Gouryuu had once again begged the magistrate for tax relief in place of their late chief, he'd told them this: The Heavens' anger could be appeased by doing Shu Keigetsu harm during her visit to their town. If they agreed to drag her to the unguarded Untouchable Village and kick her around for a few days, he was willing to cut their taxes in half. The discussion had been a contentious one, but in the end, the villagers had agreed to get on board with the plan.

Everyone wanted to escape certain doom. Having their taxes halved was too good a deal to pass up. The rice and greens he'd offered them as a down payment had been equally tempting.

"As long as we make sure to say our prayers to the god of agriculture, we won't be punished for tormenting Shu Keigetsu... right?" Despite his earlier bluffing, the fainthearted Gouryuu was already starting to chicken out. One second he'd be yelling at the top of his lungs, the next he'd be nervously begging the gods for forgiveness. Mood swings like that were a defining characteristic of people from the south. "And the magistrate *will* hide our involvement, yeah?"

"Get a grip, Uncle Gouryuu," Unran said flatly. "You just said it yourself. If torturing a Maiden were such a 'bad' thing, the kidnapping wouldn't have gone as well as it did. We left a Gen accessory on the stage, just like the magistrate told us, so all

THOUGH I AM AN INEPT VILLAINESS

the blame will get placed on them. Besides, we made him write that contract to ensure he can't cut us loose if something does go wrong."

"Y-yeah. Good point." Gouryuu nodded, relieved. "That contract is the kicker. I used to think my brother was a nutcase for teaching untouchable kids how to read, but looking back on it, his diligence really saved our hides. Right, Unran? Our chief was a great man."

The man happily sang his brother's praises, but Old Kyou's response as she dished out the congee was less than favorable. "Hmph. I wonder about that. It doesn't make a difference how smart he was if he brought disaster to our village."

"Don't be like that, Old Kyou. Back when he was still alive, you used to praise him as the finest man around, remember? And you weren't the only one. Everyone in the village used to respect the hell out of him."

"I can't seem to recall," Old Kyou replied, wrinkling her nose. "At the very least, we all stopped respecting him after he entered the Cursed Forest and unleashed calamity on the rest of us."

Her mutterings reflected the views shared by the entire village.

Gouryuu furrowed his brow, disconsolate. "Sure, it was unbelievably stupid of him to set foot in the Cursed Forest... But you don't have to—" He stopped short when Unran, the chief's own son, turned his head and shoved his chin in his palm rather than chime in. At that, Gouryuu's expression warped into one of rage. "Hey, Unran, say something! Wasn't he your own father?"

"We weren't blood-related."

"And he raised you in spite of that, so you should feel all the more indebted to him! Heartless bastard." Gouryuu pounded the table in frustration, his fists making a dull *thud* upon the crude surface.

Old Kyou set a bowl of congee on the table to alleviate the tension. "Now, now. That's enough talking about the dead. Let's think about what we're going to do to Shu Keigetsu now that we've got her captive. I can't stand haughty little girls like her who use their authority as a shield."

Steering the topic to Shu Keigetsu was her way of trying to lift the mood. Realizing this, Gouryuu picked up the bowl and said, "Good question. We've got to give the disaster-bearing villainess her due."

"Let's cut her hair. Or maybe we could lock her up in a place full of bugs. Dropping her into a cesspit isn't a bad idea either."

"Ooh, women sure can be vicious. I think it'd be best to put her to work. We can make her tend the fields all night long, and then if she makes the slightest mistake, we'll throw stones at..." Gouryuu broke into a grin as he shoveled a few spoonfuls of food into his mouth. "Whew, this hits the spot!"

"Not a bad idea. Then maybe she'll get a taste of what we go through here."

"Let's starve her out too."

"I like it!"

The pair was having a blast brainstorming over their bowls of congee.

"Then for the finale, she can let one of the village men screw her in exchange for a little something to eat," Old Kyou went on. Gouryuu shut his mouth and instinctively stole a glance at his nephew beside him. "One of the most sovereign women in the kingdom will give up her chastity for a single bowl of congee! What a riot!"

Gouryuu jabbed her with his elbow as she clutched her stomach with laughter. "Enough, Old Kyou!"

His spoon in one hand, Unran hadn't touched his congee for the entirety of the conversation.

"R-right, Unran? You agree that her plan is going overboard?" his uncle asked in an attempt to smooth things over.

"Why?" Unran said with a thin smile, ultimately tossing his spoon aside with a clang. "We all know *my* mother let a townsman have his way with her for a bowl of congee."

Unran was the child born from a townsman's rape of a village woman.

A hush fell over the table.

Unable to bear the silence, Gouryuu eventually scolded the old woman. "You're out of line, Old Kyou. It's true that the old chief was a hopeless fool, and Unran's an outsider, but they've both given their all to save our village. Don't be too hard on them. You're making *me* feel like crap over here."

"..."

Now that the chief had passed, Gouryuu was the leader of the village. Perhaps deeming it unwise to cross him, Old Kyou gave an awkward shrug of her shoulders. In a bid to ingratiate herself, she then added, "Don't get me wrong. We're grateful to you after everything you've done, Unran. You're the only one of us who could have taken on as momentous a task as setting fire to a god's altar and kidnapping a Maiden."

"'Preciate it," Unran responded with a sardonic smile, pushing his bowl across the table. He'd completely lost his appetite.

And then...

"Hey!"

Someone flung open the door and barged right into the hut, shattering the tension in the air. It was the young man who had been assigned to stand guard over the warehouse where Shu Keigetsu was confined.

"Can you come with me for a bit?" Looking drained, the man glanced over at Gouryuu, then at Unran. "It's the Maiden we captured. There was something weird about her when I peeked in through the window."

"You mean she lost her mind trapped in that bug-infested warehouse? Or did she bite her tongue?"

"No, not like that..." he answered evasively.

Unran tilted his head, puzzled. Knowing how quick she was to start screeching, he'd been sure she'd be up with the dawn barking like a wounded dog. Or was she too busy pounding on the door and wailing?

"Just come have a look, Gouryuu." A pause. "You too, Unran. You know the most about handling women, right?"

The village men avoided asking Unran for help as a general rule. If he'd made a point of doing just that, this had to be something serious. Unran and Gouryuu exchanged skeptical looks, then headed for the warehouse.

Good grief. Why's he getting so worked up over a single female prisoner?

As he was walking, it occurred to Unran that he'd missed out on his chance to have some congee. Even if he decided to have a bite later, the pot would probably be empty by the time he got back. It wasn't just Old Kyou who liked to hang around the hut; all the villagers on good terms with Gouryuu made a habit of swinging by.

Man, I'm hungry. I'm blaming this *on Shu Keigetsu too.*

Realizing how hungry he was made him all the more irritated. Unran decided to foist the blame for his whole crappy morning onto the captive Maiden.

Just being born a daughter of the Shus had allowed her to immerse herself in splendor. There was a world of difference between her and Unran, who was scorned as an untouchable and even called a "half-blood" within his own village. While he and the other villagers had survived by licking the townspeople's shoes, she had lived her life heckling the servants who groveled before her. While they fought hunger, she had no doubt indulged in gourmet meals.

Talk about unfair.

What was wrong with tipping back the unbalanced scales?

He and his people had suffered unjustly. Thus, he wanted Shu Keigetsu to suffer for how easy she'd had it. That was all there was to it.

Then, he and his uncle opened the door to the warehouse...

"Oh, good morning," the girl said brightly, glancing over her shoulder when she heard the creak of the door. Unran and Gouryuu boggled.

Around them was a dilapidated shed bathed in the weak light of dawn. Now that there was no rice to store, the place had been left in a state of disrepair and riddled with holes. Rainwater had seeped in through the cracks, rotting the wood and emitting a foul stench, and the stagnant puddles of mud were crawling with squalid insects. Even a grown man would have shuddered in disgust at his surroundings had he trapped himself there by some mistake, but the girl who had been tied to a pillar for an entire night greeted them in an exceedingly calm manner.

No, it went beyond that. Having broken free of her bindings at some point, she was wandering freely around the hut.

Unran was genuinely shocked. "What's going on here? How did you undo the rope?"

"Hm? Oh, er, I dislocated my joints to slip through. The rope was digging into my skin a little too much for comfort."

"Excuse me?"

Why did a sheltered Maiden know how to get out of restraints?

Unran was still searching for words as the girl proudly put a hand to her chest. "It's one of the few tricks even a sickly girl can practice."

"Uh... What's that supposed to mean?"

Noticing her captor's face was frozen in disbelief, she put a hand to her cheek and gave a discomfited shrug of her shoulders.

"Was escaping my bindings a taboo? I've never been kidnapped before, so I'm not sure what the rules are..."

It was then that Gouryuu noticed the wriggling millipede she was clutching in her other hand. He gulped, startled. "Wait, what are you holding that bug for?!"

"Hm? I'd feel bad if I simply imposed upon your hospitality, so I decided I'd do what I could here. First on the list was to redistrict all the bugs." As she pointed to each of the four corners of the shed, she explained, "Those are the rats, and over there are the millipedes and other many-legged critters. Here we have the worms and leeches, and I decided to take my chances grouping all the larvae, maggots included—" She cut herself off mid-sentence, a shadow of guilt passing over her face. "Was it rude of me to relocate the residents without asking? Then I'll have to apologize for tinkering with someone else's home..."

"That's not what Uncle Gouryuu was getting at. What are you gathering up all these bugs for? Planning to curse someone?"

"My!" For some reason, her face lit up at the unforeseen retort. "This conversation is really taking me back. Could you say that one more time?"

"No! Listen to me, damn it!"

"Oh dear. Hee hee hee." Her smile growing even wider, she stared long and hard at Unran. "That defiant expression and unreserved manner of speech... Your facial features and gender don't match, but you remind me so very much of Leelee. Why is it that all those with fire in their natures are such adorable people?"

He had no idea what she was talking about.

"Hey! Do you get what's going on here? We abducted you. Wouldn't it make sense to act a little more scared? To break down crying or something, maybe?"

"Erm..."

The girl gave a small tilt of her head. Unran had no way of knowing that she was thinking, *This is nothing compared to the time I almost had my soul stolen by an evil spirit.*

Thus, he just thought, *This woman has a few screws loose.* He had no idea if she'd always been like this or if it was from the shock of being kidnapped.

Unran huffed a short sigh, then brought his face right up to hers. If this were a townswoman, she would have blushed to have him that close no matter what excuses she made for it, but the girl only stared back at him curiously.

He deliberately flashed her the cruel smile of a cat toying with a mouse. "It doesn't seem like you understand the situation you're in. Allow me to explain, Shu Keigetsu."

"Sure."

"You're about to be punished—punished for having the nerve to go from talentless sewer rat to Maiden, indulging in every luxury imaginable, and then incurring the wrath of the Heavens for the clincher. You're going to be tormented every bit as much as a rotten girl like you deserves. By us Gen—" Unran thought to impress the idea that this was the work of the Gen clan as an aside, but he never got to finish telling his lie.

"Don't be silly. You're from the southern territory, aren't you?"

Shu Keigetsu corrected him without missing a beat, blinking in confusion.

"Excuse me?"

"If the Shu Maiden had truly incurred the wrath of the Heavens, disaster would befall the south. The northern Gen clan would have no incentive to root out the cause of the crisis. The idea to mete out punishment on behalf of the Heavens would only occur to those in the southern territory afflicted by the disaster, correct?"

Her perfectly logical explanation made Unran's eyes go round.

"In short, you've drawn a connection between Lady—between *me* and whatever difficulties the south is currently facing, and your plan is to curtail those by tormenting me."

The girl was so composed that it was like her tantrum in the pavilion had never happened.

"Even if the whole southern territory burns with hatred for Shu Keigetsu, no one can lay a hand on her with His Highness around. That's why you abducted me to this outback where no townsperson would go—the district known as the 'Untouchable Village.' Isn't that right?"

All she did was smile gently, yet there was something about her demure bearing that exuded an almost intimidating aura.

What's with this girl?

Unran furrowed his brow. Then, as he realized the aloof smile that more or less defined him had left his face, he felt the urge to give a frustrated click of his tongue.

"But there happen to be some very skilled military officers in the township, so I doubt your plan is going to work out. Would you mind elucidating what drove you to such reckless action? Perhaps we can make that the first step toward resolving the issue."

She stepped closer, the look on her face earnest. For a split second, Unran thought to pull back, but he instead stood his ground and glared at her. He wasn't about to let a naive noblewoman like her take command of the conversation.

"Oho?" He grabbed her by the arm and tightened his grip. Her limbs were smooth and slender, not a callus or blemish in sight. "You sure talk a big game. You want to help us out, huh? Good luck, then. 'Cause your suffering is going to be what saves us."

The damp, dimly lit space was quiet aside from the sound of the insects' skittering.

Even in a strange land, surrounded by men who openly flaunted their hatred for her—even with her arm in someone else's grip—Shu Keigetsu stared back at him with an unwavering gaze.

Rattled by the Maiden's dignified demeanor, Gouryuu attempted to talk his nephew down. "S-say, Unran. The Maiden's a lot calmer and more obedient than we expected, so maybe we ought to rethink how—"

Unran ignored him. "Maybe I'll start by cutting your hair." He grabbed a fistful of her hair with his free hand and yanked hard. "Hair is a noblewoman's everything, isn't it? I'll give you a jagged cut like mine. It'll leave your face looking a little empty, so I'll give you a splash of makeup too. I wonder what color your face would turn if I hit you as hard as I can. Red? Purple?"

A few strands of hair audibly snapped in his hand.

She was being restrained by a man larger than herself, being told at length the sort of the violence she was about to be subjected to. It would be enough to make even the most strong-willed woman go pale in the face, but the stringently sheltered Maiden didn't show so much as a flicker of expression.

Frustration mounting, Unran tightened his grip on her hair. "Nobody's coming to save you. I left evidence that ties this crime to the north back on the stage and along the road. You're going to be all on your own as the whole village makes your life hell. It's time you learned what life is like for us. You're going to be spat on, kicked, and starved. Then, in the end, all the village men will—"

"Good morning, gentlemen!"

Just as Unran was about to tug the girl toward the ground with all his might, the door to the warehouse flew open and in came an intruder.

"So this is where you were. Nobody came to see *me*, so I was getting lonely."

It was Kou Keikou, who was supposed to be locked up in another warehouse a short distance away. Even Unran was speechless.

"Wh-what are you doing here?! How the hell did you get untied?!" Gouryuu shouted in his gravelly voice.

"Hm? Oh, you know. Fighting spirit." Keikou tilted his head to one side, then flexed both of his biceps a little. "I flexed my muscles and the rope just snapped. Here, let me hand it back to you. You're the one in charge around here, right?"

Then, he pushed the tattered remains of the rope into Unran's hands with a friendly smile.

"I don't want it—"

"Oh. Gotcha."

Right when Unran was about to shove the rope back at him, Keikou dropped into a crouch.

"Wha...?!"

Unran felt an impact in his gut, and the very next moment, he was being hoisted up in Keikou's arms.

"Guh!"

At the same time, Gouryuu fell at Keikou's feet. He must have had his legs swept from under him.

Thunk!

A beat later, a hoe the guard had stolen from who-knew-where wedged itself into the floor right next to Gouryuu's groveling form. The thick, gleaming blade had just barely grazed his throat.

"Aiiieee!" Gouryuu and the surrounding men yelped in fear.

Unran gulped. Keikou was still holding him up like a sack of rice—but if the Kou man chose to slam him headfirst into the ground, Unran wouldn't have any way of stopping it.

"Believe it or not, I've seen my fair share of battle. It'd be a piece of cake for me to wipe out this entire village."

It wasn't even a threat. Something about his matter-of-fact tone lent it an even greater air of menace. Everyone could tell that he wasn't saying it as a scare tactic—it was the unadorned truth.

"With that in mind, I ask you this: What were you about to do to my precious Maiden?"

"..."

The atmosphere in the room was tense. Faced with the ultimate fighter, the men could only gape up at where Unran dangled in the air. If they told him the truth, he would kill them.

"We—"

"Goodness!" an incongruously chipper voice rang out, breaking the tension. It was Shu Keigetsu, who had moved over to the open door at some point. "What beautiful scenery. Come take a look, Brother Se—I mean, Lord Keikou!"

She seemed captivated by the landscape outside the warehouse.

"Oh? Let's see." The moment he heard her shout, Keikou tossed the paralyzed Unran aside. Leaving Gouryuu and his comrades frozen in fear, he hurried over to the doorway and oohed in agreement. "It's rice paddies as far as the eye can see."

"So this is what a rice paddy looks like!" For some reason, the girl clasped her hands to her chest and trembled like she was witnessing some sort of miracle. "Rice paddies. A land of beginnings that provides sustenance for all the kingdom's people... The surface of their water reflects the ever-changing sky like a mirror of the heavens. The modest rice fields we have in the inner court can't even compare to this grandeur!"

Before her was nothing more than rice paddies bathed in the soft light of the dawn. Yet still she nodded to herself over and over with eyes full of tears, like something about the sight tugged at her heartstrings.

"Footpaths crowded with resilient weeds. Unripe rice plants with so much growing left to do. A diverse population of insects descending upon the crops. I'm sure tending to these fields would be no easy feat..."

"Yeah. I bet it'd take a lot of work."

Beside her, even Keikou was looking out at the paddies with a fire in his eyes. There was a note of ecstasy in their voices.

"Endless weeding..."

"The thrill of defending the weak rice plants from pests..."

No one could see their faces as they gazed out at the fields. But when the man suddenly whipped around, his voice was booming. "Hey, gentlemen!"

All the men present stood straight at attention.

"It seems you guys are out to put this Maiden through the wringer. Am I right?"

He asked without rancor, but no one was going to say "yes" under the circumstances.

"N-no, I don't know about the *wringer*..." Gouryuu nervously made excuses, sweat pouring down his face.

This time, it was the girl who interjected. "That's true! Now then, I have a suggestion for how you might go about tormenting me..."

Shu Keigetsu and her guard both pitched forward, their eyes inexplicably sparkling.

Looking almost like a pair of blood-related siblings, the pair rang out in perfect unison, "How about some forced labor in the rice fields?!"

Unran was a gorgeous man, the likes of which weren't often seen in the countryside. His cynical smile held the sharp bite of a carnivorous beast, but there was also something in the way he'd occasionally cock his head and skulk over with a sweet purr that was reminiscent of a capricious cat.

Never seen without a casual smile, he was a mysterious sort of man who hadn't opened his heart to anyone. He hadn't even shed a tear over the death of his adoptive father, the only villager to ever treat him with kindness.

That day, however, he could be found crouching on the ground, one hand pressed to his forehead.

I can't believe this. What the hell is going on here?

There was a tinge of exhaustion to the eyes hidden behind his palm.

Yes. Exhaustion.

Ever since his would-be captives had offered to work in the rice fields earlier that morning, Unran had been worn down by one crazy experience after the next.

First, upon declaring their intent to tend to the paddies, Shu Keigetsu and her guard had rolled up their sleeves, flown out of the shed, and set foot in the fields with a bow and a cry of, "Pardon our intrusion!"

"My. It's true that the plants are taking their sweet time growing, considering it's already autumn," said the Maiden.

156

"Tearing into the stem with a fingernail will tell you how many days it's got left until it sprouts," said the well-muscled Kou man. "Hmm... This one's still got a ways to go."

"They're not getting enough sunlight. Disease is another concern. Looking up close, I can see the crops are planted too close together. Our best move would be to steel our hearts and thin the plants some to keep disease from spreading."

They took a look around the rice plants without getting their feet stuck in mud even once, exchanging a conversation that might make one wonder if *this* was their real profession.

"I'd say the ridges are well formed and the irrigation is ideal. They've done an excellent job here."

"Yes. But I'd say there's still room for improvement in the footpaths between the rice paddies. Growing rice is a battle against weeds and insects. I read in a book that we should clear the paths of millets to keep bugs from buzzing about the fields."

"I'd love to weed the footpaths and plant some *shiso* instead. That ought to cut down on the number of stink bugs."

"Let's take a look around the rest of the fields. We need to replant strategically, with an eye to the entire village's layout."

The pair exchanged nods like a couple of skilled farmers. Just as they were about to venture out of the rice paddy, the villagers finally snapped back to their senses.

"Hold on. Who said you could walk around the village?"

"I'm sorry, Unran. I proposed we work in the rice paddies, but that was actually a lie. I want to tend to *all* the fields, not just these. Everything on earth is connected, after all."

"That's not what I meant."

Despite apologizing to him with a look of complete serious-ness, the girl had clearly missed his point. What's more, having deduced his name somewhere in the conversation, she had taken to addressing him without a title.

"Relax, Unran. We'll do our best to accommodate your desire to torment our Maiden here. Feel free to come swinging your fists or your weapons at us all you like," the man called Keikou offered in total sincerity. But after that overwhelming display of skill earlier, who among the villagers was brave enough to rush him without a care in the world?

"Uh..."

"Erm..."

When Unran glanced their way, sure enough, he found the village men paralyzed with fear. After all, this was a man who could break through rope with sheer fighting spirit, steal a hoe without any difficulty, and subdue two men in a single breath. At the very least, they had no hope of touching him short of taking him in a ten-to-one fight. These farmers so un-accustomed to brawling shot Unran pleading looks, their will to fight in tatters.

Oh, come on! We're screwed if you all just give up.

Unran's face twitched. This was a matter of the entire village's survival. Besides, however skilled, their opponents were just one military officer and a slender girl.

I can take him once he lets his guard down.

He knew full well he was being a coward.

It was right then that Kou Keikou turned his back and bent down to dislodge the mud from his shoes. Unran grabbed the hoe left behind in the shed and flung it at the man's back with all his might. Unfortunately...

Thunk!

The hoe had traced a sharp arc through the air, only for Keikou to twist around, throw out an arm, and effortlessly catch it. "Oh, thanks." He looked back over his shoulder and grinned. "I can use this. Good thinking."

"What the...?!"

His reflexes were almost superhuman.

"Oh, can I have one too?" came the girl's adorable request as she popped out from behind him, her composure equally inhuman. And this was all before the sun had even come up.

The duo's bizarre behavior carried on undeterred. They toured the fields, assessed what was stunting the plants' growth at a glance, and plucked weeds fast enough to leave afterimages. Despite facing down the farmland without food or rest, by the end of it all, the pair was competing to find out which compost worked best, licking the soil and making comments like, "I think this one was mixed with fish meal" or "It seems like rice bran was used over here."

Not only that—the man was even laid-back enough to occasionally call over a bird flying through the sky and befriend it, cooing, "Aw, how cute."

Of course, the villagers didn't just twiddle their thumbs and watch this happen. Kou Keikou's physical prowess and

Shu Keigetsu's mettle were both unparalleled, but there were still only two of them. If the whole village had them surrounded, there was no way they could get away unscathed. Plus, true to their promise to "accommodate" the villagers, the pair had yet to strike unprovoked.

First, Gouryuu called over about ten of his friends to get them surrounded. Thanks to the hoe Unran had tossed him earlier, however, Keikou's combat ability had grown exponentially. The more times they attacked him, the more farming tools and other weapons they ended up losing, until eventually the whole group ran screaming. Unran cursed himself for ever throwing that hoe in the first place.

Next, the men tried to spring a snake on them. It was a venomous one that they'd taken a couple hours to trap in a nearby thicket. But this, too, the pair had swiftly caught and dismembered.

"Ha ha ha! Meat fell right into our laps! What good fortune!"

"No fair. I wanted to preserve it in alcohol and turn it into medicine instead of eating it... Umm, pardon me, but do you think you could find us another one?"

Shu Keigetsu's request was a meek one, but the sight of her unflinchingly skinning the snake and then asking for seconds left the villagers speechless. They'd been convinced that taking the woman hostage would leave her guard's hands tied, but *she* was the one crushing the snake's head and peeling back its flesh without batting an eye. Beneath her graceful appearance, it was clear that she was more dexterous than the average man from the village.

They couldn't even mock her grimy looks after she dove into the mud of her own accord. When they tried to dump bugs on her as a last-ditch effort, she brushed it off with "Oh, this again? Go ahead." and "I'd like to get rid of the aphids, so spiders would be my preference."

As time dragged on, the men lost their will to fight and dropped out of the "punishment" force one by one. By this point, Unran was the only one left to agonize over ways to torment Shu Keigetsu.

Granted, even he was starting to feel stupid waging his one-man battle. He thus swapped his guard shift with someone else nearby and went somewhere he could be alone—which was how he had ended up here.

What am I even doing? Why am I acting like the kid who works hard to clean the shrine all by himself while everyone else is slacking off?

The bizarre situation had thrown Unran completely off balance.

Oh, the sun's setting. It's already dusk... No, should I say it's "only" dusk? Huh? It hasn't even been a day since those guys got here? You have to be kidding me.

In the end, he hadn't bothered them at all. All he'd gotten for his efforts was exhaustion. In hindsight, he considered it a miracle that he'd managed to abduct such an unflappable duo in the first place.

His wild eyes traveled to the sky above, where he could see the sunset faintly bleeding through the clouds. The first day of the

THOUGH I AM AN INEPT VILLAINESS

kidnapping was almost over. The following night, he was supposed to head into the mountain that served as the border with the township and report back to an envoy sent by the magistrate.

He had to meet with that envoy and collect the rice and vegetables meant as their reward and hush money. Otherwise, the entire village might starve to death before the tax hike even became an issue.

"I can just tell him whatever, and he'll still give me the food. What an easy job."

For now, he'd just say that the punishment was proceeding smoothly. The magistrate and his crony had to know that Kou Keikou had come along for the ride, but Unran could always claim that they'd successfully incapacitated him—and that they were currently taking their sweet time tormenting his Maiden.

No one from the township had ordered him to provide proof, anyway. Fooling them was going to be a piece of cake. In their arrogance, it would never occur to them that the "dim-witted" untouchables could tell such unabashed lies.

That's how I'll make it through tomorrow. The military officer is only human, so he has to fall asleep eventually. If I kill him in his sleep, we'll have nothing left to worry about. Once her guard is out of the way, we can mess with the girl all we like. There's still plenty of time.

The village had Keikou outnumbered. If they took turns on the night watch, it wouldn't take long for them to find an opening. Unran's mind was sounding an alarm that the girl's mental fortitude was no less abnormal, but he chose to ignore that fact.

Once they took down the man, the helpless woman would be easy pickings. That was how things were supposed to work.

Now that Unran had settled on a plan of attack, some of the tension bled from his shoulders. Upon noticing that his legs had gone numb from crouching, he sat crisscross upon the ground. Then, he cast an idle glance at his surroundings.

It was a hill bathed in the light of dusk that sat a small distance from the plot of rice paddies. A tepid breeze blew through the area, weaving past the large stones that had been erected here and there. This was the cemetery where the villagers—and among them, those from the line of village chiefs—were laid to rest.

Unran was sitting in front of the newest tombstone, the one belonging to his father—the previous chief, Tairyuu. Tairyuu's tombstone was a good deal smaller than the rest. Whereas the grave markers of the chiefs who came before him were a composite of several polished stones, his alone was nothing but a single hunk of rock.

The other villagers had refused to help erect Tairyuu's tombstone for fear that he'd died to a "curse" after setting foot in the Cursed Forest. The ones to do all the work had been Gouryuu, who had been so petrified from start to finish that he'd barely had the strength in his arms to dig the grave, and Unran, who hadn't uttered a word the whole time. A makeshift grave like this had been the limit of what the two of them could manage by themselves.

While the rest of the chiefs' graves had been wiped clean, Tairyuu's had been left exposed to the elements and blanketed in fallen leaves. Unran reached out a hand to pluck a stray leaf that clung to the stone.

"What a sad excuse for a grave."

He stared down at the dirty piece of foliage hugging his fingers. With a grave like this, no one would believe that Tairyuu had been the most beloved and respected chief in the village's history while he was alive. The only reason his tombstone was even still standing was because Gouryuu had pacified the villagers and Unran had agreed to take on all the dirty work. The villagers' fear of misfortune was that strong.

"What a joke. You protected the village, educated us, braved the Cursed Forest to sate our hunger...and then everyone turns around and despises you."

Unran gazed down at the leaf for some time, then abruptly tore it in two in a fit of irritation.

"Say, Chief. Were you content with a life where you were taken advantage of at every turn?"

Then, he swatted the leaves and dirt free of the grave. The rainwater that had pooled in the rock's crevices trickled over the clumsy calligraphy letters of "Tairyuu" etched into the tombstone's surface. The surrounding graves were likewise inscribed with the names of the deceased: Tairyuu, Houryuu, Jakuryuu, and Enryuu.

All the men from the line of village chiefs had the character "ryuu"—meaning "dragon"—in their names. No matter how much the townspeople slandered them as lowly rabble, their names still bore a character that signified the emperor—it was the biggest show of bravado societal weaklings like them could manage.

Unran's father, Tairyuu, had been humbled that his name was "too grand for him," but the man had nonetheless carved the names of each of his predecessors into their respective tombstones. Thanks to his skillful penmanship, the calligraphy on most of the graves looked grand and majestic. Only the letters of Tairyuu's own name looked awkward and misshapen.

There was no helping it. Unran had engraved that one himself.

"I really didn't inherit a single thing from you," Unran said in self-derision, tracing his fingers over the unshapely letters barely distinguishable from scratch marks.

He'd inherited neither his book learning nor his neat handwriting. Neither his popularity nor a name ending in "ryuu." Not his integrity as a person either.

"The magistrate said that he'll lower our taxes if we torment a single girl—that the cold spell will end for the whole township if we punish the villainess who brought this calamity upon us. All I have to do is make a few reports to an envoy who'll come by the mountain, and our work will be done. Sounds easy, right, Chief?"

Instead of turning his back on his woman after she was ravished by a townsman, Tairyuu had vouched for both her and her unborn child, but he'd clearly never once thought of Unran as his own son. The fact that he'd never permitted him the character of "ryuu" in his name, instead christening him "Unran," was proof of that.

"Un"—for the clouds that shrouded the sky and robbed the village of its light.

"Ran"—for the storms that flattened the crops, never able to settle down anywhere.

That was him, Unran. The name fit him like a glove.

"I bet *you'd* never even think of tormenting a girl to protect the village...but I can do it. It's a foul plan to go with my foul soul. A match made in heaven, isn't it?"

His thin lips twisted in irony. It wasn't as though he was dissatisfied with the current state of things. This was all fine by him. In the end, he was nothing more than a "half-blood." He was an outsider in his own village—despicable, unlearned, and with no one he could trust...

"I see. So that's what this is all about."

All of a sudden, there came a girl's voice from right beside him. Unran whipped around, startled.

"Being ordered to report back on tormenting me seems to be a recurring theme."

"Wha..."

The girl—Shu Keigetsu—had clasped her hands together, solemnly gazing upon the grave.

"If you've got a reward on the line, I can see why you're so desperate to produce some results. Still, it's nice of him to settle for an oral report. You sure you don't need to show him some teeth or fingers?"

"Huh?!"

Kou Keikou was crouching on his other side. He wiped his forehead with the headscarf he'd tugged loose, then gave a polite bow before the grave.

When did they get here?!

Neither of them had made a sound.

"You people..."

As Unran stood petrified, the pair leaned toward him in a friendly manner.

"It all makes sense now. I see...so you kidnapped Shu Keigetsu in order to save your village. Sorry we ran wild without a thought to your struggles."

"I know it's strange of us to offer, but let us know if there's anything we can do to help. I've dealt with these 'reports' on victimizing Shu Keigetsu before, so I might be able to lend a hand."

"What're you—?!"

For a second, he thought this was the nobility's idea of sarcasm, but they were both dead serious.

"I'd recommend something that'll take down the magistrate who gave that inhumane order."

"Agreed. Why, I never imagined a politician with such an upstanding reputation would scheme to bring his own domain's Maiden to ruin."

"It's always the ones who seem mellow and virtuous at a glance who are hiding something," Keikou lamented, then turned back to Unran with an earnest look. "Well, I get that you gentlemen have your own position to consider. If you'd rather settle things peacefully, we could always cook up a fake report to get you your reward. Men should know when and where to compromise."

"Shall I give you some pointers on how to make the descriptions in your statement sound more extreme? He might feel inspired to give you an even better reward."

Unran had never heard of prisoners giving tips to improve their captor's torture reports. Unsure how to react, his face froze in bewilderment.

The girl rapped her chest with a look of confidence. "I've heard about various torture methods from Tousetsu...that is, an acquaintance of mine known for her gruesome depictions of violence, so please don't hesitate to turn to me."

"No thanks!" Snapping back to his senses, Unran sprang to his feet and scuttled away from them. "What's wrong with you people?! Do you understand the position you're in?!" He jabbed a finger at the pair, raising his voice.

He couldn't believe that his captives, who by all means should have been cowering in fear, were being so forward with him.

"You two were abducted! The whole village resents you, despises you, and keeps trying to attack you! You should, uh... react appropriately, damn it!"

Even he could tell that he didn't sound very threatening—or rather, it was an almost nonsensical dressing-down. What kind of kidnapper demanded the better judgment of his captors?

"Unran. It may surprise you to hear this..." As expected, the girl was unfazed. In fact, she even put a hand to her cheek and, basking in delight, murmured, "But the truth is, I get a little excited when people don't like me..."

Unran recoiled. "Damn right it surprises me!"

Just what *was* this resilient creature in Maiden's clothing?

"Um... Wait, it's not like that. It's not like I *want* people to hate me. I've simply spent my whole life sheltered, so whenever I encounter raw emotion, I feel...surprised? Touched? Anyway, it gives me this jolt in my chest...or perhaps you could say it makes me feel alive." Realizing how she had come off, the girl scrambled to make excuses, thrusting her hands before her in a fluster.

Unran clicked his tongue. "Come on!" he said, grabbing her by the hand and dragging her back down the hill. When he made it back to the fields, he found the villagers he'd instructed to stand watch. "Why are these two wandering around as they please? What happened to guarding them?!"

Scratching their noses and adjusting their hoes over their shoulders, the villagers awkwardly replied, "I mean, they told us they'd fetch water for the fields."

"They fixed the broken roof of my house too."

"The little Maiden told me I was a genius at building ridges... so I figured I'd go till the fields for the first time in a while."

"She blew my nose for me. The Maiden lady smelled nice."

The village had been totally won over in the short time he'd looked away.

A vein popped out on Unran's forehead. "Why are you guys so damn easy?!"

"S-see, Unran? These two refuse to act like proper captives."

Discomfited, Gouryuu beckoned Unran over and started whispering in his ear. "The military officer's as strong as a demon. The Maiden seems all demure, but she never lets her guard down. But for all that, they've got their own kind of charm...and they're pretty dependable..."

"So you're just gonna welcome them with open arms, huh?! What about our taxes?"

"W-well... There's not much we can do during the day, so I figured we'd wait until nightfall... No, even offing him in his sleep might be tough, so, uh, we should get him to lower his guard. We'll play nice with him 'til tomorrow. It's not like we have a strict time limit. All we have to do is fake tomorrow night's report, right?"

Unran squinted suspiciously as Gouryuu rambled on and insisted this was all a matter of pragmatism. But once he remembered that he'd arrived at a similar conclusion earlier, he just heaved a sigh. It was true they couldn't do much as long as the Maiden had such an absurdly powerful guard. Since all their attacks would be neutralized, the best they could hope for was starving them out.

"For now, just don't feed them. Don't give them water either."

"R-right! Of course not."

"If they want to work so bad, let them work themselves to exhaustion. The real fight starts once they get sleepy."

"Yeah! Damn right!" Gouryuu was eager to concur in his rumbling tones, but who knew if things would really go so smoothly.

No. I've gotta make *them go smoothly.*

Unran looked up at the overcast sky, threadbare and exhausted. If the magistrate's words were to be trusted, the clouds wouldn't part until Shu Keigetsu was hurt. On a more pressing note, the village wouldn't make it through the winter if their taxes weren't lowered.

"My! You're going to weed too? I'm so glad to have you join us."

"W-we're not joining you! We're just keeping an eye on you."

"Still, it'll be a tremendous help to have experts like you around."

"Hmph. D-don't be so sure."

Yet when he saw how pleased the men were to be the target of the girl's innocent smile, Unran had to stare off into the distance.

What the hell? he silently grumbled one more time for good measure.

"Gosh... This place truly has an infinite wealth of charm." Reirin let loose an enraptured sigh, touching her cheek with a hand caked in mud down to the underside of her fingernails.

It was late in the evening, and she was working in a rice paddy. It was the second night since she'd been kidnapped. Her body was aching all over from the nonstop farmwork she'd been doing, yet Reirin gazed tenderly upon her burning calves. Muscle soreness was her favorite kind of pain in the world.

"This is bliss..."

For a while, Reirin massaged her calves with a look of euphoria, but then her face went taut.

Ack! I mustn't break into a smile over this fulfilling farming experience. I have to look glummer.

The villagers had kidnapped her as part of a plan to harm "Shu Keigetsu." Even though she was using their scheme for her own ends—no, precisely for that reason—she had to be more considerate of their feelings.

Put yourself in their shoes, Reirin. If you kidnapped someone to torment her, only for that captive to run around having the time of her life, how terrible would that feel?

Suddenly, an earthworm crawled over the footpath in her view. Reirin gently plucked it from the ground and caressed it in her hand. She adored these lovely little critters that enriched the earth's soil.

Wait, this is no time to be admiring worms. The villagers are trying their best to hurt me. To ignore them would be a disgrace to the Kous who so value hard wo—oh, look, a frog!

Reirin tried to fire herself up one more time, only for a frog to leap by seconds later. She promptly captured it. Not only were frogs edible, but the poison in their parotid glands could be extracted and used to prepare medicines.

Oh, it's a male.

After confirming the amphibian's sex, Reirin scrunched her brow into a frown. "This is bad. There's temptation at every turn!"

Things had been following this pattern for a while now. The second she'd resolve to act more like a proper prisoner, the expanse of nature would flaunt its charms before her, sending her into another fit of excitement.

I can't help it! There's such vast soil, rice paddies, and fields!

Gardening was a hobby so ingrained into the Kou soul that it could practically be called second nature. Being a woman of that clan, Reirin had quietly set up her own field back in the gardens of the Palace of the Golden Qilin and tried her hand at pretend rice cultivation, but a miniature garden couldn't hold a candle to the real thing. Grappling with the difficulties inherent to maintaining such a large plot of land, an ecosystem more vibrant than she ever could have expected, and the unique quirks of a region ravaged by cold had all provided her a valuable learning experience.

The more she swung her hoe, the more new discoveries she made; the more weeds she plucked, the more she learned. She couldn't help getting immersed in the work.

If I were in my original body, I'd be unsteady on my feet just from breathing all this humid air, but Lady Keigetsu's body knows no limits. This is the best!

Even better, the villagers who had been so hostile to her on the first morning were slowly but surely softening up. Then again, even the way they'd spat and cursed her out during their initial meeting had seemed charming and spirited to Reirin.

Residents of the southern territory are all such colorful people!

The villagers probably believed the cold spell wouldn't end until they tormented "Shu Keigetsu." It seemed hunger had driven them to their breaking points; upon their initial encounter, the people had made a habit of shouting abuse and hurling stones at her.

Still, there was an earnestness to how they exhausted the limits of their vocabulary in their attempts to express their outrage. Their reactions to every little thing she did and said—gaping when she dodged a rock or looking bemused when she asked them the meaning of a word she'd never heard before—gave them an almost adorably pathetic quality.

"Your throw is too weak! It's not enough just to take me from behind. Pay more attention to your blind spots! You watching? Do it like this, this...and this!"

"Eep?!"

Each time Keikou turned the tables on the village men and dove straight into giving them martial arts pointers, they naturally went along with it.

"I saw a pheasant flying by just now, so I had Broth—I mean, Lord Keikou—bring it down with a rock. Frying it won't be an option without any oil, but do you think it would taste better grilled or steamed?"

"Well, aren't *you* kids having the time of your lives?!"

If Reirin struck up a conversation with the women, no matter how much they fumed, they'd still quip right back at her.

"Drop dead! You, uhh, viness who brings disaster!"

"Oh dear, I think you mean 'villainess.' Let's say it together on the count of three."

"Villainess!"

The children had picked up the adults' knack for foul language, but their impressionable natures meant they were also very compliant.

Facing the threat of famine had brought out their vicious sides, but if she took matching farming tools in hand and greeted them with all the enthusiasm she could muster, the villagers would pull back and decline to escalate things further.

What straightforward people, Reirin thought, impressed by their simplistic natures. *Come to think of it, since they're all connected to the Shu clan, there's something about them that reminds me a little of Lady Keigetsu. How adorable. Oh, right—I need to get in touch with her soon.*

Her expression clouded over as the association of ideas reminded her she had yet to talk with Keigetsu. Someone from the village had always been standing watch over her, so she hadn't had the chance to stand unattended before a flame.

She must be worried.

Though Keigetsu had been the one to tell her to run, it wasn't like they had planned for any of this. No doubt Keishou had explained the circumstances to her, but she was still bound to be feeling anxious. It probably didn't help that she was stuck playing the part of "Kou Reirin" in front of Gyoumei and other Maidens either. Reirin was concerned that the stress and responsibility might be too much for her to handle.

Still, she thought it wise to avoid using flame magic where the villagers could see. Based on the shrines erected all over the place, along with how often she saw them praying there, Reirin surmised that the villagers were fairly religious and, in the same vein, that they had a deep fear of curses and calamities. If they spotted her using the mysterious Daoist arts, then forget villainess—she'd be branded an evil spirit and burned alive.

For instance, there's that "Cursed Forest" Unran mentioned.

The name Unran had muttered before his father's grave popped into Reirin's mind. It was that of a cursed ground, one which the entire village had shunned their previous chief just for entering. Apparently, it was a dense forest that stretched across the mountainside. It looked like nothing more than a lush woodland to Reirin, but that clearly wasn't the case for the villagers.

Before catching that pheasant, Reirin had gotten hungry enough to mumble idly to herself about heading into the mountain to pick some wild vegetables. The villagers, who had seemed jovial enough to that point, had gone pale as soon as the words left her mouth. That went for men, women, and children alike.

"What did you just say?"

"You're not setting foot in the Cursed Forest on our watch."

All the friendliness had vanished from their expressions, a look of distinct loathing and fear taking its place.

"You can't go into that forest. Never ever," the children had said with unnerving looks on their faces. When she tried to ask the reason, everyone had immediately fallen silent, as if they didn't even want to mention its name.

As puzzling as Reirin and Keikou found this, they *were* guests in someone else's village. Groups with a strong sense of unity often have their own unique rules and regulations, so the siblings had been hesitant to push the matter.

"Everyone who goes in the forest dies," explained a particularly strong-willed boy among the children, glaring at them. "It's really true." He'd then clutched Reirin's arm as if to hold her back, at which she had given his hand a gentle return squeeze.

He had probably meant that as a threat to keep her from bringing misfortune to the village. But to Reirin, it had sounded almost like he was worried about her. The touch of the tiny hand he'd offered her without hesitation had felt so very warm.

Everyone is on edge because of the cold spell, but I'm sure they're much warmer and friendlier people by nature. I need to be sure I don't give them an unnecessary fright when I contact Lady Keigetsu.

Reirin could have sworn she felt the warmth of the boy's hand still lingering on her own mud-caked one. As she held her hand up to the pale moonlight, she made the earnest wish to get closer to the people of the village.

Speaking of wanting to get along with someone...

She cast a glance over her shoulder at a footpath a short distance away. There, Unran and Gouryuu were wearily watching over her. It was only the two of them left by this point. The rest of the villagers had long since tapped out, overwhelmed by the sibling tag team.

When Reirin waved to them just for the heck of it, Gouryuu waved back in befuddlement, while Unran turned his head with a scowl.

"He's so cute..."

Unran was such a perfect picture of a moody cat that Reirin's heart nearly skipped a beat. Between that and his handsome, even features, he reminded her a lot of how Leelee had been back when they'd first met.

No matter what excuses he made for it, the fact that he had gone to his father's grave inspired a kinship in Reirin. She used to pay frequent visits to her mother's shrine herself, though it had become more difficult since she'd come to the Maiden Court.

Above all else, it made her heart swell with fondness to see that, despite his brusque, feral catlike manner, he was still conscientious enough to react to every little thing she did.

"Oh, I do wonder how Leelee is doing. Being around Unran gives me the same sense of comfort as being with her. I wonder if I can find a way to make friends with him, at least for the time I'm here," she mumbled to herself with a face that meant business.

"Watch it, Reirin. You're starting to sound like a married man looking for a local woman," a voice called out to her from behind.

The man who had tied up the sleeves of his classy robe and was happily wading to his knees in the mud was none other than Keikou. Of course, he had spent the entire day absorbed in farmwork alongside Reirin.

The pair smoothly pinpointed a footpath still overrun with weeds, then crouched down as naturally as they breathed and took to plucking the grass.

"But man, this has been such a fun time. How great would it be to retire from my job in the capital and spend all my days down in the countryside dirt?"

"I couldn't agree more. Regrettably, it seems the cool summer has slowed the rice's growth..."

"But if anything..."

"That just gets us going!"

The two siblings exchanged nods as they finished each other's sentences, perfectly in sync. Meanwhile, their deft fingers never stopped working to uproot the weeds and exterminate pests with a flourish, guided only by the weak light of the moon.

"It's true that these plants aren't getting enough sunlight. Still, the villagers have demonstrated a surprising level of standards in the areas of weeding and pest control."

"The footpaths are well maintained, and the community is close-knit enough to avoid squabbles over drawing water. For all that, it's really a shame to see the plants growing so little."

"The soil itself may be barren, but they seem to be making good use of compost. Is there anything else we can try to improve the yield of rice?"

"Nah. At this point, all that's left is to keep up with the weeding and pest control and pray for sunshine."

Still crouched on the ground, the two conversed with their game faces on.

"We've done everything in our power," Keikou went on. "Only the god of agriculture can control the rays of the sun. All we humans can do is get down in the soil and work with what we have."

"And what makes those steady, unrelenting efforts possible are..."

They stood up at the exact same time, bared their biceps, and hooked their arms together.

"Muscles!"

After snorting a laugh, they gazed at each other with a sigh of wonder.

"Whoa now... This is almost too much fun, Reirin!"

"Indeed. I'm having such a wonderful, wonderful time, Brother Senior!"

Both of them were buzzing with excitement. And it was no surprise—for how close the siblings were, the issue of Reirin's stamina meant they'd never spent a full day together before. Now they could lose themselves in whatever they wanted to their heart's content, enjoying an intimate conversation all the while. How could they not be happy?

"It's been like a dream come true. I never imagined we'd be able to tend fields and grow rice together." Reirin bobbed her head vigorously, her eyes misty with joy. "No doubt the villagers' anger stems from their fear of a poor harvest. In that case, I'd like to help resolve the issue in whatever small ways I can. Of course, we won't see results overnight. But circumstances permitting, perhaps we could stay here a few more—"

Before she could finish that sentence with "days," Reirin shut her mouth.

Keikou had withdrawn his arm at some point, and now he was fixing her with a grave stare. "So you want to stay in that body for as long as possible, Reirin."

"..."

His voice was soft and deliberate. The tenderness oozing from his words was a complete shift from the playful attitude he'd had just moments earlier, and something about that frightened Reirin.

"I'm not criticizing you. I just want to know if that's how you really feel."

A lukewarm night breeze swept through the paddy. Heedless of how it tousled his hair, Keikou stared unblinkingly at Reirin—at his sister wearing another girl's face.

"Shu Keigetsu is deeply unpopular. And no matter how you slice it, it's not fair for you to bear the brunt of all this antagonism just because you're stuck in her body. I wouldn't blame you if you lashed out at me for even suggesting the kidnapping in the first place. Yet you haven't shown the slightest interest in fleeing this village."

"I mean...this was my own choice, and if I go back to the township and see His Highness, I'm sure he'll catch on to the switch. Then Lady Keigetsu would be—"

"Shu Keigetsu will be punished. And you'll become the empress. The way most people would see it, you'll be given the *opportunity* to become the empress. Yet you haven't even considered choosing your own prosperity over Shu Keigetsu's safety. No, if anything...you're actually more afraid of your own enthronement than Shu Keigetsu's punishment, aren't you?" he pointed out, voice deep and low.

Reirin's head snapped back up. "Not at all. To become empress would be the highest honor an Ei woman could—"

"So you acknowledge that it's an honor. Is it that you can't open your heart to His Highness, then? It does sort of feel like you made that bet to run away from him."

"No! His Highness—my dear cousin—is kindhearted and

182

reliable, a skilled scholar and warrior. He's almost too good for me." She made a point of calling him "dear cousin," a term of endearment she'd been avoiding as of late.

If he saw through her switch, she would spend the rest of her life as his wife and eventually his empress. But if he didn't, she was fully prepared to leave the Maiden Court altogether. Perhaps Gyoumei had interpreted the terms she laid down and her staunch insistence on calling him "Your Highness" as signs that Reirin had yet to forgive him.

That wasn't the case, though. Reirin had forgiven him a long time ago. In fact, she'd never been angry with him in the first place. Under the circumstances, it had been inevitable that he would force her into the Lion's Judgment and call her names. Those actions had come from a place of both righteous indignation and his love for "Kou Reirin," after all.

"The real reason I'm keeping up with this ridiculous bet..."

Reirin pursed her lips, then turned her back to Keikou and looked down upon the small pile of weeds she had plucked—the unnamed grasses and flowers that stubbornly spread their roots, heedless of the rice plants or the cold summer weather.

"After switching places with Lady Keigetsu during the Double Sevens Festival...I noticed something upon returning to my own vessel."

Reirin began to tell her tale piece by piece.

"I'd become remarkably healthy. I rarely ran fevers anymore, and when I did, they were mild. My whole body felt light, free of nausea, dizziness, or aches... I wondered if perhaps it was because

Lady Keigetsu's soul had purged the hotbed of maladies that is my body in flame."

"Slash-and-burn farming, eh?"

"Something like that." Reirin giggled, tickled to hear the earth-based Kou clan and the fire-based Shu clan described in terms of a field. "But," she said, cutting her laughter short and dropping her gaze, "it didn't last long. I've been suffering even worse symptoms in the aftermath, like a backlash... Hee hee, you see, I've always had this one dream whenever I'm running an especially high fever. And lately, Brother Senior, I've been having it once every few days."

When she closed her eyes, she could picture the scene in her mind. Countless eyeballs. Total darkness. Once "it" caught her, her whole body erupted into black fire, ghastly flames that clung and clung to her no matter how hard she struggled to bat them away.

A faint smile on her face, Reirin said, "I might not have much time left."

Her voice was almost quiet enough to melt into the evening darkness. Keikou swallowed hard.

"Kidding!" Reirin rushed to add in a bright tone as soon as she noticed his reaction. She bent down in the grass opposite her brother. "I'll be all right. Owing to your advice as a skilled military physician, I'm developing more potent remedies with each passing day. No matter how high my fevers get or how much my body aches, there's always medicine to take the edge off."

The pop of her pulling weeds echoed through the air. Lost for words, Keikou watched his little sister from behind.

"But, see...the empress is more than just a wife. She is the mother of our kingdom. She must produce an heir. When I consider that, I feel I shouldn't be the Kou woman to claim the position. That's all."

The Maidens were meant to be the next generation of the empress and consorts. However, that was nothing more than an unspoken agreement. If one of the girls dropped out, it would be simple to find a candidate to replace her.

But if she became a consort... If she became his "wife" officially...

"I've started to work up quite the sweat," said Reirin, pretending to wipe her brow. "Perhaps, then, I ought to hurry and step down from my position as Maiden of my own accord. But Her Majesty the Empress would never allow me to back down before a fight. Nor do I want to. It'll be all right—I can still win. The part of me that thinks that...and the part of me that thinks it's too late... Sometimes, well... Thus, I've taken the coward's way out through this gamble—"

"It's fine. I get it. You don't have to say anything more."

With a tiny sniffle, Reirin spun back around. "Say, Brother Senior, would you indulge a selfish request from your sister? Your little Reirin wants to play around in this body a tiny bit longer."

"Oh, Reirin..."

"I've been taking especially potent medicine over the past few days to ensure I don't get sick during this trip. I shouldn't cause

Lady Keigetsu too much trouble from a health standpoint, at least. The side effects will kick in after taking the medicine for about a week, so I promise to return to the township and get my body back before then."

Reirin pointed out the possibility that Keigetsu might even switch them back remotely once she'd recovered her qi. Then she added in an even softer voice, "Besides, I'm sure this will be the last time."

It was the same thing Reirin always told Keigetsu when they traded places. Each time, Keigetsu would scowl and yell, "You big liar!" How would she react if she knew Reirin was genuinely prepared for that to be true?

Keikou sat down beside Reirin, exhaled a deep breath to reset his emotions, and then went back to weeding. "Well...we all know Kou Keikou's reputation for being a sister fanatic. If my little sister comes crying to me that she's not ready for something, you better believe I'll buy her time, even if it costs our clan potential success."

"Hee hee, sure you would. I bet you're *really* thinking that it'd help the balance of the five clans if I didn't become empress."

"That's just a bonus. If you do ever end up wanting the throne, all we have to do is take the time to lay the groundwork." Keikou artfully dodged her accusation, then gave an exaggerated shrug of his shoulders. "Besides, Unran and Gouryuu cut the suspension bridge that connects the village to the township on the way here. Even I can't make it back to town without a bridge. Thus, I shall grudgingly, reluctantly stay put until help arrives in a few days."

Reirin's smile broadened. "Of course. Grudgingly and reluctantly."

She knew Keikou had chosen to watch Unran cut the rope without putting up a fight. Though her brother seemed like he acted without thinking, he was actually an exceptionally clever man.

For instance, as he moved around from field to field plucking weeds, he had been working to get a full picture of the village's layout. By now, he no doubt had a complete grasp of the village's relative location, size, and even its shortcuts.

"Exactly. In his haste, Keishou might have sent the search party in the wrong direction, but it is what it is. Let's keep our heads down and stay put for as long as the Heavens permit."

"Sure."

So many people were looking out for her.

Reirin gave Keikou a low bow of her head. "Thank you."

"Don't mention it," he smoothly replied, then stroked his chin with a muddied hand. "Still, it's lucky for us that His Highness has his hands tied as the crown prince. If the bearer of the dragon's qi got serious, he could figure out where we are in a flash, don't you think?"

"That's true. I have a feeling that His Highness has all sorts of abilities we've yet to discover."

"In that respect, as talented as they are, the Eagle Eyes and other military officers are just a bunch of common men. Provided they don't have a guy with beastly instincts who's reckless enough to act alone, they'll never be able to find this—"

Before he could finish that sentence with "village," Keikou froze. Dirt spilled from the bundle of grass he was holding.

"Uh-oh. They do."

"Um, Brother Senior?"

As her brother suddenly fixated on a certain point in the distance, Reirin tilted her head to one side. She instinctively followed his gaze past the several rows of rice paddies, looking out toward the overgrown grass on either side of the irrigation river.

"Oh," she gasped.

"Hey, Unran," said Gouryuu from where he sat next to his nephew, scratching the tip of his nose with a sigh. "How long do you think they're gonna keep working for?"

"No idea," Unran responded in a sulk, resting his elbow on one raised knee.

"My stomach's not feeling too hot, so I'd like to hit the latrine... but I guess I shouldn't leave you all on your own, huh?"

"..."

"Old Kyou's been laid up in bed all day—said she was feeling tired. She wouldn't even cook me lunch, so I'm getting pretty hungry too. I could really stand to head home, hit the hay...all that stuff..."

In other words, Gouryuu was tired of standing watch. But that went for both of them. Unran yanked a weed from the footpath in his irritation.

Shu Keigetsu had spent the last few hours in the rice pad-dies, so her sentries of Unran and Gouryuu had been forced to sit somewhere close by the entire time. No, forget "hours"—the Maiden and her military officer had been completely absorbed in farming for the past two days.

For that whole stretch of time, they'd dodged all the villagers' attempts at harassment while happily feasting on a pheasant. Meanwhile, their would-be tormentors hadn't filled their bellies in ages. To make matters worse, the pair had even afforded the luxury of covering the bird in mud and smothering the meat, as well as sprinkling it with salt they'd borrowed from a shrine when they were first abducted.

No one could blame Unran for cutting in to yell, "Don't go *borrowing* offerings to the gods!" Things had carried on like that for a while, with the kidnappees calmly going about their work and winning over the villagers with smiles on their faces, and Unran had spent almost the entire time screaming his head off.

I'm so tired… Was I always the sort of person to yell this much?

He definitely wasn't. He was supposed to be an elusive man who always wore a condescending smile on his face. Breaking character for so long had worn him out in both body and soul. As if it wasn't bad enough that the villagers kept steadily dropping out of the punishment force.

Overcome with a sense of futility, Unran stared off into the horizon, his chin still perched in his hand. He saw Shu Keigetsu and her guard knock their biceps together, then go right back to plucking grass.

"I'm amazed she never gets tired of working." Gouryuu fidgeted where he sat, apparently having given up on going home. "Look at that. They've managed to clear out all the weeds over the past two days. They've been kneading mud underfoot, fixing all the broken parts of the footpaths, squashing pests, and looking over the rice plants one by one. Who are those guys, really? A pair of professional farmers?" he grumbled, probably because he had nothing better to do.

Unran listened to him in silence. If nothing else, it was true that Shu Keigetsu and her guard were working just as hard as—if not harder than—the average farmer. Unran had considered giving them hell if they stepped on even a single stalk of rice, but so far, their work had been even more swift and thorough than the villagers'.

"Is this really the talentless, stuck-up sewer rat we heard about?"

"..."

Unran's brow creased into a frown. Based on all the rumors they'd heard from the capital, Shu Keigetsu was an unpleasant woman who bullied the other Maidens, abused her court ladies, and only cared about herself. Even judging from how she'd acted right before her dance of tribute, she looked down on her subjects enough to instinctively recoil when an untouchable clung to her leg.

So what was going on here? Ever since she'd come to the village, all traces of that attitude had vanished.

No noblewoman—no, not even a townswoman—had ever smiled at Unran or his kind before. Never mind averting her gaze from their grimy appearances; Shu Keigetsu had met their eyes, listened to them, and offered them thanks without hesitation. Instead of sneering at the untouchables' scrawny physiques or the stench in the air, she had taken in the fields and rice paddies the villagers had cultivated and nodded in admiration. Had there ever been someone like her before?

"This isn't how this was supposed to go. Not even a little. Say, Unran—"

"You're too soft. You and the rest of the villagers." Boorish though he was, Gouryuu was a good-natured man at heart. Unran had to be the one to cut him off in a tight voice. "It's obviously an act. The second she found out we were planning to torture her, she and her guard set out to win us over."

He knew full well that those two would never think like such sad, helpless prisoners. The confidence in his tone was as much to convince himself as anyone.

"Besides, the only reason they can work so hard is because they've built up their energy eating full meals every day. There's no comparing them to us, who have to get by on just a single bowl of congee. The stupid amount of pep they have is just another reason to hate them. What's so impressive about it?"

Surely they wouldn't last more than a few more hours of hard labor at most. That pheasant had fallen into their laps on their first day, but their luck was going to run out eventually. By tomorrow, they'd be too hungry and exhausted to stay on their feet. Just like all the untouchables were as of late.

"Guess you're right," Gouryuu conceded after a pause, his face falling. "We need everyone to hate Shu Keigetsu. Yeah. For your sake too."

His last comment made Unran glance up, and it was right then that Shu Keigetsu and Kou Keikou abruptly rose to their feet after hours of crouching in the footpaths and weeding, much to Unran and Gouryuu's surprise. The girl proceeded to turn on her heel and rush out of the paddy with a panicked look on her face.

Unran and Gouryuu gasped, then quickly exchanged glances. *She's making a run for it!*

I knew it, Unran thought as he took off after Shu Keigetsu. Her impressive work ethic and her humble, serene demeanor had all been nothing more than an act. Underneath that demure smile, she had been plotting her escape all this time.

"Stop right there!" he yelled.

She was faster than Unran had expected, but not enough to outrun him. Perhaps running on a damp footpath lit only by the light of the moon had been her undoing, because he caught up to her in no time.

"Where the hell do you think you're going, huh?!"

"I-It's not like that. I'm not running...or, umm, I *am*, but I'm not running from the village! I just want to hide in the warehouse! That's it, I want to go back! I want to go back to the warehouse, please!" She seemed incredibly flustered. Though her speech was as polite as ever, she was babbling incoherently. When Unran grabbed her by her slender arm, she flailed in his grip and insisted, "P-please. This is urgent. Please let me go back!"

"Not a chance, wench."

Despite the anger in his voice, Unran felt a small modicum of relief. A distressed girl and an untouchable forcing his will upon her—*that* was the shape they had all envisioned this "punishment" to take.

Unran was reassured to see the situation at last turning into something he could comprehend. "Did it finally catch up to you what position you're in? Too bad, though. You're not going anywhere. You're going to become this village's plaything, stoned by every last person you see."

"Umm, er, I'm sorry, but I must ask you to refrain from saying—"

"I'm afraid what *you* want doesn't matter here. I'll say whatever I damn well please."

As the words left his mouth, he realized something. If he took this opportunity to hold a blade to her neck, perhaps he'd be able to neutralize that terrifying guard of hers. He could take the Maiden hostage and have her guard lock himself in the warehouse. And this time, they'd be sure to tie him up with multiple layers of rope.

Unran kept the girl's arm pinned with one hand and fished around in the breast of his garment with the other.

The girl kept stealing glances behind her in the meantime. When she finally took notice of the dagger in Unran's hand, she blanched so hard that he could tell even in the black of night. "Ahhh! Um, I'm very sorry to ask this, but things could get messy very fast, so could you please put your weapon away?"

"Hah. What kind of idiot sheathes his blade on request? Should I cut you a little for a taste?"

"No—"

Relieved to see Shu Keigetsu's composure broken, Unran gripped her arm even tighter and pulled her close. And that was when it hit him.

Bonk!

He heard a dull *thud* against his side, and a few moments later, he realized someone had kicked him to the ground.

"Ugh!"

The sound of him scraping against the earth overlapped with his muffled scream.

"You lowlife," came the voice of a man just as Unran had managed to prop himself up on his elbows. He felt the chill of a blade against his neck. "You'd kidnap a Maiden, grab her by the arm, insult her, and threaten her with a blade? I see you have a death wish."

Staring down at him with the moon to his back was a man with an aura best described as calculating. For some reason, he was soaking wet from head to toe, water dripping from even the edge of his blade. He had thrust his sword before Unran with one hand and was holding Shu Keigetsu close with the other.

"Captain!"

Meanwhile, the girl who was supposed to have been rescued was looking more panicked than ever.

I never thought the captain of all people would show up!

Reirin knew that Captain Shin-u of the Eagle Eyes had been a very skilled military officer before coming to the Maiden Court.

Though he'd belonged to a different troop than her brothers, his military feats had been such that they'd reached even her ears. Now that he had shown up, there was a very real chance he could wipe out the entire village all on his own.

"How did you know where I was?!" Reirin lamented.

"The clues left behind seemed too contrived," he said matter-of-factly, having taken her question at face value. "Both the hoofprints on the road and the Gen clan tassel left behind on the stage looked like a setup. If the assassination had truly been the work of us Gens, we wouldn't leave any evidence at the scene."

It seemed Unran's machinations had backfired.

"I found it unlikely that the culprits were either Gens or bandits from a far-off land, so I had my squad carry out their own separate investigation. That's when we discovered that the bridge leading to the village had collapsed. It seemed like someone didn't want us traveling across, so I came on over."

"Why wouldn't you turn back when you saw the bridge was broken?!" Reirin retorted in spite of herself.

"Hm? Isn't that an invitation to march in?" Shin-u cocked his head with a completely straight face. "The rest of my men ended up dropping out along the way, but I managed to swim the whole way across."

In any case, it seemed that was the story behind Shin-u making it to the village all by himself. Reirin could only pray that the other Eagle Eyes were safe.

Shin-u turned back to Unran, adjusting his grip on his sword. "Now then. I plan to question you in front of His Highness, so

I won't kill you here, but turning a blade on a Maiden calls for some sort of punishment. Maybe I'll take off an arm."

"Wha—"

Reirin scrambled to disentangle herself from Shin-u's arms, then knelt down in front of Unran to shield him. "No, Captain. Please sheathe your blade. One of his bones may have been broken. We need to administer treatment!"

"Treatment? What are you talking about?" Shin-u furrowed his shapely brow. "Shu Keigetsu, not only did these bandits abduct you, but this man was ready to assault you only moments ago. Why are you protecting him?"

Out of the corner of her eye, Reirin saw her brother throw up his hands in defeat. Keikou couldn't step in to stop the captain of the Eagle Eyes. That went without saying—if her "bodyguard" of a ceremonial officer rushed over to obstruct his "ally," the situation wouldn't add up. If she wanted to keep up her "Shu Keigetsu" act, her only option was to get through this on her own.

Reirin drew her lips into a thin line, then said, "These aren't bandits. They're innocent villagers."

"Oho. You'd call the people who captured you 'innocent'?"

"I wasn't captured. These people are grappling with hunger because of the cold spell. They simply brought me here to see the situation for myself, hoping to make their plight known to their territory's Maiden."

Her far-fetched assertion earned a raise of an eyebrow from Shin-u. Another droplet of water trickled down the blade he'd thrust before Unran.

"And they bathed the stage in fire and oil for that?"

"I won't deny that they chose a forceful means of bringing me here, but that's a sign of how desperate the situation was. If nothing else, I am standing here now of my own free will," Reirin declared, looking Shin-u straight in the eye. "Whatever their intentions may have been, I came here of my own volition, and I've yet to be hurt in any manner. Why, then, is there any need for this man to lose an arm?"

Shin-u's eyes widened ever so slightly. That was almost word-for-word what the body-swapped Kou Reirin had once said as she defended her court lady. He passed the point of surprise, his eyes next blazing with uncontainable delight. Then he chuckled low in his throat.

Reirin didn't notice that, however. As soon as the blade had left Unran's throat, she'd glanced back at him in a fluster. "Are you all right, Unran? Do you feel sick? Did you hit your head?"

"That's very kind of you. I never knew you had such a compassionate heart, *Shu Keigetsu*." His eyes glinting like an eagle's, Shin-u loaded his voice with all the contempt he could muster. "I thought you'd be loath to lay a hand upon these vile *untouchables*," he said, purposely playing up his own cruelty.

"Take that back," she said automatically. Would it seem strange of her to jump on him for that remark? No, Shu Keigetsu was the Maiden of the southern territory, so of course she'd be angry to hear someone insult her own people.

Reirin couldn't hide her shock that Shin-u, a man she'd taken for fair-minded, would discriminate against Unran and his people.

198

She was likewise dismayed to see Unran, who very much resembled Leelee, with his shoulders so pitifully hunched.

Shu Keigetsu was a "villainess," so it wouldn't be strange for her to chew someone out in a fit of emotion. Making that excuse to herself, Reirin fixed Shin-u with a glare. "Could you please refrain from speaking of them that way? There's nothing 'vile' about them. Can't you see how carefully they've tended these fields?"

"Not really. It's nighttime. I can't see anything but a vile man cowering pathetically on the ground."

"Goodness, I didn't realize our esteemed captain had knot-holes for eyes. You water spinach!" she snapped, keeping her villainess status in mind.

Shin-u choked on his next words and clamped a hand over his mouth. "Pfft..."

Judging from the way he had turned his head aside and looked at the ground, that insult must have really shaken him up.

Reirin kept pushing, jabbing a finger at him. "The villagers have been unfairly forced to live in this barren land, yet still they tirelessly plow their fields. Their community is close-knit, and they tackle their rice paddies with a greater zeal than anyone else in the township. What reason is there to call them 'vile'?"

Shin-u refused to look at her, which in turn drew more of her ire.

"Take a look at these rice paddies. Don't they look beautiful? The irrigation is thorough. And look at the fields all the way back there. Do you see how the crops are arranged according to their height? That's to prevent them from blocking the sunlight, and it even takes into account the size they'll be when fully grown. This village is filled to the brim with such ingenious designs. These are the most talented farmers this entire township has to offer."

Behind her, Unran was gawking at her, blown away. Unable to see it, Reirin went on, "To call people so eager to learn, so rife with experience and knowledge 'vile'... Excuse me, are you listening?"

"I wasn't. Sorry," Shin-u responded without the slightest hint of shame.

"Why, the *nerve* of y—" Reirin leaned forward, miffed, only to swallow her next words.

When the captain turned back to her, he was grinning. "Apologies. I take it back. They aren't vile."

Shin-u sheathed his sword, then extended a bony hand to Reirin in its place. She couldn't help but stare in surprised enchantment at the first boyish smile she'd ever seen upon his face.

"And allow me to correct one other thing I said—"

Just as Shin-u was about to murmur Reirin's own name next to her ear, a loud voice cut in from behind. "Ooh, that's our promising Eagle Eyes captain for you! How flexible!"

It was Keikou. He put a friendly hand on the captain's shoulder, then peeled him away from Reirin in a motion as natural as it was assertive.

"Actually, after examining the situation from several different angles, I concluded that we ought to stay in this village for the handful of days until help arrives. After all, if we threw her over our shoulder and attempted to cross the river, Lady Shu Keigetsu here might throw a fit and end up drowning herself," he said, casually emphasizing that the woman standing before them was the Shu Maiden.

Shin-u frowned. Did Keikou not realize who she was, or was he trying to hide it *because* he knew? Either option was plausible.

"Lord Keikou—"

"Besides, I think it'd please the god of agriculture if we stayed put and saw the sights. What do you say, Captain? Let's all stay here together for the few days until the bridge is repaired and the search party arrives." Keikou hugged Shin-u around the shoulder. Then, he added in a low whisper, "Unless you want to toss her out before His Highness mid-switch and watch as he makes her his wife? You must really care about that half brother of yours."

"..."

As Shin-u stared silently back at him, Keikou flashed a cunning smile. "I hear it'll take about two more days for Shu Keigetsu to recover her qi and undo the switch. Can't returning to the township wait until then? The bridge collapsed, after all. We can't bring a Maiden with us across the river. Our hands are tied."

The broad-minded Kou clan's obliviousness to subtle emotional cues was one of their defining features. However, things were different on the battlefield. Keikou was adept at identifying his enemies' weak spots with his beast-like intuition. He could tell this world-weary looker of a man was attracted to Reirin—to the point that his empty eyes had lit up, a smile had spread across his face, and he'd almost said her name the moment he'd become convinced of who she was.

Even the man himself likely had yet to realize what he felt. It was a precarious sentiment that toed the line of irreverence to the throne, but Keikou was the sort of man who wouldn't hesitate to encourage that for his sister's sake.

"You and I have nothing to fear from these villagers. Or is the current head Eagle Eye too weak to protect a single woman without running to the safety of the township?"

A pause. "May I ask why you're so intent on remaining here?"

"It's exactly what I said earlier. If His Highness sees Reirin right now, he's going to figure out who she really is. You know about the bet, right? Reirin isn't ready to become empress yet. No brother worth his salt would force his little sister into something she doesn't want," Keikou declared, his doting sibling side on full display.

Shin-u mulled that over for a bit. Then he cast his sky-blue eyes almost imperceptibly downward. "That's a fair point."

At length, he turned aside to shake himself free of Keikou's arm. He then announced loud enough for Reirin, who was crouching by Unran's side, to hear: "True. It would be dangerous to cross the river with a girl as short-tempered as *Shu Keigetsu*. It should take about two days for the other Eagle Eyes to report back to the township, assemble a squad, and either fix the bridge or climb the mountain to meet us. We would be better off waiting until then."

Such was Shin-u's decision.

"I'll give that full marks," Keikou responded with a good-humored nod, then glanced back at Unran and the villagers who had begun to flock to him. "You heard the man, friends. From today onward, the Eagle Eyes' captain, Shin-u, will be joining our ranks. No worries—he's a high-class man, but feel free to shove him in a warehouse like us. He seems to have a surprising temper on him, though, so you might get killed if you casually take a swing at him. Watch yourselves."

"Wha..."

And thus did the pair of "prisoners" make the unilateral decision to add one more person to their team.

"For mercy's sake! Why doesn't she ever respond to my flame calls?!"

In the room assigned to "Kou Reirin" somewhere in the township magistrate's estate, Keigetsu was staring down a candle and biting her nails in frustration. It was the second night since "Shu Keigetsu" had been abducted. She still hadn't verified whether her friend was safe, let alone discussed how to undo the swap, and the suspense was driving her crazy.

"The times you're around a fire aren't matching up, that's all. She has Master Keikou with her, so I don't think she's in any danger," Leelee said as she peered into the candle from beside her, sounding like she was trying to convince herself of the same.

Keigetsu clicked her tongue and glared at Leelee. "If Lord Keishou's words are to be believed, she becomes three times as much of a handful when she's around him. Not even double for the two of them. *Three* times!"

THOUGH I AM AN INEPT VILLAINESS

"..."

Keigetsu's apprehension only grew when Leelee lapsed into silence.

Ever since the pre-celebration had been cut short two nights ago, a palpable air of tension had settled over the township. Under normal circumstances, the Maidens were supposed to spend their time freely until the main event, seeing the local sights or chatting with the townspeople over tea, but no one was in the mood for that anymore. Thus, the girls had spent the entire time holed up in their rooms, anxiously awaiting some sort of news.

The suspense was weighing more heavily on Keigetsu's mind than anyone else's. Even if she had gone along with the men for her own purposes, was Reirin really safe? Surely she had to be all right if Keikou was there, but what if the two of them were stirring up trouble for those bandits?

Honestly, that's the part I'm more worried about!

Kou Reirin was a girl gutsy enough to stand in the face of adversity and leave that adversity begging for mercy. Keigetsu was concerned that her friend was out there devastating total strangers with *her* face and, for that matter, that she might get swept up in some new, unforeseen crisis as a consequence of getting too carried away.

She'd already gotten a little too giddy at the prospect of her first-ever trip.

I'm not even married, so why do I feel like a mother worried about her kid running out of control? Realizing what she sounded like, Keigetsu silently rubbed her temples.

There was something she'd learned since getting to know Kou Reirin better: The girl wasn't a butterfly who danced about stealing people's hearts. No, she had elements of that too—but her true nature was more like that of a raging boar. She was powerful, fearless, and unstoppable. She was straightforward and single-minded in all things, whether it came to expressing her affections or fleeing a scene.

"Running off with a bunch of bandits because someone said to get out of there? How stupid can one person be?" Keigetsu groused, massaging her forehead as she felt a headache coming on. On the other hand, there was some part of her that found the stunt endearing. A large part of the reason for Kou Reirin's rash behavior lay in her consideration for Keigetsu—that is, her desire not to see her friend become the Worthy Consort or otherwise get punished.

"She's stupid. *So* stupid. Talk about reckless. I can hardly stand to watch her," she grumbled, but a more rational part of her mind said, *No, that's not it.* It wasn't that she couldn't watch. Reirin made her so anxious that she couldn't tear her eyes away.

Everything is all that madwoman's fault!

"Worrying won't do anything to keep Lady Reirin safe, milady. Your job is to maintain your body, mind, and reputation as 'Kou Reirin,'" said Tousetsu, who had just shown up with a decoction in hand. "Take this medicine, for a start."

"This is no time for that!" Keigetsu spat in her frustration.

Her tone even, Tousetsu replied, "Of course it is. This is a matter of the utmost importance to your health."

It was difficult to read emotion from the woman's face, but there was a vague air of menace to her black, doll-like eyes. In the end, Keigetsu scowled and gulped down the brew for the umpteenth time.

It tastes as awful as ever. Knowing Kou Reirin concocted this herself, I have to assume her taste buds are broken. Either that or her nasty court lady is picking on me again.

The smell made Keigetsu want to retch almost as soon as she'd swallowed it, and she reflexively threw a hand over her mouth. If Reirin's most loyal court lady had presented it to her, there was no chance the medicine was going to hurt her. Still, Keigetsu could've sworn she felt woozier *after* drinking it.

"All this medicine does is make me feel worse. It's not like I was even feeling sick. If it's just a preventative cure, could you at least reduce the dosage?" she said as she rinsed her mouth out with water.

Tousetsu's eyes widened ever so slightly. "You...weren't feeling sick?" However, she soon schooled her face back into its usual deadpan expression and ended the conversation with, "No. We can't take any chances."

Reirin had probably instructed her to administer the medicine. Even if the person inside the vessel had changed, it appeared she had every intention of continuing to prescribe it.

"Can I have a moment, Reirin?" came a voice from the other side of the door. It was Keishou, who was supposed to be off inspecting the scene of the crime as the victim's ceremonial officer. He was wearing his usual sly smile.

Puzzled by the show of politeness, Keigetsu was about to say, "Sure, get in here," but his next few words nearly made her jump out of her skin.

"His Highness is here to see you."

Tousetsu and Leelee exchanged hurried glances, while Keigetsu dove back into bed. It was routine for "Kou Reirin" to be sick. If she looked under the weather, Gyoumei might be less likely to overstay his welcome.

Keigetsu waited for the prince to show up, doing her best to emulate Reirin's tranquil demeanor. Not much later, Gyoumei elegantly graced the room. "Hello, Reirin. Sorry to catch you while you're laid up in bed."

The faint scent of a medicinal brew in the air appeared to have sold him on the idea that she was resting.

"I won't take up too much of your time, so can I have a word? All you have to do is lie there."

He sat down at the table without a hint of suspicion, taking a teacup from Tousetsu. Meanwhile, Keishou shot Keigetsu a look that said *Don't mess this up* from his place near the doorway.

"Allow me to get straight to the point..." Gyoumei began.

Relieved by how gentle he sounded, Keigetsu idly studied the prince's face. As far as she could tell, he didn't bear her any ill will. He didn't look agitated either; he was the picture of composure.

Now that she thought about it, he hadn't shown a hint of distress despite one of his own Maidens being abducted. There wasn't a trace of fatigue upon his gorgeous, fair-skinned features, nor had he upset those around him by insisting on carrying out a search of his own. It seemed he'd brought his work with him on the trip, and the way he stayed in the estate and flipped through his papers gave the impression that he couldn't care less about the whole investigation.

If anything, the township magistrate, Lord Koh, appeared far more distraught over "Shu Keigetsu's" abduction. He seemed to feel deeply responsible that such a mishap had occurred on his watch, and he drove his old bones to their limit as he fasted in prayer of her safe return. He was even pleading with Gyoumei to go join the search party himself rather than settle for giving out commands from the estate.

It was solely thanks to the magistrate getting down on his hands and knees to inspect the burnt ruins that a Gen tassel had been found at the scene a short while ago. Yet Gyoumei had barely reacted to the discovery. He'd sent further instructions for the search party, but he hadn't opened an investigation into the Gen clan.

Since Keigetsu remembered the case of the Kou tassel, she didn't want to jump to the conclusion that the Gen clan was responsible, but she still resented the fact that he wasn't taking a more proactive stance in investigating the kidnapping. In comparison, the magistrate, whom she'd previously found apathetic, looked much more humane.

Hmph. He doesn't care because it's "Shu Keigetsu" who was captured. Back when "Kou Reirin" almost died during the Double Sevens Festival, he was so furious that he held a Lion's Judgment right away. Just look at the difference in treatment.

Keigetsu's mind swam with self-deprecating thoughts. The gorgeous crown prince really didn't have room in his heart for anyone but Reirin. He was never anything less than composed, and the only times he ever raised his voice in anger were when his precious cousin got hurt. Good for Reirin, but it was hard for the Maidens lumped together as "the others" not to resent that sometimes.

Then again, if he hasn't even caught on to the switch, his feelings can't be worth all that much.

As she was getting lost in her cynical thoughts...

"Are you listening?" Gyoumei called out, giving Keigetsu a start.

"Y-yes. I'm sorry."

"It's fine. You must really be feeling under the weather. Sorry for all this." He apologized briefly, then went on to make a startling request. "So as I was saying—tomorrow, perhaps—I'd like you to have tea with the other Maidens and put their minds at ease."

"Huh?"

Drawing his own conclusions as to why Keigetsu had gone stiff, Gyoumei wistfully dropped his gaze to his teacup. "I *am* sorry to ask this of you in a time of distress. But I have to handle the arrangements and on-site inspection for the main event, not to mention command the search for Shu Keigetsu, so I don't have time to care for the Maidens."

"..."

"I'm sure the girls are disheartened to see one of their own kidnapped in a strange land. In the past, when the atmosphere of the Maiden Court grew fraught on account of bad weather or some other trifling incident, I recall you'd often serve tea to the Maidens to raise their spirits. I'd like you to do that here."

Keigetsu broke into a cold sweat. She understood why he was asking this. It was exactly the sort of thing Reirin would volunteer to do. And yet...

You want me *to entertain the other Maidens, let alone without them catching on to who I am?!*

From Keigetsu's current perspective, the idea was pure torture.

"Th-that's a wonderful idea. However...erm, in this one instance, I'm afraid I'm a little too preoccupied with Lady Shu Keigetsu. I'm in no state of mind to serve tea." Seconds from bursting into tears on the inside, Keigetsu scrambled to come up with a decent excuse. "How could I relax and sip tea when my dearest friend might be suffering as we speak? Oh, I wish I could abandon my duties as a Maiden and join the search party myself!" she said in a voice trembling with suppressed emotion.

In a sense, she was telling the truth. If she could, she'd rather run somewhere far away than live in fear of her true identity being exposed.

Still, I think I might have laid it on too thick.

She regretted saying it the second it left her mouth, but by chance, it seemed her lamentations had matched up with "Reirin's" behavior.

"That's really all it ever is with you," Gyoumei said with a rueful smile.

"Huh?"

210

"Every time you open your mouth, it's 'Lady Keigetsu' this and 'Lady Keigetsu' that. Whenever she blunders, you jump to her defense, insisting there must have been a reason for it. No matter how many people look down on her, you're always concerned enough about her to put your own well-being on hold. You're head over heels for her." Impishly, he added, "Enough to leave me in the dust."

Keigetsu was speechless. She hadn't known that. She had no idea that Kou Reirin had shown this level of unabashed concern for her.

"The sharp-witted Kin Seika, the demure Ran Houshun, or the mild-mannered Gen Kasui... There's no shortage of Maidens more suited to being your friend, but it seems Shu Keigetsu is the one you hold dear."

"Y-yes."

Her breath started to come in gasps, but Keigetsu rode it out by clenching her fists. Her ears were burning. Her eyes were tearing up. But if she hoped to play the part of "Kou Reirin," she had to nod her head like nothing was wrong.

"Lady Keigetsu...is my dearest...best friend. My pride and joy."

No doubt Reirin would be able to say that without a shred of embarrassment. Keigetsu was sure of it.

This is so humiliating.

Her heart was beating so fast she was afraid it would leap out of her chest. She thought she might combust from embarrassment.

Gyoumei's voice was what brought her back to her senses. "I see. But if that's true, Reirin, then you should have faith in Shu

Keigetsu." When Keigetsu lifted her face, she found him looking back at her impassively. "She's your pride and joy, right? Then you should trust she's all right and focus on what you need to do."

"Yes, Your Highness." With the way the conversation was going, she couldn't turn him down. Keigetsu responded with an awkward nod. "I'll do my best to allay the other Maidens' fears."

"Heh, your face is bright red. Are you embarrassed?" Gyoumei teased her as he drained his cup of tea. He probably planned to leave right away, just as he'd promised.

Keigetsu couldn't resist taking a shot at him. "You seem awfully calm, Your Highness."

"What?"

"Oh, nothing. I find it admirable that you can remain so steadfast in your duty after one of your Maidens has been kidnapped, that's all." She did her best to erase any hint of reproach from her tone, but it might have come out sounding a tad sarcastic.

Gyoumei lifted his face, then tilted his head to one side. "Does it seem that way?"

"Yes. I'm impressed by your unwavering spirit."

"I see. I'm honored."

Was his response meant to be sarcastic or not?

Gyoumei gently set his teacup down, then left the room.

Hmph. He really is a coldhearted person who doesn't care about anything but "Kou Reirin."

Once she'd heard his footsteps vanish into the distance, Keigetsu's lips twisted into a pout. Moments like this made it evident that his Gen blood ran thick. He was an inherently apathetic and infuriatingly devoted man whose emotions only wavered for one person.

But wasn't it that nature of his that led him to overlook the truth and hurt Kou Reirin last time? Ha ha, from that perspective, His Highness hasn't grown at all. He's so devoted he can't see anything else around him, and he doesn't have the patience to control his emotions!

In her petulance, Keigetsu gave him a brutal dressing-down in her mind.

She didn't have time to dwell on that, however. She had to contact Reirin with her fire magic as soon as possible, and on top of that, she had to work out a plan for this tea party with the Maidens. Seeing as socializing was Keigetsu's worst nightmare, she was already at her wit's end...and that was why she hadn't noticed one key detail.

"Uh-oh, there's a crack in the teacup we gave His Highness," Leelee said with a look of consternation as she was putting the tea set away. "These are way cheaper than the ones we have back in the inner court. We're lucky he didn't say anything."

The crack was on the outside of the cup. It happened to be right where the prince had been gripping it.

Unran hurried along the mountain path, massaging his aching stomach.

"Damn, that hurts..."

That Eagle Eyes' captain might have damaged some of his organs when kicking him around. Unfortunately, Unran had to head into the mountain that evening regardless. He had to give his report to the envoy sent by the township magistrate.

Live coals and a withered branch he could use as a wick tucked away in the breast of his garment, he hiked up the precipitous mountain guided only by the light of the moon. The mountain was a terrifying place at night. One wrong step would see him tumble over a cliff, and one wrong turn would see him wander into the Cursed Forest. But as one who had snuck out of the village to play in the mountains since he was a child, Unran could make it to his destination with his eyes closed.

The river that separated the township from the village grew wider and wider the further one went down the mountain, and at the base, it was impossible to cross without going over the bridge. To put it the other way around, however, it was easy to cross the border if you trekked partway up the mountain.

The envoy from the other side was already waiting at their meeting place, hidden beyond the dense foliage and shrouded in the black of night.

"Oh, you finally made it, Unran!"

The one to get up from the rocky ground and greet Unran with a cry of relief was a slender young man. Granted, he covered his face in a black cloth to keep Unran from remembering his features, so all he could observe of the man was his voice. Still, his meek manner of speech and timid bearing made it clear that he was both a well-to-do pampered son and a bit of a coward.

"Evening, Lord Rin," Unran responded curtly.

The man who he'd just referred to as "Lord Rin" was Lord Koh's errand boy. He was supposed to give Unran one of his rewards for tormenting Shu Keigetsu: the emergency food provisions.

"It took you a while to show up, so I was afraid you might have been attacked by a wild animal. I'm so glad you're all right."

Unran shot Rin, who ingratiated himself to even an untouchable, a look of disgust.

He didn't know much about how Lord Koh ran the township government. Neither did he know what position Rin held there. But seeing as he had been the designated envoy from the start of this deal with Lord Koh, Unran assumed he was one of the magistrate's protégés.

Rin was sophisticated and knowledgeable. The times he'd brought vegetables to Unran in the past, he'd taught him how to store the food to make it last longer and even shared fertilizer and medicinal herbs with him. Unusually for someone of a high enough status to serve the magistrate, he claimed he liked to garden. His naive personality seemed to get him a lot of work dumped into his lap, which in this instance involved hefting a sack of food deep into the mountains.

"Umm, I'm sorry to cut straight to the point...but how did things go after the kidnapping? Is Shu Keigetsu's punishment proceeding smoothly?" Rin hesitantly ventured, seemingly cowed by Unran's bad mood despite far outranking him. "None of us imagined that Lord Kou Keikou would tag along. I've heard

THOUGH I AM AN INEPT VILLAINESS

rumors that he's an expert military officer. The magistrate was worried he might disrupt our plans."

"He hasn't given us trouble at all."

The truth was that he'd done way worse than a little "disruption," but Unran bluffed his way through without batting an eye. The recent arrival of the Eagle Eyes' captain meant their plan was already falling apart at the seams, but Unran saw no reason to reveal another weakness unless Rin brought it up himself.

"He's definitely strong, but we have numbers on our side. Our men have kept him surrounded the whole time and stopped him from trying anything funny."

It wasn't exactly a lie. It was true that the men were keeping an eye on him all day long, and they hadn't let him do anything to hurt the village. He'd just left out the part where the guy happened to be tending all the village's fields.

Rin responded to his emphatic assurance with an impressed nod. "Very nice work. And things are going well with Shu Keigetsu too?"

"Of course. We've threatened her enough to make her feel like maggots crawled through her body's every pore and devoured her from the inside out, and we've glared at her so hard it's like we twisted a needle under her fingernails and watched her scream in agony."

"Eeeep!" Rin clamped his hands over his mouth, trembling, but after a beat, he tilted his head to one side. "But doesn't that mean all you've done is threaten and glare at her?"

Unran had to stop himself from clicking his tongue. *Some*

help those "pointers" were. He'd tried incorporating the examples of torture Shu Keigetsu and Keikou had suggested, but it hadn't worked at all.

"Got a problem? You said you'd leave the methods up to us. I have a contract that proves it."

In the end, he had to flaunt the existence of the contract to shut down the man's arguments.

"If you refuse to trust us, I could always have the contract in my custody sent to the township and delivered to the prince. That'd be the end of Lord Koh."

The weak-kneed Rin flew into a panic. "Please, no! I'm sorry, I didn't mean to doubt you... You're welcome to go about this however you like."

"I'd say that's leaving a little *too* much in our hands."

Unran had threatened him with the contract, sure, but even he had to wonder if the magistrate ought to have employed such a namby-pamby as his envoy.

But Rin had a surprising explanation. "The truth is, Shu Keigetsu was as good as socially dead from the moment she was kidnapped by bandits. A Maiden's chastity is her everything, after all, so as soon as she was captured by a band of lawless *men*, well... You get the picture."

In other words, all he had to do now was spread a single rumor, and Shu Keigetsu would be ousted from her position of Maiden as an "impure woman."

"Frankly, bringing me a finger or tooth as proof would only make things trickier. People might sympathize with her if she were physically harmed. It's much smarter to tarnish a woman's reputation than resort to violence. Yes, that's the ticket."

"..."

Hearing Rin make such a wild suggestion in that whiny drawl of his made Unran feel sick. He had threatened Shu Keigetsu with defilement at the hands of the village men himself, but he'd also acknowledged the gravity of the crime because he knew how horrifying it was for a woman to lose her chastity.

Yet this man demonstrated no such consideration as he blithely told Unran to deflower Shu Keigetsu. It occurred to Unran that the townsman who had ravished his mother all those years ago had probably done it with the same degree of nonchalance.

"In that respect, you're the perfect man for the job. You go through women like most men go through underwear, no? Hee hee, that must be nice. All you need to do is tell me her habits in bed or count the number of moles she has. Simple, right?"

"You said," Unran growled, his voice sounding darker than even he'd expected, "that we were free to choose our methods."

"Huh? Well, yes, but..." Rin must have been flustered by the sudden chill in Unran's demeanor. He gave an obsequious tilt of his head. "Erm, but we *do* need you to torment Shu Keigetsu."

"I know."

"If you don't, then as stipulated in the contract, we won't be able to lower your taxes. And if you don't punish the calamity-wreaking villainess, this cold spell will never end. Do you understand?" said Rin, distress in his voice. Unran's blunt response seemed to have given him cause for alarm. "Come on, please!

Your entire village's fate is riding on your shoulders. If you can't get the taxes reduced, I bet your neighbors are going to hate you for it."

"We need everyone to hate Shu Keigetsu. Yeah. For your sake too."

Gouryuu's words played back in his head.

"..."

He understood what his uncle had meant. Residents of the southern territory were emotional and selfish. They were quick to spook and quick to lean on others. They were the type to depend on someone like a spoiled child and then, upon realizing they weren't going to get what they wanted, change their tune and berate that person for not protecting them.

If Shu Keigetsu couldn't be made into the root of the calamity and the target of everyone's loathing...then their hatred would no doubt be deflected onto Unran, the village "outsider."

No, it would be worse than that.

Rin leaned forward. "Besides, haven't you just begun to restore your father's good name by taking up his mantle? If you messed this up and were branded a failed chief for the second generation in a row, I'd feel sorry for hi—"

"Enough. You're not a dog, so no need to go on yapping. I get it. I gave my report, so can I go now? Thanks for the food. I'll see you in two days."

He turned on his heel, wound a rope around the sack of rice Rin had dropped nearby, and hoisted it onto his back.

"Um, I-I'm serious about this! We heard a report that the captain of the Eagle Eyes headed for the village, so we've been really worried. The thought of one report every two days makes me too anxious, so please come tomorrow too! During the hour of the rat!" He probably didn't have the guts to chase after Unran, who was stalking off without a fire to light his path. Before the villager's back could fully disappear into the distance, he rushed to add, "How's this? I'll have more meat and greens ready for you then, and I'll arrange for the magistrate to meet you in person! If the situation ever gets out of hand, you can always come to us for help!"

The existence of the contract must have done its work because his request was an incredibly deferential one. Unran said nothing in response.

He continued down the dark mountain path. Once he was sure he'd left Rin behind, he stopped where he stood.

"He'd feel sorry for the chief?" he muttered, then gazed up at the sky. It was eclipsed by layers of trees and thick clouds, no moon or stars visible to shine their light. That tranquil expanse was meant to watch over the village in perpetuity, yet its blanket of clouds did nothing but make the residents gasp in horror.

The ominous clouds looming over the village—Unran.

"I have for ages now."

He heard the flap of a bird's wings from a distant tree.

His lips twisting in self-derision, Unran took off toward the foot of the mountain once more.

The bird glided through the night sky on powerfully flapping wings, eventually coming to a stop on a man's shoulder.

"There, there. That's a good boy," he said, petting it.

It looked like an ordinary dove at a glance. It boasted dark plumage and a beautiful chest as lustrous as a peacock's. Cooing, the dove nuzzled its head against the man's fingers. Tied to its leg was a thinly folded piece of paper.

"Look, I saved some food for you. I gathered them up on the footpaths."

The man brought an earthworm to the dove's beak. He smiled with satisfaction as he watched the animal he'd raised with such tender, loving care happily gobble down the treat.

"You full? Great. Then I've got one more job for you."

Upon giving his dove another pat, the man—Kou Keikou— squinted up into the night sky.

THOUGH I AM AN INEPT VILLAINESS

Tale of the Butterfly-Rat Body Swap in the Maiden Court

5 | Reirin Takes on a Beast

REIRIN WOKE UP to the chirping of a bird. Though the light filtering through the paneless window was weak, it told her that dawn was approaching. Once she'd finished waking up, she slipped quietly out of bed.

"Good morning..."

The reason she'd bothered with the whispered greeting was because this wasn't the warehouse.

Yesterday, Shin-u showing up in addition to Keikou had dialed up the pressure on the villagers, and as a result, Reirin had been given permission to sleep in the hut where Unran and Gouryuu lived instead of the warehouse. No, perhaps "demanded permission" was a more accurate description of the scenario. Because of that, Reirin had been forced to say her goodbyes to the warehouse bugs she'd gotten so close to.

As of now, the hut was crowded with six people: Unran and Gouryuu, the original residents; Old Kyou, the live-in cook; and Reirin, Keikou, and Shin-u.

Everyone is sleeping so soundly, Reirin thought as she glanced around. Gouryuu and Old Kyou were lying atop their makeshift bed of a straw mat laid over the dirt floor. Unran was curled up on the edge of it like a cat. *I thought they might try to kill me in my sleep, but nothing happened.*

Reirin put a hand to her unscathed neck, furrowing her brow in puzzlement. But when her gaze wandered to either side of her, she gave a solemn nod. "Oh, that explains it."

Keikou and Shin-u were sitting on her left and right sides respectively, their eyes closed in slumber.

The average farmer wouldn't be able to get past a battle formation like this.

Though their eyes were shut, Shin-u had propped himself up with his longsword, and Keikou had done the same with his hoe. Neither of them was so much as slouching. If anyone took even a single step into their sphere, the two men would instantly snap awake and strike back—or that was the aura their sleeping positions gave off, at least.

Gouryuu and Old Kyou seemed to be having nightmares, perhaps due to the silent pressure floating around the hut. Unran had eyed Reirin a few times after coming home in the dead of night, but each time she'd heard him give up with a click of his tongue. In the end, it seemed he'd prioritized getting some sleep.

Did he go out to give that report he mentioned? I hope I haven't caused him too much trouble.

Reirin hunched in on herself when she saw Unran's handsome face screwed into a frown even as he slept.

In her opinion, the village's circumstances weren't all that dire. The rice plants weren't ripe, but there was a bountiful mountain neighboring their home. If they trekked up there to hunt a wild animal or pick some fruit, it would be easy to avoid famine. Yet their fear of the Cursed Forest kept them from doing just that. Worse still, their status was such that they couldn't count on protection from the township.

The clouds never seemed to break, the rice plants refused to grow, and heavy taxes loomed in their future. The villagers were chronically short of food, had too much hard labor to do to ever get sufficient rest, and were met with perpetual hostility from every angle. How could they be expected to hold out hope in circumstances like that?

How hard would it be to lead a village that was such a hotbed of apprehension and stress?

Reirin clutched a hand to her chest as she recalled the myriad of emotion on Unran's face as he sat before his father's grave.

Is there anything I can do for them? I'd like to at least fill their bellies and put their minds at ease for a time.

Up until yesterday, Reirin had been so thrilled to throw herself into farmwork for the first time in ages that she'd barely given much thought to the village's plight. Now that she'd had two days to get her lust for agriculture out of her system, however, she regretted getting so carried away.

No, I have bigger things to regret. Reirin strode over to the kitchen, the muscles of her face taut. *I need to report back to Lady Keigetsu as soon as possible.*

Indeed. With Unran and the villagers always standing guard over her, and with Shin-u's watchful eye added to the mix, Reirin had yet to have a moment to herself around a flame. Shin-u in particular had a habit of popping up behind her when she least expected it, so it had been very difficult to give him the slip. Needless to say, she couldn't let *him* catch on to the switch or her use of the Daoist arts either.

Now might be my chance.

She waved her hand in front of Shin-u to test the waters. Judging by his lack of response, he was sound asleep.

Reirin made up her mind and walked over to the patch of barren dirt floor. Luckily, Tousetsu and her brothers had taught her how to erase all traces of her presence as she walked. If she snuck out of the hut, started a fire, and talked outside, she could avoid being noticed by anyone else. After borrowing a tool that had been left out next to the stove, she quietly slipped out the door and squinted down at her hands in the predawn darkness.

"Umm, this is the fire striker, and this is the flint. For the tinder... Oh, are these mushrooms?"

To turn the shower of sparks into flame, one needed flammable tinder. It seemed Unran and his companions used dried mushrooms to fulfill that role. It was truly fascinating to see how they made use of the local characteristics in their daily lives.

"Take that! And that!"

When they'd steamed the pheasant yesterday, she had left it to Keikou to get the flame going, so this would be her first time lighting a fire on her own since she'd been exiled to the storehouse.

It was a time-consuming endeavor, but playing with fire was so much fun that the prospect made her a little giddy.

The feeling that she was out there surviving on her own elated her. Getting washed up on a deserted island all alone was one of the go-to fantasies of main-line Kou descendants.

Reirin crouched down and struck the flint against the striker. Unfortunately, she was struggling to get a spark.

"Perhaps the striker isn't hard enough. This is a tough one."

The fire strikers supplied in the inner court were well forged and thus easily lit, but apparently that wasn't the case here. The increase in difficulty was making her impatient.

I could do with a more tempered metal here. What would work best? Something hard...

The moment the thought crossed her mind, she was surprised to see the tip of a sword pop out in front of her.

"Oh? It's steel."

"What are you doing?"

She almost reached her fingers toward the blade, only to freeze when the person holding the sword entered her vision.

"Captain..."

The man standing there with his arms folded was Shin-u, captain of the Eagle Eyes. Despite Reirin going to the trouble of erasing her footsteps and presence, it seemed he'd already noticed her absence.

"G-good morning. You're up early."

"Don't go out on your own. What, were you trying to make a fire?"

Apparently having been on alert against potential assassins, Shin-u sheathed his sword, disgruntled. Then, he snatched the striker from Reirin's hands.

"With your strength, it'll be sundown before you get a fire going."

"Ah..."

When the powerful Shin-u managed to create a spark in an instant—apparently it had been an issue of muscle—Reirin couldn't help but look like a dog robbed of its bone.

I wanted to do it...

But she knew it wouldn't be like Keigetsu to act disappointed here. After all, she was the sort to light up when other people did things for her. No doubt her cheeks would flush to see that Shin-u had gone to the trouble of starting her fire. She was an adorable girl like that.

"Wow! Thank you so much," Reirin said, putting a lid on her true feelings. For whatever reason, Shin-u covered his mouth and averted his gaze. Perhaps he was stifling a yawn. "Why don't you get a little more rest, Captain?"

"No need. I believe the bigger question is, why is the Lady Shu Keigetsu, infamous for sleeping until the hour of the dragon, starting a fire at the crack of dawn?"

"Huh? Oh."

Shin-u peered into Reirin's face, and she pulled back on instinct.

Of course, she wasn't about to say, "I was planning to contact Lady Keigetsu through her flame magic."

"I-I wanted breakfast..."

"Oho, did you? The same Lady Shu Keigetsu reputed as a slave driver is going to cook for herself? And outside, even."

"I was going to have someone else in this house cook me breakfast! Come, everyone, wake up!"

Sweating up a storm, Reirin turned on her heel and flung open the door to the hut.

The captain is hot on my trail!

Could he have figured out who she was already? No, there would be no reason for him to keep quiet about the switch. In short, he hadn't figured it out. Or he at least hadn't moved beyond the level of vague suspicion.

I have to get out of this! Now's the time to show the fruits of my hypothetical scenario sheet!

Reirin stepped down onto the dirt floor, narrowing her eyes with all her might. "What are you all lazing around for? I'm already up over here. Wake up and get breakfast started! The early bird gets the worm! Doesn't that sound great?! Come on, get up!"

The hardworking Reirin had done an impressive job imitating Keigetsu's manner of speech, but alas, she fundamentally lacked the mindset to mock other people. As Shin-u listened to her shout something halfway between a threat and a pep talk, his shoulders at last began to shake with mirth, though he kept his face schooled into a deadpan expression.

"What is it? Pipe down already," said Gouryuu, awakened by her shout. He sat up in his bed, still half-asleep. His speech garbled with drowsiness, he looked at where Reirin stood in the kitchen and complained, "The hell? It's not even dawn yet. I should kill—"

"That's no way to speak to a lady."

"Eep!" As soon as he saw Shin-u standing behind her, he sat at attention. "Y-you're up early, sir."

"Forget me. The Maiden says she's hungry."

"Uh, we weren't kidding when we said food is scarce..." He must have determined he didn't stand a chance against the captain after seeing him make short work of Unran the previous night. He was jumping at shadows, terrified of the man's blue-eyed, emotionless face. "Right, Unran? Back me up here!"

"The hell?"

Gouryuu tugged on the hem of Unran's garment for help, at which the latter grumpily stirred awake. Deprived of a full night's sleep, he shot Reirin and Shin-u a listless glare. "Given the state of the crops, we hardly have any rice left to eat after we've paid our taxes. We have to stretch our old supply several times thinner by watering it down in congee. Besides, do you think you're in a position to be demanding breakfast?"

"Do *you* understand your position? Want me to turn you into rust on my sword?"

"Please calm down, Captain. We're prisoners here," Reirin delicately chided Shin-u as he began to terrorize Unran on reflex. "We shouldn't get too comfortable. We must show more reserve and be cognizant of our role as captives. Please?"

It was a genuine plea, one borne of her regrets from the

previous night, but all it did was make Unran's face twitch. "You're one to talk."

"Then how about we fell another beast?" came a voice from the bed.

It was Keikou, who had apparently woken up at the same time as Gouryuu.

He gave a languid stretch, loosening up his stiff joints, and then stepped down onto the dirt floor. "Oh, I have an idea. This village borders a mountain. We can pick fruit and hunt animals there. That way we won't put more stress on your food supply, and it has a feeling of forced labor to it too. If you're worried we'll run off, we can all go together." He jerked his thumb at the mountain outside the door, then grinned. "I've got a taste for boar stew."

"My! Boar stew sounds adventurous indeed," said Reirin, stars in her eyes.

Gouryuu squared his shoulders, his hackles up. "Not a chance! The boars all live in the Cursed Forest!"

"The Cursed Forest..."

There it was again. Reirin and Keikou exchanged glances.

"What exactly is this Cursed Forest you speak of?" Reirin hesitantly asked.

Gouryuu's face twisted into a scowl. Only when Keikou and Shin-u prompted him with their piercing gazes did he reluctantly start talking. "It's exactly what the name suggests. Disaster befalls all those who enter. There have been a handful of fools who gave in to their hunger and ventured inside, and every last one of them

231

got mauled by a beast or died of some mysterious disease. Our previous chief among them."

According to Gouryuu, the Cursed Forest was a gloomy woodland shrouded in fog all year round. The moment someone set foot inside, they'd be greeted with an eerie sound like the wailing of a ghost echoing through the air. The area was rich in fruit trees and clean water and thus inhabited by a myriad of meaty animals, but those who ventured in to hunt them would find themselves surrounded by the beasts and mauled to death.

Anyone lucky enough to avoid being attacked would instead pass out along the road, perhaps a sign that there was miasma mixed into the fog. Those people would sometimes wake up in intense pain, finding their bodies swollen and their skin melted. What's more, they never had any idea how they had ended up like that.

With all these anecdotes piling up over the decades, the villagers had come to fear the forest and keep their distance. Yet the former chief—Unran's father—had nevertheless chosen to brave the wood and brought home a deer. The villagers had briefly rejoiced their good fortune, but a few days later, the chief and several other people who had partaken in the meat died in a fit of agony. From this, the villagers learned that bringing things back from the Cursed Forest would bring disaster not only to those who had gone inside but to the entire village—or so went Gouryuu's story.

"Sure, we could do some hunting if we went into the Cursed Forest. But we won't. It's not worth getting cursed."

Gouryuu looked genuinely terrified, but, never one to buy into superstition, Reirin met his story with a slight tilt of her head.

Those with ties to the Shu clan are very emotional...and scaredy-cats too.

Members of the Kou clan tended to believe only in what they could see and touch for themselves. She found herself questioning all these claims of miasma, screams, swelling, and cursed meat. If famine was looming on the horizon, she thought it perfectly reasonable of the chief to enter a forbidden ground and try to obtain food, but it seemed the residents of the southern territory were too afraid of divine punishment and curses to agree.

"I want to eat boar stew. I've already made up my mind. Let's go. I could use more on the job."

"I just said I ain't going!"

"Whaaat? If you're gonna be so mean about it, maybe we'll escape into the mountains all on our own. And we'll be taking the Maiden with us, of course," Keikou whined, sounding both deeply immature and nothing like a prisoner.

Still, Reirin had known Keikou long enough to know that no matter how much it sounded like a joke, he wouldn't back down when he got like this. He was as stubborn as any Kou.

"Excuse me?! You'd better stop pushing your luck with us!"

"How about *you* stop talking so big? You couldn't even touch me when I was on my own, and now we've got the captain of the Eagle Eyes here. No one can hope to stand in our path to boar stew. Just shut your yap and let us do our forced labor. Look, I even went to the trouble of framing it like a punishment."

233

"Wait, I'm going boar-hunting too?"

"I'm telling you not to set foot in the Cursed Forest! You won't be the only ones who die—the forest will be outraged to be violated and extend its wrath to our village!"

Perhaps finding Gouryuu, Keikou, and Shin-u's shouting match too noisy for her liking, Old Kyou rolled over in bed with a groan. Unran had gone silent, his arms folded over his chest.

I'm ashamed to be such a poor prisoner, thought Reirin, finding this all too much to bear. *But boar stew...* At the same time, she brought a fist to her chest as a vision of the marbled meat overtook her mind.

Reirin knew she ought to have minded her place as a captive and stopped Keikou from heading into the Cursed Forest. But she wanted boar stew. The thought of climbing the mountain itself—something she could only do in times of health—was likewise tantalizing. She worried her heart might split in two as she was torn between reason and desire.

While Reirin was struggling to make up her mind, Unran said something no one had seen coming. "Sure, why not?"

Lo, he approved of Keikou's trip into the Cursed Forest. Reirin glanced up, surprised.

"There's nothing we can do to stop you from going into the forest, and you aren't planning to let this girl out of your sight, right? I'm not about to let her escape, so I'll go with you to the mountain."

"Wha...?!" Gouryuu shouted. He grabbed his nephew by the shoulders and gave him a rough shake. "You're kidding! Do you have any idea what you're saying?! If—"

"Then what else are we supposed to do?" Unran curtly replied, drawing a gulp from his uncle.

He knew what Unran was thinking. Kou Keikou was going to do as he pleased no matter what, and he wasn't about to take his eyes off his Maiden. It was impossible to torment Shu Keigetsu as long as she was surrounded by guards from dawn to dusk. In that case, perhaps heading into the perilous mountains and splitting up their forces would give him the opening he needed to carry out his "mission."

"But—"

"I said I'd go. Stay out of this, Uncle Gouryuu."

Unran could tell that behind the excuses of "waiting for them to drop their guard," his cowardly uncle had long since given up on the plan. The situation had reached a deadlock. The only way to break through it was to take a gamble on entering the forbidden grounds. If he just continued to go with the flow, there would be no way to escape either the cold spell or tax increase, and the village wouldn't survive the winter.

Sensing the tension in the air, the girl ventured, "Um, Unran... if this is too big an ask—"

"It's not," Unran said in a lazy drawl. "Unlike the other villagers, I've always been one for hiking in the mountains. Today, I'll just be going a little deeper. Besides, what kind of kidnapper sits back and lets his captives escape?" He curled his lips into a smirk.

Gouryuu clicked his tongue, uncomfortable. "I ain't going, for the record. I've had an upset stomach since I got up," he said, bluffing until the bitter end.

Unran brushed him off. "Uh-huh."

Should I really go along with this? Reirin worried as she watched this series of exchanges.

"So, what's the deal? Are we going or not?" Unran asked her with a quirk of an eyebrow.

Despite her misgivings, her answer came immediately. "We're going!" No sane person would turn down a mountain hike.

Besides... She cast a glance at Unran's face in profile.

Reirin had a second goal in mind.

For an hour now, the group had been trekking through the dense forest, pushing branches out of their path. As he listened to the crunch of grass underfoot, Shin-u cast the occasional glance at their surroundings.

This was the Cursed Forest—a wood that was dark even in the middle of the day, the sun's light blocked by the canopy of trees. A combination of the humid climate and topography had made the area fog-prone; upon venturing deeper into the forest, they found coils of white mist dotting the air. Every time the occasional breeze swept through, there came a sound that was neither quite a shriek nor an animal's roar, lending the place a portentous air indeed. Between that and the animal carcasses that lay rotting here and there, it was understandable that anyone with a strong sense of fear would be terrified of this forest.

But as someone with little emotional range who was used to

camping out, Shin-u didn't see what there was to be scared of. Fog was just fog. The "shriek" was apparently just the wind blowing through the hollows in the trees or crevices in the rocks.

If anything concerned him, it was that there were trees bound to attract wild animals scattered throughout the forest, and it was a pain to navigate around those. If he were to accidentally crush a piece of fruit under his shoe, beasts would come flocking to them in excessive numbers, attracted to the smell.

Shin-u had been on high alert for some time now, more worried that he might get attacked by an animal and tumble over a cliff than fall victim to a curse. All that nonsense about swollen skin might indicate that there were poisonous insects or their scales floating around in the mist too.

"Gosh, look at this! Let's stop for a moment. Is the mushroom growing on this tree a lingzhi mushroom?! My, and this one is the poisonous dead man's fingers... And this here is a stork's bill weed! Oh, there are so many aconite roots and their friends!"

Meanwhile, Shu Keigetsu—or rather, Kou Reirin—kept crouching down in front of every plant or tree she saw with stars in her eyes, oblivious to Shin-u's caution. Each time, she would carefully uproot the herb and add it to a basket on her back, which looked heavy even to a sturdy man like Shin-u.

Keikou, who was leading the group, had repeatedly offered to carry it for her, but she always responded with a firm shake of her head as if the very suggestion was outrageous. More than not wanting to impose, she seemed like a child who was afraid someone was going to steal her treasure.

Whenever someone advised her to at least cut back a little, she would glance back at Unran with a smile and say something like, "But if we can plant these in the village, they'll never want for a doctor again. Isn't that right?"

Unran would then give a brusque shrug of his shoulders from behind her, neither smiling nor losing his patience. Though he was more flexible than his comrades, he was still a resident of the southern territory. It probably wasn't easy for him to be in the Cursed Forest. His laid-back gait hadn't changed, but the tension on his face was clear to see.

The reason he had tagged along nonetheless was no doubt to find an opening to harm "Shu Keigetsu." That said, Keikou and Shin-u's ironclad defense had kept him from laying a hand on her thus far. Furthermore, despite her placid demeanor, Kou Reirin herself never left any openings.

She's better at moving her body than I expected, Shin-u thought as he watched her. She never lost her balance even in the grassier areas, and she was always careful to walk in the least physically taxing manner possible.

The Maidens were some of the most exalted women in the kingdom. Most of them didn't even know *how* to get exercise, let alone get enough of it. One would expect her to collapse within half an hour of venturing into an unfamiliar mountain, but there wasn't a crack in Kou Reirin's cheerful attitude.

She'll get worn out soon enough, and when she does, I'll throw that reckless Maiden over my shoulder and double back to the village on the spot, was the development Shin-u had been subconsciously anticipating. He felt unsatisfied with this surprising turn of events, then puzzled over why he would feel that way. What was unsatisfying about *not* having someone to drag him down?

"Ugh... I must admit, this is starting to get heavy. All the soil on the roots is weighing me down."

When at last she made a very understated complaint, Shin-u made a grab for her cargo. "Give that to me."

"Ah, but—"

"I'm not interested in what's inside. I'm not going to steal it from you, so hand it over."

"I-I suppose you're right. Please and thank you, then."

Polite as ever, she dipped her head in a small bow. She was close enough that he could hear the rustle of her hair spilling over her shoulders.

She's close, Shin-u thought.

Normally, there was a polite distance between her, one of Gyoumei's potential wives and the purported top candidate among them, and him, the captain of the Eagle Eyes. Snuggling together like they had the previous night or exchanging words at such point-blank range were things the two of them never could have done back in the Maiden Court.

Neither could he have watched as she ran the gamut of facial expressions, her eyes twinkling as she rushed over to the grass.

"Oh... But I suppose this *is* the natural order of things. Go on, be a good little servant," said Kou Reirin, apparently recalling the need for her Shu Keigetsu impersonation when she met Shin-u's gaze. She gave a haughty tilt of her chin.

Her manner of speech and facial expressions were flawless mimicries, but she didn't seem to realize that bits of her own nature inevitably seeped through.

Is this her idea of a villainess? Shin-u pursed his lips. Despite being infamous for his lack of expressions, he found a smile creeping over his face with considerable frequency when he looked at this Maiden. Why was that?

"Honestly, I can't *believe* how steep this mountain is! Just walking up the path is giving my calves a good workout. Talk about wonderful. Does this mountain want me to pick all its herbs or help me train? Pick one!"

"It might want you to hunt a boar too."

"Hmph! How greedy."

Having lightened her load, Kou Reirin pulled her brother into her ongoing villainess act, while Unran watched the pair with a dubious look.

Is this her idea of Shu Keigetsu?

Shin-u averted his gaze and stifled a laugh.

Thank goodness. It looks like I managed to fool the captain, Reirin thought with relief as she glanced back at Shin-u, who was refusing to make eye contact with her. He may have boasted intuition astounding enough to live up to his title as the head Eagle Eye, but it seemed her meticulous act had successfully kept him from catching on to her true identity. *But I mustn't let my guard down. I have to be careful not to show any openings.*

The moment she relaxed, her foot nearly got caught on a tree branch spread over the ground. She quickly pulled herself back together.

When climbing the mountain came up, Shin-u had protested bringing a woman along on such a dangerous trek until the last second. Even now, he was giving off the clear impression that he would turn back immediately if she showed even the slightest sign of fatigue. As someone who had spent her life surrounded by overprotective family members and court ladies, she knew how to read the signs.

On the flip side, the same Keikou who always used to carry Reirin around in his arms and ask how she was feeling every few seconds hadn't shown a hint of that excessive concern since she'd taken on Keigetsu's form. To the contrary, he hadn't even tried to stop her from doing farmwork all day long or joining the men on their mountain hike. In all likelihood, this was the stamina level and attitude Keikou typically demanded of other people. His protectiveness of Reirin had been an exception to the rule, owing to her weak constitution.

The thought that she'd finally established a "normal" relationship with her brother made her happier than ever to be up in the mountains. Plus, the rare herbs she found growing all over the place made it a deeply enjoyable experience.

Besides...

This time, her gaze traveled diagonally behind her. Unran was walking in silence a short distance from the rest of the group.

I wonder if I can sway him to our side while we're away from the villagers.

Her secret goal in joining the mountain hike was to win Unran over.

As Reirin saw it, Unran was getting impatient because the punishment wasn't going according to plan. While the other villagers had been quick to throw up their hands and say, "Nothing we can do," he alone still seemed to be racking his brains for a solution.

What backbone. I salute him as a member of the Kou clan.

Was it because she'd seen him visit his father's grave that she was convinced he had a very strong sense of responsibility, no matter how cynical he acted around the other villagers? The brooding look in his eyes had been weighing on Reirin's mind ever since.

Besides, the fact that everyone in the village had given up on the punishment so quickly suggested that they weren't actually suited to acts of aggression. Fear and impatience came easily to them, and they tended to look for a scapegoat for those feelings in other people—but for better or worse, that was all a product of fleeting emotions, and they were probably much friendlier and warmer people at their core.

If possible, Reirin wanted to convince them to renounce their evil deeds. In order to do that, she first needed to get Unran over to her side.

No matter how you look at it, it makes no sense for the skies to clear as a result of hurting a Maiden.

At first, she thought that if it was what the villagers wanted, she could help them fabricate reports of a successful punishment to get their taxes lowered, but that wouldn't solve anything in the long run. The more logical approach was to refuse the order to inflict punishment and expose the crimes of Lord Koh, who had plotted to harm the Maiden of his own domain. Reirin would normally decline to meddle in another territory's affairs, but over the past three days, she had grown concerned enough about the village's future to push past those misgivings and get herself involved.

They do say that nothing builds unity quite like climbing a mountain together!

Nodding to herself as she eventually landed on that simple thought, Reirin clenched her hands into fists.

"Ooh! These look like boar tracks. And there's a lot of them. There must be a den nearby," Keikou exclaimed in delight from the front of the pack.

This was somewhere close to the river, where the ground was more rock than soil. A cluster of forest trees abruptly parted into a clearing, which must have been a watering hole for wild animals. Muddy footprints dotted the rocks.

"Judging by the direction the footprints are headed, I'm guessing their den is over there? All right, I'm going to go take a look."

"Surely you don't intend to leave the Maiden behind, Lord Keikou?" Shin-u must have found that *too* incautious. He cast a glance over at Unran, then frowned.

Yet Keikou just gave a carefree laugh and suggested something even more outrageous. "Of course. Why should I hesitate with my boar stew right before me? In fact, I want you to come too, Captain."

"What?"

Apparently, he even planned to drag Shin-u off with him.

"What are you—"

"Now, now, now. Don't be so fussy! Logically speaking, it'd be more dangerous to bring her to confront a horde of wild boars," Keikou said, then made a grab for Shin-u's arm. "Hey, Unran! Don't do anything bad! I'm trusting you!"

"Lord Keikou!"

And thus did he disappear into the bushes, dodging Shin-u's attempts to shake him off.

"Umm..."

Reirin felt deeply awkward to be left behind with Unran. Her brother's broad-minded personality was one of his best features, but it definitely came off like he was taking Unran too lightly—or rather, like he was looking down on the villager.

"I-I'm sorry," she said sheepishly. "He can be...how should I say it? A little too much of a free spirit."

"No kidding." Unran smiled, but it held no emotion.

Reirin leaned forward in a fluster. "Um, but he's not making fun of you or anything like that. It's just a sign of how deeply he trusts you."

"Oh?" he responded with an impish arch of his brow. His reddish-brown eyes glinted like a cat's.

"I mean it! It's a show of his faith that you wouldn't do anything bad."

"I see."

Reirin was a little concerned about the pause before he

responded, but she was pretty sure this was the first time she'd ever seen Unran smile. She nodded vigorously, hoping to further melt his heart. "Yes! Absolutely!"

"Well then. This might come as a surprise after you've said all that..."

The next moment, the smile vanished from his face, completely upending the mood. He produced a dagger in a swift moment and pressed it to Reirin's neck without hesitation.

"Take off all your clothes." The cold edge of his blade brought drops of blood beading to the surface of Reirin's skin. "Get on your hands and knees on the ground. If you scream, I'll kill you."

"My..."

As she stared back at this man with the wild look of a wounded beast, Reirin slowly went down on her knees. The clearing near the watering hole was covered in stone. One rock near the spot where she had kneeled was discolored black, and it made a sinister scraping sound when she touched it.

"That was surprising indeed."

To *no* surprise, the palms she had pressed to the rock were sweating.

"Lord Keikou! What in the world are you thinking?" Shin-u shouted at Keikou as he marched through the bushes. "You'd have to be out of your mind to leave a Maiden alone with a bandit!"

"It'll be fine. And when I get the hunch that something will be fine, I'm never wrong. Besides, hunting boars is our most pressing duty as military officers, even if we have to leave family behind to do it. Don't you agree?"

"Nonsense." Concluding that this conversation wasn't going anywhere, Shin-u shook himself free of Keikou's grip and turned on his heel.

Just as he was about to turn back down the way he'd come, however, Keikou said in an awfully dark voice, "Nonsense? Of course not. I'm dead serious."

His voice had an edge to it that sent a shiver down the spine.

When Shin-u spun back around on reflex, Keikou curled the corners of his lips into a calm smile. "Vermin need to be exterminated. Impudent, senseless animals who would raise a hand against the Heavens need to be put down."

Shin-u creased his brow into a dubious frown. "Excuse me, Lord Keikou?"

Keikou ignored him and slipped straight through the bushes. "There's a cave up ahead. Looks like there's a narrow trail leading there too. I'm sure someone's trod this path countless times, after all."

The captain followed him, feeling an inexplicable sense of unease, and found that there was indeed a cave too elegant to be a boar's den hidden among the rocky terrain.

"Found it."

"What is this?"

Keikou made a beeline for the cave, leaving that question

unanswered. He crouched down at the entrance and looked inside, then stuck in his arm and pulled out something he'd found there.

"You know something, Captain? I found it very odd that the magistrate would order the untouchables to kidnap 'Shu Keigetsu.' What good reason could he have for that?"

The previous night, the two men had spent their watch making small talk by Reirin's bedside. During that conversation, Keikou had informed Shin-u that the township magistrate was the one who had ordered the abduction.

Now that Keikou was raising the question, Shin-u gave a slight tilt of his head. "This township is suffering a cold spell. He wants to set up 'Shu Keigetsu' as the source of the disaster to deflect his subjects' discontent."

"If all he needed was a sacrifice, he could've had the untouchables fill that role. Yet Lord Koh didn't do that. On the other hand, if we assume he genuinely detests 'Shu Keigetsu' as the cause of the calamity, it's strange that he ordered her kidnapped, not killed. He settles for one verbal report every two days, and he doesn't even demand proof. It's all too sloppy."

The thing he'd dragged out of the cave with a dull *thud* was a large box. It was tightly wrapped in cloth and covered in mud, perhaps as a form of camouflage.

Keikou carefully began to unwrap it. "That means the abduction wasn't his true objective. It was a mere distraction. Lord Koh was trying to divert our attention from something by setting up this Maiden kidnapping scandal—that's the possibility that occurred to me. No, I should say someone pointed it out to me. He's truly a brilliant man," he went on with a shrug of his shoulders. He was exuding an almost sharp earnestness and intensity in place of his usual cheerfulness.

"Divert our attention from what? Who pointed it out to you?" Shin-u asked in his confusion, but the answer to one of his questions would soon become clear.

"There's a handful of things a government official might want to hide: a rebellion brewing, a past slipup, or..."

His rugged hands dexterously untied the knot and pulled the cloth free. What emerged from within was an imposing lacquered box.

"Fraud."

Removing the lid revealed a large quantity of gold inside.

"No way!"

"Lord Koh seems to have saved up quite a bit. The lacquered box is a commonplace product distributed nationwide—probably to prevent it from being traced back to him—but sadly for him, the tie-dyed pattern on the cloth is unique. I've seen it around his estate."

Ignoring Shin-u's gasp, Keikou inspected the box for hidden tricks or evidence with the practiced hand of a competent military officer. "It seems 'Shu Keigetsu's' abduction was part of a much more complicated conspiracy."

Shin-u was awestruck by Keikou's nonchalant tone as he adroitly closed in on the truth. He was supposed to be an eccentric man who was always off on conquests and rarely stuck around the capital. Rumor had it that he was a doting brother, overzealous, and incapable of playing politics—but he was exactly what one would expect from the nephew of the empress and the brother of Kou Reirin.

He was not to be trifled with.

Shin-u watched him from behind for a while, until he abruptly lifted his face and said, "Lord Keikou."

"What's up? Is the captain going to lend me a hand? We don't have to take the money with us, but I want to remember how much there was and the state it was in. It'd be less reliable if it were just one man's testimony, so come be a witness with me."

"I don't mind, but we have more important matters to attend to right now," Shin-u said in a low voice.

"Come on," Keikou whined. "Are you going to tell me to head back to Reirin's side this instant? In a healthy body, she could easily take on a guy or two from the village. Tousetsu and I both trained her in self-defense, after all."

"No, it's not that," the captain matter-of-factly replied, then drew his sword. "I believe you stepped on a hardy kiwifruit earlier. Thanks in part to that...a horde of boars has come for a visit."

"Huh?!"

Keikou whirled around with a start, and there he saw several boars staring them down with drool spilling from their mouths, enraged to have found a pair of intruders encroaching upon their den.

"C'mon, strip. Your underwear too. All of it."

"I can't..."

A blade to her neck, Reirin broke into a cold sweat as she groped the rough surface of the rock.

I've made it through a lot of dilemmas as of late, but this is a new kind of crisis.

Her chastity was on the line this time.

Reirin had been put in the same cage as a beast and nearly cursed to death, but she'd been treated like a Maiden throughout it all. She'd never been faced with an emergency like this one before.

In hindsight, however, there was a very real risk of a female prisoner being sexually abused. The fact that the possibility had never even occurred to her made her realize just how naive she had been.

"Um, please calm down... I understand why you would be so enticed by this beautiful, robust body of mine, but such acts should be reserved for married couples who share mutual—"

"Hah! You think I'm lusting after you? Don't be so full of yourself," Unran spat, cutting off the girl's attempt to smooth things over. He tightened his grip on the dagger in his hand. "I hear that an untouchable like me stripping you naked and counting the number of moles on your body is all it'll take to 'kill' you as a Maiden. Isn't that nice? You get to have a quick and painless death."

In other words, the point was to reduce "Shu Keigetsu" to the status of a woman defiled by a lowborn man.

"Be grateful that I'm not getting rough with you."

250

"Why should I be grateful for that?" she shot back.

"Oh?" Unran laughed, then knocked her hard against the rocky surface. "Sounds to me like you *want* me to get rough."

"No!"

Reirin struggled against him, but he was quick to cover her mouth with the hand of his holding the dagger. He then used his free hand to hold her wrists together and pin them against the rock. Next, he straddled her and trapped her legs in place, leaving her completely helpless to resist.

Her pulse quickened.

"This is where a normal girl would get beaten." Unran gazed down upon his wide-eyed victim, his face close enough for her to feel his breath. He removed his hand from her mouth, but to make up for it, he brandished his dagger in threat. "Her bones would be broken, her robe torn, and once she was too scared to speak, she'd be deflowered. Implanted with a child she never wanted." His gaze suddenly dropping, he murmured, "It must have been terrifying."

Reirin gulped. "Un...ran..."

Unran raised his head again, then smiled. "But you're a Maiden, so all I have to do is see you naked. Lucky you."

He seemed unstable. His tone was a mix of low and threatening and something almost innocent and childlike. One wrong move, and she would set him off. That feeling rendered Reirin speechless.

When she did nothing but stare straight back at him, Unran gave a small tilt of his head. "Huh, you aren't crying. Color me surprised."

251

"..."

"Here I figured a Maiden would break down bawling at a time like this. You're such a good little girl." He brought his face right up to hers, then said in an exceptionally low growl, "But you'd better start crying soon."

The hatred and frustration simmering in his voice made Reirin's flesh crawl.

"Beg me for mercy. Get on your knees and apologize. Tremble in fear."

Thump!

In a fit of rage, Unran thrust his dagger into the rock right beside Reirin's neck. Her face tensed. Yet still she refused to shed tears.

An irritated smile rose to her assailant's face. "Still won't cry? You've got some real balls."

"..."

"Always so happy-go-lucky... Just watching you makes me sick. You're not scared to be kidnapped, and you want to make nice with your abductors? What a joke. Well, I guess you've got nothing to fear when you've got guards like *that* looking out for you. You don't get it at all, do you? You have no idea how desperate we are."

He let go of the dagger, grabbed a fistful of Reirin's hair, and forced her to look up at him.

"You don't know what we'll lose if we don't bring you to ruin!"

"What will you lose?" Reirin asked softly, staring him right in the eyes. "What are you most afraid of losing, Unran?"

"Wha—"

"You won't hurt me. You've simply been scared and conflicted all this time."

Taken off his guard, Unran's eyes went round. "Huh?"

It happened the second he opened his mouth to sneer at her.

The girl, who had been staring up at Unran without the slightest hint of resistance, sat up lightning fast...and shoved something into his mouth with frightening precision.

He felt something hard touch his palate. Some sharp object had stopped just short of piercing the back of his throat.

"Don't move. Unless you want me to slit your throat from the inside."

The girl was holding a sharp shard of rock.

Sweat trickled down Unran's skin. This wasn't even comparable to having a sword held to his neck. There was nothing quite like the fear of being forced to swallow a blade. Quite literally, one wrong move—no, one *word* or even a swallow—would see the most tender part of his body sliced open.

When she saw he had stopped moving, the girl with Shu Keigetsu's face flashed him an uncomfortable smile. "Say, Unran. You do realize you were just conflicted, right? Because if you truly had your heart set on hurting someone, you would skip all the preamble and get it over with quickly. Just like I have right now."

There was something terrifying about the gap between her gentle smile and her radical actions. Unran found himself hopelessly intimidated by this so-called sheltered noblewoman.

When did she manage to pick up a weapon?

She must have read Unran's question from the look in his eyes. Holding the shard in his mouth with her right hand, she patted the ground with the other.

"Are you wondering where my weapon came from? It was right here."

Her slender fingers indicated a rock discolored black. The larger part of the rock was buried in the ground, but the outer section was splintered, almost like its shell was peeling back. She had made a swift grab for one of those shards and used it in place of a dagger.

"Rocks can splinter like this if they get too hot. Someone must have built a fire here and failed to properly extinguish it. The firewood turned to charcoal and slowly, steadily heated this rock. It's quite sharp, isn't it?"

The tip of the shard nearly bit into the back of his throat as she tilted her head a fraction.

"Ghk...!"

"I'm sorry, I don't mean to frighten you. Oh, but..." She almost withdrew the blade in a fluster, but rethinking that move, she instead impishly brought her face close to his. "Could this be what they call 'turning the tables'?"

Meanwhile, she used her left hand to pull out the dagger Unran had thrust into the rock's crevice and tossed it aside. His bewilderment only grew.

"I've learned that men don't tend to listen if you simply ask them to. I'm sorry to have to threaten you like this, but would you be willing to hear me out? No?"

The way her face fell in dismay looked cute at a glance, but there was no hesitation in how firmly she pressed her blade forward, nor did she allow him an opening to escape.

Unran stared back at her, his whole body tense.

"Haven't you noticed, Unran? This rocky stretch of land is free of tall grass and has an abundance of fresh water. I'm sure plenty of animals come here to rest."

He couldn't say so, but he failed to understand what her point was.

"That would go not only for animals but people too. Drawn to the allure of fresh water, I imagine an explorer might settle down here and think to satisfy his hunger. It's easy to picture someone building a fire here. So who built that fire, I wonder?"

When he at last realized what she was getting at, Unran gasped.

The girl looked at him with a gaze as steady as the hand of hers holding the blade. "If your words are to be believed, the only villager to ever venture this far into the Cursed Forest before you was your father. And the fire he once started splintered this rock and saved me."

Her voice was gentle. She wasn't threatening him, but her words sank into Unran's heart like some kind of divine oracle.

"Isn't it almost like your father is telling you not to kill me?"

Unran's eyes went wide.

People of the south were impressionable, as prone to love as they were to hate, and clung to miracles. This description of his people that Unran had once spat in frustration naturally applied to him too.

The chief's actions had protected the Maiden. It couldn't have been more than a simple coincidence, but the fact hit Unran with a hefty weight.

His father had protected the girl in front of him.

"If you think of it as your father's dying wish, will you be a little more willing to hear me out?"

She gently extracted her blade from the paralyzed Unran's mouth, then let it fall to the wayside. He kept telling himself to strike back now that she had dropped her weapon, but he was too stunned to move.

"First, I must apologize. I am truly sorry if my attitude has offended you and the other villagers. It's true that I got a little carried away between the excitement of my first trip and the vast fields of rice paddies." The girl with Shu Keigetsu's face gave a meek bow of her head. Then she awkwardly placed a hand to her cheek. "If you'll allow me to make an excuse, 'always keeping positive' is an expression of my own resolve. I absolutely must be happy, after all."

It seemed the sharp rock shard had cut into the skin of her own palm. Awed by the sight of her taking not the slightest notice of her bleeding hand, Unran stared at her in silence.

"You know," she said, casting her eyes downward, "I lost my mother a long time ago. In exchange for my own life. I mustn't ever bemoan a life gained by using my mother's as a stepping stone. 'I'm so happy, every day is so much fun'—I'm sure my mother would turn in her grave if I didn't think that."

Unran wasn't sure how to react to this unexpected confession.

Perhaps embarrassed that she'd said too much, Reirin flashed him one of her usual smiles to cover up her secret. "Unran," she said, reaching a bloodied hand toward him, "isn't it the same for you? You're distressed that someone like you was appointed your father's successor, and you're convinced that you've disgraced his legacy."

She touched his cheek with her warm, blood-soaked hand.

"Isn't that why you're so desperate to protect the village and clear his name? You believe it's the only way you can make amends."

"Hah... 'Course...not..." As if he could ever be so selfless. "You think I'm that noble a person?" he finished, his voice cracking.

"Yes," the girl said, shutting down his argument with a tone of finality. "Haven't you noticed, Unran? You looked upon your father's grave with eyes full of anguish. Plus..."

Her next words made Unran's heart beat faster.

"I saw the characters you carved on his gravestone. A complicated character like 'ryuu' isn't something an illiterate farmer can learn how to write overnight."

"The character 'ryuu' symbolizes the emperor."

Something Tairyuu had told him a long time ago played back in Unran's mind.

"In other words, whoever has 'ryuu' in his name is the ruler of this village. Pretty big deal, right?"

Tairyuu had loved to learn, which was a rare quality in an untouchable. In an effort to educate the villagers, he used to gather up the children and teach them how to write. Granted, the

students in question would always complain that they'd rather spend the time plowing the rice paddies, so they never absorbed much of his lessons.

"The 'u' in your name means 'something big.' The 'shi' in yours means 'a potent herb.' Ain't that amazing? You kids ought to be proud."

He would nab the kids itching to go play one after another and happily impart his knowledge.

Yet he'd never given one of those lessons to his own son. That was because Unran had never set foot inside the warehouse his father had dubbed the "lecture hall."

If the rest of the kids had to sit in the same room with Unran, they would get upset and leave. Having a "half-blood" like him around would just earn his father the disdain of even the village children. Because Unran knew that, no matter how eagerly Tairyuu had invited him, or no matter how many people had lost patience with him for it, he had stubbornly refused to show up to those "lessons."

Still, sometimes he would lean back against the warehouse wall and catch snippets of his father's voice from outside.

"Even if we're untouchables, we've all got impressive names. We even have a ruler. I swear I'll protect this village no matter what."

Unran had no paper, wooden tablets, or brushes to work with. He'd write the characters in the dirt by his feet based only on his father's instruction, then erase them again and again. Whenever the deluge of loneliness became too much to bear, he would flee into the mountains.

259

The villagers had complained that the half-blood Unran never bothered to plow the fields. That he did nothing but play around. That he wouldn't even listen to his own father's teachings.

That was fine. He didn't have a place in the village because he was lazy. That reason was much easier for him to accept. He didn't want anyone to know about all those years he'd spent watching from afar as his father laughed with the other children.

"Say, Unran. It looks to me like you've been suffering for a very long time," a voice rang out from close by, snapping him out of his reverie.

The girl was looking at him with a penetrating gaze.

"You loved your father, didn't you? You felt sad for your mother, didn't you? You wanted to be accepted as a member of the village, didn't you?"

"..."

"Then you mustn't resort to underhanded methods to protect the village. I'm sure you realize that yourself. That's why you could never bring yourself to lay a hand on me."

Her unclouded eyes stole the words from his mouth. The hand on his cheek was warm enough to make him melt. He needed to fight back—or at least *argue* back.

So he told himself, but in the end, what left his mouth sounded like a child's excuse. "Then what am I supposed to do, huh?"

The rock that Tairyuu might have splintered. The girl's soft-spoken speech. Memories of the distant past. Everything came together to shake Unran to his core. He no longer had it in him to act tough enough to deny what she was saying.

"Yeah, I wanted to pay the chief back for what he did for me. Is that so wrong? For someone who gave his all for the village, who raised a 'half-blood' like me, who was so stupidly kind...to be treated like a blight and not even given a burial...is just messed up!"

His voice was trembling. The sight of Tairyuu's shabby grave came back to him when he closed his eyes, bringing rage and sadness to well up in his throat. Once the emotions he had locked deep in his heart came spilling forth, it was like lava erupting from a volcano.

"He just wanted to protect the village...but because he went into the Cursed Forest and died, all his contributions, all his popularity, *everything* came to nothing!"

Tairyuu had always worried for the village. Even with the cold spell looming, he had tried his best to find food instead of shifting the blame onto someone else. Then he'd set foot in the Cursed Forest and lost his life.

It had all been for the good of the village. Yet the moment he died, rather than thank Tairyuu, the villagers had chosen to cast stones at the fool who broke a taboo. All because they were afraid of some curse.

"If I torture you and protect the village...the chief and I will be heroes."

Unran had always hated himself for being a half-blood. He'd never been anything but a disgrace to the chief, and he'd never been able to blend into the village no matter how hard he tried. Was it his mother's fault for being defiled by a townsman? Was it his own fault for being born an unwanted child?

Tairyuu had shown affection even to someone as undesirable as Unran. Unran had wanted to give something back to him, even if it was a small gesture. But as unlearned, unpopular, and grimy as he was, this was the only way he could do that.

"Do you truly believe you can end the cold spell by tormenting a Maiden?" the girl asked him in a hushed voice.

"Then what else am I supposed to do?!" Unran shouted to silence her.

This was his only way forward. If he couldn't end the cold spell, if he couldn't ruin Shu Keigetsu—if he didn't set her up as the root of all disaster, then the villagers' hatred would remain focused on the old chief.

"This...is all I can do!"

This was the limit of what he could do as one without "ryuu" in his name—as a halfwit who hadn't inherited a single thing from the chief.

"Unran."

The girl did something surprising in response to his blood-curdling scream.

"Can you read these characters?"

She sat back down and scrawled something on the rock. There, she had written two characters using the blood from her palm: Unran.

"It's my name," he muttered.

She broke into a smile. "About the second character, 'ran.' It may bring to mind a gust of wind that flattens the crops, but it originally referred to the lush mountain air."

"…"

"As for the first character, 'un,' the radical meaning 'rain' was added to it later. It started out as a much simpler symbol." She painted over the part that meant "rain" with her slender fingers, then gently pointed to the character that remained. "The horizontal stroke at the top represents the clouds drifting across the sky. The part underneath it signifies a dragon winding and twisting its long body."

"Huh?"

"Unran. There's a dragon hidden within the clouds."

The moment he heard those words, Unran gave a soft gasp.

A dragon.

As he sat there stunned, the girl gently went on, "In the imperial capital, no one ever gives their child a name with the character 'ryuu' in it. The dragon is the ruler of the Heavens. Bestowing a child with such a grand character would rob them of their fortune. I'm sure anyone who could read would avoid picking a name with 'ryuu' in it."

Those words of hers made Unran think back to Tairyuu's bashful smile. To how he had recited his and his ancestors' over-ambitious names with a look of embarrassment.

"Pretty big deal, right?"

Before he knew it, Unran's clenched fists had begun to tremble.

"A cloudy sky is a hiding place. A sanctuary for the luxuriant. In a place teeming with the abundant swell of qi that marks a prelude to something bigger, there lurks a powerful and noble dragon."

Some of her vocabulary was too difficult for him to under-stand, but the beautiful string of words stirred Unran's very soul.

"Don't be afraid of the clouds looming overhead. You are a brave man who volunteered to become the villain to protect your village."

The look on Tairyuu's face had been so gentle. Even when Unran rejected him or turned his head, his gaze had always been warm. Why hadn't he ever realized the truth?

"Are you not the dragon who rules over the clouds shrouding this village?"

He had been accepted from the moment he was born into the world so long ago. His father had counted on him to succeed him as the ruler of the village.

"I..."

When he ceased to scowl, it became his undoing. His eyes swam with tears as soon as he relaxed his glare.

With his face contorted in sorrow, Unran said in a quivering voice, "I...loved him."

"Yes."

"I...wanted to call him my father. I wanted to succeed him... and protect this village."

He thought of his father, who was such a far-off existence now. He was a noble man who gave so much of himself and asked for nothing in return. He'd treated Unran with unending patience, never once holding his bitterness against him. He'd loved his village, supported his wife, protected his son—and in the end, died bathed in scorn.

Unran had never even had the chance to express his gratitude.

A rush of intense emotion coursing through his being, Unran buried his face in his hands. "I wanted to be his real son!" he said, shouting the feelings he'd kept hidden all this time.

The girl cradled Unran's head into an embrace. "You still can."

Her words had the force of the shining sun.

"Let's protect the village in a way that would make your father proud." She cupped his face in her hands and forced him to look at her. "Come to my side, Unran."

She was as dazzling as the light breaking through the clouds. Unran stared at her wordlessly as she took her time speaking.

"I swear to protect you no matter what, so you must protect this village as its ruler. Instead of defiling a woman to cover up your frustrations, you must strike back at the township that hatched this dastardly plan."

The action she was telling him to take was extreme. It was neither virtuous nor benevolent. The way she incited him to start a fight could surely classify her as a villainess.

Yet as she held his face in her hands and looked him straight in the eye, Unran found her more beautiful, earnest, and sacred than any woman he had ever seen.

"You..." Unran let some of the air out from his lungs. He wasn't sure what sort of face he ought to make, but he soon found his lips curling into a wry smile of their own accord. "You're insane."

"I get that a lot."

"Who would invite the man who tried to assault her over to her side?"

"Don't be silly. *I* assaulted *you*," the girl shot back delightedly, then giggled. She picked up the shard she had left abandoned on the rocky surface, thrusting it before him with a mischievous smile. "You've been extorted by a wicked woman, Unran. Surrender and join me."

"Pfft...!" Unran cracked up. His shoulders shook with mirth for a while, until at last he got his laughter under control and pushed back his hair.

He would renounce the punishment, betray the township, and join this girl's side. By all accounts, it was an outrageous decision, but his heart felt as clear as a summer sky.

"Fine. I don't stand a chance against you."

"Very good." The girl smiled like a flower that had burst into bloom and then, for some reason, readjusted her grip on the rock dagger. When her threatening stance drew a frown from Unran, she flashed him a frightfully cheerful smile. "Say, Unran. I'm truly glad that you've decided to join our team. This might come as a surprise after we've only just reached an understanding..."

"What?"

He'd known her for scarcely a few days, but he somehow knew that whenever this ballsy woman smiled like that, something bad was about to happen. When Unran followed her gaze over his shoulder, sure enough, his face froze.

"Ahhh! Sorry! I let one get away!"

"I'm going to throw my sword! Get down!"

A drooling boar sprang from the bushes, and soon Shin-u and Keikou came barreling after it.

The boar's eyes were bloodshot. This wasn't looking good.

"But I suggest we all hunt boars as a team," she finished at last. "Come, let's do this with a bang!"

"That..." As he scrambled to pick up his dagger, Unran yelled, "That was surprising indeed!"

THOUGH I AM AN INEPT VILLAINESS

Tale of the Butterfly-Rat
Body Swap in the Maiden Court

6 | Reirin Seduces

THE SURFACE OF THE WATER rippled in the light of the setting sun.

"Whew..."

Upon scrubbing all the dirt from her body, Reirin had closed her eyes and relaxed in the tub for a short time, but she eventually shook her head and stepped barefoot out of the vat. She peeled off her drenched undergarment and slipped into the hand-me-downs a village woman had lent her.

Since she hadn't dried herself off first, the clothing clung to her skin. There was nothing to be done about it, though. As she gathered up her wet hair and wrung it out, Reirin peered at her surroundings.

She was near the outskirts of the village, now dyed in the light of dusk.

There were several ponds scattered throughout the village. Reirin had picked the one that was the smallest and had the most brush cover, then requested the villagers bring her tub there. She'd been itching to cleanse herself of all the animal blood.

It had been half a day since the boar hunt in the Cursed Forest. The game killed by Keikou, Shin-u, and Unran had been safely carted back to the village and processed.

Reirin had aided the fight, of course, and thus she was covered head to toe in blood.

Unran worked hard for us.

The thought of her new "companion" brought a smile to her face. Though his face had been frozen in horror the whole time, he had joined the hunt right alongside the two military officers who so skillfully wielded their weapons. When a stifling silence threatened to fall as everyone concentrated on the fight, he was the one who livened up the scene with his mighty battle cry. That never would have happened with just the unflappable Kous and the apathetic Gen around.

Reirin giggled to herself as she reflected on the lively journey.

I'm so glad I managed to talk him over to my side.

Granted, in retrospect, it wasn't like she'd solved things with a peaceful chat. In fact, she was pretty sure she'd shoved a blade down his throat and threatened him.

Then again, her brothers *had* always told her, "It's fine to get pushy with a man." Above all else, Unran himself looked like she'd taken a weight off his shoulders with that stunt, so it was probably fine.

It's also great that the villagers accepted us.

Her smile broadened when she recalled the villagers' reactions.

Upon their return from the Cursed Forest, Gouryuu and the rest of the villagers had at first looked upon Unran and the game he'd hunted with transparent fear. Yet as Keikou flaunted his artistic field dressing techniques, those skeptics had slowly but surely begun to flock to him in fascination.

The sight of Keikou and Shin-u dressing the boars all by themselves had no doubt helped to relax the villagers' guard. But what had eased their fears more than anything was the two men's detailed explanations regarding the dissected animals.

"Listen up. See this boar that looks so exceptionally young and healthy? I know these white spots on the meat look tasty, but they're all parasites—bugs. If you eat 'em, the bugs will chew on your guts and sometimes kill you."

"This one with the swollen gullet is no good either. It's diseased. You'll die if you eat it."

Their ample camping experience had made them experts at preparing wild meat. The men explained which meat was safe to eat and which wasn't. What was dangerous to do and which rules would keep people safe. Their concrete and practical commentary utterly outstripped the villagers' knowledge.

"But the deer the chief hunted looked nice and clean. We made sure it was cooked real well too."

"Oh. In that case, there were poisonous mushrooms growing in clusters around the Cursed Forest. Those're toxic enough to make the skin swell up just from touching them. If a deer eats one of those, the poison'll spread to its flesh and organs. Do you remember the color of its poop? That's how you can tell. By the way, this boar here is safe."

"I didn't know all that..."

As all of their questions were swiftly addressed, the people began to understand the truth: The previous chief had died after eating a deer from the Cursed Forest because it was either infected or poisoned. In short, there was an identifiable cause for it—and it wasn't a curse.

"The fog, the sounds, the inflammation, and the dangerous animal meat... We have a good explanation for most of what was considered to be the forest's curse. With the proper preparations, they're all things that can be avoided," Reirin calmly explained as the villagers began to regain their composure.

Eerie noises, trees that attracted animals, and poison that could inflame the skin. From her perspective, all the "curses" the forest brought about seemed man-made. Chances were good that someone had taken advantage of the villagers' superstitious nature to create the legend of the "Cursed Forest."

Someone who didn't want anyone going near the forest.

Lord Koh, if I had to guess.

It was still nothing more than speculation. Opting to keep that theory under wraps for the time being, and thinking to herself that she ought to consult with Keikou as soon as possible, Reirin smiled at the villagers. "It's true that the forest is a dangerous place that warrants caution. But starvation is an even greater danger. We should take the proper precautions and be thankful for the blessings we're given."

Staring up at the boars hanging from the eaves with a gulp, the villagers obediently nodded their heads. It was possible to obtain such a huge amount of food in less than a few days. And if they trained enough to venture into the forest, they could get their hands on even more. They couldn't help but cling to this shred of hope that had suddenly manifested before them.

The first one to speak up was a village woman cradling an infant in her arms. "Umm... Would you mind sharing some of that boar with me? My husband caught a cold, and I want to help 'im build up his strength. You'll want to get out of that bloody robe soon, right? I can trade you for a change of clothes..."

That ushered in a flood of people requesting boar meat in exchange for all manner of goods, including a tub, fresh water, and old farming tools.

When Reirin's group agreed to share without demanding anything in return, the villagers became even friendlier. They watched over the long dressing process with smiles on their faces, eventually began to lend a hand, and by the end were even roaring with laughter at jokes and slapping their guests on the shoulder.

Reirin and Unran had to exchange looks over the villagers' blatant show of self-interest, but they let it go with a rueful smile. Still, Reirin had noticed then that the look on Unran's face as he shrugged his shoulders was softer than she'd ever seen it.

They're emotional, sociable people.

Overcome with a wave of bashfulness, Reirin scooped up some hot water. As a Maiden revered by all those around her, Reirin had never actually had much experience working in a group. Each time she was exposed to their unguarded smiles, their good-humored jokes, or their friendly pats on the shoulder, deep emotion and joy welled up within her.

This has been...such fun.

Their unadorned smiles made her happy. She knew they weren't her own subjects, but she couldn't help feeling like she wanted to see more of their smiling faces and grow even closer to them.

The same was probably true of Unran. No matter how much he pretended to have given up, he knew his neighbors were warm people deep down and couldn't help but want to be part of their circle.

I hope Unran can take this chance to deepen his bond with them.

At this rate, it might not be long before he completely integrated into the village. After all, once the villagers had changed their attitude, they'd become thoughtful enough to actively encourage the blood-soaked hunters to take a bath.

"Hey now, that can't feel too pleasant. Go wash off in the river. Or how about I boil some water in a tub?"

"Hey, Old Kyou! How long are you gonna sleep for? Get to work already!"

"Right, you'll need a change of clothes too. Do you want some of my hand-me-downs? The Maiden can wear mine... But Unran is so tall, I'm not sure my husband's clothes will fit..."

Once they'd decided to go all in, the villagers had stormed Unran's hut and told Old Kyou to boil some water. Both Unran and Reirin had balked at how the villagers closed the distance in an instant upon finally warming up to them, but ultimately, they'd let themselves be pushed into getting clean.

However, while the men had the option of simply going to the riverside and washing themselves off, it wasn't quite so easy for a woman like Reirin. There was a nearby pond the village women used as a shared bathing area, but since it seemed that water was also used for washing clothes and other daily necessities, they were hesitant to contaminate it with animal blood.

Thus, Reirin had instead borrowed a large tub and headed for a small pond on the outskirts of the village, where she was at present.

Here I can bathe without too much concern.

Reirin slowly crouched down. A fire had been lit right next to the tub for boiling the pond water and drying her wet body.

And I can finally talk to Lady Keigetsu.

Indeed. She had been looking for a chance to stand alone before a flame for ages now.

She leaned backward to steal a glance at the bushes in the distance, where she could see Shin-u standing with his back turned to her. As opposed to Keikou, who had sent her off with nothing more than a "Have a good soak," the captain had insisted on standing watch over "Shu Keigetsu" while she bathed and refused to take no for an answer.

He'd claimed that no matter how much the villagers had softened their hearts, there was no telling when someone might turn a hostile blade against her or if she might drown. When she told him she wanted to take her time, he'd said, "I'm used to waiting around," and when she told him she didn't want him to see her skin, he'd said, "I would never do something so improper." Considering the captain already had his pick of women, it was indeed hard for Reirin to imagine him stealing a glance at a Maiden, let alone "the court nuisance," so she'd ultimately consented.

He'd been very efficient in setting up the tub and fire for her, which she *did* appreciate.

Weh... His kindness is so overbearing. Do I really seem so unreliable?

Reirin heaved a sad little sigh as she held her hair over the fire to dry. When she switched bodies, people were supposed to be more willing to leave her to her own devices. Yet as soon as she tried to become independent and take care of other people, suddenly they would be trying to take care of her.

Earlier, Reirin had felt a pang of sadness when Unran snatched the heavy meat from her hands and hung it from the eaves, huffing, "This is no job for a Maiden."

It's cute to see Unran working so hard... It is *cute, but still...* She wanted to be the one doing the doting and protecting.

Reirin slumped her shoulders, but she was wrenched from her reverie by a drop of water trickling from the ends of her hair. This was no time to be moping.

"Lady Keigetsu! Can you hear me, Lady Keigetsu?"

As she pretended to dry herself off, she peered into the flickering flames. It wasn't like they had agreed on a time to talk. It was currently close to dinnertime, so there was a good chance Keigetsu wouldn't be around to pick up.

Can I get away with sticking around for about half an hour on account of my hair, I wonder? Please don't let him notice anything!

In an effort to keep her distant sentry, Shin-u, from catching on, Reirin kept her voice to a whisper and hid as much of the fire as she could with her body.

"Please use your flame magi—"

"*Took you long enough!*"

As a matter of fact, the flame call connected before she could even finish her sentence. The red contours of the fire billowed and swelled, then quickly died back down. In the dead center of the flickering flame was her own scowling face—or, in this case, Shu Keigetsu's. She was keeping her voice down, but she leaned toward the flame with a look of extreme intensity.

"*I've tried over and over and over again to reach you with my flame spell! What have you been doing all this time?!*"

"*So this is flame magic! Can you hear us, Lady Reirin? Are you all right? Wait, why are you all wet?!*"

"*We were sincerely concerned for your well-being...but you've been enjoying a relaxing bath, I see.*"

Leelee and Tousetsu popped up from where they'd apparently been waiting on either side of the screaming Keigetsu. It looked like the trio was sitting in a circle around a candle. To Reirin, it felt like she was getting a lecture from every angle.

"I-I'm sorry. I haven't been lounging around, I promise. I was just cleansing myself of all the blood," she tried to explain.

"*The blood?!*"

All three girls gasped.

"Yes. I've been getting my fill of farmwork since I came here, and today I even hiked a mountain and hunted some wild boars. The filth was getting to be too much to bear."

"*Farmwork?*"

"*Mountain?*"

"Wild boars?"

All traces of expression vanished from their faces in an instant.

Keigetsu spoke for the whole group when she asked in a very slow and deliberate manner: *"No matter how independent you are...you are being held captive by bandits, right? Why does it feel like you're enjoying a life of retirement in the countryside? Why were you going for a merry little hike up the mountains?"*

"Uh..."

Reirin went stiff. Keigetsu was furious with her.

"G-good question. Why *did* I hike a mountain? Because the mountain was there, perhaps?"

"Forget it. Listening to your drivel won't get us anywhere," said Keigetsu, pinching the bridge of her nose. *"Just give me a simple answer to my questions."*

"Sure," Reirin agreed with a meek nod.

"First of all, are you all right?"

"Yes. I'm doing great. I've been sleeping well, eating well, and enjoying my time here."

"Glad to hear it. Next, who were those bandits, and where are you now?"

"It was the people referred to as 'untouchables' within the township who kidnapped me. They abducted me to their village as part of an order to torment 'Shu Keigetsu,'" Reirin replied as matter-of-factly as she could manage.

Keigetsu gulped. *"What did you just say?"*

"I'm sorry to have to tell you this...but it was the residents of the southern territory who kidnapped 'you,' not assassins from another land. It seems the magistrate Lord Koh put it in the people's heads that this cold spell is the Maiden's fault. He claimed that the Heavens' anger would be appeased if someone tormented the root of the misfortune, and that he'd lower the villagers' taxes if they took on the task."

Keigetsu lapsed into stunned silence as she listened to Reirin's explanation.

"So Lord Koh searching so desperately for me was all an act, and the antagonism he displayed at the start was his true feelings." Eventually, she hung her head in self-derision. *"Why? Because I'm a 'sewer rat'? Because an untalented girl couldn't possibly bring good fortune to her own domain? Even the residents of my own territory treat me like the root of all disaster. It's absurd to think one person could be so hated."*

"No, Lady Keigetsu," Reirin cut her off firmly. "This isn't a matter of good or bad. You haven't done anything wrong. The townspeople were desperate, and a bad man took advantage of that. That's all there is to it." When Keigetsu lifted her face and looked at her in plea, Reirin leaned forward. "In fact, the villagers have begun to open up to me after spending only a few days together. Everyone was just hungry, anxious, and looking for someone to take out their frustrations on."

Keigetsu drew her lips into a thin line, her eyes watering ever so slightly.

"So please don't hang your head, Lady Keigetsu. Let us instead punish the fool who pushed these people into a corner. And let us think of a way to save Unran's—that is, this village and the entire southern lands. That is our role here."

At length, Keigetsu nodded like she'd found her resolve. Reirin was relieved to see it. *"You're right."*

"How are things going on your end? I hope Brother Junior is doing a good job of supporting you."

"'Supporting' isn't the word I'd use." The moment Keishou's name came up, Keigetsu dove right back into a sulk after she'd just found the will to hold her head high again. *"He harasses me all day long. It's always 'You'll give yourself away with posture that terrible,' or 'Oh my, the esteemed Kou Reirin can't even serve her brother a cup of tea with a smile?'"*

Evidently, being stuck around a man as condescending as Keishou was proving too much for Keigetsu to handle.

"He never has anything but rambling praise for you, but it's always rambling insults for me. Plus, his snide remarks are getting nastier by the day. He's a flippant, clingy jerk."

Leelee scrambled to pacify the Maiden putting the man of another clan on blast.

Reirin, meanwhile, took in her comment with wide-eyed surprise. "Goodness! It sounds like he's taken quite a liking to you, then."

"Say what?"

"Brother Junior is the type to start out mercilessly bullying someone he's taken a shine to. He'll needle them and needle them, and if they have the backbone to stay standing by the end of it all, he'll accept them as one of his own and cherish them to bits."

Keigetsu stared back blankly, then shuddered. *"That's insane. Is everyone in the Kou clan a freak? There's something wrong with—"*

"His relationship with Lady Keigetsu aside, Master Keishou has been playing his part well." Tousetsu leaned over and put the conversation back on track, interrupting Keigetsu before she could say something gravely irreverent. *"He used a Gen tassel found on the stage to lead the search in that direction. I see he planted that as a tactic to keep the rescue team from heading into the village."*

Reirin gave that a moment's thought, then shook her head. "No. Brother Junior shouldn't know where we are either. Our captors left the tassel behind on the stage to disrupt the investigation. They admitted to it themselves."

"I see."

"But thinking about it...even if they had orders from the magistrate, I have to wonder how ordinary citizens could get their hands on another clan's tassel," muttered Reirin. Gazing into the fire, she gave a recap of everything that had happened to that point.

The south had suffered a cold spell. The townspeople had grown anxious, and that had probably given the magistrate cause for concern. He'd then pushed the blame onto Keigetsu and attempted to turn his people's malice on her. Left with little other option, the villagers had kidnapped Reirin in the form of "Shu Keigetsu" and tried to torment her.

"In addition to the Gen clan tassel...there was a Kou one left near the ceremonial robe, as I recall."

Come to think of it, were Unran and Gouryuu the ones who slung mud over Keigetsu's robe? She'd forgotten to ask.

If that were the case, it would mean the villagers—or the magistrate who had given the orders, perhaps—had to be in possession of multiple tassels. Tassels were worn only by noblemen. The items were so rare that only a select few craftsmen were allowed to make them, and the magistrate of a backwater township wouldn't know what one looked like to counterfeit it.

In short, someone of a high enough rank had used their extensive enough breadth of knowledge to prepare them beforehand.

"The magistrate was pulling the strings of the impoverished villagers. But it seems there may have been someone pulling *his* strings too."

"*So you mean there's a mastermind who wants to use the Shu clan to bring down 'Shu Keigetsu,' then foist the blame onto the Kou and Gen clans?*" Leelee chimed in.

It was just like when the former Noble Consort, Shu Gabi, had posed as a Kin court lady and given the order to kill Keigetsu.

Someone was looking to torment another without getting their own hands dirty. Having been wrapped up in a similar situation once before, Leelee was quick to understand what was going on here. "*Give me a break... Why do those in power always turn out to be such bastards?*"

"*Then should we assume the mastermind behind this is from neither the Kou nor Gen clan—in other words, someone from the Kin or Ran clan?*" Tousetsu asked.

Reirin shook her head. "It's too early to jump to conclusions.

First, we should confirm what the magistrate is after. If nothing else, he's definitely the one who pushed Unran's people over the edge, so we have to make sure he regrets it."

"Who's Unran?"

"A young man from the village who was the main culprit in this kidnapping. He's the former chief's heir, and his strong sense of responsibility made him determined to somehow save his people from starvation."

As Reirin explained with a tender look in her eyes how he'd locked her in a warehouse, denied her food, and made her work in the fields all for the sake of his village, the three girls inferred what had happened there: *Oh, it's the thing where he was seriously trying to victimize her, but she wouldn't act scared at all.*

"Hee hee. He's an adorable person. His responsible nature is the spitting image of Leelee. He tried to assault me at one point, but he ended up changing his mind right after. The whole time we were dressing boars together, I was thinking about how glad I was that we'd made friends and how much I wanted to protect his smile."

Everyone's faces froze in horror at some of the more disquieting terms she'd thrown in there. But the bottom line seemed to be that this Maiden had escaped her predicament with her usual methods.

"I remain impressed with your resolute magnanimity in the face of all circumstances."

"Damn seductress…"

Ignoring the mumblings of the two court ladies, Reirin put a hand to her cheek in a fluster. "Still, as determined as I am to get back at the magistrate, I can't find out who's controlling him from here. I assume it must be someone who keeps in close contact with him."

"About that." Keigetsu was the one to speak up this time. *"As it happens, I'm going to be holding a tea party tomorrow. I might be able to gauge what the other clans are up to through their Maidens."*

"A tea party? Why?"

"The other Maidens are anxious about 'my' kidnapping. His Highness asked me to do something to put their minds at ease. He's coming by later to help me plan for it. Admittedly, I'm worried about whether I'll be able to pull it off." Keigetsu heaved a melancholy sigh, then lifted her head as if something had just occurred to her. *"Wait, if you make it back safe, won't we have to put the whole party on hold?"*

"Ah."

"Can you head back now? The Untouchable Village is just one bridge over from the township, isn't it?"

"Oh, did no one tell you?" Reirin blinked. "Unran and his uncle cut the suspension bridge. We'd have to go all the way around the mountain to get back, so it would be about half a day's trip for a girl like me."

"Oh... Then I guess I'll just have to do my best."

"Or shall we go ahead and undo the switch now?" Reirin hesitantly offered. "Though you *would* have to spend a few days in the village, of course."

Keigetsu gave a rueful shake of her head. *"I've got plenty of qi stored up, but it has such a strong fire bent that I haven't managed* to mold it just right. If we want to stay on the safe side, I shouldn't cast the spell until tomorrow at the earliest."

"Oh, too bad."

"Also, I have to be in physical contact with whoever I cast the spell on. If I'm too far away, it might not cover the full target. I could end up switching only one part of our bodies, like our birthmarks or wrists." Reirin's eyes went wide, surprised to hear this was possible. Keigetsu shrugged her shoulders in embarrassment. "It's actually a lot more difficult to cast a spell to switch a specific part of the flesh than to simply detach and switch two souls, not to mention it takes more qi. I normally couldn't do it. But this is the place I have the greatest compatibility with, a land abundant in fire qi. Anything could happen."

"Goodness, Lady Keigetsu... You're a truly skilled practitioner of the Daoist arts."

"As long as my powers don't run out of control," Keigetsu answered with a hint of self-deprecation, evidently harboring mixed feelings about her magic. "When I first started learning the Daoist arts, I made a lot of mistakes. I'd try to float and end up crashing, or I'd try to mind control a cat and turn my own arm into a cat instead."

"That sounds incredible," Reirin murmured in spite of herself.

Also, she had to scratch her head over how harsh Keigetsu's own self-assessment was.

"I bet you're the only one on the entire continent who can do something like that. You're almost like the Great Ancestor who was said to bear the dragon's qi and possess divine powers. It's a wonderful talent."

"Now that's just blasphemy. The dragon's qi is a divine favor, but the Daoist arts are about drawing power from the gaps between yin and yang using curses. That's exactly why cultivators have been suppressed. Anyone who's outed as a practitioner in this day and age will become a target of persecution. That's what brought my father to ruin." Keigetsu shuddered.

That explained why she'd hardly told anyone else about her powers until now. Her complete lack of self-esteem likely also stemmed from how no one had ever praised her for her magic.

"Anyway," Keigetsu went on anxiously, *"try to make it back by tomorrow. Based on what you've said, you're a prisoner in name only, right? Since Lord Keikou knows what's going on, couldn't he get you out of there any time you asked?"*

"I suppose that's true. But the captain doesn't know about the switch, and since we agreed to stay in the village until help arrives, I'm not sure how I'd broach a sudden change in plans without arousing his suspicions..." Reirin mumbled to herself, pressing a hand to her cheek.

"Excuse me?" said Keigetsu, staggered. *"Why are you bringing up the captain?"*

"Oh? Did no one tell you that either? Last night, the captain zeroed in on the village and crossed the river all by himself to join us."

"What?!"

The flame swelled, sending Reirin into a tizzy. "Um, he's standing guard from some far-off bushes right now, so please calm dow—"

286

"*How do you expect me to be calm?! You mean to tell me that you've been under His Highness's surveillance all this time?! He has to have heard about the switch from the captain already!*"

"Th-that's not true!" Had Keigetsu's shout reached Shin-u's ears? Casting nervous glances behind her, Reirin did her best to calm her friend down. "The captain is right here. He can't report back to His Highness."

"*Even if he can't do it now, he's going to tell him we switched bodies later! Thanks a lot, now all my hard work was for nothing! I'm the one His Highness is going to punish in a fit of rage, remember?!*"

"As I said, he doesn't even know about the switch!" Reirin rushed to say, keeping the volume of her voice as low as possible. "We'll be fine. The captain is utterly convinced that I'm Lady Keigetsu. I've been training day and night and even drawn up a list of hypothetical scenarios, after all. The accuracy of my impression is second to none. Right, Tousetsu?"

"*O-of course.*"

Reirin was stunned to see her head court lady and most loyal retainer avert her gaze. "Tousetsu?"

"*Erm. Is it possible that he figured out who you are a long time ago...and he's just letting it go for now?*" Leelee was the next to nervously venture. "'*Cause, uh, you're garbage at playing the villainess. It's hard to believe he wouldn't see through it.*"

"I'm garbage..." Reirin choked up upon hearing this shocking revelation from the court lady she so loved to dote on. "You're terrible, Leelee. That's how you've been looking upon my efforts this whole time?"

"Wait, uh…! I don't mean to make fun of you or anything! It's more like, um, a plain fact?"

Clutching her chest in sadness, Reirin got defensive enough to argue back. "I'm doing fine! I take care to routinely insult him, and I endeavor to keep Lady Keigetsu's clipped manner of speech in mind too."

"It's not an issue of how she talks. Are you still playing around with pill bugs out of habit? I sure hope you're not happily sticking your hands in the mud or playing nice with your inferiors either," Leelee said, squinting in suspicion.

"Uh…" Reirin gave a start. Every last one of those things the girl had mentioned rang a bell.

Keigetsu glared daggers the moment she caught that gulp. *"See?! So much for accurate! He* **has** *to know!"*

"Th-that's not true. If he knew, why wouldn't he say anything? He has no reason to keep quiet about it. That means he hasn't—"

"Get your ego in check. Oh, I can't believe this! Even I managed to fool someone as overzealous as Tousetsu for a full week, and you can't even last three days. Talk about incompetent!"

"Weh… I said we'll be fine… The blade of your words cuts deep, Lady Keigetsu. My heart is aching…"

Reirin was the unflappable sort, but it was hard not to feel upset about being called "incompetent" to her face for the first time in her life. A pained look clouded her expression, both her heart and ears aching.

"Hold on, haven't I warned you about the pill bug thing before? Why don't you ever learn? Are you stupid?"

"Ouch!"

"She's right! Don't get so carried away, you big idiot!"

"Ouch! Ouch! Ouch!"

Their emotions getting the better of them, Keigetsu and Leelee came at Reirin with all the outrage they could pack into their hushed voices. As someone who had never been subjected to worse than Tousetsu's dispassionate lectures, Reirin reflexively covered her ears and wailed, the Shu girls' onslaught of verbal violence too much for her to take.

However...she shouldn't have done that.

"Hey! Are you all right?!"

Why? Because it brought Shin-u springing out of the bushes with a face blanched in alarm.

"What? Captain?!"

Reirin boggled at him before immediately curling into a ball and pulling her robe more tightly around herself. She was wearing nothing but a thin hand-me-down that might as well have been an undergarment, one that also happened to be clinging to her wet skin.

"Wh-wh-why did you come over?!"

"I heard a scream. I thought we were under attack, but it looks like no. Did a wound start acting up?" It seemed Reirin's attire hadn't even registered to Shin-u, however, and he simply glanced around with his sword held at the ready. Then, he narrowed his gaze as he looked down upon Reirin's crouching form. "It must be that injury you sustained during the boar hunt. Let me have a look."

289

"Pardon?!"

Oh. It's because I yelled "ouch"...

He had probably been too far from the flame to catch the other girls' voices. In other words, from Shin-u's perspective, a girl who was fresh out of the bath and warming up by the fire had abruptly curled in on herself and started screaming in pain.

N-no wonder he was worried! Oh, what have I done?!

Reirin's gaze flicked to the fire in a panic. The girls must have figured out what was going on as soon as she'd said the word "Captain" because they'd stepped aside to where they wouldn't be reflected in the flame.

As relieved as she was to see that, her heart was still thumping wildly in her chest. To put a finer point on it, she didn't want Shin-u seeing her in her good-as-underwear outfit.

"N-no! It's all right! I'm not hurting anywhere. My wound is just fine! No need to be concerned! Now, please don't mind me and take your leave at once!"

"Why are you so panicked? Are you hiding something?" Alas, her reaction had only deepened Shin-u's suspicions. He scrunched his shapely brow and fixed her with an even sharper gaze. "Don't tell me: Did you get hurt somewhere besides your palm? A sword wound or a sprain, perhaps? Whatever the case, we should tend to it right away. Hiding it and leaving it to fester will just make it worse. This place isn't as well equipped as the inner court."

"I-I'm really not hurt. Excuse me, Captain, but I'm dressed in little more than an undergarment at the moment. It's very embarrassing to be seen like this. I really must ask that you leave."

"Which matters more: your safety or how you're dressed? I'm not some rookie fresh out of his first battle, so it'd take more than this to get a reaction out of me. Now show me the wound you're hiding."

Why was it that the more Reirin laid out the facts, the more he became convinced she was injured?

"You *do* have a habit of pushing yourself too hard sometimes."

The statement was a reaction to the time she had drawn the Bow of Warding until she passed out, but that hint went over Reirin's head.

"No, regardless, I need you to go—"

"Oho."

In the face of her persistent urging, Shin-u stroked his chin and took a step back. Then, he dropped a slow and deliberate glance upon her.

"I recall that when Kou Reirin once hurt herself with the Bow of Warding, she stubbornly rejected the concern of those around her... How curious. I know you're Shu Keigetsu right now, but something about the way you're acting—"

"Inspect me as much as you like."

Reirin solemnly rose to her feet and held out both arms to Shin-u.

Hrk... I get the feeling the captain is toying with me.

She gritted her teeth in spirit. Was it possible she was being played for a fool?

Then again, if a man as faithful to his duties as Shin-u had seen through the switch, he would need to get her word on it so as to report back to Gyoumei—which meant he would be pressuring her to confess to the swap herself. There was no reason for him to overlook it or let it go.

Then that has to mean he doesn't know.

When she flicked her gaze upward, she locked eyes with Shin-u as he diligently inspected her entire body. His experience with women showed in how he indeed didn't bat an eye at her state of undress, checking the various parts of her body as nonchalantly as if he were inspecting a weapon.

"I don't see any gashes besides the one on your palm, true. But what happened to your neck?" he asked upon finishing his checkup, his eyes narrowing in threat. His slender fingers indicated the spot where she had bled when Unran held a dagger to her throat.

"A cat scratched me."

Shin-u glared when she jumped to Unran's defense. "Lying won't do you any good. Tell me the truth."

"No," she said firmly.

Looking miffed, he grumbled, "Can't you ever just do what someone tells you to?"

"My. Why should I obey a man who is neither my husband nor my family?" Reirin couldn't help but retort.

It was then that Shin-u froze.

"..."

In reality, his heart felt like it was on fire.

It was for purely professional reasons that he had stood watch as this Maiden bathed. He had kept his back politely turned to the glimpses of her visible past the bushes, and in practice, he hadn't been struck with the slightest hint of temptation. He'd simply stood there, all his attention focused on whether the girl might drown in an unfamiliar tub of hot water or if wild dogs or hostile townspeople might attack.

Then he had heard her stifled scream. As his hand flew to his sword, the first thing that had popped into his head was the time she'd drawn the Bow of Warding.

She never showed weakness in front of other people. She'd stand tall even when she was sweating buckets and smile even when she was bleeding, only to pass out after the fact—that was the kind of woman she was.

He thought that perhaps she'd sent everyone away on purpose. Then, only once she was alone, she'd let loose the screams she'd been holding back. If it was an attack, he could strike down any enemy, and if it was a wound, he'd get to the bottom of the matter and see that she was treated this time.

That had been his plan when he rushed in, at least, but she'd been as stubborn as ever and merely treated his concern as a nuisance.

And to top it all off, she'd even called him a man who was neither her husband nor family.

She's right.

It wasn't the scathing nature of the remark that shook him. It was that he found the words so correct as to be irrefutable.

This girl was a Maiden. One of the girls who would become Prince Gyoumei's wife. If there was any man she was meant to obey, it would be her family and the prince, not him.

"Captain?" The girl standing before him looked up at him nervously.

Her wet hair clung to her nape, and her slender body was clad in naught but a flimsy robe. As he watched droplets of water trickle down her temple and drip onto her collarbone, something dawned on Shin-u.

He would never be the one to stroke her hair.

He would never be the one to hold her tender body close.

If this strong-willed woman ever allowed herself to cry in front of others, Gyoumei would be the one to wipe those tears, not him.

"If I were your husband..." Before he knew it, he found himself reaching for the waterdrops trickling down her cheek. "Would you obey me?"

"Huh?"

"If I took you as my wife...would you obey me?"

He was the captain of the Eagle Eyes. One of the few positions of prestige a man could aspire to in the inner court. It was a position that allowed him to be gifted the lowest-ranking consort.

"Then maybe I will," Shin-u murmured as he placed a hand to her cheek.

Well now.

Meanwhile, Reirin had gone stiff as a board with Shin-u's hand on her face.

Is it just me, or did the captain more or less propose to me just now?

Had Shin-u and Keigetsu had a much more positive relationship than she'd realized?

No, no, no! This has to be what you'd call giving tit for tat. He certainly took me by surprise!

This was, after all, the same Reirin who had been picked to be Gyoumei's wife before she'd even turned ten. She'd never been wooed by a man before, and she hadn't the slightest clue how to act in a situation like this.

"That's quite enough joking around..."

"Joking? No." When she turned away from him, Shin-u scooped up a lock of her hair as though in pursuit. "I'm actually quite serious."

His voice was low, but it was thick with passion.

"I—"

She almost replied with an innocuous "I see," only to stop herself mid-sentence. This wasn't the sort of topic to be brushed aside.

Wh-what do I do?!

As belated a reaction as it was, she was suddenly very conscious of the fact that Shin-u was close enough for his breath to graze her ear. His tall figure as he closed in from right behind seemed so terribly vivid and real, and the hand holding her hair exuded a palpable heat without even touching her skin.

First, I need to get him to let go. Umm... Stay calm, maintain eye contact, and slowly back away... Wait, no, that's for encountering a bear in the forest.

As she quietly panicked over this unprecedented dilemma, the firewood popped near her feet. The sound snapped her back to her senses.

This is no time to be flustered!

Keigetsu and the court ladies were "watching" this very conversation from the other side of the flame. The thought almost made her blood boil with shame, but even more than that, it filled her with a strong sense of purpose.

Her friend had been so upset because she was certain Shin-u had seen through the switch. Reirin had to assuage her concerns by putting on the perfect "Shu Keigetsu" act where she could see it.

Didn't I make a list of detailed hypotheticals for exactly that purpose? Get it together, Reirin!

She gave a tiny nod of her head, steeling a resolve that would have had Keigetsu screaming, "Don't bother!"

It was going to be all right. She'd asked Keigetsu's thoughts on this exact sort of scenario just the other day.

If a man confesses his love to you...seduce him!

She recalled the answer Keigetsu had been so proud to give, her eyes narrowed with a smirk.

"What would I do if a handsome gentleman made a move on me, you asked? Why, I'd use every trick in the book to seduce him into becoming my personal love slave."

She would expect no less of the Shu Keigetsu who lived so true to her heart's desires.

Reirin would stand there stock-still, lost as to how even to react to another's affection, but Keigetsu would relentlessly strike back. How truly brilliant.

Frankly, Reirin couldn't think of a single wile to use on him, but she was determined to make an effort to come as close to Keigetsu as possible.

"Take *me* as your wife?"

Reirin turned back to Shin-u, flashing him a smile that dripped with every last drop of confidence she could muster. Staring straight back at him as his eyes went wide, *she* reached out to *him* this time.

"I'll give him my best bedroom eyes, run my fingers over his skin, and never let him take his eyes off me for a second."

Then, she brushed that hand over his cheek.

"You think I'd obey even my husband? Surely you jest."

When Shin-u gulped, she responded with a provocative tilt of her head.

"You'll obey *me.* I'll show you no mercy if you don't offer your everything to me, Master Shin-u."

Once she'd delivered that clincher, Reirin cast a brief glance over at the fire.

How was that, Lady Keigetsu?!

Little did she know that pandemonium was unfolding on the other side of the flame.

"Wh-wh-what is that idiot *doing*?!" came Keigetsu's stifled scream as she backed away from the candle. She really wanted to yell at the top of her lungs, but she couldn't do that in case the pair reflected in the fire overheard.

No, she knew what Reirin was thinking. If one had to guess,

she'd taken to heart what Keigetsu had told her the other day, and now she was trying to seduce Shin-u to get into her role as "Shu Keigetsu."

How?! How is it that you're so bad at being bad, yet you still manage to destroy me without the slightest hint of malice?!

She only wished she could leap out from the flame and shake Reirin around by the shoulders.

"Th-that's some provocation... Uh, you don't think he's going to take her on the spot, do you?"

"Also, didn't that comment about 'pushing herself too hard' imply that the captain already knows who she is?"

Leelee and Tousetsu watched the spectacle unfolding in the flame with sweat pouring down their faces.

The girls wanted nothing more than to put out the fire and pretend this wasn't happening. But they couldn't do that. They also itched to shout something across the flame and make Reirin stop this instant. But if they did *that*, the switch would be out for sure. The trio was too caught up in a maelstrom of inner conflict to so much as move.

"You want my *obedience?"*

On the other side of the flame, Shin-u had snatched Reirin's hand from his cheek, his gaze narrowed. It was clear even from a distance that those eyes so often described as "frosty" now burned with an uncontainable heat.

He was like an eagle before his prey.

He would corner the poor little bird with an overwhelming tenacity...

299

"*That's right*," said Reirin, lifting her chin in a gesture that screamed "Shu Keigetsu."

The three girls clasped each other's hands and gave a voiceless shriek. *Eeeek!*

They were all thinking something along the lines of, *Stop. Please stop. Don't you notice the passion emanating from the man standing before you? Do you think you can light a fire under a man from the Gen clan, those known for the strength of their obsession, and get away unscathed?*

"**If you're not up to the challenge, don't suggest something so outrageous.**"

You don't want *him to be up to the challenge!*

Oblivious to the three girls' despair, Reirin and Shin-u fell silent on the other side of the candle, gazing into each other's eyes as if gauging what the other would do next.

"Now this is a convenient spell."

That was when an ice-cold voice rang out, giving the trio a start.

"Eek!"

It came from behind, just as they'd let their guard down.

Standing there was none other than Gyoumei, his arms folded and a gorgeous smile on his face.

Beside him was Keishou, whose usual thoughtless smile was nowhere to be found. "Sorry," he mumbled, scratching his cheek.

Eeeeeek!

All three girls went white as a sheet.

"It's H-H-Hi-Hi-Hi...!"

"That's quite enough laughter, thank you," he said, silencing Keigetsu as she came close to blowing bubbles. He gracefully strode up to the candle, then held up a finger to inspect the flame. "Is this happening over there as we speak? Can Reirin and Shin-u see us?"

"Uh, erm..."

"Answer me."

"Y-yes. Um, ours is a candle flame, so they can see less of us than we can of them... But if you get close enough, your image and voice will be channeled to the other side," she answered, feeling like a frog staring down a snake.

That was when it hit her. He'd just called the "Shu Keigetsu" reflected in the flame "Reirin." He wasn't questioning how Keigetsu could wield fire magic either. That meant only one thing.

"Wait a minute, Your Highness... Does that mean...?"

Gyoumei slowly narrowed his eyes. He didn't even wait to let her finish her question. "Did you really think I hadn't noticed?"

That was her answer.

Keigetsu felt ready to collapse to her knees. "But...then why... didn't you say anything?" she asked, gasping for breath.

Gyoumei tore his gaze from the candle to glance back at her. His beautiful face still held the gentle smile of a model crown prince. "It's in the nature of the Gen blood to lose all semblance of control when a loved one is hurt. We want to protect our beloved by locking them away in our arms. That's only a natural desire, and it's the way we ought to be. That's what I used to believe."

"Right..."

"But I was wrong. I lost control of my emotions, and in my haste to punish her enemies, I made my beloved's predicament worse. And at the same time, the sight of the crown prince dancing to the tune of one select Maiden shook the balance of the five clans."

Keigetsu gasped. She couldn't have been more wrong about him not growing since the previous switch. He regretted more than anyone that he'd pushed Reirin's back to the wall and lacked the self-control a prince ought to have. Behind his untroubled expression lay a passionate whirlwind of remorse, self-reproach, and resolve that couldn't hope to be measured from the outside.

"I'll never lose sight of what's happening again. Nor will I ever cast the other Maidens away to run to Reirin's side. For I am the crown prince of the Kingdom of Ei."

For the brief moment when he uttered the words "crown prince," the smile on his face tightened and he cast a penetrating gaze toward the flame.

"Eek!"

Keigetsu saw a wind rage before her very eyes.

No—this illusory gust that neither jostled the bamboo blinds nor shook the flame of the candle had to be his dragon's qi. For one fleeting moment, the room was filled with an aura powerful enough to steal the breath of all those present.

Gyoumei was curbing his fury out of regret for his past actions. Still, even that small glimpse of raging emotion he had shown was enough to shock not just Keigetsu but even the composed Tousetsu, cocksure Leelee, and flippant Keishou into silence.

"Shu Keigetsu. I assume this switch took place before I forbade it. If that is indeed the case, I won't punish you for this transgression." He looked down at where Keigetsu was slumped on the floor. "However," he went on, inclining his head as he gazed at the candle's flame. He had already regained his usual self-possessed smile. "This threat to my Maiden's chastity is a different matter. The uninhibited girl herself, the man who wooed her, or those who allowed the situation to happen—who should I punish here, I wonder?"

Keigetsu didn't respond. No—she couldn't speak. The smile on his face somehow looked even more dangerous than the wild look he'd once had as he summoned a blanket of rain clouds. "Um..."

"I'd already received news of where Reirin's been taken. But I mustn't run into things half-cocked ever again. I'll go rescue her only once I have a clear picture of the situation."

"Received from who? What's the situation?" Keigetsu asked in a quivering voice, but she never got an answer.

"Hey, we have a problem!" came a sudden shout from the other side of the flame. *"You're done bathing, right? Sorry to cut you short, but I need you to come back fast! Your Kou clan guard is calling for you. He said you know a lot about taking care of the sick."*

Upon whipping around to look, the group saw that it was a man with one section of his short hair tied into a bun who had come running up to Reirin and Shin-u in the middle of their staring contest. His grungy appearance aside, he was a gorgeous man.

The girls assumed this was the "Unran" Reirin had mentioned, the son of the village chief.

"Old Kyou's been feeling sick since morning, and she started vomiting a little while ago... But it's not just her. Uncle Gouryuu, our neighbors, and the other villagers started throwing up one after another, and their diarrhea won't stop."

Unran was breathing hard, his handsome features twisted into a grimace.

Swallowing down his trepidation, he said in a cracking voice, *"Help us. This...has to be a plague."*

7 | Interlude

O<small>N HIS KNEES</small>, Lord Koh glared balefully at the approaching twilight. "Damn it..."

He was praying at the shrine located next to the drum tower. The residents of the southern territory were by and large a pious sort who prayed to the gods for every little thing, and so too was the magistrate in the habit of visiting the various shrines he'd had built around the township. Now in particular, he was praying for Shu Keigetsu's safe return, fasting, and extolling the Heavens all day long—or that's what it looked like, at least. There wasn't a shred of sincerity to any of it.

"Damn it, damn it, damn it..."

All he felt was panic over how things weren't going the way he'd planned.

"Why won't the crown prince take action?" The voice that usually crafted such polite webs of words had been reduced to an irritated croak.

And it was no wonder why—despite all the fuss Lord Koh had raised with this Shu Keigetsu kidnapping scandal, Prince

Gyoumei had yet to show a crack in his composure. He was even staying holed up in the estate and engaging in small talk with the townspeople.

His own Maiden was kidnapped! Why won't he focus his attention there? If he stays in the estate too much longer and starts looking into my account books...

The magistrate just barely managed to keep his face from contorting in resentment.

He'd already disposed of the account books. From the start, he'd maintained a policy of only keeping his closest relatives by his side.

There should have been no means for the truth to come to light—that is, that he had lied about the population of the township to engage in tax fraud.

Damn it... If it weren't for the cold spell, I would have pulled it off without a hitch.

Gazing up at the leaden clouds that shrouded the sky even at dusk, Lord Koh clicked his tongue where he kneeled.

After his marks on the civil service examination had been less than impressive, he'd found this backwater region dumped into his lap. There was only one reason a man like him—someone with a lot of self-esteem and little to show for it—hadn't objected to his post: The township was located a good distance from the center of the kingdom, thus making it the ideal place to line his pockets.

Taxes were calculated according to the census reported to the imperial capital. Therefore, Lord Koh had reduced the number of recorded households over time until the taxes levied upon the township had become a fraction of what they were meant to be paying.

Lord Koh kept the leftover rice for himself. He distributed it to the neighboring eastern territory and turned it into gold, which he then hid in a cave deep in the misty mountains. He'd even gone to the lengths of creating a superstition about a "Cursed Forest" to keep anyone from going near it. He'd drilled holes into the trees so that the wind would make eerie noises, and he'd planted a variety of fruits popular with animals so that people would be more likely to be attacked by wild beasts. His most ingenious idea had been during the first few years, when he'd sent in assassins to knock out the hikers, then smeared poison all over them before sending them home. Nowadays, not a single soul from either the township or village was brave enough to set foot there.

Over the course of these many years of scheming, Lord Koh had saved up quite a bit of funds. Unfortunately, the past two years had been marked by a drought and a cold spell in quick succession, resulting in a sharp drop in the crop yields.

It was good to have a smaller nominal population in times of peace because it meant lower taxes, but the drawback was that it made things harder when the township ran into food shortages. The amount of aid sent from the capital in the form of congee, salt, and clothing was likewise calculated based on the census.

As a result, the townspeople had grown discontent when they saw that they weren't getting as much congee as the other territories. That was all well and good as long as they directed their anger at the capital, but there was the danger of an uprising if they caught on to his fraud.

Normally, he would have sacrificed the Untouchable Village to distract the townspeople from their problems. After all, that was the only reason he had bothered to leave those repulsive people alive.

Lord Koh understood the nature of the southern towns-people all too well. They were emotional and all too quick to blame someone else for their struggles. That was precisely why he had provided them with a "scapegoat" in the form of the Untouchable Village. He had imposed heavy taxes on the village while lowering those on the township, and he'd even reinforced the sense of discrimination by dictating what the untouchables could wear and how long they could keep their hair. In the lean years, he would lure in village women and let the townsmen most likely to revolt have their way with them. That was all it had taken to keep Unso rebellion-free for the past twenty years.

Thus, he'd been hoping to get through this particular predica-ment with his usual methods, but about half a month ago, he'd been faced with an unexpected disruption.

"Blast it! If only that accursed man hadn't set his sights on—"

"Oh, praying again? Now that's devotion."

Just as he had started grumbling under his breath, a youthful, elegant voice suddenly called out to him from behind. Lord Koh gave a start.

The voice belonged to a military officer clad in a robe with a blue motif. He was a slender man whose defining feature was the mole under his eye.

His name was Ran Rinki. He was the second son of the Ran clan, who had come along on the trip as the ceremonial officer to the Ran Maiden, Ran Houshun. His skill was such that he was rumored to have the upper hand over the eldest son in the Ran clan's succession struggle.

"I'm not a particularly religious man myself, but we *are* neighbors. Let's pray together," he said blithely, then kneeled right next to Lord Koh. The perfect picture of a refined nobleman, he picked up a stick of incense and dropped it into the burner dedicated to the god of agriculture. "May Lady Shu Keigetsu be found and rescued as soon as possible."

Lord Koh's mouth twisted into a grimace as he watched the man close his eyes and rattle off prayers he didn't mean without a care in the world.

Almost as if he'd sensed this, Rinki opened his eyes and flashed the magistrate a smile. "Hee hee. The truth is, it'll be over for you if this kidnapping case is resolved too quickly, hm?"

"..."

As if to corner Lord Koh as he averted his gaze, Rinki went on, "It looks like His Highness is a much calmer man than we anticipated. Even after his Maiden was kidnapped, he's remained a steadfast leader no matter who calls him callous for it. He didn't jump on any of the evidence you planted either." His thin lips curled in amusement. "My prediction that he would spend the entire Harvest Festival getting jerked around by the kidnapping scandal was off. I'm afraid that if his levelheaded investigation keeps up, your tax fraud may come to light in the process."

"Excuse me..." Lord Koh just barely managed to keep his choice of words polite, but his voice dropped a little too low in his efforts to stifle his anger. "*You're* the one who convinced me to have her abducted."

Indeed. It was Rinki who had approached Lord Koh when he was starting to grow anxious over the poor harvest.

Given its location on the southern territory's outskirts, part of Unso shared a border with eastern territory ruled by the Ran clan. Though their lands were separated by a mountain, the two sides still exchanged goods much more frequently than with the far-off imperial capital. Hence, when Ran Rinki made an incognito trip to the township, Lord Koh had given him a warm welcome.

Yet he had come bearing an unforeseen threat, as well as a deal.

"*You're committing tax fraud, aren't you?*" he'd begun, as if making a round of small talk. "*You're falsifying the census to reduce your taxes. It's a good idea when the crops are abundant, but there's been a cold spell this year. If the census numbers are less than your actual population, you'll get less congee from the capital, and your people will starve. I imagine your subjects won't be very happy about that.*"

At first, Lord Koh had kept his cool. He had his trump card of the Untouchable Village to make the townspeople's discontent disappear. However, Rinki's main point lied in the next thing he'd said.

"*Also, this region was chosen as the site for this year's Harvest Festival. Our crown prince is a very diligent man. He'll be sure to look into the history of the township chosen as his destination. And then...you know what will happen."*

Lord Koh felt like he'd just been plunged into a dark abyss. Even a backwater magistrate like him knew how brilliant Prince Gyoumei was. What would happen if the prince were to conduct a detailed investigation into the region? If his fraud were exposed to the state?

Placing a hand on Lord Koh's shoulder as he lapsed into silence, Rinki had smiled and gone on, *"We are neighbors. I have a proposition for you."*

His plan had gone as follows.

First was to divert the townspeople's frustrations by setting up Shu Keigetsu as the bad guy. He just had to tie the cold spell and lack of congee back to her dearth of talent.

Next was to abduct Shu Keigetsu during the Harvest Festival. He could kill her or torment her—it didn't make a difference. What mattered was that he drew everyone's attention in that direction. That way, the crown prince would be forced to split his attention and inevitably relax his investigation into the tax issue.

"We'll be partners in this. You'll maintain your clean reputation, and we'll get to ruin Shu Keigetsu. Once this is all over, we'll even welcome you as the magistrate of an eastern township much larger than this one."

The carrot that came after the stick had sounded irresistibly sweet to Lord Koh's ears. As rich in wood qi as it was, the eastern territory never had a bad harvest. The townspeople were docile and submissive, which supposedly made it a very easy region to govern. Lord Koh had never felt much attachment to his own backwater township beyond the fact that it made tax evasion easy. He believed without question that his talents would be better served in a larger, more prosperous area.

If he took Ran Rinki's hand, he could avoid ruin. No, even better—he would be entrusted with the rich lands of the eastern territory. It wasn't his own territory, no, but it was a region he'd had plenty of dealings with. He was sure it would work out.

Or so I thought...but the plan is in ruins.

In practice, as one only familiar with the world of bureaucrats, Lord Koh had underestimated the skills of the military officers. He'd never imagined that Kou Keikou would tag along to protect the Maiden. He'd assumed that if he planted a tassel, the Gen clan would become the target of the investigation. To make matters worse, he'd heard reports that, despite leading the search, the Eagle Eyes' captain Shin-u had headed into the village all on his own.

The perpetrators were coming to light several times faster than Lord Koh had planned.

In retrospect, he regretted drawing up that makeshift contract to force the job onto the village chief's son. He'd counted on being able to "silence" the man after the fact, but with the crown prince's eyes perpetually on him, he couldn't do anything that might arouse suspicion.

I have to dispose of the whole village before Kou Keikou or the captain finds out about the contract.

Time was of the essence, but he didn't have a way forward. If the untouchables were to suddenly die now, all it would do was attract even more attention.

"What do we do? If the truth gets out, you won't get away unscathed either. If I'm apprehended, you'll go down with me as my accomplice."

Rinki gave a light shrug in the face of Lord Koh's threat. "Oh dear, no need to glare at me like that after I prepared the perfect solution for you." Then, he fished something from his breast. It was a small, folded piece of paper.

"What is this?"

"A threatening letter from the untouchables who kidnapped Shu Keigetsu."

Lord Koh cocked his head, skeptical.

"Or so the story goes. It's fabricated, of course," Rinki added. "The kidnappers' demands are written here. 'The cold spell has impoverished our village, and disease is spreading. Hence, we abducted the Maiden. If you don't want her to die, send us medicine' is more or less the gist of it."

Lord Koh made a dubious face at the sudden mention of "disease," but he figured out the intent soon enough. "I see... So we provide ourselves a justification for burning the village to the ground."

"Exactly. We can't have them bringing disease to a township where someone so exalted is staying. You'll have no more grounds to protect the untouchables you've left alive out of the kindness of your heart, and thus will the ever-rational magistrate steel his heart and set fire to the village. The end."

"But what about Shu Keigetsu and her military officer, Lord Kou Keikou?"

"We'll say the Maiden took her own life in despair after she was defiled by the untouchables. Lord Keikou followed suit for the crime of failing to protect her," Rinki smoothly explained as Lord Koh nodded his head along.

It was true that a Maiden prized her chastity above all else. It would make sense for her to commit suicide if she were kidnapped by untouchables and even came down with a disease. Her military officer likewise wouldn't be able to face the crown prince if he shamelessly allowed a Maiden to be violated and catch ill.

I see. If it's too difficult to silence them in secret, it's better to dispose of them out in the open and make up an excuse for it.

All that washed over Lord Koh was relief and admiration. Not a single pang of remorse.

"Still, untouchables don't usually write letters. Won't His Highness get suspicious if we burn down the village based only on a single ransom demand?" he asked cautiously. "If by chance Kou Keikou survives and testifies that there was no disease—"

"Don't worry about that." Rinki narrowed his gaze with a smile. "I've already spread the sickness."

"You what...?"

"Hee hee. During the pre-celebration, I incited an untouchable to bring the source of the sickness back to the village. Though *they* won't know where it started, of course. I believe the disease should be making the rounds as we speak," said the fair-skinned man, beaming with delight.

It seemed he'd already had this "solution" in place since the pre-celebration. Lord Koh felt a tinge of irritation that Rinki had hidden so much of his hand from his so-called accomplice. Still, since that far-sighted scheming had saved his own hide, Lord Koh had no choice but to butter him up.

"You're a force to be reckoned with."

"Hardly. My *master* is the one who came up with the idea."

"The patriarch of the Ran clan, I assume? I've heard he's a man of sharp intellect indeed. Seeing what a keen mind his son has, I'm sure the Ran clan's future is in good hands. That's a world of difference from the Shu clan, who put all their hopes on Noble Consort Shu—a *woman*."

Lord Koh had a much higher opinion of the Ran clan compared to the Shu main line and their constant dependence on women.

It had been an effort to play on Rinki's ego, but the man just smiled thinly. "Why, thank you."

Was it Lord Koh's imagination, or did he see a hint of disdain in those intelligent eyes?

"Now then, my dear magistrate. I need you to 'coincidentally' summon the ceremonial officers of the Kin and Gen clans. Tell them you received the aforementioned ransom demand and want to make the deal in private so as not to trouble His Highness, but that you wouldn't feel safe with only the township guards to protect you. Ask them to come with you to the meeting place. Then, if an unsuspecting untouchable shows up and tells you all about the disease—well, I trust you can figure the rest out?"

"So the idea is to have the ceremonial officers bear witness to the disease running rampant in the village."

"Exactly. Someone with the status and credibility of a military officer will make for the perfect witness here. It would be inconvenient to bring someone as sharp-witted as His Highness along, so we're looking for people easier to manipulate. I'm sure the Gen whose clan is being framed for the crime will be especially eager to attend the meeting."

Lord Koh furrowed his brow as he briefly chewed over the plan. "What about the untouchables? Do you really think a villager will conveniently show up to explain the situation?"

"Oh, he will. This is exactly why I've been having him report to me in the mountains in exchange for food."

Rinki took a handkerchief from his breast to wipe the incense from his hands but, struck with a sudden idea, he wrapped it around his face instead.

"'Oh, you finally made it, Unran!'" When Rinki whined pathetically with his face half-hidden like that, his delicate features worked to make him look like a first-class coward. "Or something like that," he said, pulling the cloth away with a chuckle.

A shiver running down his spine at the young man's unfathomable behavior, Lord Koh chose to cut the conversation short when he saw a bird flapping its wings across the sky. "Is that right? Then I'll go call for the military officers posthaste."

"You do that. Oh, but don't include the ceremonial officer from the Kou clan. He has close ties to His Highness."

"Understood."

Ending the conversation there, the pair exchanged polite nods and took their leave. From a distance, they surely looked like nothing more than a magistrate and a military officer who had been kneeling in prayer of the Maiden's safe return.

Lord Koh went back to his estate, failing to notice that when the bird soaring across the sky—a dove—reached its destination at the top of the drum tower, a certain someone standing there turned to look in his direction.

8 | Reirin Nurses

Upon returning from the bath, Reirin and Shin-u quietly gasped at the sight that awaited them in the chief's hut.

"Urp!"

"Blegh..."

People were vomiting into tubs, their backs hunched over. Many had stained the bottoms of their garments, a horrible stench filled the air, and the agonized wails of children and infants echoed throughout the room.

"We've had food poisoning in the summer before, but we've never had everyone collapse one after another so suddenly. It'd be scarier for everyone if we kept them apart, so I gathered all the sick in one place for a start."

"What is...?" Reirin murmured, stunned, as did Shin-u.

"Dysentery," Keikou answered them from a corner of the room. He had wrapped a cloth around the bottom half of his face, and he was passing out tubs to the villagers who were retching nonstop. "No matter how humid it is, there hasn't been much sun this summer. I doubt heatstroke caused this. It's either food poisoning or water poisoning."

Reirin frowned. "Dysentery... I didn't know it could progress so fast."

Dysentery is the general term for illnesses whose main symptom is severe diarrhea. Mild food poisoning and life-threatening infectious diseases can both fall under this umbrella. Given the amount of vomiting, not to mention how many people had come down with it at once, this appeared to be a case of the latter.

Among the afflicted were some of the women who had asked to split their boar meat earlier. It hadn't even been a few hours since then. If such a rapid progression was left unchecked, there was a chance the entire village would fall ill within a few days.

But why? Could it be...the boar we cut up earlier?

The thought flashed across her mind for a fleeting moment, but no, the onset of the disease had been too fast for that to be the explanation. Besides, if the raw meat had caused it, it wouldn't make sense for Reirin and her men to be fine when they'd been the ones doing most of the handling.

"We still don't know what caused it, but it sounds like Old Kyou and Gouryuu have been suffering chest pains and diarrhea since last night. Those ladies were probably sick this morning too, but they just hadn't realized it yet," Keikou suggested.

That made Reirin think back to the woman who had mentioned her husband catching a cold.

"If all these people looked after their families in that condition... I imagine we're going to have a few more patients on our hands."

"Yeah. I've seen stuff like this happen in the army. If we can't nip it in the bud now, it's going to turn into a real problem."

Having several years of experience with communal living on unsanitary battlefields, Keikou knew how to keep his cool in situations like this. Despite not even hailing from a line of doctors, he had such a strong caretaker nature that he even served as a pseudomilitary physician. Some of Reirin's knowledge of medicinal herbs had come from her brother's introductory teachings.

"You haven't been drinking unboiled water, have you?" Keikou asked Reirin. The sharp look he shot her was a big departure from his usual broad-minded attitude.

She shook her head. "No. I haven't consumed anything except the food I've obtained for myself. Nor have I touched my mouth with unwashed hands, as I've been instructed since I was little."

"Don't even touch your mouth with *washed* hands in here. Any water we use has to be boiled."

"I know. I should still have the stork's bill weed I picked in the forest. I'll go make a decoction."

"Please do. I'll do what I can to keep the vomit and feces from flying all over the place."

"Be careful. I'll bring you some boiled water later. Liquor too, if we have any."

"Thanks."

The siblings each confirmed their respective roles through that short exchange.

Reirin turned on her heel and headed for where she'd left her herbs outside, firing off orders all the while. "Is there any strong liquor in this village, Unran? If there's any that's been distilled multiple times, please bring it here at once. Captain, prepare some firewood. Could I ask you to fetch some water from the river—preferably upstream—and boil it in large quantities?"

"I'll help, sure. But...is a Maiden like you really going to tend to these villagers?" Shin-u asked in a stern voice.

Reirin cast him a quick glance over her shoulder. "Is there any reason not to?"

"Of course there is. Show some more awareness of your exalted status. Do you *want* to get sick?"

"You're right. I mustn't allow *this body* to fall ill. Hence why I'm going to tend to them," she asserted to the same Eagle Eyes' captain whose presence could overwhelm a grown man, putting a hand to her chest. "Disease—and especially dysentery—can spread in the blink of an eye through excrement, vomit, and contaminated water and food. This is a small village. It's precisely because I want to protect myself that I must act before the sickness can spread to the whole area."

Neither her voice nor her eyes wavered. Her slender body exuded a will reminiscent of the solid earth, and that strength was enough to overpower even Shin-u.

She didn't want to save the people in front of her out of some fleeting sense of morality. It was an instinct coated in resolution. No matter how he tried to argue with her, she would refute him in an instant.

If nothing else, she seemed to have enough self-control to not endanger Shu Keigetsu's body. In that case, he had no choice but to give her a warning and watch over her to ensure she didn't fall victim to disease.

Once he'd done those swift calculations in his head, Shin-u nodded. "But if you do anything even a little bit reckless, I'm taking you straight back to the township, even if it means throwing you over my shoulder and crossing the mountain to do it."

"Thank you very much. I'd be willing to accompany you half of the way to pick some herbs, at least." She dismissed even the greatest concession he could make with a tinkle of a laugh, then urged him one more time, "Please get us that boiled water as soon as possible. You're going to devote your every effort to me, aren't you?"

"I am? Since when?" As indignant as he was, he complied.

"Hey." When Reirin made to head through the doorway for a second time, it was Unran who called out to her. "This...is just a mild illness, right? Everyone's going to get better soon?"

There was a hint of tension in his reddish-brown eyes that not even his forced smile could obscure. The real question he'd stopped himself from asking was clear: *"This isn't a curse, is it?"*

"Unran." Reirin turned around and met his gaze. Resisting the urge to reach out and caress his cheek, she said as slowly as she could, "We still don't know the severity, scope, or cause of this sickness. All we know is that if we don't take proper care of those who are currently suffering, the disease will spread even further. Looking at it another way, if we do what needs to be done here, we can control the spread."

"..."

Those willful eyes of his wavered with emotion. When she saw that, Reirin realized that these villagers weren't used to "facing" these frightening, unknown situations.

The people of the southern territory were rich in emotions. While their abundance of imagination surely lent itself to dabbling in the Daoist arts, it could also make them too in tune to the suffering of others, breed fear, or even birth hatred from that fear.

"Unran... Isn't this happening...'cause you went into the Cursed Forest?" a weak voice suddenly rang out from the back of the room.

The one who had spat those words in a quivering voice was a woman clutching a tub. She had been the first one to ask for some boar meat earlier.

Drool trickling from the edges of her mouth, she pointed a trembling finger at Unran. "Didn't we all get sick...right after we cut up those boars?"

"The chief died after he ate a deer from the Cursed Forest. We shouldn't have messed with the forest...after all..."

Adults who had been curled up all throughout the hut raised their faces one by one. Tubs in their hands, they glared at Unran with bloodshot eyes and faces full of resentment. All this despite laughing with him, slapping him on the shoulder, and dressing boars alongside him just hours ago.

"The hell..." Unran said in a voice low enough to sound like a moan, gritting his teeth. "You were all convinced the curse was a lie just earlier. You all admitted that the chief didn't die to a curse but because of some kind of insect or poison."

Almost like this comment had set them off, the villagers around them grew even more vehement.

"Then why are we all sick when we haven't even eaten the boar yet?!"

"The big shots who said there's no curse are just outsiders! They don't get that there really are curses in this village—in this world! *Hurk!*"

"This is divine punishment! It's all because we didn't punish Shu Keigetsu... We're all suffering divine punishment because you let that villainess trick you into waltzing into the Cursed Forest!"

"This is all because of you and Shu Keigetsu!"

They must have been suffering. They must have been in pain. Since their feelings were so easily influenced, they couldn't help but expel their emotions outward when they were pushed over the edge.

And their hatred given shape would spread.

Much stronger and faster than any disease.

Just like a darkness fell over the rice paddies when clouds blocked the sun, the eyes of all those in the room were stained with the color of hate.

Unran turned around and cast a pleading look toward his uncle on instinct, only to gasp at what he saw. The man who had always come to his defense when all was said and done was now glaring at him with an ashen face.

"Give me a break..." Gouryuu seemed to be deep in pain as he clutched his tub. His breath coming in ragged gasps, he screamed at Unran like he couldn't hold it in anymore. "Would you and my brother both give me a goddamn break?! Stop wreaking disaster on the rest of us!"

"Uncle Gou—"

"Didn't I try to stop you, huh?! You and Brother both! Yet you both went into the Cursed Forest anyway, looking so goddamn proud of yourselves as you spread your misfortune everywhere! I'm sick of cleaning up your messes!"

Gouryuu's insults utterly crushed Unran's spirit.

He was gruff, but a good-natured coward. Even if he complained, he'd never spoken ill of either Tairyuu or Unran. Unran didn't want to believe *that* was how he'd felt about him all this time.

"That's right! Like father, like son—both of them do something stupid and rash and end up causing havoc for the rest of us!"

"Our first mistake was ever accepting an unwanted child like you into our village!"

"We don't even know which townsman's son you are! You damned half-blood!"

"You and Shu Keigetsu did this!"

The other villagers joined Gouryuu in shouting whatever they pleased, having lost sight of the plot.

"Don't make the village suffer! Get out, curse man!"

Swoosh!

Caught up in the emotion of the moment, a child took the flint lying next to the stove and threw it at Unran. It was the same boy who had told Reirin about the Cursed Forest just the other day.

"Look out!" Reirin jumped out in front of Unran to shield him.

Shing!

But the rock never hit her. It fell to the ground, spraying a few sparks.

"You've all got a lot of spirit."

Shin-u had drawn his sword and deflected the stone.

"If you've got the strength to be throwing stones, I assume you don't need to be tended to. Get out. Go die a dog's death." The captain had coolly but mercilessly threatened a child.

The boy snapped back to his senses, burst into tears with a squeak, and covered his head in a feeble attempt to protect himself.

A silence fell over the hut, followed by a woman's voice. "Everyone, please calm down."

It was Reirin.

She grabbed the boy's trembling arms and gently set them down by his sides. "It's true that the mind grows vicious when the body is in pain. All the same, you mustn't waste your strength on getting angry right now."

The boy looked up at the Maiden with a start. No, not just him—all the other adults in the room did too. Neither tearful nor enraged over her treatment, the gentle tones of her voice somehow seemed to ooze into their ears.

"It's fine if you want to assign blame for this illness. But please blame me, not Unran. Aren't I the terrible villainess who brings disaster to the southern territory?"

Yet far from a villainess, she smiled with the quiet dignity of the priestess who passed on the will of the dragon.

When no one said anything back, she looked at everyone in the room one by one. "Do you want revenge? Do you want someone to blame, throw stones at, and curse? Then be my guest. But all that must wait until after you've recovered."

Even those who had been vomiting too much to look up from their tubs stared back at the Maiden, forgetting their symptoms for a fleeting moment in the face of her powerful presence.

"I have the name of 'Shu Keigetsu' at stake. Upon this glorious name, I swear I shall not let even a single one of your lives slip through my fingers," said the so-called talentless girl dressed in old hand-me-downs who nevertheless exuded the dignity of a ruler. "Do prepare yourselves. I plan to hold your noses and pour enough decoctions down your throats to leave you drowning."

She then turned on her heel, grabbed the petrified Unran by the arm, and marched out the door.

"Unran, I'm going to boil some stork's bill weed. I want you to go around to every house in the village, gather up liquor, and look for more victims," she said, glancing back at the man who had let her drag him out of the hut without putting up a fight. When she made it to where the herbs were hanging from the eaves, she briskly gathered the ones known to work against diarrhea into a draining basket. "Dysentery is largely transmitted through excrement, fingers that have touched said filth, and water. Be sure to bring those who have exhibited symptoms to the hut to isolate them. And take care not to touch your mouth when you do."

"…"

"Cover your mouth and nose. Don't touch any vomit or waste. Wash your hands with alcohol and boiled water as often as possible. As long as we take proper precautions, we won't catch ill from tending to the sick."

"What's the point?" Unran muttered from where he stood behind her. His voice was shaking like never before. "Why even bother with all that?"

"Oh, Unran..."

"This village is always like that. They'll turn to you, depend on you, and then the moment you stop being useful, toss you aside and resent you. Sure, they'll be grateful if you save their lives...but if even one person dies, it'll be all your fault!"

His tone shifted from strangled to a bloodcurdling cry. Reirin heard him out without turning around.

"They'll turn to you like it's nothing, and they'll hate you like it's nothing! What's the point of working so hard to please them?! I'll always be an outsider. All the chief's work will be meaningless!"

She was sure he wouldn't want her to see him abandoning all traces of his aloof attitude and letting tears blur his vision.

"No matter how much you run yourself ragged—"

"You mustn't wipe your tears with your hands, Unran," she said just as he was about to scrub his face in frustration. When Unran froze, shocked that she almost had eyes in the back of her head, she reached a hand to the eaves and slowly went on, "You mustn't rub your eyes. You mustn't blow your nose either. That's how the disease spreads. If a tear falls from your eyes, dry it by looking up to the sky."

"Wha..."

"Those tending to the sick—those working to save others—don't have the time to cry."

Her voice was tender, yet there was a sternness to it that would brook no argument.

Unran fell completely silent. Reirin considered something for a moment, then brushed away the soil clinging to an herb. "I happen to know someone who's a very proud man—a born ruler of sorts."

"There's no point leaving out his name. It's obviously the emperor or crown prince," Unran muttered.

Reirin brushed his comment aside. "The thing that makes him proud is his sense of responsibility. He's tough on those he deems his enemies, but he's exceptionally kind to the weak. Whether they're criminals or have a complicated lineage, whether they're fools or rebels, he'll hold them in his arms and protect them as if it were the most natural thing in the world."

He was stubborn, and he wouldn't hesitate to subject even a woman to death by beast if she was his enemy. Still, he was an honest man who was harder on himself for his mistakes than most and who always kept his promises. Just thinking about the devoted yet sometimes awkward prince brought a smile to her face.

"And he never asks the people he protects to love him back. He simply protects those he must protect because it's the right thing to do." At that, she finally turned around to meet Unran's stare. "See, Unran, a ruler doesn't protect his people because they respect him. He protects them because they are his people. Wasn't your father the same way?"

A ruler.

That word penetrated Unran to his core.

She's right...

No matter how much Unran rebelled against his father, the chief had continued to protect him. So too had he patiently led the villagers who were so emotional and quick to complain. No matter the hardships he had to face, no matter how much unreasonable abuse his so-called community heaped on him, his father had been a "ruler" until the very end.

"Unran," the girl called out to him, as solemnly as if she were performing a rite. "You must live true to your name."

As she looked him straight in the eyes, Unran felt something that had been coiled deep inside his heart spring into motion.

"Unran."

His own name echoed through his mind.

Unran. One who bears the dragon in his name.

He who shelters the ruler of the Heavens in the abundant clouds and guides the lush mountain air. He had a feeling his name was pointing him to the path he should take.

I'm going to protect this village.

Even if no one thanked him for it, even if they cast stones at him for it. Even if they never saw him as one of their own. He'd do it because he was the village's "ruler," the one his father had appointed his successor. It felt like a light had suddenly broken through the clouds. His view of the world expanding before his eyes, Unran steeled his resolve as a matter of course.

"I see you've calmed down." The girl flashed Unran an impish smile as he exhaled a slow breath. "Come now, time is of the essence. Go take a look around the village. Let's do this with a bang."

"Yeah." Unran nodded, feeling a heat beginning to burn in his chest as he placed a hand to it. It was a heat that called his whole being to action.

As someone who had spent his life wandering the village, he knew who would be doing what and where like the back of his hand. He needed to check on all the villagers within the hour and root out those who weren't feeling well. His duty came to him so easily now.

Also... That's right, I have to report to Rin.

Having regained his composure, he suddenly remembered about the envoy from the township—that young man who seemed like such a cowardly pushover. He was supposed to meet him in the mountains tonight.

He did say I could come to him for help if the situation got out of hand.

He recalled what Rin had said to him. It was no doubt part of his carrot and stick approach, but if nothing else, that meant he valued Unran enough to try and win him over. If he took advantage of that and negotiated well, maybe he'd be able to get medicine or a doctor out of the man.

As Unran watched the girl so industriously gather up herbs in those slender arms and shake them free of soil, he clenched his hands into fists. He wanted to do more than just watch her from behind and get protected.

"I'm going to take a look around the village. Once that's done, I'm going up the mountain one more time."

She glanced back at him, concerned. "What? It'll be nightfall soon."

"As you know, I've got good night vision. You need a bunch of these herbs, right? I'll go pick some more." He nodded vigorously.

"But—"

"As long as I've got a torch, I'll be fine. That forest is basically my home. Hell, maybe I'll be able to bring back something even better."

He would threaten the township via the envoy and get his hands on more herbs. He was sure he could do it.

The girl leaned toward him. "Unran..."

"'Let's do this with a bang,' right?" he replied, silencing her with her own catchphrase. When her face fell with worry, Unran lifted the corners of his mouth into a smile. "I could stand to learn from your cheekiness."

"A-am I cheeky?"

"How else would you describe a woman who can take all those insults without batting an eye?" He left her at a loss for words, turning on his heel. "I'm off, then."

Unran raised a hand in farewell before slinking off like a cat.

"Goodness." Reirin sighed softly as she watched him disappear into the distance without the slightest trace of hesitation. "There's no stopping those with strong fire qi once they've made up their minds."

In her mind's eye, she saw images of Leelee and Keigetsu alongside Unran.

The residents of the southern territory had intense personalities. They were impressionable and quick to hate, but at their core, they had profound faith in other people. And they ran straight ahead with a burning love in their hearts.

"He called me cheeky."

Reirin giggled, then turned back to the eaves of the house. For a while, she went back to adding the herbs dangling there to her draining basket, until all of a sudden, she let a few plop to the ground.

"Ah..."

She almost picked up the herbs with an "Oh no," but she found herself holding her tongue.

The fingers she'd reached for them were ever so slightly trembling.

"How embarrassing."

Reirin clenched her hands into fists and pressed them to her chest, but it did nothing to stop them from shaking. She couldn't let anyone see her like this.

I'm sorry, Unran. Despite the pompous lecture I just gave you, when the villagers berated me... She bit her lip. *I was sad.*

Reirin could still feel the hands of the boy she'd soothed against her fingers. His arms were small, warm, and had once reached out for her in concern. Yet with that same hand, he had cast stones at her.

I was such a fool.

As she gazed down at where her herbs lay sprawled over the ground, the voices of the villagers played back in her mind.

"Well, aren't you kids having the time of your lives?!"

"Would you mind sharing some of that boar with me?"

"Do you want some of my hand-me-downs?"

The more she talked to them, the more jovial the villagers had seemed. They'd laughed with their mouths wide open and gotten friendly enough to hug her around the shoulders. The moment they'd shared food and clothes with each other, Reirin was sure they had become friends.

"I was a big idiot."

She couldn't even force her lips into a rueful smile.

Why did I get so complacent?

Reirin was so sure they had come to trust her. Some part of her had believed that if she always received people with cheer and met them with sincerity, she could make friends with anyone. She could survive even a torrent of malice—because she had the determination and backbone to have fun in any situation. She had entertained that delusion.

"That doesn't have to be a bad thing! Just picture the critter and its adorable little squeak!"

"I get a little excited when people don't like me."

Reirin grimaced as she thought back on the things she'd said in the past.

"I was so wrong..."

I'm sorry, she muttered to Keigetsu in her heart.

She keenly wished she could apologize in that moment.

Has Lady Keigetsu harbored these feelings in her heart all this time? I had no idea. I didn't know being hated by someone could be so terrifying...and so sad.

The reason she was so afraid to be hated was no doubt because she had taken a liking to them. She'd let them into her heart and offered them her affections. That was why it hurt so much to not have those feelings returned.

Keigetsu was so afraid of being hated because of how strongly she yearned for others. She loved people from the bottom of her heart. It had taken Reirin so long to realize something so obvious.

"..."

She balled her hands into fists.

The villagers' glares hit her all the harder for having seen their warm smiles before. Their voices had been filled with hatred, and their arms had pitched stones without hesitation. Reirin was ashamed to realize their relationship was so shallow that this was all it had taken for them to turn on her.

Reirin stared at the ground for some time, but as soon as she registered that she was hanging her head, she lifted both hands and slowly bopped her cheeks.

"Chin up."

That was a vow she'd made a long time ago.

Chest out, deep breaths, gaze forward.

She had to do things with a bang—and always keep a smile on her face. Otherwise, how was her mother supposed to rest in peace?

"I'm fine."

If she said that to herself, her emotions would eventually catch up to the words.

Reirin lifted her head and forced her usual smile onto her face. That gentle, tender smile so overflowing with hope.

I swear to protect both Unran and this entire village.

A ruler protected his people. Even if his feelings weren't returned. Then the same applied to the Maidens who supported that ruler.

"You had it backward, Unran. I'm the one who should learn from you."

Despite being hurt much more deeply than her, Unran had managed to get right back up again. However much comfort he had derived from her humble words, the courage his attitude had given Reirin had to be equal to or even greater than that.

Besides, this body belonged to Keigetsu. Reirin couldn't tarnish her name by sitting back and letting the villagers die.

"Let's do this with a bang."

Her hands weren't trembling anymore. Reirin picked up the herbs for real this time, squeezing the bundle she had gathered up into her hands.

It made her sad to be hated. She understood that now. Still, she'd already decided to protect them. She would make sure they heard her feelings loud and clear.

"Dysentery is a very painful disease. I'm sure the people who insulted my darling Unran were suffering so much they simply lost control of their emotions."

Snap snap snap!

337

The roots and grass tore with a muffled sound.

"I'd better make them the most bitter and potent medicine I can."

The glint of a strong will dwelled in her eyes as she looked upon her herbs.

"I'll cure you all in a single night," Reirin muttered darkly before heading back inside.

"Looks like I made it first tonight."

Upon arriving at the meeting place—the entrance to the Cursed Forest—Unran wiped his sweat and caught his breath. He was physically exhausted after all the running he'd done to that point, but his heart was filled with a sense of accomplishment like never before.

He estimated the time by looking up at the moon hidden behind a thin layer of clouds. It must have been about six hours since he'd told Shu Keigetsu he was heading off. For that entire length of time, he'd worked himself to the bone going around the village, bringing patients and liquor back to the hut, heading into the mountains, and picking herbs. It might have been the first time in his life he'd spent a full day applying himself so hard.

Though he had to shrug at his own out-of-character behavior, he clutched a hand to his chest in the same motion. That was where he was keeping one more example of uncharacteristic sentimentality.

"Watch over me, Chief."

Wrapped in a shabby cloth and tucked into the breast of his garment was a small splinter of rock. It was the "blade" that the Maiden had turned on him when he tried to assault her—the one that had flaked off because of his father's fire. It had been stained with both her blood and the blood of boars, but Unran had rinsed it off in the river and secretly taken it home with him.

Now he'd decided to treat it as a memento of Tairyuu.

I bet she'd say, "Oh my, what a lovely memento. It can make for either a flint or a blade."

He gave a little chuckle as he thought of the slightly off-kilter Maiden who was pragmatic in the strangest of ways. The girl who was supposed to be the talentless, disaster-wreaking sewer rat of the southern territory. Despite the facts, he found himself placing all of his hopes on her. Seeing her gentle smile and steadfast courage in the face of all adversity filled him with courage.

Everything was going to be fine. He could push through any predicament eventually.

"Oh, I'm sorry to have kept you waiting. I was just so busy with work."

It was then that Unran saw a flicker of light from behind the bushes, and with it came a man holding a torch. It was Rin, the envoy from the township. His face was swathed in black cloth like always, and he opened the conversation with some casual small talk.

Unran cut him short and got right down to business. "There's a disease going around the village. If you don't want me to show our contract to the prince, send us medicine and a doctor."

"Huh?" An expression of such blank surprise rose to Rin's face that it was discernible even through the cloth. "Sorry, a disease? What? What about the contract?"

"It's dysentery. It's spreading like wildfire. This is no time to be tormenting Shu Keigetsu." As Rin fell speechless, Unran leaned forward to threaten him. "We're backing out of the punishment, but we still have the contract. The one that proves you coerced us into the crime. I'm telling you to bring us medicine if you don't want it going public."

Rin looked stunned for a few moments, but once it dawned on him that Unran meant business, he visibly started to panic. "Y-you can't spring this on us so suddenly... You're accomplices to the crime, and the ones who actually carried it out. If you sell us out, you'll be punished too!"

"Yeah. But we'll take you down with us," Unran shot back smoothly.

The envoy looked lost for words, but eventually he opened his mouth to moan, "I...I don't have the authority to make that call."

"I'll bet not. So could you hurry back to the township and let Lord Koh know? Tell him to bring medicine and a doctor here by noon tomorrow. That'll give him half a day. If he refuses, I'll make sure the crown prince finds out—"

"I'd rather not," Rin cut in, casting Unran a pleading look. "Could you inform the magistrate yourself?"

"'Scuse me?"

"As I believe I mentioned yesterday, I brought the magistrate to the foot of the mountain tonight. Though it turned into a bit of a pompous affair, since he brought a few guards with him." When Unran looked surprised to hear this, he explained, "The magistrate has been really concerned about all this too. And he has all the more reason to be if there's an illness going around. You're always so quick to threaten us with the contract, but the township would consider a disease ravaging the village a big deal on its own merits."

"Wow, is our esteemed magistrate so distressed by the plight of us untouchables?" Unran said with a hint of sarcasm.

Rin gave a solemn shake of his head. "It's not that. The crown prince and Maidens are staying in the township right now...all very important dignitaries."

The township and village were separated by only a single suspension bridge. If disease was running rampant in the village, there was no telling when it might spread to the town. If by chance the crown prince fell ill, the responsibility for that would fall on the township's shoulders.

Unran smirked as he considered how much the magistrate would panic if he heard about the disease. It was annoying to think the man cared more about a select few people getting sick than an entire village's plight, but it's not like he couldn't understand the logic.

He agreed to meet with the magistrate right away. There wasn't much time. He headed for the foot of the mountain with Rin. Though he stayed alert to his surroundings, he made it to a forest clearing without a single ambush along the way.

"Good. You made it."

There stood Lord Koh, the pale-blue moonlight to his back. He looked the part of an upright man, speaking politely to even an untouchable and standing with impeccable posture. Still, Unran was dismayed to find a handful of men with bows and swords standing behind him—probably the "guards" Rin had mentioned—and all hiding their faces in cloth to boot.

Rin hid his face because he didn't want an untouchable like Unran to know what he looked like, but what reason did Lord Koh and his guards have to disguise themselves?

"We had to sneak out without His Highness catching us. We decided to wear disguises to make ourselves a little harder to spot," Rin whispered from behind Unran, picking up on his confusion.

It seemed like a pretty makeshift disguise to Unran, but he understood why they wouldn't want the prince finding out about their deal. Lord Koh seemed awfully concerned with what the monarch was going to do. In which case, Unran was starting to think Rin might have been right that stressing the severity of the outbreak was a better move than going on about the contract.

"We're not friendly enough to bother with long-winded introductions," Lord Koh began. "Let's start with what you have to say."

"There's a disease spreading around the village," Unran said, getting straight to the point. "It's dysentery. The vomiting and diarrhea won't stop. People are collapsing one after another, young and old alike. It sounds like the illness isn't any sort of curse but something passed on through vomit and contaminated water."

He was careful to keep his tone calm. He had to emphasize that he knew the sickness wasn't the result of any curse or

misfortune but had an identifiable cause and a path to spread—
that he couldn't be manipulated through fear anymore.

"We're making do with herbs we picked from the mountain,
but that's not enough. Share the herbs stored in the township
with us. We need nutritious food and a doctor too. Or else..."

At this point, Unran had the choice to threaten him by either
flaunting the contract or hinting at the infection spreading to the
township.

Before he could decide, the magistrate asked, "Are you sure
you aren't exaggerating?"

"What?"

"All the herbs in our possession are top-notch items purchased
from the agriculturally advanced eastern territory. Are you sure
you aren't just making a fuss over this disease to rob us of our
supply and line your pockets?"

Unran's eyebrows shot up in disgust. "Like hell I'd do that."

Perhaps Lord Koh saw the untouchables' plight as someone
else's problem after all. Or maybe he was trying to make the situation
appear less dire to the men around him.

Whatever the case, the best way to scare him would be to
stress the severity of the illness and emphasize its possible impact
on the township. "The whole village is suffering. Men who were
walking around in good health just hours ago are writhing in pain
and spraying their crap everywhere. The kids are crying and the
women are haggard. At this rate, every last villager will die."

The magistrate and the men behind him gasped. Unran
leaned in even closer.

"Don't act like this isn't your problem. Dysentery is transmitted through water. The village and township are separated by a river, but guess what? That means it runs through both of our homes. We use the same water for our rice paddies and daily necessities. Don't you get what that means?"

The moment Unran took that verbal shot, the magistrate's expression grew grim and he glanced back at the men behind him. "This is an emergency. Please report what this man said word for word to His Highness. You can leave my page and this gentleman here to protect me."

"Yes, sir!" they promptly replied, then ran off toward the township, leaving only Rin and a single bow-wielding page behind.

"Well said, Unran, son of the chief."

Once Lord Koh had made sure his guards were gone, he turned back to Unran and held his head high. The solemn air about him was enough to bring Rin to his knees beside him.

Not the least bit offended by the way Unran was standing stunned, he said, "We'll make arrangements for those herbs. A doctor and some food too."

"What about Shu Keigetsu?"

"Don't bother with her anymore. You're free to back out of the deal. I'll work out a way to cut your taxes as well." It was a once-in-a-lifetime bargain. As Unran's eyes went round, Lord Koh flashed him a benevolent smile. "Even the Untouchable Village is part of the township. It's important to take steps to deal with a health crisis. I'll likewise take measures to ensure the village isn't implicated in what happened to Shu Keigetsu. I apologize for having taken advantage of you."

He was such a man of character that Unran didn't know how to react. He'd assumed the magistrate to be an arrogant man who only wore a false mask of virtue, but it seemed his dignity as a politician shone through in the right situations. Unran was struck with the sense that this man was likewise the "ruler" of his township.

"Now then. I'll have the herbs delivered later, so head back to the village for the time being. I'm sure everyone is anxiously awaiting your return."

"Will do."

It was hard to talk tough with the magistrate being so nice to him. Regardless, it seemed this man was the sort to maintain a polite demeanor even with the untouchables. Unran didn't know if the man's concept of morality was to blame or if he was just drunk on his own virtue, but as long as it stood to benefit him, he didn't care which.

This way, I'll be able to protect the village without putting everything on her.

Feeling relief and a sense of satisfaction, he picked up the basket of medicinal herbs he'd set down.

"Oh, one more thing, Lord Koh. Now that we've given up on the punishment, when can we let Shu Keigetsu—"

Thud!

In that moment, Unran felt an impact in his chest and landed hard on his back. Both his basket and herbs went flying, and he felt a burning heat along his side.

"Goodness, why did you have to turn around all of a sudden? You made me miss," came Rin's repulsive mutter as he wrung his hands.

An arrow was sticking out of Unran's chest where he lay on the ground, while a dagger was lodged in his flank. It took him a few moments to understand that the page had shot him in the heart and Rin had stabbed him in the side.

"Urk... Guh...!"

Rin kicked him away like a piece of trash as he writhed in pain. He crouched down beside the wheezing village man and removed the black cloth around his face for the first time.

"You were a very good boy, Unran."

This revealed the face of a fair-skinned man with a distinctive mole under his eye. There was a smile playing upon his thin lips and not a trace of cowardice left about him.

His usual whiny tone nowhere to be heard, he drawled, "Thank you for stressing the horrors of the illness without ever bringing up the contract."

"Wha..."

The pain was consuming so much of Unran's mind that it was hard even to breathe. He instinctively reached out a hand, which Rin smacked aside like something filthy before rising to his feet.

"Now I won't have to worry about a scolding from my master. There have been so many disruptions in the plan that I was getting nervous."

Unran had no idea what he was talking about.

As Rin began to walk off, this time it was Lord Koh who kneeled before him. "I thank you for your guidance in this matter, Lord Rinki."

For some reason, he was calling Rin by a different name.

The man called Rinki turned to Lord Koh with a gracious nod. "Oh, I hardly did anything. You're the one who took care to ensure the other ceremonial officers didn't find out I was acting as your envoy. That was a big help."

"Not at all, milord."

Hadn't Rin been Lord Koh's errand boy? Why was the magistrate the one bowing to him?

Dazedly following the man's figure out of the corner of his eye, Unran asked in a trembling voice, "Why...?"

"Oh, you're still breathing?" Rin's—no, Rinki's—smiling voice sounded so far away. "Then I'll tell you as a reward for being so good: Why were we so deferential and accommodating of your demands? Why, because we *knew* about the disease ravaging your village."

Those words stirred Unran's rapidly fading consciousness into motion. "Huh?" His heart beat faster.

Gazing down upon Unran's breathless figure, Rinki chuckled. "Come now. Providing a lowly untouchable with a contract, demanding no proof, leaving the methods entirely up to you, paying you upfront, and allowing you to back out anytime you wanted... Didn't you ever think the deal was too good to be true?"

"Wha..."

"You could figure it out if you gave it just a second's thought. With a bargain like that, you're definitely going to get killed as a loose end."

Unran blanched as it finally dawned on him what the man was implying. "You wouldn't!"

Then, the reason Rinki had brought Unran to meet the magistrate...

The reason he'd tricked him into describing the village's plight before an audience...

"I appreciate you giving us good cause to burn your village to the ground."

Now that he had no more use for them, he was planning to burn the village down to keep their mouths shut.

"Wait—"

"I'd love to report back to the township with the corpse of the 'culprit,' but the story wouldn't add up if I brought back a diseased untouchable. Sorry, but you'll have to settle for a dog's death out here. See you," Rinki said, then took his leave.

Unran writhed in pain for some time, until at last he ground his molars together.

Damn it...

He was soaked in a clammy sweat. His limbs were shaking, and he felt like he could pass out any second now. But he was still conscious.

"Hah... Hah..."

Unran stopped himself as he was about to pull the dagger from his side. If he tugged it free, blood would come gushing out and drain his life along with it. In that case, now wasn't the right time. Instead, he gingerly groped around his breast.

He did it to retrieve the rock shard the arrow had hit and shattered. The page's arrow hadn't managed to reach Unran's heart because of the shield of stone blocking it.

"Hah... Hah! That was some blessing...right off the bat..."

He tried to force his lips into a wry smile, but the corners of his mouth were trembling. As he held the shard aloft with an unsteady hand, he could have sworn he saw his father's face within the darkness of the sky still so far from dawn.

"Dad..."

Shu Keigetsu had said that she didn't believe in curses. Yet even she had subconsciously seemed to accept the existence of miracles—of coincidences that had to be the will of the Heavens themselves. Then wasn't he allowed to believe in miracles too?

Did you protect me, Dad?

He pressed a hand to his stomach and rose to his feet. He couldn't die yet. He had to warn the village about the impending arson.

"Please, Dad..."

He raised his voice...and took a step toward the mountain.

Beyond that mountain was a village he had to defend.

"Help me protect the village..."

A light in his eyes, he turned back toward the village from whence he came.

Soft light shining through the hut's window informed its inhabitants the day was breaking.

Reirin's face fell at how weak the light of the morning sun was. "It looks like it's going to be another cloudy day. Not a very good day for laundry, I'm afraid."

"Not that we have the clean water to spare for that, anyway," Keikou blithely replied from beside her. Despite his tone, there were dark circles visible under his eyes, the only part of his face that wasn't hidden by cloth. "Jeez, it's one person vomiting after another in here."

"Well, it *is* dysentery. We're lucky that you and the captain are such experts at boiling water."

Reirin gave a demure nod, but her voice was likewise marked with exhaustion. It was no surprise, seeing as her team had barely slept or eaten up to this point.

One night had passed since the multi-person outbreak. Reirin and her guards had spent that time diligently changing out the tubs, brewing herbs and giving the villagers their medicine, boiling water, and sterilizing tubs and robes.

If the children wore themselves out crying, Reirin would have them drink water with a pinch of salt to replenish their bodily fluids. There was never enough hot water on hand, and Shin-u had likewise stayed up the whole night going all the way to the upper reaches of the river, drawing water, and then boiling it.

Thanks to Unran's efforts to gather all the sick in one place, there had been too many people to fit inside the hut by twilight, and they had been forced to lay straw mats outside and have some of the patients sleep there. The chorus of moans and the stench of filth hanging in the air were so appalling that new patients could never hide the fear on their faces when they were first brought in. Still, the team's conscientious nursing had helped those people to slowly but surely regain their composure.

There's always an underlying cause for dysentery, like food or contaminated water. Don't touch excrement. Don't drink unboiled water, and be sure to expel any poison that enters the body. You'll run a fever eventually, but it will pass. It's dangerous to lose too much body water, so be sure to drink the decoctions, even if you have to take it one sip at a time. The medicine will provide relief for diarrhea and fever.

As their caregivers provided explanations before anyone could even ask and shoved a decoction into their hands time and time again, the people began to relax. Disease was terrifying, but knowing what was going to happen ahead of time and having measures in place to deal with that gave them some peace of mind.

Among the earliest patients brought in, Old Kyou had been the first to show symptoms, and her diarrhea and vomiting had already begun to subside. It had helped for the other villagers to see that. The sickness would subside in a day or two—there was an end to their suffering in sight. Knowing these things for a fact allowed them to keep calm. There were still a great deal of villagers whose symptoms had yet to improve, but the situation was looking up.

"It probably helps that we prescribed these decoctions in the early stages, but I'm glad to see this was a relatively minor case of dysentery." Reirin nodded sagely.

"Ha ha ha! You've got guts to call this 'minor,' I'll give you that," Keikou replied with a laugh.

The slightest disturbance could be fatal on the battlefield. Even the mildest of stomachaches could slow the troops' march if several soldiers came down with it at the same time. So too had this been a sufficiently "terrible" epidemic, in which even the slightest misstep had the potential to unleash the chaos of panicked villagers spreading the disease to each other.

"I'll go take a look at the patients outside. I'll leave the ones in here to you."

"Sure."

The siblings nodded to each other, then moved to their respective stations.

Due to the time of day, the majority of villagers were moaning amid the sounds of their sleep. Reirin had been sitting back and keeping an attentive eye on them, but when one patient reached out with a groan and made a gesture asking for water, she hurried over to him.

The one who had just woken up was Gouryuu.

"Here you go."

Upon confirming he wasn't about to vomit, she helped him drink the water. After she'd watched him gulp down a few mouthfuls, she very smoothly switched the bowl out for one filled with a decoction.

"Blegh," came Gouryuu's immediate cry. "Tastes like shit..."

"That's because it's a very potent medicine."

"Tastes like despair..."

"That's because it's a very potent medicine," Reirin asserted once more with a smile, then plugged his nose and poured the contents down his throat.

"Ugh... Gimme water..."

"Drinking too much water at once might make you throw it back up, so it'd be best to hold off for now." She gently denied even his request for a palate cleanser.

Gouryuu clamped his hands over his mouth and moaned, but it seemed both his vomiting and diarrhea had subsided without incident.

"This tastes way too nasty to be safe for consumption... You sure you didn't poison my bowl specifically?"

"Of course not. You can feel yourself getting better, can't you?"

"But the other folks...didn't seem to mind theirs as much..."

"Well, everyone has different tastes," Reirin answered with a smile.

Incidentally, the man who had insulted Unran as a "half-blood" *really* hadn't seemed to agree with the medicine, but to each their own. It was entirely out of Reirin's control, of course. Entirely.

"Or would you have preferred to forgo the decoction and lie here spewing your own waste?"

Gouryuu closed his eyes in resignation, then lay back down again. A listless sigh escaped his lips. "You're mad at us, aren't you?

353

You must think we're a bunch of selfish bastards," he eventually muttered. When Reirin declined to answer, still smiling, he heaved another sigh. Then, he tacked on an apology soft enough to melt into his languid exhale. "Sorry."

There were circles as dark as bruises under his sunken eyes. Even the way he coughed up phlegm oozed with an overwhelming exhaustion and sadness.

"I was jealous of him."

It was immediately clear who he was referring to.

"When the chief... When my brother died, I was sure I'd be the one to take over from him. So when he didn't pick me, his own little brother, to be his successor...but a kid with the blood of a townsman...I was really bitter."

Reirin paused as she was wiping his mouth clean. "I see."

Gouryuu turned his face aside as if to escape her quiet judgment. "We're all untouchables. We're surrounded by nothing but enemies. If we don't stick together, we'll get trampled in an instant. That's why we all cling so damn hard to each other, no matter how suffocating it gets. But...*he* always acted so distant." He sniffled once, his mouth twisting into a grimace. "Even if we treated him like an outsider, he just brushed it off. He basked in my brother's affections but never paid him back for a damn thing. No matter how much he was hated or ostracized, he always looked like he couldn't have cared less." In a whisper, he said again, "I was *so* jealous of him."

It wasn't just him, he said. All the villagers had envied Unran for being the only free spirit among them.

"But, y'know..."

Was even the weak morning sunshine too dazzling to a man who had just woken up? Gouryuu threw an arm over his eyes as if to block out the light filtering in through the window.

"I think my brother made the right call. 'Cause after everything we said about him...he still offered us a helping hand."

A stifled sob echoed through the silent room.

"He really is...my brother's son."

"Yes." Reirin nodded, this time with a sincere smile. Then, she diluted his decoction with a splash of plain hot water. "Please tell Unran the same thing when he gets back."

Setting the bowl down beside the whimpering man, Reirin rose to her feet. The patients here were going to be all right now. She needed to clean up and recover her own strength while most of them were sleeping. Though she'd been careful not to get any waste matter on her, her robe was soaked with sweat and she had very dark circles under her eyes. If she let too much fatigue show on her face, she was sure to come under fire for lacking the dignity of a Maiden.

She didn't want to provide even the slightest of grounds to link "Shu Keigetsu" to misfortune. Nor did she want to give anyone reason to attack Unran. Yet the moment she quietly turned on her heel, her legs wobbled beneath her.

"Ah..."

Of course. She was sleep-deprived and exhausted. Reirin sucked in a breath when she felt herself toppling over, but for better or worse, she was used to passing out. She reflexively pulled a leg back to keep herself from falling, then crouched down on the spot.

I almost hit my head just now.

The dizziness faded as she buried her head in her knees and got her breathing back under control. But the moment Reirin lifted her head in relief, her eyes lit up.

Gouryuu, who had been lying down just moments ago—*all* the people who she thought had been sleeping around her—had sat up in their beds, each of them reaching out with a look of dismay.

"Oh."

Upon making eye contact, they pulled back their hands with a start. But that merely went to prove how "instinctively" they had reached out to her. When they saw Reirin about to collapse, they had sprung into action without even thinking.

"Erm..."

The way they sat there awkwardly with their arms half-outstretched had none of their friendliness from the previous day. In its place, their faces were tinged with bitter contrition and hesitation. Indeed, these open and unreserved villagers were conflicted about whether or not they had a right to extend a hand to the girl in front of them.

"I-I know we've got no right to ask this..." the woman who had been the first in line to blame Unran hesitantly began. "But, uh...are you all right?"

"Huh?"

"I mean, you've been up all night long. Taking care of everyone, comforting the children...putting up with us as we cursed you out." The woman who had once ranted until she was blue in the face was suddenly much less articulate. She spoke each word like she had to squeeze it from her mouth, until at last she exhaled a frustrated sigh. "Never mind. I was right the first time. It's not our place to ask." Then she clenched the hand she had almost extended over her chest.

She wasn't the only one; the same went for all the men around her too. No—*everyone* who was lying in the hut had woken up, looked around, and then dropped their gazes guiltily when they realized what was going on.

It was in their nature to solve minor conflicts with an unabashed apology and a reconciliation. The reason they weren't doing that now, hesitating to so much as reach a hand to her in support, was no doubt because they'd come to realize how opportunistic their behavior was. They knew how it looked to get attached to whoever fed them, berate that person once they fell victim to disease, and then thank them after they were nursed back to health.

An awkward silence fell over the room.

It was a young voice that broke the tension in the air. "I'm sorry."

It belonged to the boy who was lying on the straw mat next to Gouryuu—the boy who had thrown the stone yesterday. Despite finally feeling well enough to get up, he was hanging his head low. He was quick to retract the tiny hand he had once reached out to Reirin in plea, almost like he had given up on her forgiveness.

"I'm sorry for saying it was your fault...even though you looked after us until you couldn't stand up straight." Tears welled in his innocent eyes. "I'm sorry for throwing a rock at you."

The adults grimaced and looked at the floor one after another as they listened to his apology. Now that the worst of their illness was behind them, they were painfully aware of how hotheaded and unreasonable they had been last night. Yet Unran and the Maiden had devoted themselves to their care despite all their selfishness.

They wanted nothing more than to offer their apologies and gratitude. But that would be far too self-serving. Guilt and self-loathing had robbed them of their usual familiar ease.

"Goodness gracious," a light voice rang out with a sigh.

The villagers looked up with a start, only for their eyes to go even wider when they saw the look on the Maiden's face.

"You're so opportunistic."

She was wearing the rueful smile of someone dealing with a troublesome child.

"It's difficult to stand, so could you please lend me a hand?"

The smiling girl reached for the boy. She laid a hand on the arm he'd pulled back from her, then tried to get back up using him as a crutch. When he scrambled to grab her arm in return, she broke into a smile and slowly rose to her feet.

"Thank you for helping me. I'll consider that enough to make amends to me. Please save the rest of your apologies for Unran."

Reirin gazed gently upon the boy who was staring up at her with his mouth hanging open.

Bonds with others are such a fascinating thing. Things never quite go the way you expect.

She gently caressed her own arm. She could still feel the warmth of the boy's hand where he had gripped her so tight. She'd made friends with them only to be easily cast aside, and now here she was standing hand-in-hand with them again. She knew their fickle attitudes ought to have come across as insincere and selfish; was it strange of her to find something about their ever-changing cycle of colors so deeply moving?

It was a relationship that was neither pretty nor simple. But that was precisely why it impressed a hefty sense of reality and vividity upon her heart. Better to cherish their awkward words of apology than the unguarded smiles that had been so easily won—or that was how Reirin saw it, at least.

"Actually, no, let's do this. All those who regret their attitudes last night should drink this decoction right here. Make sure it's all gone by the time I get back."

"Huh?"

When she held up the earthenware teapot she'd left next to Gouryuu, everyone's faces went stiff. And who could blame them? It was a decoction mixed only with an eye to efficacy, bitter enough to leave the taste buds crying.

"But, um...we're all feeling a lot better, so there's no need for us to take more medicine..."

"It tastes like a mix of a rotting bug carcass and water wrung from a rag."

"Just drink it, hm?" Reirin emphasized.

The villagers obediently nodded their heads. "Yes, ma'am..."

She giggled, this time catching her breath and getting to her feet for good. "Come, let's do this with a bang."

She'd shaken all her sleepiness. Her whole body felt light, and it was like the world had suddenly opened up around her. She needed to take advantage of her newfound momentum to wash her hands and change clothes. After that, she'd have to perform a checkup on each individual villager and change their sleeping spots according to the severity of their condition. It would be a problem if the wind carried the poisoned qi from the tubs, so she had to clean those too.

Tasks to be done popped into Reirin's head one after another, filling her with energy anew.

Oh, but I also need to get back in touch with Lady Keigetsu soon, she abruptly thought as she headed out the door and gazed upon the fiery red sunrise shrouded in thin clouds.

Last night, between Shin-u barging in and the news of the disease, she'd had to cut the flame call in a hurry. She hadn't had a moment to spare for a secret conversation while she was brewing herbs, and Shin-u had guarded the fire the entire time after that, so there hadn't been a good time for Keigetsu's flame magic.

In the end, she hadn't spoken to Keigetsu since their conversation by the pond. No doubt her friend was getting anxious.

I'll leave my nap for later and let the captain get some rest first. I did leave him in charge of boiling all the water, after all. And that way, I can use the fire. Oh, I know, I should have Brother Senior take a nap too!

Just as she had worked out a plan in her head, Keikou came back. Reirin opened her mouth to call out to him—until she noticed the deep frown upon his face.

"What is it, Brother Senior?"

"I've been trying to figure out what could have caused the dysentery outbreak for a while now." Keikou gave a jerk of his chin that said to follow him. He took off in a particular direction, then said in a hushed voice, "It couldn't be food poisoning if the villagers haven't been eating anything but congee as of late. There were some vegetables they received as payment for this kidnapping, but based on what I heard, none of those were the type to carry illness."

"I've also wondered about that. Is it safe to assume it was something in the drinking water, then?"

"Not quite. At first I also thought it might have come from drinking unclean water, but it's weird for this many people to come down with symptoms this bad all at the same time. So I went around talking to everyone who got sick."

It seemed Keikou had been conducting interviews at the same time he was tending to his patients. According to what he'd learned, Old Kyou had been the first to show signs of vomiting and diarrhea. Gouryuu's symptoms had manifested a little later—perhaps due to the difference in their physical resilience—but chances were good that he also had dysentery at that point. Despite living under the same roof as them, Unran never caught the illness.

Some of the others to start vomiting first had been a man

THOUGH I AM AN INEPT VILLAINESS

from a neighboring family with a newborn and a child from a different neighbor's home. They hadn't eaten the same food, but they did have one thing in common.

"The infant had soiled his diapers, so the man went to the washing area while his wife was cradling the baby. The kid had been running around and working up a sweat, so he bathed using the same water."

They had both used the water from the largest of the ponds.

"Could the baby's stool have contaminated everyone's water source?"

Reirin frowned. The pond water used for both laundry and daily necessities wasn't kept separate from the drinking water, so she had been afraid something like that might happen.

Yet Keikou shook his head. "It's been a rule since the previous chief's time not to return used water to the pond. Since people got fewer stomachaches as a result, the villagers came to believe the god of agriculture who dwells in the pond likes his water clean and have followed the regulation to the letter."

"Then why...?" Reirin murmured.

Keikou came to a stop, then pointed to something in the pond. "It's that."

At the far end of the pond that glistened in the faint morning sunlight was a small shrine. It was dedicated to the god of agriculture who protected the district's rice paddies. The shrine was a simple stone structure, but there was something tied to its pillar and fluttering about. It was red, sparkling, beautiful, and largely submerged in the water.

As soon as Reirin strained her eyes to see what it was, she let out a gasp. "It couldn't be...!"

"Yeah. It's the ceremonial robe the Kin clan gave as their offering for the festival. Or its sash, rather."

She started to ask what something like that was doing here, but she came up with the answer in an instant. "Old Kyou was in the township on the night of the pre-celebration... She must have stolen it."

"Right. She told me as much herself. She took advantage of the feast in the township to steal some food and valuable items. She ate what she could and offered the inedible garment to the god of agriculture. The robe to the shrine on the mountain and the sash to the shrine in the pond. She was feeling a little deferential after her group had set fire to the altar on the stage." At that, Keikou dropped his gaze and said, "There's this military tactic called a 'sick gown.'"

"What is it?"

"You rub the feces or sweat of someone infected with dysentery over a robe, then give it to an enemy soldier or captive to wear. It's a strategy to spread disease through the enemy camp— one of the prohibited moves in the game of war." When he saw his sister's eyes go wide, Keikou grimaced in shame. "I know. The battlefield is a dirty place. I don't like these sorts of tactics either. I once got into a fight with the adjutant adviser from another clan over it. He loves doing things that way. Says it's logical."

Reirin looked back at Keikou, pale. "You don't think...the Kin clan gave out a disease-ridden robe?"

But she soon rejected her own suggestion. The reason being that she recalled the Gen clan tassel left behind on the stage and the Kou one left in Keigetsu's room.

Misdirection.

Just because there was a clue pointing to the Kin clan didn't mean they could jump to conclusions.

"What clan was the adjutant who liked 'logical methods' from?" she asked with a gulp.

Keikou nodded, knowing where she was going with this. "The Kin clan values pride. The Kou clan likes to fight head-on. The Shu clan is too emotional to have any semblance of strategy. Each member of the Gen clan is so individually skilled in the military arts that they'd never even think to play tricks. Thus, everyone says the Ran clan is best suited to the role of strategist."

He must have remembered some of the conversations he'd had on the battlefield; his scowl was obvious even beneath the cloth.

"The Ran clan's attribute is wood. They're typically mild-mannered and rational types. But given the clan's academic excellence and appreciation of reason, it sometimes births people who don't understand emotion and can kill in cold blood. This adjutant was one of those types."

"And his name...?"

"Ran Rinki," Keikou answered in a low voice. "The Maiden Ran Houshun's older brother."

Reirin fell silent, lost for words. So many thoughts were racing through her head at a tremendous pace.

The ceremonial robe was originally meant to be worn by "Shu Keigetsu." She had been planning to wear it to the main Harvest Festival rite and offer a prayer alongside Gyoumei. Had the Ran clan turned the Kins' robe into a "sick gown" as part of a plan to kill Keigetsu? Was it just a coincidence that the villagers had brought it back with them? And then, they'd just happened to use the water contaminated by the sash to cook and do their laundry...?

Then why? No, if that *was* the case...

Reirin pursed her lips for a moment, then began, "Here's what I think—"

She was interrupted by a man's sharp cry. "Hey, pull it together!"

A quick look over her shoulder revealed that it was Shin-u shouting somewhere near the hut. He had cast aside the firewood and tubs of water he'd collected to prop someone up on his shoulder. It was a young man with only one section of his hair tied into a bun—Unran.

"Unran!" Reirin shouted in surprise, rushing over to his side with her brother. "Unran! You made it back! Goodness, there was no need to pick herbs to the point of—"

Before she could say "exhaustion," she clamped her mouth shut. She noticed he wasn't holding his basket of herbs. No, beyond that...

"Unran?"

The path he had been walking was dotted in blood.

"Why...?"

Unran had collapsed in Shin-u's arms, his knees buckling under him. Reirin could see there was something in his side. It was a dagger.

When he heard Reirin's loud gasp, he made one feeble attempt to lift his head. "Hur...ry..."

"Unran! What happened, Unran?! Where did this blade come from?!" she shouted.

His ice-blue lips quivered weakly. "Every... Run..."

"Run? Unran?! Unran!"

With one last thin exhale, Unran fell limp to the ground.

9 | Keigetsu Suspects Something

L ET'S TURN BACK the clock a bit—to just after Keigetsu had heard news of the plague via her flame magic.

"You're kidding..."

She sat there, stunned, as wisps of smoke curled from the candle in front of her.

Reirin had cut the call short. As soon as she'd realized the gravity of the situation, she had poured water over the bonfire with a hurried apology of "Sorry, I'll be sure to get back in touch," and then taken off running.

Gyoumei was likewise nowhere to be found. His expression had turned grim upon hearing the report of the sickness, and then he'd briskly exited the room.

The only people left at Keigetsu's side were Leelee and Tousetsu, whose faces were taut with worry.

"What am I supposed to do?"

She instinctively shoved both hands into her hair and curled them into fists.

A plague. And worse, it was dysentery, an exceptionally filthy disease that saw the afflicted spew their waste everywhere. If one of the Maidens so prized for their nobility were to contract such a sickness, it would spell her doom. Her reputation would be too thoroughly damaged to ever recover. Keigetsu was trembling just as much for fear of her own social death as she was for the village and Reirin's well-being.

"What am *I* supposed to do about any of this?"

No, she knew exactly what she had to do. Gyoumei had given her the order right before he left, after all. When the distraught Keigetsu had begged him to send help to the village at once, he had answered thus: "Now isn't the time to run to her rescue. You still have a tea party to see through."

Then when is he going to dispatch a rescue team? And why on earth does he want me to hold this tea party amid such an emergency?

Keigetsu had naturally objected to this, but Gyoumei hadn't entertained her protests. His argument had gone as follows.

If the other clans knew "Shu Keigetsu" had been caught up in a plague at her kidnappers' whereabouts, they would be sure to take advantage of that—in other words, they'd try to drag her down by establishing her as a "sullied" woman. Thus, the idea was to get one step ahead of them with this tea party and prevent "Shu Keigetsu's" reputation from being ruined. In short, this was information warfare.

Keigetsu had screamed that she wasn't capable of that, but Gyoumei had left before she could make any further argument.

Though she had no idea what he could be thinking, if it was the prince's order, she had no choice but to obey. She knew as much, but she'd still sat there in shock, her mind unable to catch up with what was going on.

"Well, *that* was unexpected," came a voice blithe enough to feel out of place.

The moment Keigetsu cast a slow glance over her shoulder and saw who it was, she made a face. It was Keishou. He'd apparently come back after escorting Gyoumei out.

He strolled back into the room, heedless of the petrified girls, then sat down in front of Keigetsu without bothering to ask her permission. Perhaps for lack of anything to do with his hands, he plucked the extinguished candle from the candlestick and rolled it between his fingers.

"Say, Lady Shu Keigetsu..." he began after a long pause.

Keigetsu braced herself for what was going to come next.

What, is he going to say, "What are you staring into space for?" I don't think I can handle his snide remarks right now.

Over the past few days, Keishou had stuck to Keigetsu like glue, giving her guidance to keep the people around her from catching on to the switch and sharing investigation updates he'd learned as a ceremonial officer. She was positive now that he hadn't been the one to sling mud on her robe, and as someone who knew the full situation, he was about the only person in the estate she could talk to without walking on eggshells. Still, she didn't think she could deal with his unique brand of needling at the moment.

"Listen, now's not the—"

"Sorry."

When Keigetsu attempted to shut down the whole conversation, he abruptly came out and apologized, taking the wind out of her sails.

"Excuse me?"

"I never would have guessed His Highness had figured it out from the start and was just letting it slide. And here I was giving you acting lessons and getting on my high horse about making absolutely sure you don't get caught... How embarrassing for me. 'Surprising' doesn't even begin to describe this development."

Apparently, what had seemed like a deliberate attempt to drag this out was just him feeling awkward. Keigetsu felt her guard drop as she watched him scratch his cheek in embarrassment.

At the same time, all her pent-up anxiety and irritation came flooding out in one huge burst. Keigetsu didn't hesitate to take the ground Keishou had conceded and lay into him. "That's for sure! How are you going to make this up to me? I might have gotten off lighter if I'd come clean from the start, and I wouldn't have felt so trapped all this time."

"True."

"His Highness is furious, Kou Reirin is caught up in a plague, and I've had this tea party dumped in my lap. Things couldn't be worse!"

"Maybe so."

Keigetsu knew full well that being so quick to blame others was her biggest flaw. Even so, she tore into Keishou to her heart's content, unable to stop the torrent of her emotions. The truly surprising part was that he just sat there and took it all.

"Hmm, but I'm not convinced. His Highness did say he would overlook the charge of switching bodies."

What's more, he even offered her words of comfort.

Yet, unable to accept his kindness without a fight, she shot back, "Sure, but I bet I'll take the fall for Kou Reirin's crime of 'infidelity.'"

"His Highness isn't that petty. Plus, we don't know that Reirin will fall ill."

"We don't know that she *won't* either."

"And Tousetsu and I will both help you out with the tea party, so I'm sure that part will go well."

"There's no way!" she finally screeched when he kept telling her to look on the bright side. "You've said it yourselves. I'm a talentless 'sewer rat'! I can't do anything, and I don't have any strengths. How could I possibly pull off a tea party?!"

"I'm not so sure about that one," he replied in his usual calm voice, striking Keigetsu into silence. "I think you can do it." Keishou wore a sober look in place of his usual elusive smile.

"What?"

"I mean, think about it. You never run from anything." He gave a light shrug of his shoulders. The way he said it, like he was stating the obvious, robbed Keigetsu of any argument she could make. "I realized it after watching you for the past few days. You're quick to yell and quick to cry out. You're always complaining about how you want to run away or how you wish the world would give you a break. But the fact that you're still screaming means you *haven't* run away yet. You might throw a fit, but you always stand your ground in the end."

He chuckled, perhaps thinking of his little sister. "By contrast, look at Reirin. She never whines about wanting to run away, but as soon as things look bad, she makes the spur-of-the-moment decision to run off with bandits. Though I suppose that's gallant in its own way." He tacked on, "And besides, we *did* give her the idea."

Unsure what to make of his speech, Keigetsu averted her gaze. "I was the first one to run. On the night of the Double Sevens Festival, I tried to escape this body by stealing hers."

"At first, yes." Keishou wouldn't budge. Still smiling, he returned the candle to its holder. "But if I had to guess, I'd say you learned your lesson from that. You've been nothing less than commendable since then. You try your best in your own clumsy way, and you stood strong in the face of our nasty comments. When you accidentally set off another switch, for all your wailing, you met His Highness head-on."

"I just couldn't find a chance or way to escape."

"Sure, but the end result is that you didn't run."

When Keishou smiled at her, Keigetsu suddenly noticed how much his features resembled Reirin's. The two were definitely brother and sister, right down to the way they only ever cared about the ultimate outcome.

"I'm sorry for calling you a 'sewer rat.' It's true that you might not measure up to the others in terms of talent yet. But you have the courage to face your flaws and fight."

Oh, Keigetsu thought as her face almost contorted with

emotion. How was it that each and every member of the Kou clan managed to toss out the words she most wanted to hear?

"In short, you have backbone. That's the most important thing there is. A dazzling backbone!"

"..."

And why were they all so obsessed with backbone?

The corners of Keigetsu's lips twitched a fraction. "Backbone alone won't do anything to fix a problem."

"But without it, you won't even manage to take the first step. Backbone is the foundation of everything. Very impressive stuff." Keishou gave her a friendly pat on the shoulder, then left the room without further ado. "It looks like His Highness has given up on toying with us, so I'll go ask him what he's thinking. Good luck with the tea party," he said as he walked off.

Did he come all the way back just to tell me that?

In the end, Keigetsu watched the uncharacteristically amicable man go without further comment.

"Shall we prepare for the tea party, Lady Keigetsu?" Tousetsu called out from behind her, perhaps having waited for her chance to ask.

By the time Keigetsu turned back around, the nod she gave came perfectly naturally. It was a total departure from her earlier attitude. "Good idea."

She was going to do this. She would believe she could do what she could.

But it's not because Lord Keishou cheered me up or anything, she thought to herself.

It wasn't that she was happy or feeling better—she just had to do it.

She had to run this "information warfare" tea party to confirm what clan had ties to Lord Koh and keep the hostile Maidens in check.

"Come give me a hand," Keigetsu said.

Tousetsu and Leelee exchanged glances, then responded with an emphatic, "Yes, ma'am."

It was four hours later, and the dead of night was fast approaching. Keigetsu staggered out into the garden and stared up at the moon hanging high in the sky.

"I'm exhausted..."

"That's because you tried to take on too much all at once," Leelee pointed out with exasperation from behind her. She was tired enough to stifle a yawn herself.

It was understandable. The girls had spent the last few hours carefully picking out tea and sweets, arranging the furniture, preparing incense, and accounting for all possible threads of conversation to ensure the tea party would be fit to be hosted by "Kou Reirin."

Tousetsu had gone to perform a final check of the tea room, while Keigetsu and Leelee had stepped out for a breath of fresh air.

"Normally, we'd be holding banquets every night of the trip, but we've been on total lockdown due to the kidnapping incident," said Leelee.

"True..."

The pair mumbled a conversation as they looked out over the quiet courtyard of the estate. The lights were off in all the Maidens' rooms that could be seen from the cloister. According to the rules, the ceremonial officers of each clan were supposed to be standing in front of their Maiden's room around the time the date changed over, but there was no one to be found.

Keigetsu assumed—with a touch of disdain—that they must have found the lack of a banquet so disappointing that they'd gone straight to bed. She used to have a vague infatuation with the ceremonial officers, but she'd changed her tune upon learning that they would barely even help with the investigation of another Maiden's kidnapping. That was why Shin-u was the only one who had managed to track down "Shu Keigetsu," even though she'd been right under their noses the whole time.

In the end, being from different clans made both the Maidens and the ceremonial officers nothing more than cunning enemies of hers. The only exception to the rule had to be the unconventionally and impossibly good-natured Kou clan...

"Oh?"

Keigetsu and her attendant stopped in their tracks as they spotted two figures emerge from a garden pavilion behind the bushes. She was surprised to realize who one half of the pair was: Kou Keishou.

"It's Lord Keishou and...Lady Houshun?"

Upon confirming the identity of the second person, the girls' eyes went even wider. The one who had stepped out of the pavilion with Keishou supporting her weight was none other than the Ran Maiden, Ran Houshun.

For a moment, Keigetsu had to wonder if she had just witnessed a secret tryst, but the way the Ran court ladies were bowing their heads to Keishou with looks of humbled gratitude, combined with how Houshun was wobbling on her feet, told her that wasn't the case.

"Should we assume Master Keishou looked after Lady Houshun when she was feeling ill, then?" Leelee asked, frowning.

Keigetsu nodded. "It doesn't look to be anything scandalous, at least."

Almost as if to prove this, Houshun lifted her face upon noticing the pair and broke into a delighted smile. "Hello, Miss Reirin. What are you doing here?"

Keigetsu forced the mask of "Kou Reirin" back upon her face and replied, "I couldn't sleep, so I came to get some fresh air. What are *you* doing out so late at night, Lady Houshun?"

"It's embarrassing to admit, but I pushed myself so hard on such a humid night that I started to feel sick... Master Keishou just happened to be passing by, so he took care of me for a bit," Houshun squeaked out with the timid demeanor of a small animal.

"You 'pushed yourself too hard' in the middle of the night—and not even back in your room but out in this pavilion?"

"Yes... Umm, see..." The petite girl hesitated, looking up at Keigetsu with puppy-dog eyes.

Keishou cut in from the side to explain for her. "Lady Houshun was transcribing the *Thousand Character Classic* as something to offer to the Great Ancestor in prayer of Lady Shu Keigetsu and my brother Keikou's safe return. I'd expect no less from the Maiden of the clan known for their wealth of knowledge. Her calligraphy was truly a sight to behold."

"N-not at all. You flatter me." Living up to her shy reputation, she covered her face with both sleeves. "I feel bad that this is all I can do..."

"I was especially charmed that she showed the diligence to do it outside by the light of the moon rather than burn a candle in her room late into the night." Keishou continued to praise her. "Why, it was enough to make me think the other Maidens should aspire to her example."

"No, umm, er..." She blushed so hard it was visible in the dark, falling all over herself to argue back. "Please don't say things like that. If, say, Lady Seika were to find out, um...I don't think she would appreciate it..."

No kidding. I bet Lady Seika would say something like, "My, you certainly know how to flaunt your virtue."

Keigetsu suddenly understood why Houshun had bothered to do her transcription in secret under the pavilion. One with such a unique sense of aesthetic and self-importance as Kin Seika hated inelegant acts like grinding away at something for another person's sake. Once, when Houshun had gone to the trouble of calling upon her court ladies to sign a card for Seika's birthday, the latter had even mocked her and refused to accept the gift.

Houshun and Seika had been assigned neighboring rooms in the estate. She must have been worried about what would happen if the Kin court ladies caught on to her act of "virtue."

"I did it for my own sake because I wanted Lady Keigetsu to be all right... I feel truly terrible that I caused trouble for the member of another clan in the process," Houshun said, her eyes damp with tears.

Keigetsu found the sight heartwarming.

I thought she was nothing but timid, but she's actually pretty nice.

At the very least, Houshun had to be the only Maiden other than Reirin concerned about "Shu Keigetsu."

Come to think of it, her polite way of talking and knack for triggering the protective instincts remind me a lot of Kou Reirin.

To begin with, wood and earth temperaments were said to share a lot of similarities.

Getting the same feeling she did when Reirin smiled at her, Keigetsu made a rare show of calmly praising another clan's Maiden. "You're so kind and modest, Lady Houshun."

"N-not at all!" Houshun flapped her hands back and forth. "*You're* the kind and modest one, Miss Reirin. I truly look up to you. I know you've been worried sick over Lady Keigetsu amid everything. Not even her disregard for her chastity or shameless comments could keep you from caring about her..."

"What do you mean by 'disregard for her chastity'?" Keigetsu asked automatically, picking up on that concerning choice of words.

"Oops." Houshun went pale and threw her hands over her mouth.

This piqued Keigetsu's interest even further. "And what shameless comments?"

"No, umm..." Her round eyes swimming with tears, Houshun cast a glance toward Keishou. By the time she changed her mind and said, "Never mind," Keigetsu was starting to get irritated.

"Please answer me, Lady Houshun. When has Lady Keigetsu ever disregarded her chastity?"

Keigetsu had heard all the gossip before: She was talentless, she was tactless, she toadied to authority, and so on. But she had no recollection of doing anything that would bring her chastity into question.

"I-I'm sorry. It was...a slip of the tongue."

"No one could make that sort of mistake. I won't get mad, so please tell me," Keigetsu pressed, leaning forward.

Houshun at last answered her question with the air of a kicked puppy. "I...heard something. That is...Lady Keigetsu said she was lusting for the ceremonial officers."

"She what?" Keishou was the one to ask this time.

Houshun screwed her eyes shut, looking ashamed. "Lady Keigetsu loves dignified gentlemen, apparently. So people like the handsome captain of the Eagle Eyes and the other ceremonial officers look, um...irresistible to her. She said she might take advantage of her position as hostess to talk with them and slip them an aphrodisiac."

Keigetsu was utterly speechless.

"She said that she's going to end up the lowest-ranking consort who can be 'gifted' either way, so she ought to be allowed this much 'fun.' It took me by surprise... I tried to admonish her in secret, but she made me promise not to talk."

Keigetsu's whole body went cold. What was Houshun talking about? She had never said anything of the sort.

"Are you sure Lady Keigetsu said that?"

This was the girl as adorable as a small animal, the most harmless of the Maidens, Ran Houshun. Considering all that, it was possible someone had fed her a lie. Maybe someone was using her.

And yet, tears of sorrow welling in her eyes, Houshun asserted, "Yes. I heard it for myself. I even caught her casting lascivious glances at the ceremonial officers during the carriage ride."

Keigetsu's heart raced. What was this girl after? Why would she tell "Kou Reirin" this kind of lie? What was her goal in making "Shu Keigetsu" out to be such a sexually uninhibited woman?

Keigetsu stared at the petite girl in front of her, forgetting to breathe for a moment.

"The magistrate was pulling the strings of the impoverished villagers. But it seems there may have been someone pulling his strings too."

Reirin's thoughtful murmurings played back in her head.

The soiled ceremonial robe. Keikou and Keishou hadn't been the culprits. The Kou clan tassel left behind at the scene. A clue pointing to Gen clan. Fragments of information came to her mind one after another, then vanished once again.

Who in the world was out to ruin "Shu Keigetsu"?

"Umm, but those with strong fire qi are said to be open-minded about sex by nature...so it may have been the Shu idea of a joke. Please don't worry about it too much. I'm really, really sorry for not only troubling Master Keishou but making you uncomfortable as well," Houshun added at the end. She then thanked Keishou for taking care of her one last time and left.

Keigetsu watched her go in a daze.

Afterword

HELLO, Satsuki Nakamura here. We've made it to Volume 3 thanks to all of your support. Thank you so much.

In this third volume, I was so determined to live up to my readers' expectations that I introduced a bunch of new characters, delved deeper into Reirin's psyche, and put my all into writing the thing...but I got *so* into it that, as I'm sure you've noticed if you're finished reading, I, uh...didn't manage to wrap it up in one volume.

Despite all the extra linage I was afforded, I've once again packed the volume so full that I only have one page left for the afterword. It wasn't the word count that ran over so much as my love and enthusiasm. I'm afraid this was inevitable. The story will continue in Volume 4.

If I had to sum up the theme of Volume 4 in one word, it'd be "counterattack." Please look forward to seeing how Reirin will escape her greatest crisis thus far and what Keigetsu will do next in light of her surprising growth. Oh, Gyoumei and Shin-u will have their time in the limelight too! Uh, I do feel like I have to announce that...especially for Gyoumei...

THOUGH I AM AN INEPT VILLAINESS

Once again, I would like to thank my editor for always keeping me in line.

I likewise extend my thanks to my designer, Kana Yuki-sensei, for the wonderful illustrations (I love this volume's color inserts so much that my heart nearly leapt out of my chest), and Ei Ohitsuji-sensei for the amazing manga adaptation (each month's issue of *Zero-Sum* is what keeps me going these days).

And the biggest thanks of all go out to my dear readers. Let's meet again in Volume 4.

—Satsuki Nakamura, November 2021